WHEN A RED LIGHT SHINES

by

David Wilson

Published October 2012 by Links Books Ltd.

First Edition

Published by Link Books Ltd
www.linkbooks.co.uk

ISBN 978-0-9572876-0-0 Paperback
ISBN 978-0-9572876-1-7 E Book

**Visit the author's website at
www.dmcwilson.co.uk
Follow David Wilson on Twitter @DaveDmc111**

Politics and the Police

The murky cut-throat world of politics has always fascinated me since joining the police in the early 1980s. As a young rooky, I didn't realise how closely policing and the world of politics were linked until I started working the streets of Inner London.

Policing has always had a political slant in the way the organisation operates, but in recent years it has become so politicised that I feel this has had a detrimental effect on how police carry out their duties. Instead of being left to do their job, their hands have been tied to such an extent that 'the job' has become so sanitised. A disease has spread through the organisation, just as it has in many walks of life – political correctness. Many people criticise this new phenomenon, and at the same time embrace it.

People from all classes commit crime, and they all have different motives. Some are driven by greed, some by power and some by sheer desperation and real poverty.

One thing is for certain, it will always feature in daily news bulletins because it is a simple fact of life, and as a consequence, law enforcement doesn't get any easier.

Acknowledgements

In particular, I need to mention Bill Rogers,
author of the Tom Caton crime series.
His knowledge and help
have been invaluable to me.

Dedication

This book is dedicated to my wife Janet and
my children Jack, Lewis and Robyn,
and of course, my Mum and Dad.
I cannot thank you enough.

'Corruption is worse than prostitution. The latter might endanger the morals of an individual; the former invariably endangers the morals of the entire country.'

Karl Kraus

**Part I of the Detective Chief Inspector
Jack Edgerton series**

*Constitutional Hill, London
Tuesday, 27th September 2011*

Another early start as the newspaper seller prepared his stand. Pulling on his white jacket, he made his final preparations for what would be a typically busy day in the capital. He took the felt-tip pen from his pocket and laid the headline sheet on top of his rickety stand, placing a stone on each corner to stop it blowing away in the northerly wind that swept through the busy thoroughfare. Studying his surroundings and checking for punters, he cleared his throat in anticipation of another shift bellowing to passers-by.

Rubbing his hands to warm them and donning his woolly cap, he completed his final task before waving a bunch of the first editions above his head, and wrote the headline for the day in big bold letters.

*MP's report into misconduct – the Foreign Secretary
Robert Bamford acted inappropriately*

He held the sheet up to check it and then placed it firmly in the display behind the metal grill.

This is where the story begins…

Chapter 1

Detective Chief Inspector Jack Edgerton lay back on his sofa.

It was his rest day, and he watched the Central London skyline from his bay window in his Primrose Hill residence located on the northern side of Regent's Park in London. With a clear view of Central London to the south-east, as well as Belsize Park and Hampstead to the north, he was right in the centre of one of the most exclusive and expensive residential areas in the city. It was supposed to be a rare moment of relaxation for the hard-working detective. Unshaven and alone, he rubbed his fingers over his chiselled features, contemplating what lay ahead.

His complex mind was in overdrive, but at the same time he was overwhelmed by feelings of anger and revenge as he flicked through the pages of his tea-stained daily newspaper and an old pathologist report he had found in his desk. Time had not been a great healer for the seasoned detective. Now living alone since the amicable split from his wife, he had moved on and his thoughts about this murderer were foremost in his mind.

He was finding it hard to unwind as he read the paper.

This person was abhorrent … he was narcissistic … this killer needed to be caught. A chilling description of a person, but whoever had committed these acts deserved the label.

Not easy reading. The crime correspondent had penned an article that morning reminding the public that two high-profile double murders remained unsolved. The headline was a stark reminder to its readers.

Unsolved double homicide has London on the edge
The Metropolitan Police, on the third anniversary of the double murders in Mayfair and Camberwell, are renewing their appeals for new information…

Edgerton threw the newspaper in the waste bin. He was no longer involved in the investigation since his promotion to Chief Inspector, but it reminded him of his association with a case that had frustrated him more than any other case he had investigated.

He wasn't annoyed with the paper or the article's author, far from it. The journalist was trying to help the police and inject new life into the investigation, but Edgerton was a proud man. The whole saga had been a game of cat and mouse, and he didn't like to lose.

He had been involved as a Detective Sergeant on the Murder Squad three years earlier with a case that to this day still haunted him, and he hoped one day it would be solved for the sake of the families, and indeed the Mayfair and Camberwell Grove residents who had been rocked by the murders. Two wealthy couples had been repeatedly stabbed in the privacy of their homes for no apparent reason.

The murders showed all the hallmarks of a serial killer – locks of hair cut from the head of each victim; no apparent motive, since valuable items were left in situ; not a trace of evidence left behind; and all the victims had died as a result of deep lacerations to the aorta. These were crimes that were committed by an individual who was equally as cunning as Edgerton, and forensically aware. They had given the killer a nickname – *The Barber*.

Only basic information was ever released to the press. Command had made a conscious decision to remain tight-lipped; such detailed information had to remain confidential. The case would never close.

However, like all major cities, life in London carried on as normal. Jack Edgerton had moved on...

Chapter 2

The Houses of Parliament – Portcullis House
Monday, 3rd October 2011

The completed Select Committee report lay on his desk, hot off the press and meticulously prepared for prying eyes. The recipient, however, was instrumental in the preparation of this two-hundred-page document.

HOUSE OF COMMONS
Committee on Standards and Privileges
An investigation into the conduct of Robert
Bamford MP – Foreign Secretary...

His hand caressed the glossy cover and he slowly turned the first page, ensuring that his title had been presented correctly. He steadily donned his spectacles as he turned every page to examine the content.

Current Membership
Mr Brian Beaumont MP (Conservative, Oxford) (Chair)

He quickly turned to the conclusion of the report. Brian Beaumont MP mumbled to himself as he read the extract and, as a raging anger took hold, he cast the report across the desk. It wasn't the result he had hoped for, or anticipated. Several members of the Select Committee he had chaired couldn't agree on all the evidence, and the report's content was open to interpretation. That would have serious ramifications for the newly promoted politician. The division amongst several committee members was clearly evident in the report for everybody to see and made it vulnerable to criticism from certain quarters, in particular those who supported Robert Bamford. The report merely criticised the current Foreign Secretary for his associations with Russian businessmen.

The Committee, in its conclusions, fully accepts that the role of the Foreign Secretary involves meeting with foreign dignitaries regularly, but House of Commons procedures in relation to such meetings must be adhered to at all times. We feel that the current Foreign Secretary has not followed such procedures and has acted naively in his association with certain officials from the Russian Embassy.

There were several meetings over a period of months that took place at the Russian Embassy that were never officially recorded, and this is unacceptable. However, the Committee was divided as to the reason for these omissions, so we must therefore give Mr Bamford the benefit of the doubt and accept that they were not recorded due to administrative errors, as his evidence before the Committee pointed out.

The report continued.

The Committee refers to the following paragraph in the Ministerial Code that clearly states:

Meetings with external organisations (Code 8.14 refers)

Ministers meet many people and organisations, and consider a wide range of views as part of the formulation of government policy. Departments will publish, at least quarterly, details of ministers' external meetings.

As the report had been released on the House of Commons website, it was already in the hands of the media. Its content would be scrutinised and dissected down to the last full stop. This matter was not going away. In some people's eyes, Robert Bamford MP had quite literally got away with murder, but for how long? Beaumont was confident the scandal wouldn't just disappear.

A consequence of a weak report meant that Robert Bamford received the full support of his Labour Prime Minister Charles Chillot, much to the frustration of Beaumont and the Conservative party. The Russian Ambassador, Andrei Loktev, would also remain in post. As far as investigative journalists and Beaumont were concerned, the matter should not be left to lie.

Whilst certain politicians reeled in Westminster, and Bamford, the egotistical Foreign Secretary, carried on as normal, Edward Fahy, a freelance investigative journalist, a man who held a deep-rooted hatred for Bamford, couldn't let go. He would continue to follow Bamford at every opportunity and log every minute detail relating to his activities. He was a good ally for certain members of the establishment, but he was also a loner, and the way in which he conducted business was no different.

As Fahy proceeded, keeping his findings a total secret, he would wait for his moment of glory, but first he needed time to relax.

Chapter 3

*The West Coast of the Sinai Peninsula
– Close to the Red Sea
October 2011*

Edward Fahy had arrived in paradise. After a pleasant journey to Naama Bay, Sharm El Sheikh, he was looking forward to a dive he had planned for several years as he loaded his diving equipment and laptop onto the boat he had hired.

Abasi, the boat's owner, greeted him with an embrace.

'It's been a long time, Edward. Where have you been?'

Fahy, also pleased to see his old friend, replied, 'Work, my friend, and my mother's been ill.'

Offering him a glass of Qasab, his favourite drink, his friend was keen to accompany Fahy on his trip.

Fahy was a little hesitant and declined. 'No thanks, my friend, I need a little time alone, but we can catch up after the dive.'

It was a boat journey that would only take Fahy a couple of hours. This would give him time to view the surrounding beauty and periodically check his laptop.

He had an important story to run, his greatest scoop nearly completed; this would be the calm before the storm. On his return to England, he would sell it to the highest bidder. A scandal would surely be uncovered when he revealed his secret to the nation. Robert Bamford was his target, a man he had followed day and night, vowing to expose him.

Cruising at a leisurely pace through the calm waters of the Red Sea, it wasn't long before he approached the west coast of the Sinai Peninsula, the very spot he had researched in detail and read about in his diving magazines. As the sun started to rise, he took a deep intake of clean sea air into his lungs and anchored the small boat.

Thirty metres beneath him lay the wreck of HMS Thistlegorm. He took his lighter and ignited his Gitanes, his favourite smoke, and lay back in the boat on the deserted waters.

His descent into this beautiful habitat was imminent. He realised this might be his last moment of normality before he returned to the chaos of London.

After one final check of his diving equipment, he wrapped his laptop in a towel and straddled the edge of the boat, leaning backwards towards the deep-blue waters. After a short pause, he pierced the surface, descending slowly to the seabed, and as he looked up, the sun's rays were starting to penetrate deep into the sea, giving him a panoramic view of his stunning surroundings. In a matter of minutes, the journalist had made contact with the seabed, and as he navigated the numerous ledges, he was confronted by a spectacular multi-coloured coral reef.

Fahy was astounded by its beauty and splendour as he paused, tempted to touch the sharp coral with his bare fingers. He deliberately waved his hands back and forth through the warm sea water, and progressed towards the damaged hull of the infamous HMS Thistlegorm. As it came into view, it offered him everything that he had expected. It was as if time stood still as he moved towards the twisted wreck. He thought to himself that this was just as he had imagined. He started to kick furiously as his excitement got the better of him and his desire to reach the wreck quickly took hold.

All his anxiety about the story he was about to break seemed so far away as any worries he might have had slowly diminished. He was in isolation for the time being as he continued to study different areas of the wreck.

Above sea level, the journalist's boat remained anchored to its spot as a high-powered boat approached, slowing down to avoid detection. It remained some distance away. The occupant of the boat was alone, and he carefully checked for other divers in the immediate vicinity. The conditions were perfect for the rogue diver to launch his strike as he entered the calm waters. He was some distance from the wreck and would make a slow and deliberate descent, working his way deeper until he found Fahy alone.

The Second World War wreck was now within touching distance for the diving enthusiast as he decided where to enter the boat. He patrolled around the area, visually examining the damage caused by the explosion which had sunk the ship so many years ago. Old artillery and boxes of ammunition were spread around the wreck, along with other remnants of a war that he had waited for so long to examine in person. Disturbed by the odd lionfish, he continued to weave in and out of the mangled steel – the result of a catastrophic explosion caused by enemy fire – and to his surprise, he suddenly encountered a school of black-spotted sweetlips taking shelter from the currents in the remains of this timeless war machine. The boat's upright position pointing to the surface reminded him of an underwater skyscraper, shard-like, illuminated by the raging sun.

Although Edward Fahy was an experienced diver, his first visit to the wreck didn't disappoint. He continued to swim around, reaching out to touch the fish. They were just as curious as him, keeping a safe distance as he controlled his flippers.

He gazed ahead as the sun's rays continued to light up the varied species which moved from side to side like a cascading rainbow. It was akin to an art form as all the different colours clashed, and the fish, now used to human interaction, engulfed him as he swam around the boat. Pointing his powerful underwater torch in the direction of the damaged stern, which had been separated when the vessel sank, he made a decision to visit that section of the ship at the end of the dive.

The natural light from above penetrated deep, lighting up the wreck, and exposed piles of soldiers' boots and shoes strewn across the holds as a result of the huge blast. As he approached hold number five, he turned to examine the damage inflicted on the vast ship and ran his hand along the jagged edges as he tried to imagine himself there at the time of its demise. He could imagine the eruptions in his head, the screams of injured sailors and the chaos as men fought for survival; the boat had been hit by two bombs, igniting the ammunition within its bows.

He finally entered hold number one and swam through the wreckage, and HMS Thistlegorm's inner secrets were gradually revealed. It was a treasure trove. BSA motorbikes and armoured trucks lay in this war grave and the whole experience overwhelmed him. He felt a deep sense of sadness, but on the other hand a feeling of bliss. The many species of underwater life still circled him as he weaved in and out of the hold, exploring the various air pockets.

Encountering the odd soldierfish and sweeper, he continued to swim alone apart from these curious creatures fascinated by his presence. Fahy now felt part of their family and free to explore, just like his hero Jacques Cousteau had done many years ago when he had rediscovered the doomed vessel. But unbeknown to him, another diver was watching his every move.

Gently touching the windscreen of a lone armoured truck in the hull, still intact after all these years, he adjusted his regulator and entered a storeroom that was void of any natural light. It was an eerie place. This was the perfect position for the diver, and he approached Fahy from behind like a shark moving in for the kill.

He struck swiftly, and as he held the journalist in a lock, he turned off the air supply from his tank. Fahy attempted to turn back to one of the interconnecting doorways, but he couldn't move. He was trapped. Alone and without any help, he began to panic as his breathing became frantic. He tried to free himself, believing he had become entangled. He wriggled, twisted and pushed, and then realised that he was no longer alone. In a moment he thought another visiting diver had seen him in trouble and come to help.

Every breath he took became laboured as he struggled for air. It was a moment of sheer terror as he grasped and clenched his regulator, holding it tightly to his mouth. There was no air supply. Fahy was weakened by the struggle and started slipping slowly into unconsciousness. He tried once more to free himself from the wreck and the imposter who had cut off his oxygen.

The diver, strong and athletic, kept a tight grip that was so powerful in such a small area that it made it impossible for him to move. As he looked up, he could see the daylight steadily fading away, as did his last breath. The bubbles rising to the surface slowly disappeared.

It was early in the morning and the wreck site was still unusually quiet – two divers remained deep in the holds, one alive and one dead.

The killer stayed for a while to catch his breath after this monumental struggle and then placed Fahy's leg into a nearby railing, carefully trapping the foot. It would be seen as another diver who had lost his life pursuing a dangerous hobby. Gradually turning on the oxygen supply to the tank, he released the air from the regulator until it was empty.

The diver had one last task to complete – to return to the journalist's boat and remove his laptop. His assignment would then be successfully completed.

Fahy's boat remained anchored at the surface and would do so until late that afternoon, when his body would be discovered by a passing fishing boat and divers on a day trip.

The site would be closed off as an investigation started to examine the death of a freelance journalist – his secret would die with him, as his possessions were taken from the boat and returned to a grieving wife.

The Red Sea had claimed another victim. The story would run in the online magazines and again, divers would be warned about the perils of diving alone. He was a respected journalist, and his obituary would be posted in all the newspapers.

Chapter 4

Portcullis House
Tuesday, 25th October 2011

Brian Beaumont MP peered through the window of his Westminster office, overlooking Big Ben. As midday approached, the renowned chimes of the great clock rang out, drowning out the noise of heavy traffic. Beaumont loved the life in the cauldron of politics, and he stood a proud man as he gazed at the clock face.

It had been a long road. He had just been promoted to Shadow Home Secretary, and it gave him time to mull over the last six months as he prepared to resign from his post as Chairman of the Select Committee. He could hear the wind whistling through the window and noticed how quickly it carried the autumn leaves through the air, a sure sign winter was on the horizon. He hoped it would be a warmer winter than the previous one and he had a good feeling about the remainder of 2011. He was an ambitious politician, with a prosperous future ahead of him.

Pen poised, he was ready to thank his colleagues in his resignation letter, but on a day when he had been promoted by his leader, John Cotterhill, there was a profound inner feeling of disappointment that continued to dominate the politician's thoughts.

He continued to look through the window, rolling his pen in his fingers, giving a great deal of thought to how he should word his letter.

Suddenly, there was a loud bang at the door.

'Come in,' he shouted.

'Hello, Brian. Congratulations on your promotion! I thought I'd come to see the new Shadow Home Secretary.'

The speaker of the house, Arthur Betram, entered the room and embraced him.

'I can't hide my pleasure. The rate you're moving, you'll be in No. 10 in no time at all.'

A fellow Tory MP and ex-rugby player from South Wales, Betram was a huge man with a big wispy grey beard, long grey locks – always gelled – and a loud piercing voice, which could be heard across the corridors of Westminster as he brought the house to order daily. He was a loveable character, ever the eccentric.

He looked at Beaumont and mused.

'You're supposed to be ecstatic. Instead, you look like you've lost a fiver and found a penny. Cheer up!' His grin was so wide it made Beaumont laugh.

However, he was still deeply disturbed by the report, and it showed.

'I know I should be happy, Arthur, but the Select Committee's findings were farcical and that still weighs heavily on me. I'm so bloody frustrated – I've just been reading through the final report, and I have an interview this afternoon with the BBC and ITN News about the damn thing. Not to mention the broadsheets.

What do you say to them?'

'Brian! Shake yourself down,' Betram barked. 'You must get over this one. I know you're frustrated, but you could only work with the information you had, and the evidence wasn't there.' He paused. 'Do you think Labour's come out of this smelling of roses? Because I don't think they have. It's put the PM in an unenviable position. I don't think the matter's closed.'

'Yes, but they should have gone with a full public inquiry in the first instance.'

Betram agreed. 'What they should have done and what actually happened are two different things. You know how it works.'

Beaumont approached his decanter and replied, 'Let's have a celebratory drink.'

Betram raised his glass. 'That's more like it. You know, the public aren't that stupid, and I think they'll make their own minds up at the end of the day.'

Beaumont paused. 'Do you really think this is the calm before the storm?'

'My instinct tells me it's not over.'

'I suppose you're right,' replied Beaumont, clearly consoled by Bertram's encouraging tones. 'But I'm going to push for a full inquiry. I'm not letting this go and I don't think the papers will either – there's no smoke without fire. All the circumstantial evidence points to corruption, and I just think we lacked the killer blow and never got that vital piece of evidence, so they got off scot-free.'

Betram twisted his beard with his fingers and looked at Beaumont, raising his bushy eyebrows.

'If you think there's mileage – and I know you better than anyone – then you must keep pushing and use your influence wisely. I don't think it will harm our party if this snowballs. You know what I mean, don't you? Perhaps there's a smoking gun hidden away, waiting to be revealed.'

'I think there's a lot more to be revealed, I really do.'

'Just remember, you'll be upsetting a lot of people, so watch your step.'

'I know, but it's a risk I'm prepared to take,' Beaumont replied.

'As long as you consult Isabel and tell her what's happening. I know what you can be like.'

Chapter 5

The Prime Minister's black Jaguar entered Downing Street, and as the security gates closed behind them, John Smith, the Prime Minister's advisor, sat in the rear next to Charles Chillot, holding a copy of the Select Committee report.

Charles Chillot looked at Smith and said, 'Well, what do you think, John?'

'Nothing of any substance.'

The Prime Minister was guarded.

'Well, I'm not so sure. Knowing Beaumont, he'll push this.'

Smith loosened his tie. 'He will try to, Prime Minister, but he needs evidence, so at this point I think you can back Bamford.'

Charles Chillot was in a pensive mood and listened. He knew Beaumont's capabilities.

The Right Honourable Brian Beaumont MP had now been a Member of Parliament for over a decade, having previously worked as a corporate lawyer in the City of London. He was moving rapidly through the ranks within the Conservative party and his recent promotion had most definitely placed him in a position to one day become the leader of the party. After all, he was regarded by many in politics as a future prime minister, and if the Conservative party could hold its momentum in the polls and win the next general election, then Beaumont's pedigree would stand him in good stead.

He had always dreamed of a life in politics. Born into a farming background in the Oxfordshire countryside in 1960, it became abundantly clear from an early age that he would not follow in the footsteps of his father, Edward, and was most certainly destined to reach greater heights.

His primary school teacher had spotted his potential early on and once informed a packed assembly hall on a school awards day that Master Brian Beaumont would one day be 'a successful public figure'. Miss Ledger had not been wrong in her assessment of Master Beaumont. A highly intelligent individual, he progressed quickly and went on to be educated at Eton and then Oxford University, where he graduated with a first class honour's degree in Business Law. It was only a matter of time before he became a successful lawyer in the city. His intelligence was matched with a vibrant personality and good looks. Larger than life, he had a big personality, and when he entered a room, people felt his presence immediately and listened to him.

He continued to cut a popular figure both with his peers within the party and the public at large. Not a luxury John Cotterhill enjoyed as the current leader of the party faithful. It was simply down to personality, and many considered Beaumont had that wow factor necessary for the world of modern politics.

That's when he had formed a close relationship with Patrick Sands, who had written a piece on him when he emerged into the world of politics. Sands was no doubt drawn to him and they became close.

Beaumont had unsurprisingly excelled at Oxford University and became president of the students' union. At times, the young man could be quite rebellious, but this did not detract from his love of politics born from his travels as a young student, when he loved to travel to London in his formative years and sit for hours at Speaker's Corner, listening to a whole host of speakers from the sublime to the ridiculous. He didn't mind rubbing people up the wrong way if he thought he was right. Popular and successful in the financial capital, he eventually became tired of the monotonous daily grind of dealing with complex fraud cases and wanted to return to his true love, the world of politics. The corridors of Westminster beckoned...

During the years of relentless studying and working in the city he had gained a reputation as a ladies' man, but this changed when he eventually met his wife Isabel, ten years his junior. Isabel's intelligence, wit and beauty were irresistible to Beaumont and, according to many of his peers, she had a big influence on his change of lifestyle and meteoric rise within the Conservative party. Having become acquainted with her four years previously at a Law Society dinner at the Guildhall in London, and after a whirlwind romance, they married in Oxford – his birthplace and constituency.

Even the opposition spoke about Beaumont in positive terms. Charles Chillot, Prime Minister, had recently been quoted in The Times during an interview – *Everything Brian Beaumont touches turns to gold.*

A naive statement from a seasoned leader about an opposition MP, especially to a journalist, but he did speak his mind.

Both the Beaumonts were successful in their own right, and this meant they had busy schedules. As a consequence, they could sometimes only muster a few hours together each week. There were no children – the subject of starting a family had never been a popular topic of conversation.

Isabel was born in Manchester and studied law in her home city, then moved to the capital where she eventually set up her own legal practice in Islington. It had become so successful that the firm had now relocated to Regent Street at the heart of the West End. She had been a star pupil at Manchester Grammar School and wasn't bad on the sporting front either, excelling in volleyball and hockey.

Both careers afforded them a lavish lifestyle, and they loved the hustle and bustle of Camden Town, where they settled after Brian's election to Parliament.

Beaumont was rapidly approaching his 50th birthday. He knew that time was running out and felt at some point he should mount the challenge to become leader of the party. He had calculated that if he timed the move precisely, there was a possibility he could become Prime Minister. The current scandal involving the Foreign Secretary would not go away and rising unemployment coupled with bad press had eroded the lead held by the Labour party. Times were good for the Conservatives. If the Tory Party was in the ascendency, then so was Beaumont.

He sat outside on the terrace of the Houses of Parliament mid afternoon. He was deep in thought while he smoked his favourite cigar and sipped his pint of Guinness. It was an unusually warm autumn day as he looked in the direction of Westminster Bridge, admiring the view while he reflected on events in recent weeks.

His moment of tranquillity ended abruptly as his secretary, Jane McEwan, approached and tapped him on the shoulder.

'Hello, Brian. I wondered where you were, I've been looking for you.'

'Is it urgent? You've caught me by surprise. I was having a quiet moment to myself.'

'No. Leslie, the new intern, has been tidying up the cupboard and we've found a bundle of old Select Committee reports in folders. We don't want to discard them or send them to the archives without your say-so.'

'Thanks, Jane,' Beaumont replied. 'I think I need to go through them before we do anything with them, and I do appreciate that my filing system, which I must say works for me, is not everybody's cup of tea.'

Jane smiled.

'I didn't want to put it that way, but since you have broached the subject, it is very untidy.'

'I promise you, cross my heart and hope to die, I'll help you tidy up, but make sure we can put aside a full day.' Beaumont was repentant. He always was when his disorderly ways were discussed.

Jane had raised the subject with Isabel at several social functions, but it had little effect on his habits.

'Thanks, Brian, I will hold you to your promise.'

Beaumont paused and stubbed his cigar right in the middle of the portcullis emblem in the base of the ashtray as he continued to drink his pint.

'Would you like to join me and we can discuss some matters, and I might be able to help explain the content of some of the older Select Committee papers? We can also indulge in idle banter, I suppose.'

Jane flicked back her long blonde locks.

'Of course, that would be nice. Mr Beaumont, if I didn't know you better I might think you're flirting with me.'

She suddenly remembered an article she had read in the paper that morning and tapped Beaumont on the shoulder.

'Oh, before I forget, did you know a journalist called Edward Fahy?'

'No, I don't think I know…'

'Eton, does that ring any bells?'

Beaumont had a puzzled expression on his face. 'Oh yes, I think I may have heard the name.'

'Come on, think.'

Beaumont had to dig deep. 'Ah yes, come to think of it he was a couple of years below me, but I didn't know him personally. I think he played for the cricket team. Why, what's happened?'

'He was a freelance journalist…'

Beaumont impatiently interrupted. 'Well, is he being knighted or does he wish to speak to me?'

Jane prepared herself and replied, 'Well, that won't happen. He's been killed in a diving accident in Egypt. I just thought I'd let you know … I thought you'd know him.'

'Well, that's sad, but I didn't know him. There are lots of ex-pupils from Eton that crop up from time to time. It's sad.'

Beaumont was visibly shaken, but he wiped any negative thoughts from his mind very quickly.

It would be a relaxing lunch for him. Even with his

continued success, he was still far from comfortable with the allegations of corruption hanging over Westminster. He had a deep sense of duty. He wanted the Foreign Secretary, Robert Bamford, to stand up and be counted.

He wanted Jane's opinion on the whole affair. It mattered to him.

'What did you think of the Select Committee report, Jane?'

She was receptive. 'I thought it made some good points. It's a pity you weren't backed up by some of the MPs, but nothing in this place surprises me any more.' She paused for a while and looked at him. 'I will say something though, and I hope I don't speak out of turn, but since you have asked for my opinion, then I shall give it.'

'Please do.'

'I've never liked Robert Bamford. He has a dark side, and you can call it a woman's intuition, but I think he's a creep. If you keep digging, then you will find something. I've seen him around Soho several times, and he's denied seeing me the next day.'

'Bloody hell, I didn't know that.' Beaumont was pleasantly surprised.

'C'mon, you know we have the same views.'

Beaumont knew he was on the right track and held court. He was also aware that there was still a mistrust of most politicians and the popular media would always be waiting to pounce at any sign of impropriety by any member of the House. Another man's downfall could open the gate for him. After all, he was a politician, and he knew how to play the game.

He took his seat and sighed.

Jane observed Beaumont. 'It's about time you relaxed and took a holiday with Isabel.'

Clearly frustrated, she added, 'Let's get back to business. You're not in a relaxed state of mind, are you?'

'I'm fine,' said Beaumont as he held his knife and fork, inspecting the steak that lay on the plate before him.

Jane was experienced in the workings of Parliament. She had been around long enough to know that her boss was ambitious and more than happy to go along for the ride. She always relished the thought of possibly one day being secretary to the leader of the party. She encouraged Brian to push forward as they both sat together in the restaurant.

Beaumont made a brief call to his wife Isabel and then contacted his close friend, Patrick Sands. It was unusual for Beaumont to have such a close relationship with a journalist, but that's the way it was. They were inseparable.

Beaumont answered, 'Hello Patrick?'

'Brian, I need to talk to you about your Select Committee work. Something's come up, and before you say anything, it's nothing to worry about.'

Beaumont calmly replied, 'Why, what's it about?'

'I don't think we should discuss the matter over the phone, if you get my drift. Can I see you today? The Clarence on Whitehall would be a good place, and we can chat.'

Concerned by Patrick's sombre tone, Beaumont said, 'When?'

'ASAP!' Sands shouted down the phone.

'I've got to tie up some loose ends, so I'll see you about 5 p.m. That'll give me half an hour.'

'Fine.'

Beaumont placed the phone back into his Barbour jacket and started to feel rather agitated. He was not normally the worrying type. However, he had known Sands for many years, and one thing he did know was that if he said the matter was important, it would be. He would waste no time in preparing for the meeting with his friend. The short walk back to Portcullis House would be a good time to consider what news Sands might have in store.

Counting the cracks in the pavement and making the odd call, Beaumont finally reached his office and was greeted by Leslie, the new intern. Jane, now back at the office, was surrounded by brown envelopes and box files. Beaumont realised these were the Select Committee files. He had no intention of hanging around.

'You're back so soon, Jane?' he asked.

His greeting fell on deaf ears and he laughed.

'I didn't realise there were so many. We will get it sorted out, I promise, but not today.'

It would be a fleeting visit to his office. He collected his case and left the girls as they tried to put the mountain of files in some sort of chronological order.

Beaumont never drove when he was in Westminster, preferring to take the tube or walk, and as the Clarence was only minutes away, he took the brisk walk up Whitehall towards the public house close to Great Scotland Yard.

He loved the Clarence Public House. It had an atmosphere – sawdust on the floor, the smell of beer mixed with an aroma of the cooking food – and since being elected he had always regarded it as his local.

En route to the pub, Beaumont was acknowledged several times by strangers. He was now a well-known public figure, and it surprised him when he was stopped by the public for the odd autograph or even a photograph. He couldn't take the new celebrity culture too seriously – he was confused as to why a politician could be treated this way, but deep down he enjoyed the attention. Isabel would tease him over his newfound status.

As media speculation regarding his calls for a public inquiry grew, so did his image as the volume of media work increased. Jane had complained recently about his new Twitter account he had decided to launch. Thousands of followers resulted, and he didn't even know how to interact with them.

The Clarence was packed when Beaumont finally arrived. He couldn't find Patrick Sands, so he sent him a quick text and bought himself a Guinness and the usual brandy for his friend. He found a comfortable chair in a quiet corner and waited. He didn't have to wait too long.

'Hello, Brian,' shouted Sands in a loud penetrating voice that echoed across the room.

Sands seemed to be in an upbeat mood. The fact that Beaumont had bought him a drink may have cheered him up. Eventually sitting down after exchanging the usual pleasantries, the subject of the inquiry was broached and with that the mood changed quickly. Their conversation, almost boisterous, soon turned into a more sombre whisper and Sands broached the subject.

'Brian, I've been speaking to a contact regarding another story and, in passing, he mentioned your name and your push for an inquiry into corruption. He'd been reading the papers.'

'Does he know we're close?'

'Oh yes. It's not a problem, but I wanted to tell you about it.'

Brian whispered into Sands' ear, 'Can you tell me who it is?'

'Not yet. I don't think it's all that relevant. However, I can tell you he's straight and a reliable source. I'll do some digging for you. As you know, I'm speaking to you as a friend, but he has warned me that your calls for a public inquiry are ruffling feathers with some big players within the establishment.'

Beaumont paused and let out a long sigh. 'Well, who might that be I wonder?' He took a drink from his glass. 'I realise this. It was always going to happen. Is this guy who you know involved? Is this a veiled threat from him?'

'No, not at all,' replied Sands. 'He overheard a conversation in a gentlemen's club the other night and passed it on to me.'

'Who were they?'

'He said he didn't know, but they were obviously important and your name was brought up on more than one occasion.'

'I'd love to know who they are.'

'Don't worry, my contact has asked his friend to find out because even he didn't know. When I hear anything, I'll get back to you.'

Beaumont smiled and said, 'Interesting, very interesting indeed.'

Concerned for his friend's welfare, Sands replied, 'It is interesting, but my instinct tells me to warn you to tread carefully.'

Beaumont, unperturbed by Sands' warning, said, 'Don't worry, I will. This is why we need to get into government. At least then I would have an armed officer to watch my back, but at this moment in time I'll just have to fend for myself.'

He laughed hysterically, which seemed to have a calming influence on his friend and confidant.

'I'll keep my eyes and ears close to the ground,' Sands reassured him. 'You're a good friend, Brian.'

Beaumont thanked Sands. 'I appreciate your help, but in the meantime I'm going to keep pressing for this inquiry.'

'Well come on, what's the state of play?'

'I think there will have to be an announcement soon by the Prime Minister, but if there isn't, then we will apply pressure as a party. The only way to have any sort of transparency, especially in this matter, is to hold a full public inquiry.'

'But what about the Select Committee?'

'Patrick, it was a load of bollocks, a non-starter. The whole matter needs to be looked at by a prominent member of the judiciary. The findings of the committee I chaired weren't unanimous and certain individuals bottled it. When that happened, the report had no weight. However, there are certain quarters within the media that want to keep this running and won't let it drop, and I'm going to board their train.'

Sands agreed. 'I know, but Labour won't want this inquiry, surely?'

'Definitely not, but if they don't, pressure will grow and PMQs will become a farce. As you know all too well, the papers are after blood – this whole push for a public hearing needs to hold its course. It's in everyone's interests.'

Sands' attention was alerted. 'There could be some mileage in this for you and your party, Brian.'

Beaumont smiled, paused, took a deep breath and said, 'Politics is a dirty game, Patrick, and this could be an election winner for us.'

'I've heard rumours that the tabloids are still gunning for Bamford, and I think Edward Fahy had been interested in him for years, but he died recently in a diving accident.'

Beaumont's ears pricked up. 'Did you know him?'

'In passing, yes. He was a very private man. Bit of a loner, some might say, but a great investigative journalist. He was like a dog with a bone, and if he thought he had a lead he wouldn't let go. Changing the subject, though, you're right about politics, and if you play your cards right it could be a winner.'

Beaumont grinned.

Sands had a knowing look on his face. 'Mmm, the straw that broke the camel's back, so to speak.'

'I couldn't have phrased it better myself. Let's get drunk.'

It was surprising how alcohol eased the tension.

Chapter 6

Brian Beaumont's campaign to call a public inquiry was still gathering pace, and the media coverage was intensifying. John Cotterhill, the Tory leader, remained surprisingly quiet as Beaumont took the lead in this campaign.

The Right Honourable Charles Chillot MP had just finished a Cabinet meeting at Downing Street and was sat in his office with his trusted advisors. He was preparing for the weekly press conference and had a good idea of what was going to be the topic of the day.

The Prime Minister was in a frosty mood; if it wasn't a grilling in the papers, then it would be a ravaging at PMQs at the hands of the opposition MPs – the pressure was relentless. John Smith, the Prime Minister's advisor, was close by, also consumed by the tension within the walls of Downing Street.

The Prime Minister said, 'John! Before he leaves the building, I must speak to the Foreign Secretary. I need to be fully briefed before I speak.'

'Yes, Prime Minister. I'll phone the Cabinet Room

now,' replied an uneasy Smith.

Chillot stood away from his desk and started waving newspapers at his bemused audience as they sat back and relaxed on his settee. This posse of civil servants had seen it all before.

'Look at this press coverage – all negative.'

The silence and relaxed mood within the room ended abruptly. The Prime Minster ranted…

'I've got Brian Beaumont all over me like a rash – letters, phone calls, and then he briefs the press every day about a public inquiry he wants me to call. I cannot see how we can push this one aside … if I find out there is anything wrong and Labour MPs are found wanting, I'll throw them to the wolves.'

His remarks were met with a wall of silence. No one dared to speak when the Prime Minister was in this mood.

'Where's fucking Bamford? I want to see him now, John.'

His main advisor, standing well back, replied, 'Prime Minister, he's on his way.'

Chillot said, 'You know, John, I can't wait for the reshuffle. I'm going to get rid of some of the deadwood.'

Sleeves rolled up and his tie loosened, Chillot paced around his office. A knock on the door was followed by a quick response from the unsettled leader.

'Come in.'

Robert Bamford entered the room. He looked nervously at the Prime Minister; he wasn't his usual boisterous self.

'Robert, we need to speak about this ongoing story. Beaumont is still pushing for a full public inquiry, and

I'm going to get another mauling from the press this morning. I need assurances that there has been no wrongdoing before I go in and defend you.'

Bamford was quick to respond.

'With all due respect, Prime Minister, we have gone over this before. I will again repeat what I said previously.'

Chillot detected that Bamford was fed up with the whole saga.

Bamford was forthright. 'As you know, I have had meetings on a number of occasions and have attended various dinners and functions with the Russian Ambassador and some of his friends, and I cannot vouch for every person who comes into contact with me. The Select Committee looked into the matter and could find no wrongdoing on my part. I accept that allegations have been raised, but I still categorically deny them. I have a happy marriage and a family. Yes, mistakes were made and perhaps I was naive, as the Committee has pointed out, but I have never had any relationships with prostitutes, and to think I am courting certain members of the Russian Mafia is absurd. I am prepared to put this in writing if you wish, but I cannot add any further to the report I have previously submitted.'

Bamford was ready to walk out of the room. The Prime Minister stopped him in his tracks.

'Robert, we go back a long way and I regard you as a friend, and I will back you, but the pressure is intensifying so much it's becoming an unnecessary distraction for the government.'

'Would it be easier if I resign?'

'No. I'll back you for the time being, but be prepared

for a public inquiry – this train is running fast, and I can't stop it. The media aren't letting go.'

'Forgive me, but I shall be frank. From where I stand, I don't detect much support.'

The Prime Minister was furious. 'Nonsense, you're talking absolute rubbish. However, if we are throwing insults around and you question my loyalty, then I suggest you choose your company more wisely in the future.'

Bamford stared at the Prime Minister, his eyes penetrating deep into his line of vision.

He stood his ground and replied in a defiant tone, 'Don't worry, Prime Minister, I'll choose my company wisely.'

Chillot sighed and, in a deflated tone, said to his advisor, 'John, you must keep me briefed on all press regarding this matter.'

Bamford said, 'Thank you, Prime Minister. I understand your position.'

'Okay, but I would prepare for a rocky ride, and watch out! Beaumont is an intelligent man, and he has an agenda. His ambition is to be standing in this very room after the general election. In fact, he's a fucking pain in the arse that won't go away – a smart arse of the highest order.'

There was another pause, and the Prime Minister took a deep breath.

Bamford laughed sarcastically and said, 'Yes, Prime Minister, the very man you chose to commend in your recent article. A very smart move, I'd say.'

Chillot walked towards Bamford and said, 'Don't preach to me the rights and wrongs of politics, Robert. Now fuck off out of my sight.'

Smith had never seen the PM so angry. Chillot quickly calmed down and turned to his advisor.

'Right, John, I had better go downstairs and feed these wolves.'

Robert Bamford left the Prime Minister's office and headed to the top of the stairs, where he gazed at the pictures of previous Cabinets and Ministers, his picture being the closest to the PM's office. Would Bamford survive this barrage from Brian Beaumont MP and the press?

Chillot walked briskly down the steps on a mission, papers in hand, and approached the main hall where the press waited. There was a sudden flurry of activity within the room; flashlights and bodies ducking beneath his lectern, eager to get their microphones close to the leader.

He took his position, looking for familiar faces, and after a short introduction from Smith, the questions began. They came thick and fast. The media machine was in full flow.

Charles Chillot was now well into his first term as Prime Minister and these were challenging times. He had made his way up through the ranks of the Labour party slowly. His wife had given up a promising career in the oil industry and was seen as instrumental in his success. She had shaped him into the man he was. He would now have to use his skills to get out of possibly the worst crisis he had faced as Prime Minister.

Born into a mining family in Golborne, Lancashire in 1950, Chillot would follow a different path than that of his father, Eric, a face worker at Parsonage Colliery, a small mine in the industrial town of Leigh, Lancashire. He had witnessed the decimation of the coal industry in his town – an act he still believed was orchestrated by the Conservative government – which in turn had brought hardship to his family and many others who had been affected by the mass pit closures.

After finishing his studies at Leigh Grammar School, Chillot moved to the capital and studied at the London School of Economics, and subsequently worked as a lecturer at Edinburgh University where he met his wife, Jean, at an oil industry conference in Aberdeen. His political views never changed. You couldn't get a stronger Labour man than Charles Chillot. His opposition and disdain towards Tory policy was stronger than that of any of his colleagues.

He often cited in anti-Tory speeches and media interviews the decline of the NCB and the destruction of the board's HQ, Anderton House in Lowton as an example of Tory attitudes towards the north and its inhabitants. That's why his party faithful were so surprised when he complimented Brian Beaumont in the newspapers. Was it a mistake or a compliment from a man who recognised potential?

Chillot still had a strong northern accent, which had mellowed during his time spent in the capital. His wife regularly poked fun at his northern twang, but he wouldn't change, not even for her.

The Prime Minister had always had an interest in the Trade Union movement and was actively involved in their affairs wherever he worked. He was a good speaker and a motivator. The skills he had attained would now be tested to their limit, and he was poised at the lectern, ready. The Prime Minster was assertive.

'Yes, you,' he said, pointing at the fresh-faced journalist. 'First question. Yes, you, Alastair, fire away.'

The journalist delivered his question. 'Thank you, Prime Minister. I must start by quoting Brian Beaumont this morning in The Times. He has again said that you must set up a public inquiry into corruption and that you are stalling.'

Chillot didn't hesitate in responding. 'Thank you, Alastair. I'm not stalling at all, quite the contrary. I am once more looking into the matter and stand by Robert Bamford, who has been given some very negative press in the last few weeks. The Foreign Secretary has assured me there has been no wrongdoing, and I must point out that the Select Committee, originally chaired by Brian Beaumont himself, didn't really unearth any real issues. Bamford is a hardworking MP and has been a dedicated Foreign Minister, in particular when pushing through our foreign policy. Not to mention his negotiating skills, which have been invaluable in dealing with nations embroiled in civil war at the recent UN conference. I have nothing further to add on this matter.'

The journalist, waving his biro, continued. 'I agree, Prime Minister, but the leader of the Conservative party, John Cotterhill, has also called for a public inquiry and has pointed out that when you were elected, the main header in the manifesto described the need for total accountability and clarity within the government. Has he got a point?'

The journalist waved the Labour manifesto above his head.

Chillot leant on the lectern and lowered his spectacles, making eye contact with the reporter.

'I can assure you accountability is high on the government's agenda, and I have never ruled out an inquiry into this matter, but I am confident that if there is such an inquiry, nothing will come of it and the Foreign Secretary will again be totally vindicated – I believe in total transparency.'

The questions kept coming and coming – some related to the poor state of the domestic economy, some to foreign policy, but the vast majority related to Beaumont's call for a public inquiry, and they were fired at the Prime Minister one after the other. It was relentless, and a tired Chillot was looking forward to the end of this press conference and his forthcoming trip to Chequers, where he could regroup and speak to his close advisors. He wanted to be away from the spotlight of No 10 Downing Street.

He would also be able to spend some valuable time with and confide in his most trusted advisor, his wife Jean.

A testing time lay ahead for the Prime Minister … it would be a long, cold winter.

Chapter 7

November 2011

The office, occupied by Detective Chief Inspector Jack Edgerton, was in close proximity to Downing Street, but poles apart in the way business was conducted.

As the enigmatic detective sat back on his reclining chair, he raised his feet and slammed them hard on the windowsill.

Staring out of the large window behind his desk, he sighed and said loudly to himself, 'What am I going to do with myself today? Why's it so quiet? It's driving me insane.'

In a pensive mood, he looked out over the River Thames, looking in the direction of the South Bank towards the London Eye, watching pedestrians walk along the bank going about their daily business.

The freezing fog was hanging over the landscape, slowly crawling along the river's surface. There was an occasional glint of sunshine, which reflected back off the River Thames, causing the detective to squint. Bored, he reached for his binoculars and slowly focused in on the Battle of Britain bronze memorial.

'Absolutely fucking amazing,' he said loudly to

himself. 'I wonder how long it took to create this ... fantastic!'

He scoured every inch of its surface and then put the binoculars back. The protruding bronze figures captivated the detective's imagination, as did the stunningly beautiful blond with large breasts and long, lean legs that slowly came into his view as she passed the memorial.

'What a sight,' the detective whispered.

Edgerton was comfortable in his new but unusual surroundings. While renovation work was being carried out at his old office in Scotland Yard, the Murder Squad had been temporarily moved to the Ministry of Defence buildings in Whitehall, which he enjoyed, although it had certain operational drawbacks. It meant that he wasn't in the same building as his immediate supervisor, Detective Chief Superintendent Robert Watkins, but that arrangement suited him.

Watkins had just returned from a brief spell at Bramshill Police College on a senior command course and was a flyer, unlike Edgerton. The experienced detective had come up through the ranks the hard way. Edgerton thought Watkins had changed for the worse since his return from the college. That's the way he saw it, and so did many of his colleagues – Edgerton was a popular and a formidable figure. The view from his office on the fifth floor afforded him an enviable view of London.

The sound of his athletic frame hitting the windowsill must have alerted the officers sat in the main incident room outside his office. The door opened, and he was greeted by Detective Constable Chloe Moran.

'Are you okay, Guv?'

'Chloe, it's too quiet for me. When I start to think about how I will spend my retirement and staring through binoculars, something's not right.'

'Never say it's dead, Guv, you're tempting fate,' replied Moran as she sat on the end of the desk.

There was a silent pause, and Edgerton relaxed and closed his eyes.

He drew breath and shouted out, 'I wandered lonely as a cloud...'

Moran interrupted sharply, and in a quiet voice continued, 'That floats on high o'er vales and hills, when all at once I saw a crowd, a host, of golden daffodils; beside the lake, beneath the trees, fluttering and dancing in the breeze...'

She continued to recite William Wordsworth's classic poem to its conclusion.

Edgerton sat up in astonishment, and before he could say anything Moran said, 'I knew my degree would one day impress you, Guv!'

He remained silent, his face glowing with appreciation and affection. He didn't need to utter a single word.

'Where is the boss, Guv?' Moran whispered.

'Not sure, and quite frankly at this moment I couldn't give a toss. When he's not here he's out of sight, out of mind.'

There was a slight tension between the two detectives, and Edgerton regularly showed his disapproval of a system which he thought promoted the privileged public schoolboy with a university degree. He found it difficult to relate to some of the politically correct ideas which the force had now adopted and which Chief Superintendent Watkins appeared to embrace.

He didn't like the Bramshill way of training. He thought it was a form of brainwashing. He would often moan in the pub to some of his trusted colleagues after a few pints and deliver his favourite line: 'They couldn't nick themselves shaving, never mind arrest a hardened criminal.'

Rocking the boat didn't frighten Edgerton; after all, it was the least of his concerns. His adolescent years playing on the tough streets of his birthplace, Bermondsey, moulded his personality. An area in South London adjacent to the Elephant and Castle and close to Peckham and Brixton was a place few outsiders visited.

As a young boy he regularly watched his favourite team, Millwall, at the old Den in Cold Blow Lane, New Cross with his father, Ian. That was an experience in itself during the years when hooliganism was rife. Edgerton still watched his team occasionally in the New Den, when he had time. The club had come a long way in recent years and he loved to take his daughters on the odd occasion. Football was in his blood.

The Detective Chief Inspector never closed his door. He loved nothing more than to mingle with all the different ranks.

DC Moran decided to leave the office and said, 'I'll need to sort the exhibits from the Jenkins case, it's up for committal at the Inner London Crown Court in the next couple of weeks.'

'Yeah, it needs to be boxed off, but the exhibits were moved yesterday – sorry, I forgot to tell you.'

'Oh! Where are they?'

'I had an email from Watkins, and they've relocated them back to the Yard. It's probably easier for us in the long run.'

'Nice of them to give us notice.'

Edgerton didn't reply, and just gave Moran an agreeable nod.

Moran showed her displeasure and said, 'Who's running the show then at the Yard?'

'DS Brian Martin – do you remember him? He was the old court sergeant at the Old Bailey, then he worked for the Diplomatic Protection Group. His tenure was up, so as retirement beckoned, he got this sideways move.'

Moran frowned. 'I know him. I thought he would have had a cushy number at court.'

'Not my cup of tea, I must say.'

The Jenkins case had had a profound effect on some of the officers on the Murder Squad. It had been a particularly unpleasant domestic murder, which had left two youngsters without a family.

Edgerton had decided it was time to have a team-bonding exercise. Another terminology he might have used was 'an almighty great piss-up', which would normally end at the curry house in Pimlico.

While things were quiet in the Murder Squad office, he decided to take a walk to clear his mind. Sometimes a brisk walk up to Trafalgar Square and on to the Mall would suffice, but today he decided to hop on the Number 12 bus from Whitehall and visit his old stomping ground near the Elephant and Castle. Once he hit the Walworth Road, he would do what he normally did when taking a walk and just follow his instincts. It would be a therapeutic exercise.

As he approached Whitehall, it reminded him of his days as a young probationary constable walking the beat and the fun nights he had at the police section house in Soho with his colleagues. After all, it was his home for several years, and at three quid a month rent it was the cheapest flat anyone could have in the heart of London.

Edgerton treasured his time in Soho, and wished he could have turned the clock back to rekindle those moments and to relive the nights he spent in the smoky Brahms and List jazz club near Bow Street nick, drinking copious amounts of Rioja. Not to mention the long list of women he escorted back to his room for nights of passion.

The bus soon arrived and he settled quickly on the upper deck after a quick flash of the warrant card to the bus driver. He always sat upstairs, as it afforded him a better view. It was a swift journey to the Elephant and Castle, and as he approached the Walworth Road, he began to feel rather excited at the prospect of his little adventure, even though he knew the area like the back of his hand. Before he got off the bus, he took a quick glance at his phone, but there were no missed calls and no messages.

His principal port of call would be Carter Street Police Station, his first posting after completing his training at Hendon as a young trainee and cadet. Carter Street had recently closed, with a new station opening around the corner – which seemed to be order of the day, as the Met wanted to modernise its operation. He was rather saddened that they had renamed it Walworth Police Station. Carter Street had a much more traditional edge to it and for years had a fearsome reputation amongst even the hardest of criminals.

Edgerton was always open to change, but still wondered whether some of the recent transformations actually improved the efficiency of the force. He believed in the good old-fashioned method of policing – talking to people and mixing and working closely with informants in the most unlikely of places. He felt the job had become overly sanitised and restricted, and the expectations from the bosses at the top were unrealistic.

As he approached his old workplace in Carter Place, the slight breeze carried the waft of pigeon droppings from the nearby railway bridge, which brought back memories. He had spent many an hour cleaning bird crap off his beloved Ford Fiesta XR2 after a shift, and with his colleagues had spent an equal amount of time firing stones into the rafters to get rid of them, but like all pigeons in London, they were resilient creatures and always returned to their nests. Even the regular train that passed from Elephant and Castle train station on the hour, which nearly shook the bridge to its foundations, had no effect on the birds.

He wanted to check under the railway bridge one last time. He didn't need to – he could still hear the warbling coming from the voids up above him, and the familiar tackiness on the pavement coupled with the ever-strengthening stench. It was time for him to make a sharp U-turn.

The aged police station was almost unrecognisable now that it had been converted into flats – if the residents knew the history of the building he wondered if they would have ever moved in, but on inspection they did look rather splendid.

Edgerton didn't want to reminisce about this Old Nick, or he would have been there all day long. It was time to head up East Street Market to the Old Kent Road. He loved the hustle and bustle of the market – this was a place in policing terms which had everything. As he walked into the crowded street, he placed both hands in his pockets and held onto his wallet – experience had taught him to be suspicious. The smell of bacon oozed out of the extractor fans from nearby cafés into the atmosphere, and the shouts of local market traders plying their trade rang in his ears.

East Street Market was like a small town against the backdrop of a vast concrete jungle. It was the notorious vast Aylesbury Estate. With a huge expanse of council flats, it was one of the biggest council estates in Europe and one of the few places that really daunted Edgerton. Built in the early 1960s, the estate housed around ten thousand residents and totally dominated the skyline of Walworth. It was like a spider's web, interconnected by narrow walkways that were well above street level, making it a haven for criminal activity. Edgerton knew the layout, but always felt intimidated when wrapped in its clutches. The whole aura that the estate gave made it an ideal natural film set for crime movies. It didn't need much preparation to make a film – it was a ready-made film set. Its mere existence made it a mecca for film directors, especially when night fell.

Over the years, the estate had deteriorated and Edgerton had been involved in the investigation of numerous incidents. He knew only too well that the chances of reaching a satisfactory conclusion were marred by the complex workings of one of Europe's biggest housing estates.

Walking along the walkway next to Wendover House, Edgerton heard someone shout, 'Oi.' He turned around and saw the place was deserted, so he carried on.

'Jack, get off my patch.' Another yell came from the flats that bounced off all the walls.

He turned around again, frustrated at not knowing where the shouts were coming from. Then he saw a figure hiding in a doorway with his police helmet under his arm. Still not recognising the officer, he approached.

As he got closer, he said, 'Smithers, you tosser, you shit me up!'

'How are you, Jack? It's been a long time.'

'Not bad, Joe,' Edgerton replied. 'What are you up to?'

'I'm just carrying out some house-to-house enquiries. There was a robbery the other night, you know, the usual.'

Edgerton was instinctively nosey when it came to police work. 'Why, what happened?' he asked.

'An old lady had her bag nicked.'

Edgerton and Joe Smithers had worked together previously as beat officers at Carter Street, and Joe was coming up to retirement. He knew the estate like the back of his hand – every nook and cranny, every villain, every snooping neighbour, every informant.

Smithers said in a surprised tone, 'More to the point, what are *you* doing here, Jack? You'll get lost. Did you bring an A-to-Z?'

'Cheeky sod! I'm on a trip – one of sentimentality. Just thought I'd come back to the old stomping ground.'

'How's the Murder Squad?' Smithers quipped.

'It's quiet at the moment; probably the lull before the storm, so you take these moments and treasure them, pal. We're just tying up some loose ends on the Jenkins case before it goes to the Old Bailey, and then we shall wait until the next one drops on the desk.'

'I vaguely remember reading about that case in the Evening Standard.'

'It was a difficult one, for the family and the troops.'

'Who's your boss at the Yard?'

'Well, we're not at the Yard at the moment; they've stuck us in the MOD buildings in Whitehall, which as it goes is alright for me, but Watkins is running the show.'

A grimace appeared on Joe Smithers' face. It was a knowing look.

In a surprised voice, Edgerton said, 'I'm surprised you know him.'

'Oh, I know him. Mr PC.'

'So, you know him well,' replied Edgerton. He couldn't stop himself laughing.

'I'll fill you in another day, over a pint perhaps in the Beehive, just like the old days. But I've got to go back to the nick now.'

Edgerton waved and turned in the direction of the Old Kent Road.

Just as Smithers started to leave his vision, he screamed, 'Joe, perhaps you might like a stint with us before you go off to the knacker's yard.'

Smithers turned towards Edgerton and waved, chuckling. Both the officers went their separate ways.

Smithers may have thought Edgerton was joking, but he was deadly serious. Smithers would be a valuable asset to Jack Edgerton's team.

Edgerton had decided to take a walk and see where his legs would take him, so he continued to head towards the Old Kent Road, looking skywards and scanning the walkways and flats above him. He hadn't forgotten his instincts, even though he had long been out of uniform – the last thing he wanted was a fridge or old cooker to be thrown in his direction from a window up above.

Some of the local residents could sniff a policeman a mile away; it had become part of their culture to play a game of cat and mouse with the cops, and the stakes were high. It didn't make a difference whether you were in uniform or plain clothes – they had a sixth sense, and any policeman was fair game.

Every now and again, an overpowering smell of stale urine would blow towards him from the entrances to the flats, so bad he held his handkerchief to his nose and mouth.

He always carried a handkerchief soaked in his favourite aftershave. He often used it at murder scenes and post mortems. He had never become accustomed to the smell of death and had a fragile stomach. He hated that sweet smell of death that would stick to your clothing and secrete itself in your pockets, only to jump out at you weeks later. He scurried away and found fresh air.

In front of him he noticed an old lady creeping towards him with her walking stick, almost bent double and walking at a snail's pace. As he watched her closely, he wondered how people so frail could be allowed to live in such places, where the only mode of transport was by foot. Why should they have to negotiate steps daily and then have to suffer the indignity of having to stand in a graffiti-covered lift, time after time, to reach a flat perched high up in the sky? Not to mention having to contend with the smell of piss and discarded refuse as well.

This life was worlds apart from the surroundings he had left in Central London – glamour and despair was his most powerful thought. As far as Edgerton was concerned, this estate was run by a pack of organised criminals who preyed upon the weak, and the rest had to suffer. He hated criminals, and they hated him. He was happy with that arrangement. It drove him on.

A well-commended officer, he didn't suffer fools gladly and was sometimes accused of being aloof and rude by certain senior officers, but they knew his experience was invaluable. Jack Edgerton believed that the first priority of policing was to uphold the law and let the other organisations pick up the pieces. He had complained to Chloe Moran recently that he was spending too much time on irrelevant politically correct courses that were getting in the way of his real work. The only course he had any time for were his regular visits to his firearms re classification classes with his old friend and colleague Detective Inspector Philip Palmer. While sat in a classroom Jack always felt he was wasting valuable time neglecting the real task at hand. He hadn't joined the police to be a social worker or community leader. He just wanted to feel collars.

Edgerton had a caring side, and under his tough exterior colleagues would say that he could be the kindest of men and had a great rapport with victims of crime.

He had a quote that he regularly preached to his colleagues: 'I will arrest the baddies and then leave the rest of the shit for everybody else to clear up.' Not everybody agreed with this view.

Of course, the new addition to the squad, Chloe Moran – a graduate from Bath University – liked Edgerton and had become close friends with him. Nineteen years his junior, Chloe had decided she liked his methods better than those that were taught at training school. Perhaps she had been attracted to the other side of his personality.

Edgerton was tall, handsome and athletic, but was from time to time oblivious to the attention of the opposite sex, especially when embroiled in his police work.

Winter had arrived, and he was now feeling the cold as he walked through the South London streets. Through the misty sky, the sun had started to appear to brighten up his dull surroundings as he approached Bagshot Street. *What a shithole*, he thought. The area was full of heroin addicts, affectionately known as skagheads, running around like rats in a sewer. It was worse now than when he was a probationer. He could still see the used needles littering the stairways and the burnt tin foil, all remnants of heroin abuse floating in the light breeze. It made his blood boil. *The root of all evil*, he thought.

He found the whole world of drugs sickening and had a deep-rooted hatred for the dealers who dealt this deadly chemical. He had witnessed too many youngsters grabbed by heroin addiction and seen first-hand the lengths they would go to, to get their hands on it. Young kids, some from loving families, who would steal, prostitute themselves and betray their families to get their next fix.

He had as much contempt for the politicians, who he thought had no idea when it came to legislating against the drug barons. The world of drugs was far away from their sheltered existence. Did they know how it ruined people's lives? Edgerton wasn't sure – he didn't play party politics.

He often fought verbally with some senior officers who saw his views as somewhat extreme when it came to the administration of justice. Those around him avoided talking about the new ideas within the police service because it would surely provoke a heated discussion.

He didn't want to hang around in Kinglake Street any longer than he had to – he looked out of place, especially in his suit and pristine overcoat. Having eventually arrived in the Old Kent Road, he felt the familiar vibration of his phone in his trouser pocket, followed by the deafening ring tone provided by The Clash, one of his favourite bands. It was ironic he had chosen 'I Fought the Law' as his latest ringtone.

He quickly grabbed the phone, looking at the display screen to see who it was. The picture of an anteater appeared and it could only be one person – Chief Superintendent Robert Watkins, such was the dark wit Edgerton possessed. He thought for a brief moment about dumping the call, but decided to answer.

Edgerton had a picture for most of his colleagues on his phone and didn't hide the fact. His Detective Chief Superintendent, for all his politically correct views, found it quite amusing. He often said to Edgerton, 'What picture shall I have on my phone to tell me you are calling, Jack?' And Edgerton would often reply, 'An Adonis would suffice.'

'Hi, Guv, how are you today?'

'I'm okay, Jack, where are you?' replied Watkins.

His mind going into overdrive, Edgerton had to think quickly. He was always mindful that his boss might be checking on his whereabouts.

'I'm in Walworth, near to the Old Kent Road, seeing an informant about some information on an old case.'

'Okay; is it something I need to know about?'

'No, not really. I wouldn't want you to panic.' Watkins was always inquisitive. 'C'mon, you can tell me, I'm not going to bite your head off.'

'It's some information I'm seeking in relation to 'the Barber' murders. I'd love to get my teeth into it again. I'm sure the killer's still out there.'

'I'm fine with that, but the murders just stopped. I still think the killer died.'

'Perhaps that's the case. Anyway, what can I do for you, sir?'

'Can you come and see me at the Yard today?'

'No problem, what time?'

'About 1600 hours.'

Edgerton replied sarcastically, 'You mean 4 p.m. – I'll be there.'

After saying goodbye, he disconnected the phone and placed it back in his trouser pocket.

He muttered to himself, 'Another late night.'

Edgerton suddenly found himself standing outside the old Dun Cow public house, now converted into a GP surgery. He had not visited the Old Kent Road for a while, apart from passing through in his car, and it made him feel rather sad. Walking on foot gave him a totally different perspective of the place. Was this the demise of this great road that had found its way onto the Monopoly board?

He had spent many a night in his earlier days on the Old Kent Road. It was always a hive of activity, with the vast array of pubs situated on both sides of the highway. As he stood contemplating his next move, a man walked past and gazed at him. He looked like a down-and-out and surprisingly gave him a wide berth.

Edgerton was taken aback when the tramp said, 'Awight, my son? Good day to you,' in a strong South London dialect. It was a nice gesture, and he returned the greeting.

It reminded him of one of his favourite films, 'A Little Princess', in which Shirley Temple sang in cockney slang.

He loved the different characters that made up the borough of Walworth. For all the things the people had to endure and the downsides that parts of the inner city had to offer, he still loved its ambience, and he too had experienced the lows of living in the area as a child. There was a flip side though. He knew how the complex inner-city clock ticked, and how certain people used and stole from their own. He could sometimes understand what drove particular people to commit a crime. He could have chosen that road, like a lot of his old school friends, and knew how sheer poverty could send someone into a world of criminality, but he struggled to have empathy with those who committed crime for greed and showed no regard for others.

His walk in the streets of South London had certainly made the mind work overtime. It was getting late and he had to meet Watkins, so Edgerton flagged a black cab and made his way back to the MOD buildings. He made himself comfortable in the rear seat as he travelled through the Elephant and Castle towards Westminster, loosening his tie. Putting his hand into his junk-filled pocket, he rooted around until he found his earphones. *Time to listen to some tunes*, he thought.

Edgerton loved all music, but he'd never lost the appetite for punk; after all, he had been one during the seventies. The anticipation of what tune would play on his iPhone intrigued him as he pressed the play button. Today's random choice would be 'Waltzinblack' by The Stranglers. A very soothing melody as he closed his eyes and meditated…

Who would have thought? Jack Edgerton, a punk rocker in his teens. He'd seen them all – from The Clash to The Ramones, and had still not recovered fully from the shock of watching the demise of the old Roxy Club he used to frequent.

He wanted to speak to some of the members of his squad before he went to see Watkins at the Yard. He liked to be briefed before he saw him, and didn't want to go into the meeting cold. His favourite saying was 'forewarned is forearmed'. He always got the impression his Chief Superintendent was trying to catch him out – whether this was the case didn't matter to him. There was an old saying when he joined the police that it was the three Ps that would get you in the shit. The first were prisoners, then property, and of course prostitutes.

Edgerton added a fourth piece to his jigsaw – those in superior rank above him. He often found that when he spoke to officers the biggest stress they faced was dealing with senior officers who had no bottle. They almost felt alone, bombarded from both sides of the fence. He had some empathy with them.

He had warned Chloe recently about trusting career men within the force and had told her that the great comfort, at least when dealing with criminals, was that at least you knew where you stood. He had learnt through experience not to trust most bosses.

Edgerton returned to his office in the Ministry of Defence building, which had become rather a strange experience. He had seen more army officers in the last few months than he had in his whole life. They were everywhere, followed closely by a posse of civil servants who all seemed to be wearing the same suits. There was an atmosphere of formality which, lately, he hadn't experienced at Scotland Yard.

In the last decade, he had noted to others that discipline had become slack within the force, but felt that they had become more accountable, possibly caused by the advent of 24-hour news and the World Wide Web. The Web was a double-edged sword for Edgerton. Hence the saying 'knowledge is power'. He wasn't particularly over-enamoured with all the red tape and form filling.

The main Murder Squad office in the MOD building was now taking shape. The back wall of the incident room was taken up by a row of large translucent Perspex boards still displaying remnants and pictures from the Jenkins case, all carefully laid out and planned by Detective Inspector Palmer and Chloe Moran. The office was conventional, but it had everything Edgerton wanted and he looked forward to his next case. History had taught him he wouldn't have to wait long…

He entered the office, and Detective Inspector Palmer griped about the state of it.

'Everyone must listen to me!' Edgerton said. 'Can

we clear all this mess up please? It's starting to annoy the cleaners and myself included, so let's be ready for the next one. I have a feeling.'

All the heads popped up from around the HOLMES 2 computers, alerted by his shout.

Jean, the office girl, said in an eloquent voice, 'Mr Edgerton, would you like a brew?'

Edgerton snapped back, 'Let us get our priorities right.'

She looked nervously at him, expecting a good old-fashioned rollicking.

Smiling at her with a mischievous expression, he said, 'Yes, let's do that first – a nice brew.'

A detective constable sat close to the Detective Chief Inspector looked up at Edgerton with a 'what if I said that?' expression.

Edgerton looked back at him. 'I know what you're thinking.'

At times, Edgerton could be the strictest of officers if the need arose, but he felt it particularly difficult to lambaste females – he just found it hard. It would have to be a serious issue for a female officer to seek his wrath.

As he prepared to leave the simple surroundings of the Murder Squad office, the Russian Ambassador Anton Loktev sat in the palatial surroundings of the Maisky study inside the Russian Embassy residence in Kensington. As he sat at his desk, he began to write rough notes on headed Embassy paper with his fountain pen. They were very basic.

Make contact with Anton Zonov and ask him to monitor Beaumont and Sands. Then contact third party and arrange fees. AZ to report back all information...

The Ambassador then placed the unfinished note into his safe. A plan to follow the politician was now hatched and in its infancy.

As Edgerton returned to his office, he grabbed the remote control and turned on the television attached to the wall. He liked to catch up with the news as he did with work; there was nothing of interest to the detective. Briefly glancing at the television, he started to sift through various papers on his desk and came across an old Sunday Times. Edgerton wondered how it had ended up on his desk. He thought perhaps someone had used his office over the weekend while he was off. He had often wondered whether it was used as a doss house during weekend refreshments when officers would watch the TV. He didn't mind as long as they cleared up.

He checked the date and noticed it was a week old. The headline read:

Pressure mounts on Prime Minister and Bamford over vice scandal

Edgerton was no different from any other man and he liked scandal in small doses, especially when it involved politicians. He was not remotely interested in politics, but liked to keep abreast of developments. He mistrusted most of them anyway and didn't believe there was a right or a left any more. As far as the officer was concerned, he felt they didn't back up the police, apart from the odd Member of Parliament that would rarely stick their head above the parapet and make a pro police statement.

He believed it was the order of the day to bash the cops. The tide had changed and in the current climate he believed the 'the tail was now wagging the dog'. He felt that it didn't really matter who ran the country, because as far as policing was conducted it didn't change much from government to government. After working at the Yard and now the MOD, he was even more convinced that the civil servants ran operations and the Ministers were mouthpieces.

Edgerton, still holding the crumpled Times newspaper, decided to read the article, and he examined every detail. It was juicy. So much so that he thought he would follow this one closely.

It was time to go to Scotland Yard and see Watkins, so he shouted to Chloe Moran, 'Can you take me to see the Chief Super, Chloe?'

'No problem. I'll wait for you while you're with him.'

'No need,' he replied.

In a forceful tone, DC Moran said, 'I insist, Guv.'

'Okay, but only if you take me for a drink afterwards.'

Enthusiastically she replied, 'It's a deal.'

'Pick me up outside the Monty statue. I think that will be the easiest pickup point today. You go and get the car, I need to see someone.'

It was only a short drive to the Yard for Edgerton as long as the traffic was quiet. He would normally choose to walk, but on this occasion the thought of having a drink with DC Moran after the meeting soon changed his mind.

He had no real home life since his divorce four years earlier, and his two daughters had now moved away and were studying at university. He sometimes felt lonely and yearned for company, but his career and hectic schedule still filled the void in his life. At times, some of his colleagues watched him walk what appeared to be a lonely road and felt sorry for him. This frustrated him. He didn't want sympathy from anybody – he was content. Detective Inspector Palmer, Edgerton's closest friend, was always on the lookout and had someone in mind.

By the time he arrived at the statue, he could see Chloe Moran parked up in the black unmarked police Vectra, which shone brightly as the sun started to disappear. The temperature was dropping rapidly.

Rubbing his hands vigorously, he ran to the car and jumped inside. The warmth sent shivers down his spine.

'Someone's just stepped on my grave,' he said, laughing.

Moran was ready at the wheel.

'Well, Chloe, this should be fun,' he said in a sarcastic tone.

'Suppose these meetings have to happen; after all, he's got to justify his existence.'

She slowly made her way through the traffic to Scotland Yard.

As the couple approached the embankment traffic lights, they came to a sudden halt and heard the thunderous roar of an Aston Martin DB5 as it pulled up alongside their unmarked car. The engine ticked over and its body shone brightly. As it started to move away, Edgerton saw a constellation of light flicker along the polished roof onto the tinted window as the sun's rays connected with its highly polished black surface. As he gazed in awe of this car, with the London Eye prominent in the background, it reminded him of why he loved London. The glamorous side of the city certainly appealed to him.

He turned to Chloe and said, 'I wonder how people afford these luxuries – where do they get these vast amounts of money from? I'm in the wrong job.'

'Are they happy, though, that's the million-dollar question?'

DC Moran's quiet, sophisticated voice always had a soothing effect on Edgerton, who sat back and said, 'You're probably right, all's not what it seems.'

After negotiating the mid-afternoon traffic, they eventually arrived outside the iconic revolving Scotland Yard sign.

For some reason, whenever he went to the Yard Edgerton always felt his stomach begin to churn – like he was about to see the headmaster for the cane.

When he arrived at the reception, the security guard recognised him and said, 'Hello, Detective Chief Inspector Edgerton, where have you been?' He came around from the desk and shook his hand.

'How the devil are you, Dave?'

'I know you're at the MOD, but we miss you around here, you know – you can pop in and have a brew anytime, Jack.'

'I'll hold you to that. Can you bell Detective Chief Superintendent Watkins for me? We have a meeting at 4 p.m.'

'Anything for you, Jack. Please take a seat.'

Edgerton sat down and waited. Eventually, the call came from Watkins' secretary, and Edgerton, hands in pockets, strolled into the office where the boss sat at his desk.

'Hello, Jack, how are you feeling today?'

'I couldn't be better, sir.'

'Right, let's get started. The first thing is your appraisal.'

Edgerton showed his displeasure and sighed.

'Well, they need to be completed, it's force policy. So I need to have a meeting with you next week, if that's okay?'

'Yes, that's fine, sir. I've completed the observations section already.'

'Are you happy, Jack?'

Edgerton laughed. 'Oh yes! The Commissioner and I have something in common. That was the conclusion I came to.'

Watkins looked puzzled. 'What do you mean?'

'We have both reached the pinnacle of our careers, which means you're stuck with me until I hang my boots up, unless I drop a bollock.'

'Well, I gathered you had no intentions of applying for a Senior Command course.'

Edgerton laughed. 'No, leave me where I am, solving murders, it's what I do best. I'll leave the political stuff for you guys to sort out, sir.'

Watkins remained in his seat, rather bemused. He was a different animal to Edgerton. Dressed in his pinstripe suit and crisp white shirt to which a silk tie was pinned with a small Metropolitan Police badge, he looked more like a barrister than a policeman.

Watkins was a child of the accelerated promotion scheme and had risen quickly through the ranks to Chief Superintendent. At forty-one years old, he was still young in policing terms, and Edgerton didn't pull any punches when it came to reminding him of their age difference and the paths they had taken to reach their respective ranks.

Watkins had respect for Edgerton – he had to. His record when it came to solving homicides was exceptional and his boss played the game – if Edgerton looked good and performed, then so did Bob Watkins.

As Watkins ruffled a pile of papers on the desk, Edgerton spoke up.

'By the way, sir, we'll be having a drink soon, and after that a curry – a team-bonding exercise – and you are always welcome to join us. Later we can indulge in swapping unpolitically correct jokes, but only if you promise not to report us.'

Watkins lowered his head and spectacles towards Edgerton and shook his head.

'Jack, stop being mischievous – and yes, I will go, but having a good time doesn't always have to end up with gutter talk, does it?'

Edgerton defended himself. 'Sir, please! My jokes are about actual life, real people, situations I deal with every day, and I know the truth sometimes hurts, but that's life.'

Watkins was tired of Edgerton's cynical attitude. 'I know, but … well, I don't need to tell you we have been here before.'

Edgerton interrupted. 'As you have reminded me on several occasions. But why can't we have a laugh any more and say it how it is?'

'Plain and simple – I don't make the rules. That's the way it is.'

'Oh, why don't you let your hair down and say what you think? This PC bullshit is madness, sir, and you know it. Anyway, where does it actually originate, because everybody I speak to doesn't agree with it?'

Watkins' impatience was obvious. 'Let's change the

subject, Jack. We're poles apart on this one.'

Edgerton was becoming more frustrated and said, 'Well … we will just agree to disagree, but remember, you're a number just like me – nothing more, nothing less. But when you fall in the shit it's from a far greater height than me.'

The room went silent. Chief Superintendent Watkins had learned to allow Edgerton the final word in such discussions, despite his seniority. He again lowered his glasses and looked at him in the eye.

'You will be in the MOD building for a short while, possibly up to twelve months, so if you need anything just tell me – the budget's healthy at the moment and there's quite a bit of money in the pot, so all things are fine on that front. By the way, is there any update on the Jenkins case?'

'Chloe Moran is sorting out some exhibits, and the rest is just fine. I've got a case review in the next few weeks with the CPS. Would you like to come?'

'Yes, I would. I'm pleased about the case. The Family Liaison Officer has been contacted by a relative who wanted to pass on his thanks for the way your team dealt with this sensitive matter.'

'Thank you, sir. How about a commendation? It always helps morale.'

'Good thinking; let's wait until after the trial and then review the matter. Please don't let me forget. Well, that's it for me, Jack. Unless you have anything else, I'll speak to you in the next day or so.'

'I think it might be a guilty plea.' Edgerton stood to attention and smiled. 'Thank you, sir, I'll send you the Pimlico date – and please keep your diary free.'

'I will, Jack,' replied Watkins.

'Would you like a vindaloo when we go out, Guv?'

Watkins snapped back with a smile, 'You're taking the piss, Jack. See you later.'

Chapter 8

Chequers Court, Buckinghamshire

Parliament was now in recess until 22nd November 2011, and Prime Minister Charles Chillot headed off to Chequers to regroup with his advisors.

It was possibly the most vulnerable he had been since his premiership began. He needed time to think, and more importantly to look after number one. He thoroughly enjoyed his time at Chequers. If he had his way, No 10 would be demolished and he would spend all his time in the Buckinghamshire countryside.

He stood alone in the Long Gallery while he pondered and contemplated his next move. He looked at the stained-glass window and read the inscription:

This House of peace and ancient memories were given to England as a thank-offering for her deliverance in the great war of 1914–18, as a place of rest and recreation for her Prime Minister forever.

It was a poignant moment for Chillot. He may have come for a rest and possibly some recuperation, but he was far from the relaxed state of mind he thought this trip might give him.

His Foreign Secretary, Robert Bamford, was staying

in Chevening, the Foreign Secretary's official residence, meeting an official from Sudan. He wondered what Bamford was thinking. Was he telling the truth about his private life, and did he have a plan? Both men were currently under considerable pressure, and Chillot was now resigned to the fact that he would possibly have to call for an inquiry to put the matter to bed.

His advisor, John Smith, entered the gallery, his metal-tipped shoes clicking on the marble floor alerting the Prime Minister.

'Hello, Prime Minster, they said you would be in here.'

'Hello, John,' Chillot replied in a sombre tone. His usual commanding voice had almost disappeared. 'Let's talk about the inquiry.'

'Prime Minister, would you like my advice on the whole matter?'

'Of course, go ahead.'

Smith wanted to take control. 'We're currently approaching a critical point in this whole affair, and I believe Robert Bamford has resigned himself to the fact that an inquiry is now inevitable. I know you both go back a long way, and perhaps you feel some allegiance to him, but I think it's time to take the bull by the horns and kill this dead. We should invoke the inquiry under the 2005 Act; then the matter is out of your hands, and as a government we cannot be accused of being involved in a cover-up.'

'I agree, it makes sense to follow this course of action, and I think we must talk this through. I don't want to rush this and make a rash decision. I just need some time alone, but please do not take this as a refusal to listen to your advice. I'm a pragmatist just like you, and when I return to Westminster I have no doubt that an inquiry is the only way forward.'

Smith showed no emotion. 'I think you're making the right decision, Prime Minister – you must protect your position and that of the Labour government.'

'I know, but what I'm about to tell you may not go down well. I will tell you this once, and we must never repeat it – I have a bad feeling over this matter. Why? I don't know, but my instinct tells me that there is something not quite right, and we're heading for stormy waters.'

Smith paused and slowly walked away, then turned to the Prime Minister.

'I echo your feelings, but I must stress to you, there's no other avenue. You have no choice.'

The Prime Minister was dejected. 'The sad thing is I don't believe Bamford, and I should do. God, I shared an office with the guy for years and know him inside out. I'm in personal turmoil, but if there is impropriety on his side, then he's had every opportunity to wriggle out. He's a stubborn bastard.'

'I know, Prime Minister,' replied Smith.

Chillot turned and followed Smith, saying, 'Have you seen Jean?'

'Yes, she's in the Long Room.'

Chillot made the short walk to where Jean was sitting reading her newspaper.

'Hello, Charles. You look like a man who needs some comforting.' Jean approached her husband, hugged him and whispered, 'Remember, we discussed that at some point you would reach a rocky road; well, here we are! We shall shake ourselves down and fight this head-on. The most important thing in this matter is that you have committed no wrong. You've been dragged into this mess because you are the Prime Minister, and I suppose it comes with the territory.'

Her words certainly comforted the Prime Minister and he kissed her.

'Thank you, Jean.'

'Remember, I'm behind you.'

Her strength invigorated Chillot.

As he looked at the walls, he said to his wife, 'You know, Jean, in this room there's a diary that belonged to the late Admiral Lord Nelson. If we were to read it, would it contain nothing but happy memories?'

'We're a team, and all the great leaders have one thing in common – inner strength. You have it in abundance, and Nelson's diary would no doubt chronicle the dark moments as well as those of triumph.'

Still embracing each other, they kissed.

Charles Chillot had made up his mind.

'Jean, call John and let's get the ball rolling.'

John Smith eventually entered the room and said, 'Have you made a decision, Prime Minister?'

Chillot smiled. 'We need an inquiry.'

Smith was ecstatic and said, with a beaming grin, 'I think you've made the right decision.'

'Let's get this mess sorted out, and I'll make an announcement in the House after the recess, but Robert Bamford needs to know the position. I'll phone him immediately.' After a short pause, he added, 'And by the way, keep this quiet for the time being. I don't want this to leak.'

Chillot hadn't felt so nervous since he won the general election. But he had to make the call to his old friend and knew it was his only way out of this mess.

Smith and Chillot stood together as he prepared to make the call. Before Smith left the room, the Prime Minster beckoned him to come back.

'John, the first priority is to inform the Lord Chancellor and Secretary of State for Justice and give them a brief outline of what we want. Just tell them I will catch up with them at a later date.'

Smith raised his thumb and said, 'Consider it done.'

As the Prime Minister looked out over the grounds of the estate through the leaded windows, the snow started to fall. Cold days lay ahead.

Chapter 9

Sunday, 20th November 2011

Chillot stood in the Long Room staring at the phone poised, and took a deep breath. His wife stood by his side and comforted him.

'Jean, I need to make this call alone,' Chillot said quietly.

She affectionately stroked his hand and left the room.

Chillot dialled Bamford's number and waited patiently for a reply. It came quickly.

'Hello, it's the Prime Minister. Can I speak to the Foreign Secretary?'

After a short pause, he was connected to the Foreign Secretary and Chillot took another deep breath.

'Hello, Robert, how are you?'

'Hello, Prime Minister.'

'Robert, I don't think this will come as any surprise, but we've come to a point where this scandal is not going away. As I said previously, we need to get on and govern the country, and the whole matter has snowballed and become an unwanted distraction.'

Bamford was prepared, or so it seemed, as he

replied, 'I know, Prime Minister.'

'It's only fair to tell you now, so you know. After the recess, I will be making a full statement to the house, and we will be setting up an inquiry under the provisions of the 2005 Inquiries Act.'

'It is deeply regrettable this whole situation, Prime Minister, but I accept your decision.'

'It is sad day for me. Be very cautious about what you may say to the press – they will be watching you like a hawk.'

'I am aware, Prime Minister,' Bamford snapped. 'I have been around a long time, you know.'

'Robert, can I ask you this question as a friend one more time?'

'Go on.'

'Have you been to any brothels and frequented with prostitutes?'

Bamford replied in a defiant tone, 'You doubt my integrity, Prime Minister?'

Chillot remained silent. He was uncomfortable with this whole situation.

As young MPs they had shared time together, and it was Chillot who promoted Bamford when he was installed as the leader of the Labour party. Although they didn't socialise together, Chillot had regarded Bamford as an ally in past campaigns, but this whole affair had had a profound effect on the Prime Minister. He had a bad feeling about his former office mate. The friendship was heading for stormy waters.

The Prime Minister continued as he gazed through the window. 'Obviously there will be considerable press speculation and coverage, but I think this will put the matter to bed.'

Bamford sat at his desk with his fist clenched. 'I hope so. I am disappointed that the original Commons inquiry didn't really find anything, yet the matter has constantly been dragged up by Brian Beaumont. No one sees through this whole conspiracy to out me. This man plays party politics, and his own leader really doesn't get it, does he? Does Cotterhill not realise the bastard's after his job? He must be a naive man. He backs Beaumont to the hilt and has done so in his calls for this inquiry. It has nothing to do with morals, it's about getting through the big black door – your door not mine. It's turning out to be a sideshow, because that is what it will become. My patience with politics is somewhat diluted at the moment.'

'I agree with some of your points, but let me play devil's advocate for one moment. Would we do the same if this situation were presented to us as a party coming up to an election and hoping to get into power?'

'We would, Prime Minister, but I have a lot to lose here, and if it all goes wrong, there will be consequences that are beyond my control.' Bamford's mood was changing.

'You have always said you are innocent of these allegations, so why bother?'

'I am just warning you. I will not be responsible for any fallout from this.'

The Prime Minister gathered his thoughts. It had become evident throughout the conversation that they would never be close again, but he was rather surprised by Bamford's defiant attitude.

After a pause, the phone went dead. In a fit of rage, Bamford had hung up the telephone.

Both men were tired. Bamford reached immediately

for his whisky, a drink he would become familiar with in the coming months.

Any feelings of sympathy from the Prime Minister slowly began to evaporate. Charles Chillot's emotions changed to a feeling of anger towards his Foreign Secretary, whom he had supported. It was evident after their recent conversations that Bamford thought otherwise.

It was two months away from a Cabinet reshuffle, and their now strained friendship had broken down. There would be no going back. The Prime Minister's advisor would now become his most trusted ally.

John Smith, the younger brother of Derek Smith MP, was hands-on and a former researcher for the party, but most of all he was streetwise. However, Smith had aspirations to go far in politics and played the game.

Smith sat calmly in the hallway next to the Long Room and realised the muffled sound of conversation had died. The lull in proceedings was suddenly interrupted by the scraping of a chair across the floor, and he could hear the unsettled Prime Minister ranting loudly to himself. He stayed put and listened with his ear close to the old wood-panelled door.

'What a fucking arsehole! I give you everything, and this is what I get in return.'

Smith entered the room. The Prime Minister was on the offensive.

'Calm down, sir,' Smith begged. 'Just forget it, keep focusing.'

Smith had never seen Chillot behave like this in all the years he had advised him. He was now acutely aware they were entering trying times.

Chapter 10

John Smith, preparing for the inquiry and still at the Prime Minister's country residence, was sat at his desk when the Prime Minister entered the room and sat beside him.

Smith's Blackberry beeped loudly.

'Sorry, Prime Minister, I thought I'd switched it to silent,' he apologised as he checked the text message. It was from Robert Bamford.

Hi John, give me a call when you can. RB.

'Anything urgent, John?'

'No, Prime Minister, just a message from my mother. I'll phone her later.'

He watched intently as Smith drew up a list of possible people to contact – he switched between his notes and his laptop.

'It's been difficult. I think we should have a brandy. Join me on the terrace and we can both have a cigar.'

'That would be nice, Prime Minister; it's been a ball, hasn't it?'

Chillot produced two cigars and Smith gasped with excitement. In that moment, all their troubles seemed to have vanished.

As Smith examined the tubes, he said, 'They're the

biggest I've ever seen. I must confess, I was expecting the usual Crèmes!'

Chillot replied proudly, 'Yes, 9.2 inches long to be precise, and they were given to me by the President when we visited Camp David. I thought I'd keep them for a celebration, but in light of what has taken place in the last few hours … well, I thought better now than never.'

'They look expensive.' Smith had never smoked a cigar this big.

'Arturo Fuente Opus X 'A' at 80 dollars each, I am led to believe – enjoy.'

Both men stood with their cigars puffing away in the cold night air. The Prime Minister looked over the snow-covered gardens.

'You know, I often wonder when I'm at Chequers if I was ever really meant to be here. I think of the great prime ministers who have stayed here – I even thought of Winston Churchill smoking his cigars on this terrace during the war years, until I found out he never used the damn place. That shows my real knowledge of political history. I sincerely hope that whatever happens in the future, history will be kind to me and the party … and indeed you, my friend.'

Smith replied defiantly, in a positive tone, 'At this time we must be strong, and we will pull through – I've never thought about the future really, Prime Minister. Anyway, let's be honest, we'll all be six feet under. Who cares?'

Chillot gave a wry smile. 'I've never really looked at it like that. Stop me from being negative, let us look forward. We need to look at the inquiry and appoint somebody urgently, and perhaps some panel members to assist. It will have to be a judge, I suppose?'

Smith was prepared. 'I have already made some calls and prepared a list for you. I do, however, have someone in mind, sir.'

'Well, who's the man?'

'Lord Justice Rameau.'

'I vaguely remember the name – I must have read about him at some time.'

Charles Chillot, in fact, knew his father well, but he would hold court.

Smith continued. 'He's a well-respected judge, sir, and the Lord Chief Justice has no objection to him running the inquiry.'

'Thanks, John. We need to move quickly with this inquiry and set it up as soon as we can. I intend to make an announcement to the House when we return from the recess. However, I do not want to encourage a media frenzy, so can you make the statement short and to the point?'

Smith looked at the Prime Minister through the smoke belching from the cigars, took a sip of brandy and said, 'I've already written a draft statement for you to look at. It should only take a couple of minutes.'

The Prime Minister patted him on the shoulder and thanked him.

Smith's skills and experience would be needed in this time of crisis. As his advisor and close aide, he had a burning desire to fly through the ranks, and it was highly likely his goal would be achieved. He was an ideal press secretary for the Prime Minister, and his former editorial skills would be vital if Chillot were to avoid any embarrassment. Smith had it in his mind to brief the press against Beaumont if he had to. Whether this would be an easy task only time would tell, as most papers were pushing in the same direction as the farmer's son.

Chillot had plans for Smith and liked to keep a tab on his life, in particular his relationship with his older brother, Derek Smith, a long-serving Labour MP and close friend of the Foreign Secretary.

'How is Derek lately?'

'I don't really see him, Prime Minister. I don't have a particularly close relationship with him.'

'I've seen him in passing, but not had chance to speak to him for a while. He is quite friendly with Bamford, isn't he?'

Smith became a little uneasy. 'I think they are close, but we don't get on and I don't really like Derek's wife. I think they might be having some problems, and now that Mum and Dad are dead there's no reason for our paths to cross.'

Chillot was sympathetic. 'That's sad, I hope you can patch things up.'

Smith was eager to change the subject. He was uncomfortable talking about his brother with the Prime Minister.

Derek Smith had been a backbench politician for several years and was relatively unknown. He lived in Cumbria where he served his constituents, but was still a Londoner through and through. His relationship with Bamford was unusual, as they were completely different characters, Smith being much quieter.

Chapter 11

Recess had now ended and it was time for Parliament to attend to business – Chillot and Beaumont were ready. It was a clear, cold, sunny day in the capital, and the Shadow Home Secretary was in good spirits.

'Good morning, Jane,' Beaumont quipped as he entered the office.

'You're lively today, Brian.'

'I am indeed, ladies, and I cannot stay too long. I am in an excellent mood. I have it on good advice that there will be some breaking news.'

'That sounds very juicy, what is it?'

'I would have to kill you first, my dear … but to put you out of your misery, it is indeed good news for us all.'

'Well, that's fine. Don't worry about keeping us in the dark.'

As she handled the usual mountain of envelopes that had been delivered that morning, she threw them on the desk.

Beaumont looked on and asked, 'What are these – surely not all for me?'

Jane passed them over to the intern, Leslie, who said, 'They are – you should have a fan club.'

Brian laughed. 'Don't be silly, girls, most will be from the constituents. The usual moans and groans about daily life in Oxford.'

Leslie fumbled with a brown envelope. 'This is big – let me guess,' she said as she ran her fingers down the length of the package.

In a typed format, it read:

Brian Beaumont MP (By hand)

Above, in a childlike scrawl, there was another heading in red ink.

Private and confidential – must be opened by Mr Beaumont

Beaumont was mystified as to what was in the package, and he quickly opened it with his letter opener. Inside was a blank CD in a plastic wallet and a typed note on plain paper.

'Good God, Brian, be careful,' Leslie said. 'Anything could have been inside the envelope – you must be careful.'

Beaumont broke out into hysterical laughter. 'Why, do think someone is trying to kill me? Stop fretting!'

Jane scowled at Beaumont. 'If the head of security saw you he'd have your guts for garters.'

Beaumont opened the plain white folded paper and read the note inside.

Mr Beaumont – within this package is an art form – a tale to tell – in a place – in the city – where a red light shines – dig deep and explore, and you will find the jewel – your passage to power and glory – the road to all things great – a tale of giants swirling within a cavern of sin and greed. Enjoy, my friend, but tread carefully.

Leslie was puzzled. 'Well, what is it?' She could see the look of surprise on Beaumont's tanned face.

Jane joined in. 'Come on then, don't keep us in suspense.'

Beaumont didn't reply and the girls looked at each other, bemused by his reaction.

Beaumont read the passage again and it confused him. He felt uneasy. Whether it was good news or bad, he had no time. He placed the package in his inside coat pocket and turned to Leslie.

'Leslie, I'm going to the House of Commons and I'll be there a while. The Prime Minister's making a statement to the House – I suggest you switch on the TV and digest.'

She didn't waste any time, and grabbed the remote control and turned on Sky News.

'And by the way,' Beaumont shouted, 'get ready, your phone's going to be hot this afternoon.'

'Brian!' Leslie shouted.

It was too late. The door had closed. Brian Beaumont was on his way to Parliament.

As he walked through the corridors to the main chamber, Beaumont stood tall – he knew what was coming and could sense the tense atmosphere. He entered a now packed chamber, combed his hair back and took his seat alongside his Shadow Cabinet colleagues. They all turned and smiled at him in sync. He returned the compliment.

He sat motionless until the last Member of Parliament took his seat. It was sheer coincidence that today he would be sat immediately opposite the Foreign Secretary, Robert Bamford.

Bamford stared straight at him; he could feel his eyes

cutting through him. The look portrayed his sheer hatred, but Beaumont was not a man to cower. He returned the compliment and eventually Bamford backed down. It was a battle of wills.

The chamber was now becoming increasingly rowdy as MPs from both sides of the House were waving papers furiously above their heads.

'Order, order!'

Arthur Betram stood to his feet. Again, he dug deep and shouted, 'Order! The Prime Minister wishes to make a statement to the House.'

The noise was deafening, with jeering and boos bouncing off the walls in the great hall – it had reached a level that even Beaumont had never experienced as an MP.

Charles Chillot stood at the despatch box, papers ready.

'Mr Speaker, I am today announcing a public inquiry into the ethics of ministers, Members of Parliament and government officials following recent events and ongoing allegations, which will be chaired by Lord Justice Rameau. There will be a panel of members assisting him, and they will be announced shortly. All members of the public inquiry team have been carefully selected for their expertise, impartiality and independence. The terms of reference are as follows: firstly, to look at the relationship between ministers, Members of Parliament and government officials when dealing with foreign embassies, and part two of the inquiry will consider the extent of malpractice or improper conduct by ministers in dealing with the Russian Embassy. I am aware that allegations have been levelled at the Foreign Secretary, and he assures me that he is innocent of all allegations.'

The House erupted and Betram again was forced to intervene.

'Order! Order – stop this nonsense!' He shouted across the House. 'Let the Prime Minister finish. What will the public think when they hear you all shouting like infants? Order!'

Charles Chillot stood back from the despatch box and raised his arm.

'There will be a further announcement, but I expect the inquiry will commence very soon.'

He sat down and folded his arms, his speech ending as quickly as it started.

As some members of the House left the chambers, Bamford took his place behind the despatch box. Chillot left to attend to his diary, but the room remained packed.

Bamford stood up and was greeted by cheers and boos from the opposing party, led by Brian Beaumont, but he remained composed.

'Mr Speaker, I have opted to stand in front of the House today to make an announcement in light of media speculation about my private life.'

Bamford was interrupted as the House erupted once more. Hands were raised and Betram once again had to intervene.

'Order, order, order! Please let the Foreign Secretary complete his statement.'

As the House slowly returned to order, Bamford continued.

'I will make this statement brief. I have read the contents of the Select Committee report and accept some of its conclusions, but the facts are that I have not been found guilty of any misconduct. I accept the criticisms and thank the Prime Minister for his support.'

The House listened, and you could hear a pin drop.

Bamford continued. 'I welcome the public inquiry for one reason, and that is because it will show that I have acted correctly in my role in Public Office. I am confident I will be vindicated. I will not resign, and I continue to have the full support of my family and all my colleagues, in particular those who work tirelessly with me in the Foreign Office. We live in a democracy, and that means we should allow due process to take its course, which is why I will continue to serve as Foreign Secretary.'

Beaumont immediately stood up and booed the Foreign Secretary, joined by his party members, whilst Bamford looked on helplessly.

Bamford's ordeal was over – for the moment, anyway. The opposition would prepare to launch an attack in the next few months.

As the House eventually emptied, Beaumont walked from the chamber totally satisfied with the day's proceedings and went to the toilet to refresh himself. The room was quiet and he was alone, or so he thought. As he stood to wipe his face, he looked in the mirror and Robert Bamford appeared. He leaned towards Beaumont and whispered in his ear.

'Cherish this moment, Mr Beaumont and enjoy it. We are in the game of politics, and I know you, I can read you like an open book. Perhaps your leader will hopefully see through your plans, but again, let me remind you of your fragility as a human being. You have made an enemy of me, my friend. Whatever you do, whatever you say, wherever you go, look over your shoulder. Your time will surely come.'

This was a chilling threat from a Foreign Secretary desperate to hold on to power.

Beaumont smiled and remained silent. He was unperturbed.

One of the cubicle doors opened suddenly and Bamford made a hasty exit. It was a fellow MP, Christopher Tomkinson.

'Fucking hell, Brian, was that Bamford? What was that all about?' He was rather shocked by what he had just overheard.

Beaumont shrugged his shoulders. 'Forget it, Chris. It never happened.'

Chapter 12

Charles Chillot was exhausted after his speech as he looked out of the window overlooking the rear garden at No 10. He could see John Smith huddled with a group of advisors on the snow-covered lawn.

He was putting the final touches to the public inquiry and assisting Lord Justice Rameau in compiling a team of lawyers to assist him through the whole process. It would be a lengthy investigation. Chillot had a connection with the Rameau family, albeit rather remote. He had met Rameau's father, Alfred, on two occasions in Paris when he completed his last state visit to France.

Lord Justice Jacques Rameau was an Englishman through and through, born to Alfred and Alice Rameau, who had made their fortune in the vineyards of southern France. Prior to the birth of Jacques, the family had moved to London, having set up a chain of small supermarkets in and around the capital which eventually expanded to parts of Europe. This venture was to prove even more lucrative than the vineyards.

Jacques had been born into immense wealth and opulence, and although very British, he still had the traits of a typical Frenchman. Most of his early years were spent in various boarding schools in England.

Those adolescent years were a strain on a young and impressionable Jacques, and he didn't particularly enjoy the experience, which would sometimes be a source of strain between the judge and his mother. Alice Rameau was a pushy mother and was determined that her son, having been born in London, would grow up to be the quaint Englishman, and she certainly achieved her goal.

Chillot was more than happy with this appointment and hoped it may stand him in good stead. Surely, Jacques' father would mention his acquaintance with the Prime Minister when they spoke next time. Chillot continued to keep quiet about Rameau's father. He considered it a minor issue which had no bearing on any possible outcome, and in any case, Rameau was known to be a highly independent judge.

The Prime Minister walked into the garden to find John Smith now alone.

'Hello, John, what are you doing in the cold?'

'I needed the fresh air to clear my mind. Anyway, everything is now in place for the inquiry. I had a call the other day from the Lord Chief Justice, who was happy with Rameau. I had phoned him during the recess and he suggested we go with him.'

Smith paused as Chillot listened intently. He then continued while checking his notes.

'It's all in hand, and a team needs to be assembled by Rameau to assist him. I'm sure he has a few people in mind.'

'That's fine. Have you heard from Bamford?'

'No, I've not, but my eyes and ears in the Foreign Office have reported back and he's not happy, as you would expect.'

'It doesn't surprise me; he's under pressure. Anyway, where is the inquiry going to be held?'

'I think they will want to use the Royal Courts of Justice.'

'That's fine. I know it well; I've been there a couple of times.'

'Prime Minister, are you happy with the choice of Chairman for the inquiry?'

'Yes, I am. I think he is a fair man. He has a good pedigree, and I've had a look at others and there are few judges more experienced in England. After all, it's a daunting task, and the Lord Chief Justice admires him, and I've met his father in Paris.'

Chillot had made a sudden U-turn, but didn't want to elaborate on his relationship.

Smith didn't look concerned with the Prime Minister's confession.

'Where does he reside, John?'

'He resides in Islington, alone. I think he's a bachelor.'

'I know he's a career man, probably never has time to hold down a relationship. He took his silk very early as a barrister, which is unusual, so he must have been exceptional.'

'I spoke to the Attorney General, and he holds him in high regard.'

'Did you know, that most QCs need to have about fifteen years' experience before they are appointed? He took his silk with only nine years' experience. Quite remarkable.'

'I didn't know that. Perhaps that's why he's a popular choice,' Smith replied.

The Prime Minister continued his tribute to the

newly appointed judge. 'And when he was appointed member of the Privy Council a few years ago, he was the youngest member they'd ever appointed.'

'I heard that,' Smith replied.

'John, I need to announce his team via a press release when you have drawn it up. Obviously I'll have a look first and liaise with the Lord Chief Justice – we wouldn't want to have someone on his team who doesn't like the government, would we?'

'No, Prime Minister.'

Both men laughed.

'And keep me posted with Robert Bamford … he concerns me.'

'I will,' replied Smith.

Chillot wondered what Beaumont's next move would be. He admired the man and knew he was a considerable threat. Although he was in opposition, he liked his style, although he still regretted praising him in the popular press. It was a move that may come back to haunt him.

Chapter 13

Still exhilarated by the Prime Minister's announcement, Beaumont immediately left Parliament, but he had only one thing in mind – the package in his pocket. He raced back to Portcullis House, to the sanctity of his office – he felt like a boy with a new toy.

As he entered, he noticed all the staff had gone home, so he locked himself inside. He didn't want to be disturbed – whatever was on this CD was important. He carefully pulled it from the case and placed it into the drive on his computer. There were two files – a video file and a Word document. He opened the Word document first.

Watch the CCTV footage and enjoy – be careful.

His hands were shaking, so he took a deep breath and opened the video file. He checked the counter; it was half an hour in length, but there was no sound.

The film was time and date stamped, and he could clearly see the people in the foreground involved in sexual activity. There were two MPs and the Russian Ambassador in the brothel, and he noticed money changing hands. In the background, there were two other men, but the picture was so grainy he couldn't identify them. This frustrated him.

However, he felt vindicated – the main player, Robert Bamford, was there as clear as day. As he sat on a chair with the naked working girl, he spoke to the Russian Ambassador Andrei Loktev and took money from the Russian.

Bamford had very close ties with Loktev and had been spotted several times socialising with him at the Embassy. There was no doubt that in his capacity as Foreign Secretary he had to meet Loktev, but this had become more than a professional relationship, one which started in New York at the United Nations. It was rumoured that Bamford had been involved in a brief fling with Loktev's interpreter, an accusation he always denied.

He thumped his fist on the desk. 'I knew he was at it. Time to play hardball.'

Beaumont's elation soon changed. He also knew that this smoking gun would have serious ramifications for the Prime Minister and the Labour government. He didn't know how he should feel in such circumstances. He had to regroup. After all, this is what he had been striving for. He needed to take stock, but his first task was to take a number of copies on several discs and place them in his safe.

He had to speak to his friend and confidant Patrick Sands. Beaumont found his mobile phone and tapped in Sands' name. He was so nervous his hands were visibly shaking.

Sands answered and sounded upbeat.

'Hello, Brian, I was just thinking about you. You did it! Just watched the news.'

'Thanks, Patrick,' replied Beaumont, but he was jumpy.

'Bloody hell, you sound like a right miserable bugger.'

'I've been sent a CD with some footage, and I need to see you in the next few days – I can't say too much at the moment.'

Sands was intrigued. 'Sounds good. Is it controversial?'

Brian paused. 'It's what I've been waiting for. I knew it was out there.'

Perplexed, Sands didn't know whether to cheer or not. 'Well, who sent the damn thing?'

'I don't know. I'll phone you to arrange a meeting. I trust you like a brother, but don't tell a soul – I'm not telling Isabel, so be warned. Just you and me. It must go no further.'

Beaumont hung up and left Sands to brood.

Chapter 14

Jack Edgerton flicked through every page relating to the Jenkins case, studying every word and every statement. He was determined to see his officers commended as a team for their work on the case. He didn't want any accolades. It had to be recognition for everyone. So he sat pen poised, with his report forms ready. It would be long and detailed, but he didn't mind. He didn't like to work in an office with low morale. He had already decided this would be his finest commendation report for the attention of his boss, Chief Superintendent Bob Watkins. It had even crossed the detective's mind that upon receipt of their certificates from the Deputy Assistant Commissioner, his officers might even buy him a drink as a token of their appreciation.

Edgerton was always the first to arrive every morning, so he completed the report and waited until nine o'clock when the office would be full. He hoped Chloe had told the staff about the night out.

He wondered if Chief Superintendent Watkins would be in at this time, so he phoned the Yard.

'Good morning. Robert Watkins,' came the reply.

'Good morning, sir, how are you?'

Watkins was in a good mood. 'How are you, Jack? I

see you're in nice and early as per usual.'

'Sir, there is no snooze button on a cat who wants breakfast.'

Watkins laughed. 'I don't know where you get them.'

'You need to read, sir, and you will find them.' Edgerton laughed. 'Let us read, and let us dance; these two amusements will never do any harm to the world.'

Watkins shook his head.

Edgerton continued. 'Anyway, Guv, it's not business, it's about the curry – I will arrange it for tomorrow night, if that's okay? I fancy a few after the meal in the West End. Are you up for it, sir?'

'Yes, I am. Are the troops okay with that?'

'They will be, but if there are any problems, I'll phone you around ten o'clock. I've done a report for the Jenkins case. I think the officers deserve a commendation. It will be with you soonest.'

He didn't give Watkins the opportunity to answer and placed the phone firmly back down. He was looking forward to a night out. He needed it, and he looked forward to catching up with Chloe Moran in a social environment so they could talk. Two different personalities, but they had a good chemistry, and Edgerton loved her sharp, intelligent humour.

He was becoming increasingly bored and thought about what the day ahead might hold. He thrived on action and liked to work with tight restraints, and it was an unusually quiet time for his Murder Squad in their temporary accommodation.

As he awaited the arrival of his team, he switched on the news. He took immediate notice. The headline news that morning was all about the Prime Minister's announcement to hold a public inquiry.

Edgerton sat back in his chair and sighed. He continued to watch the report with interest.

'Well! Beaumont finally got his own way, the crafty bastard,' he said to himself.

He had met Beaumont on a number of occasions at parliamentary charity functions and liked him. They had similar views on law and order, which Edgerton had found at odds when he had met with previous politicians.

As he continued to watch the news, there was a knock on the door and in came the office manager, Detective Inspector Philip Palmer.

'Good morning, Philip.'

'Good morning, Guv, how are you?'

'Fine. I'm just catching up on the news.'

Looking up at the TV, Palmer said, 'Oh yes, this palaver with Robert Bamford and the prossies.'

'Oh, so you're following it?'

'I am, and I read a good article in the Mail about it the other day. I think it was only a matter of time – I think Bamford's luck might be running out.'

'It could be.' Edgerton paused. 'Worth following. Just hope the cops don't have to get involved.'

'Not sure about the ins and outs, but I suppose it depends what's been going on.'

'On to more important things, I've just spoken to the boss and we're having a night out tomorrow, so rally the troops and sort it.'

'Already done, Guv, and it'll be a good turnout. I'm pleased everybody's going. I think boredom is creeping in. I've not known a quiet period like this one. We moan when it's busy and moan when it's quiet. It's a funny old world.'

'My thoughts exactly. I'm sure something will change soon. After all, Philip, this is London.'

Chapter 15

Anton Zonov had recently settled into his new apartment in Hampstead Heath and it was a beautiful sight. Known locally as The Heath, the large ancient London Park, covering 790 acres, was an ideal grassy public space for the Russian immigrant.

Having left Moscow, this would be his first Christmas in England and he looked forward to it. It was going to be filled with excitement and more importantly it could be a lucrative time for him. It was a far cry from the Khrushchev slums in Moscow where he had grown up with his mother as an only child. He was now very much part of the Russian set in London, but kept a low profile.

If one asked Zonov what he did for a living, the answer would be vague. Nobody seemed to know what he actually did, but he was a fixer with a fearsome reputation, and had money to back it up. A child of the new Russian democracy, the 1980s had been kind to him – he had taken advantage of the changes the country had experienced and prospered, but not to the same extent as some of his fellow oligarch compatriots. The period of market liberalisation under the reign of Mikhail Gorbachev had been kinder to them, but

Zonov couldn't complain. He took his slice of the pie and intended to further his reputation while he was in London.

While in the capital he had formed strong links with the Russian Embassy through his connections with the Russian Mafia. It was a mutually beneficial relationship, and both sides prospered. With the support of Andrei Loktev, the main man at the Russian Embassy, Zonov started to mix in powerful circles and rubbed shoulders with people in high places, and he didn't look out of place.

As he lapped up his new surroundings, he was feeling rather frustrated, as he would have liked to go for a stroll on the heath on this nice clear winter's day, but he was waiting for a special delivery. The contents of the package would help towards the down payment on his new flat in North London. It was a package from Andrei Loktev via a client he had never seen or met.

Anton Zonov always preferred to do business through a third party, with little dialogue. Loktev had the contacts and fulfilled that role quite nicely. This made his work clean, and he could remain undetectable. Zonov was clinical and had a reputation for getting his work done in a quick and efficient manner. If a hit was required, then he delivered, but this assignment might be slightly away from the norm.

The KGB was interested in him, so he was always on his guard. He was suspected of committing several murders within Russia and the Ukraine, but the authorities could never pin him down. Not a shred of evidence could ever be found, and some believed he still had contacts from within who were on their payroll. Zonov was, it seemed, untouchable.

As he waited patiently, the doorbell rang and the postman handed the Russian his package. Zonov meticulously opened it with a pair of scissors and, not wanting to leave any prints, donned his rubber gloves.

It was a simple package wrapped in brown paper, and inside was a note.

Meet a man in Hampstead Heath at midday – Kenwood House – outside the front door – his password – hello, lone ranger – you reply – a busy lone ranger – he will know you and supply expenses and info.

The note was simple, but that is how business had to be conducted. You played by Zonov's rules or hired somebody else to do your dirty work. It might be a complex plan, but for all involved there could be no comeback – no connection to their crimes. And the end goal? To be rid of their problem.

At eleven thirty, Zonov donned his suit and overcoat and made his way to Kenwood Hall situated in the heart of Hampstead Heath.

At midday precisely, a man approached Zonov wearing a hat and scarf around his face and said, 'Hello, lone ranger.'

As per the instructions he had received, Zonov replied, 'A busy lone ranger.'

The thick brown package exchanged hands and both men left without any further dialogue. Zonov felt the thick package and made his way back home.

On his return to his flat, he opened the package and examined the contents. He looked at two small photographs, on the rear of each were addresses and detailed information followed by simple instructions to follow the men and report back to Loktev when further contact had been made.

Inside was another envelope containing £10,000 in UK sterling – he flicked through the banded used notes and placed them inside his jacket pocket. He looked at the two photographs more closely and memorised the two faces – Brian Beaumont MP and Patrick Sands. He recognised Beaumont from the newspapers.

Armed with the information, it was time for Zonov to start his next assignment and prepare meticulously, as he always did.

Chapter 16

Ice Wharf, King's Cross

Patrick Sands was relaxing at his desk in his houseboat on the Ice Wharf, writing his latest script, when the phone rang. He struggled to maintain his footing as the boat bobbed up and down on the choppy waters. It was his close friend, Brian Beaumont.

'Hi, what are you up to?'

'What are you doing?' replied Beaumont tersely.

'Well, I'm writing at the moment. I always fancied writing a script if I ever got some spare time, so that's what I'm doing. It's a short play.'

Without any words of encouragement for Patrick's new venture, Beaumont changed the topic. He was in his own little world since the arrival of the CCTV footage.

'Patrick, I'd like to meet you, with this disc.'

'Name the time and place, and I'll be there.'

Sands decided to ignore Beaumont's terse manner, knowing his friend had something on his mind.

Beaumont continued. 'I'm in Parliament at the moment, so could I meet you in St James' Park and we can have a coffee?'

'Okay, where abouts?'

'The small café called Inn the Park; I'll be outside waiting,' came the reply.

'I know it – I think we've been before. It's the wooden restaurant, as I like to call it. What time?'

'Midday. Don't be late.'

Patrick laughed. 'If you're buying, I won't be late.'

He needed to meet Patrick, but he had chosen what would be a hectic day. After finishing a meeting with the BBC political editor, Beaumont went back to Portcullis House to collect the CCTV footage from his safe along with his laptop, before walking towards St James Park along Whitehall. En route, he stopped at the old Whitehall Theatre to book a show. He then walked through Admiralty Arch and made his way to St James' Park. The walk would normally take him twenty minutes, but with the snow freezing, it was particularly slippery underfoot.

He grew increasingly excited in anticipation of his meeting with Patrick. He thought about the conversation he had with the Speaker of the House, Arthur Betram, and the words of wisdom he had delivered in his office. As he strolled along the Mall, he was totally oblivious to the fact that he was being followed by Anton Zonov.

The plan to follow the politician and his friend was now in motion, with a view to finding out as much information about the two men and what they knew in relation to the upcoming inquiry. Certain members of the Russian Mafia based in London had anticipated that the inquiry would prove to be a futile exercise and wouldn't harm their operation.

Zonov continued to follow Beaumont from a

distance, stopping occasionally, but it wasn't a difficult task. The West End was busy with tourists, shoppers and workers, so it was easy to mingle in the crowd. Beaumont was an honest citizen – he wouldn't be surveillance conscious. It was so easy, in fact, that Zonov had time to stop at the newsagents and buy a paper while still watching him.

Beaumont finally entered St James' Park and approached the café, with Zonov close behind. He hadn't had chance to eat yet, and spoke to the waitress, Anka, whom he knew very well.

Pleased to see him, she said, 'Good morning, Mr Beaumont, how are you today?'

'I'm well thank you, Anka. And how's life treating you?'

'Very well,' she replied.

'I'll have a latte, but I have company today, so a large coffee as well and two blueberry muffins.'

'No problem, Mr Beaumont. Where are you sitting?'

'I'll be outside under the heaters.'

As Beaumont turned, he bumped into Anton Zonov. Zonov looked down at him and smiled.

In a quiet, calm voice, Zonov apologised. 'Sorry, sir.'

'No, it was my fault,' Beaumont said politely.

Zonov would be in close proximity when he met Patrick Sands, and would watch every movement and eavesdrop on their conversation.

Patrick Sands was a man of his word and arrived promptly at midday to join Beaumont. Beaumont's laptop was open and powered up, ready to show him the footage.

The journalist was out of breath.

'Brian, let me settle. You're like a cat on hot bricks.'

Beaumont was eager to start the footage.

'No, wait until you see this. Christmas has come fucking early this year – I won't get a better present.'

Beaumont loaded the CD and was raring to go.

Sands cleaned his reading glasses on his jacket and put them on. He watched intently as the file opened.

'What do you…?'

'Let me watch,' he interrupted, his eyes fixated on the screen. He was stunned by the footage. 'Jesus Christ, Brian, this is serious – who the fuck has sent this?'

'I don't know,' replied Beaumont.

Sands stopped the film. 'Well, Bamford's in it right up to his ears. He's always denied this, hasn't he?' As he restarted the footage, he continued. 'And look at him screwing away like there's no tomorrow… and surprise, surprise, his partner in crime is Derek Smith MP.'

'Do you know Smith?'

'No, I don't know him personally.'

'He's a close friend of Robert Bamford.'

Sands seemed disinterested in Derek Smith until Beaumont elaborated.

'There is an interesting connection. Derek Smith is the older brother of John Smith, the Prime Minister's advisor, but they don't socialise. They share the same political views, but Derek mixes in different circles. I think John has more ambitions than Derek, and of course being close to Chillot, he possibly has a brighter future.'

Sands' ears pricked up when he heard this revelation.

As he continued to watch the film, he said, 'There are a couple of blokes in the background, but I can't make them out.' He tried to wipe the screen, but the picture was still fuzzy.

Beaumont pulled the laptop across the table to have a look.

'I'm not bothered. I think they are probably small fry in the great scheme of things.'

As the footage progressed, Beaumont couldn't take his eyes off Bamford's movements within this seedy club. Suddenly, his attention was alerted as he reached a particular part of the footage.

'Patrick, did you see that?'

'Yes, he's paying the chap.'

'He's not, he's taking money. You know, this is damning footage.'

'Go back, go back and rewind it.'

They examined the film closely, and both stared at each other.

'This puts another dimension on it, Brian. What's the fucking moron doing, is he mad?'

Beaumont didn't reply, still in shock.

'Anyway, where do you think the building is located?'

Sands looked at the screen, squinted and said, 'There's no name anywhere, but it looks like a club … it's got a bar. Let me think.' He paused. 'I'll find it, don't worry. I know the West End better than anybody. Shame there's no name.'

'Well, it won't have a name, will it? It's a brothel, knocking shop, whatever you want to call it. If you look at the mirror closely you can see outside, but the picture's so grainy.'

Patrick leaned back and placed his hands behind his head.

'It's a shame the picture isn't better, but CCTV is never that great. In fact, it's a waste of time, isn't it?'

Sands smirked at his friend. 'In the next week we'll get a clearer picture, if you know what I mean?'

'No, Patrick, what do you mean?' Beaumont replied, a puzzled expression on his face.

'I've got a plan,' he replied.

Beaumont replied impatiently, 'What plan? Come on.'

'A few years ago I did an article for the Washington Post about a serial killer and met the lead detective, Roger Fischer; a great guy, and he works for the FBI from Langland Virginia.'

'That's the main HQ.'

'You're right, and I visited him there on several occasions. They can clean up CCTV images, and I'm sure they do a lot of work for the British Police. I don't know the ins and outs, but it's surprising what they can do, and it's only a little fuzzy.'

Beaumont pulled out the CD and handed it to Sands.

'Whatever you do, Patrick, don't lose it.'

Sands inserted the CD into his pocket and said, 'I'll put this on my laptop and get the footage sent.'

Zonov, comfortably placed at the side of them, continued to listen.

After a pause, Sands said, 'This is the plan. I'll send this to Roger today via UPS, and we can probably get it back in a week, or he will be able to email me the cleaned-up version to save time. Then we're laughing.'

'Look, this is going to come out at some point, so be very careful.' Beaumont laughed. 'If it breaks, you might as well do the story.'

Sands held up the evidence and waved it. 'You don't get a bigger scoop than this – I could retire.'

There was an eruption of laughter on both sides.

Beaumont continued. 'But seriously, you are the only man I can trust on this one.'

If only the conversation had been private. Zonov sat contently, blending into the background drinking his green tea, having listened to both men exchange words. Like a sponge, he had absorbed every snippet of information and was ready to report back to Loktev.

Beaumont and Sands had been indiscreet, but they had no idea they were in any danger. Why should they? After all, they were close friends, and as far as Beaumont was concerned, it was their secret. This information would only be revealed by him when the time was right and it would be a purely political decision.

Chapter 17

St James' Park

Zonov continued to watch Sands and Beaumont closely while he retreated to make contact with Loktev. He had not expected them to reveal so much information at such an early stage, but he was experienced enough to know that he must act quickly before time ran out.

He fumbled with his Blackberry and tried to phone the Russian Ambassador. Zonov became increasingly frustrated as he struggled to get a signal, so he tried to reposition himself nearer to St James' Lake. The Russian still couldn't get through, so in desperation he sent a text to the Ambassador's mobile phone.

Watching our targets and have important information. I need a decision quickly. Speak to your contact and get back. They have CCTV – could be very damaging.

Zonov waited patiently for a reply as he continued to watch both men as they sat at their table.

The phone rang, and when he answered, Loktev said, 'Anton, what have you heard?'

'They have footage, but it's not great quality. The politician's friend is sending it away to get it enhanced.'

'We can't take any chances. We must get that footage.

I will phone you back shortly.'

Zonov held his position and waited. The next call came almost immediately.

Loktev, in his usual assertive tone, said, 'I've spoken to the contact. This footage is a problem and it changes the whole plan. Put the journalist to bed as soon as possible and get the footage. Leave the politician – repeat, leave the politician. The time is not right yet. We will meet soon. Keep me updated.'

'Have you anything in mind?'

'I'll keep this brief. If this footage is going to cause irreparable damage to our operation within the UK and any politicians on the footage, then this cannot leak. Complete the assignment as you see fit, and as I said earlier, you must try to recover any footage and copies. We need to know what is on those tapes.'

The plan had now changed drastically and Zonov felt a sense of relief. He was a cold-blooded assassin, not a surveillance operative, and he was now in familiar territory; and, of course, his fee would increase.

His phone rang and he answered it straight away.

'Who is this?'

'Anton, my friend, it is Vitaly. How are you?'

Zonov was happy to hear from his friend. 'Where are you, Vitaly? It has been a long time.'

'I'm still in the Algarve with the girls; I'm coming to London soon.'

'Are you still in Villamoura, my friend?'

'Yes. How are the boys at the club? We must all meet up sometime.'

'The operation is running smoothly at this moment in time. We shall meet up and celebrate old times – all of us – in London in the Soho club.'

'Yes, this will be excellent. Plenty of girls – they'd better be good. '

Ending the call, Zonov said his goodbyes to his long-time friend and continued to remain close to his subjects. The cold wind was starting to bite through his lightweight coat he had decided to wear, and he wished both men would retire and head home. It reminded him of a Siberian winter.

Chapter 18

Patrick Sands took a sip of his coffee and spluttered, 'My coffee's cold, Brian, buy me another, it's the least you can do. I need a breather after taking all this in.'

Beaumont left the table to buy the drinks.

Zonov was now happy with his day's work in St James' Park and decided to execute the second part of his plan. It was time to check Patrick Sands' address at Ice Wharf and to follow Loktev's instructions.

After Beaumont returned to their table, the men discussed the footage further.

Sands, now becoming increasingly nervous, said, 'Remember what I told you about the gentlemen's club?'

'Go on…'

'Well, people are concerned about the inquiry, and you are the one pushing it. Don't take this the wrong way, but you are upsetting a lot of people. I admire what you are doing, but we must be cautious. I wouldn't trust anyone, not even John Cotterhill. Don't forget, he may have his own agenda.'

'I totally agree with you. I wasn't that interested in who the other people were in the footage, but I think this runs a lot deeper than we initially thought.'

Sands folded his arms. 'I'm interested to know who sent the footage. Bear in mind they might be getting us to do their dirty work.'

'You have a point. I think the sooner we find out where that club is located, the better.'

'Well, whoever sent the tape had access to the club.'

'I'm totally confused,' replied Beaumont. He could sense that Sands had something on his mind. 'C'mon, Patrick, let it out.'

'I've found out who was talking in the gentlemen's club the other night, and I think you'd better know.'

Beaumont shouted, 'C'mon then, who was it?'

'I spoke to my contact, and after making some discreet enquiries he found out it was in fact Robert Bamford, and John Smith, the Prime Minister's advisor. Apparently, they are in the same lodge, but he doesn't know which one. Why they were in the club, God only knows.'

Beaumont remained calm. 'That's one to keep under wraps.' After a short pause, he added, 'I just wish you had told me earlier.'

'I couldn't. He's only just found out, and I didn't know it was that important.'

Beaumont stood up and looked around the park.

'Well, Patrick, I'll have to love you and leave you, my friend.'

Sands started to head home to his new houseboat moored up at Ice Wharf Marina in King's Cross. He took the quick walk to Charing Cross tube station, closely followed by Zonov.

He didn't have any aspirations to live in a large house – he had never married, so the lifestyle on the boat suited the journalist. He was a free spirit and always had been. After buying the boat from a friend the previous year, Isabel and Beaumont had enjoyed sitting on the deck and soaking up the atmosphere of the wharf during the summer months. Isabel particularly liked Patrick and had tried to match him up with women on several occasions, but it never worked.

She thought he couldn't keep his women. Beaumont knew otherwise and was discreet. Patrick wasn't remotely interested in long-term commitment and the arrangement suited him. He and Beaumont were the ultimate drinking duo. Beaumont often moaned that he had never had any relationship with his sisters, Annabelle and Bernadette, because they simply didn't get on. He had told Patrick on several occasions that he was like a brother, and the only friend he could trust. The feeling was mutual. They both needed each other.

His tube journey nearly over, Sands' mind was all over the place as he thought about the day's events. He was oblivious to the fact that Zonov was sat opposite him. In fact, he was in a bubble, all alone, and looked forward to the peace and tranquillity that awaited him. He arrived at the boat around 8 p.m. and it was particularly cold. He decided to continue his writing, so he sat at the table and opened the curtains so that he could look out onto the wharf. His new script, 'Nowt Funnier than Folk', was slowly taking shape.

Zonov stood outside on the cobbled street, watching the boat and Patrick's every movement through the small windows. He wanted to get closer before he made any attempt to assassinate him.

Although the Russian had received information about Beaumont and his friend, he still didn't know a lot about the journalist. He was intrigued and still a little confused as to how close they were. He wondered whether Beaumont's closest friend was a police officer or another government agent. If he continued to keep a close eye on him, he hoped that would lead him to the footage.

Sands tried to write, but he had developed writer's block. His mind cluttered, he needed to see the CCTV footage again before he made contact with FBI Agent Roger Fischer in Virginia. As he checked the grainy images, he focused closely on a reflection from a mirror within the club which pointed to a window. If he could get a clear picture, it may indicate where Bamford and his cronies had been meeting. He again examined the pictures thoroughly and determined that the room was upstairs. He paced up and down the barge, thinking about how this whole affair would end.

Although he had never met Bamford, Sands was aware that rumours had always been floating around regarding his extramarital affairs, but nothing had ever been proven. Bamford had always brushed them off and portrayed himself as the happy family man, with two daughters. And as most politicians had done in the past, he made certain people believe in his innocence.

Sands was acutely aware how dangerous Bamford could be. A Geordie, he was a successful businessman and a self-made millionaire, having accumulated his wealth during the property boom in the 1980s. From an early age he'd always dreamed of a life in politics, and success in business served as a stepping stone. He was heavily involved with construction in Dubai and built apartments in the exclusive European ski resorts. He was a slight man, but famously had an ego the size of a giant. With a tan courtesy of his love of sunbeds, he was also known for his dapper dress sense and was a well-known face in Saville Row. Although he came from a working-class background, since his rise to power he was regarded by many as a champagne socialist. He had come from nothing and made his way to the top through sheer determination, and possessed a ruthless and callous streak.

Many words were used to describe him, few being over-complimentary, but he was a talented negotiator on the world stage, and with strong ties and connections worldwide, Charles Chillot had worked closely with him in their formative years in politics and he had spotted his potential. When Chillot won the general election, Bamford was an ideal candidate for Foreign Secretary and he didn't waste any time appointing the Geordie.

It was ironic that as Sands was writing, he couldn't stop thinking about the Foreign Secretary and the footage.

Suddenly, the phone rang. It was Beaumont.

'Hello, Brian,' Patrick greeted.

'Patrick, I forgot to mention an incident the other day.'

'And what was that?'

'It's not a problem, but I was confronted by the Foreign Secretary.'

'When?'

'Throughout Chillot's announcement, Bamford stared daggers at me and then followed me into the toilets.'

'What did he say?'

'It was a veiled threat, and I didn't think much of it at the time.'

'I'm glad you told me. He doesn't know about the

footage, does he?'

Beaumont was hesitant. 'No, he doesn't. Well, how could he? The threat was overheard by a colleague, who was in one of the cubicles at the time. I think it put the shits up Bamford, because when he heard the toilet door open he scarpered. It was too late, though, because the threat must have bounced off every fucking wall in the place.'

'Do I know the MP?'

'Chris Tomkinson, one of the backbenchers. Well, I thought I'd tell you … it was on my mind. But I'll leave you to get on with whatever you're doing and speak later.'

As Sands scribbled doodles on his notepad, he said, 'It's worth knowing. Why would Bamford, being the seasoned politician he supposedly is, sit there and stare at you when the whole thing is being televised? It's bizarre.'

Beaumont ended the call, and Sands continued to work late into the night.

The wharf was now quiet as Zonov departed. He walked from King's Cross to his flat in Hampstead Heath, a journey of about 4 miles, but it gave him time to think.

Eventually, he reached Heath Street and lady luck happened to be on his side. Feeling hungry, he approached one of the local pizza shops and noticed an Audi TT parked up outside, engine running. Being the opportunist he was, and surprised to find no one at the wheel, he placed his hood over his head and slowly advanced towards the vehicle. He saw that it was empty and the keys were in the ignition. This was the perfect opportunity.

As the owner of the car remained in the takeaway reading a magazine, waiting for his food, he would have no idea that his car was about to be stolen.

Zonov steadily crouched down, sat in the car and adjusted the seat. The owner couldn't see the Russian as he reversed the car quietly away from the shop. In no time at all, Zonov had left without a trace.

He drove back to his flat, where his lock-up garage would house the car overnight.

Chapter 19

The next day, Sands woke at around 7 a.m. after a few hours' sleep. He was exhausted after tossing and turning all night, thinking about the CCTV footage. He was eager to contact Agent Fischer, but it was still 2 a.m. in the United States; not a good time to phone and ask for a favour. So he sent an email instead. He couldn't wait any longer – the clock was ticking, and each minute was precious. He was impatient at the best of times, but he wanted to help Brian. He was also fully aware that this story would be his best scoop.

Once the send button was pressed, he scrawled on a piece of paper:

Things to do…

Chase up Roger – after email.

Check CCTV footage again and see if there is anything else.

How can I break this story? See Brian…

Bamford … and the others in the footage – expose – no mercy – CONNECTIONS – Who owns the club and where is it located? Find it!!!!

Keep positive!!!!!!!!!!!!

This was a typical note written by Sands on a large yellow post-it note – his eccentric way of reminding himself to complete his daily tasks.

He had only just sent the email when he got a response from Agent Fischer.

 Hi there, buddy. How are you? I'm still awake, although it's very late here in the USA … give me a call...

Sands reached for his phone and dialled.

Fischer answered immediately. 'Hello Patrick?'

Fischer sounded happy to hear his voice. 'Patrick, great to hear from you, man. It's been too long. I keep meaning to contact you and ask you to visit. We could do some hunting.'

'How are things at the FBI?'

'Well, after 9/11 it's been a busy time for everyone, and I'm still here in Virginia, so I love it. I miss the field a little, but hey, I get to see the kids most nights and play baseball with 'em, but they always kick my butt.'

'It sounds like you've found a great place to be.'

'I'm happy. And what are you up to, buddy?'

'I'm still writing, my friend. I will come to visit, and the deal is you come to stay in London – you'd love it here. It's a shame you couldn't get when I did the piece with you.'

'I know, it would have been great. I promise, I will come.'

'Roger, please forgive me if I sound rude, but I need a big favour.'

'Go for it.'

'I won't bore you with the details, but I have a friend, Brian Beaumont. He is a prominent Member of Parliament and a public figure.'

'Yes, I recall this guy.'

Sands hesitated. 'Okay, I couldn't remember if I'd told you about him.'

'Oh yes, I remember. It's a coincidence, buddy, but I was on the plane to Washington recently and read about him in The Times – it was a free paper, you know. Something to do with corruption and an inquiry – it sounded quite tasty – and at the time I thought of you.'

'Well, this is all connected. I'll come straight to the point. Can you clean up images on video or CCTV?'

'No problem,' replied the agent.

'I've got a copy here and it's on CD. It's sensitive and must be kept secret, that's the problem I have. No way can I have this done in the UK.'

Fischer's tone changed. 'Sounds like deep shit, Patrick.'

'It is – it's CCTV footage recorded in a brothel. One of the customers is a member of the government.'

Fischer burst into laughter. 'Jesus! Son of a bitch! What the fuck's going on in the UK? I thought everything was squeaky clean.'

Sands laughed. 'I don't think so.'

Fischer was still laughing. 'Here we go, sounds like another Watergate. Okay, send me the footage and I'll look at it myself. When it's cleaned up, the new version will be marked and placed on a new disc. Address the package to my home, and I suggest you get an encrypted stick with a password. You don't want this ending up in the wrong hands.'

'I'll send it tomorrow by UPS.'

'Okay, bud.'

'Thanks, Roger. You should get it in the next few days. Can you keep me posted?'

'Yes, I will. Don't worry, and be lucky, Patrick. I'm going to bed.'

After the call ended there was no way Sands was

going to sleep, so he meticulously prepared the footage to be copied for Fischer so that it would be ready the next day.

Suffering from insomnia, it would be a long night as he drank copious amounts of coffee. He was tempted to call Beaumont, but decided he would wait.

Chapter 20

10th December 2011

Patrick Sands was in the middle of a dream, and as he fell from a great height, the sensation woke him immediately. Momentarily he wondered where he was, and as he wiped his eyes, he noticed the time – 10 a.m. He jumped out of bed and made another coffee.

He immediately sent a text to Beaumont.

Brian, spoke to the guy at the FBI. Everything is fine. I'll get the footage sent today by courier.

There was no time to waste. Sands showered, changed and left the barge, and headed to the West End. He decided he would get the package collected from the boat later that afternoon. He locked the door and made his way to the landing area. As he came out of the barge, his attention was drawn to a black Audi TT parked close to the wharf. It was strange to see a car parked so close to the boats, so he made a mental note of the registration.

In the past few months there had been several burglaries, and vehicles had been used in the commission of the crime. The area was restricted, and the sign clearly stated no vehicles must enter. He was tempted to approach the driver, but decided against it.

As he walked alongside the car, he tried to look in the windows, but frustratingly they were blacked out. He carried on towards King's Cross train station where he would catch a black cab into London.

Zonov sat in the car, his face concealed by his hood.

Patrick tried to call Beaumont, but it went straight to voicemail.

Once inside the black hackney carriage, Sands said to the taxi driver, 'Covent Garden, please.'

The Audi TT, driven by Anton Zonov, started to tail them. It wasn't difficult. It was a typical London day, and the traffic was moving slowly.

The cab driver, a large West Indian with a Rastafarian haircut, was in a jovial mood and tried to make conversation with Sands, but he was totally preoccupied reading and eventually, the man gave up. They soon arrived in Covent Garden.

'That will be ten pounds, sir. You look like a troubled soul.'

Sands looked at the taxi driver and a sudden air of calmness descended upon him. The man had a warm, kind voice. It soothed him, and he felt guilty.

He handed over fifteen pounds and said, 'Forgive me for being rude, just thinking about things.'

'I know the feeling, sir. Have a good day, and thank you.'

The ground was freezing and Sands took great care to keep his footing on the icy pavement as he slowly made his way into Covent Garden Market to look at the stalls. The artic conditions were almost unbearable, so he decided to have a coffee, and the strong aroma of hot waffles drifting through the busy marketplace made him hungry. He adored the smell, and quickly found a café nearby and took a seat.

Sands was a highly intelligent man, so much so that it had probably held him back. To his detriment in the past, he had been on the verge of having a big scoop and then hesitated, only to see colleagues beat him to the post. He wasn't a natural risk-taker, and he decided this time he was going to take the bull by the horns. However, it didn't sit easily with him. He was fully aware that there was going to be massive fallout when this story broke. As he approached his forty-seventh year, he felt he wouldn't get many more opportunities like this, and he was well aware that his friend Brian Beaumont was also going to benefit. He wondered what lay ahead as he sipped his coffee.

There was only one other journalist who had come remotely close to breaking a story about Robert Bamford, and Edward Fahy never lived to tell his tale. The secret he held died with him.

While Sands sat in the café, Zonov stood at the entrance to Covent Garden watching closely.

Beaumont, keen to contact Sands and get an update on any progress, tried to call him, but his phone was in silent mode as he relaxed in the café. Beaumont was left wondering...

As Sands made notes and devoured his waffle, the peace and quiet would soon be broken by the sounds of a busker playing his guitar. The out-of-tune notes destroyed the morning calm. It was time to leave and find an Internet café.

Sands was rather frustrated by the busker's antics and uttered an obscenity in his direction as he passed the man en route to his destination, where he could hook up on a PC and arrange the collection of the footage later that day from his boat.

Having visited the café, he finally left the central market and walked along Russell Street, crossing the junction with Wellington Street and Bow Street, still walking gingerly on the frozen snow as he looked up at the Theatre Royal. The streets were unusually quiet. The snow had caused considerable chaos in the capital. Sands continued to stroll aimlessly through the alleyways and streets.

The silence then ended unexpectedly. He could hear the sound of a car revving its engine, and it was so loud that he turned and noticed a black Audi TT.

He didn't stop to think and carried on walking. Moments later, it slowly dawned on him that it was the car he had seen previously when he was leaving the boat. His deliberate walk quickly developed into a jog. He felt uneasy.

Then he heard the wheels screech and realised the car was now driving towards him at speed.

Realising the gravity of the situation in which he found himself, he tried to sprint with his head down, struggling to grip the footpath. He slipped on the ice and moved onto the salted road, but there was no escape. The car mounted the pavement and was only yards behind him.

In a matter of seconds, the car was upon him and he jumped. The car tossed him into the air. He somersaulted and landed hard on his back, and felt a sharp pain in his left arm. It felt like an eternity as he writhed in agony on the cold icy road surface.

He looked up and saw that the car had stopped, engine still revving. To his horror, the reverse lights illuminated and again, the wheels screeched. The car reversed towards him and he lay helplessly as it ran over his leg. The pain was unbearable and he started to feel nauseous.

Zonov, confident he had killed Sands, left the scene.

Patrick looked up at the clear blue sky and felt a sudden warmth followed by hot sweats. He couldn't move and felt dizzy. He fell into a state of semi-consciousness before finally passing out.

Zonov had one thing on his mind and that was to retrieve the footage from the boat. As he approached Ice Wharf in the stolen Audi, he heard sirens, and in a state of panic he headed towards a derelict building close to King's Cross station and torched the car.

After sending a text to Loktev, he returned to Patrick's houseboat in a cab. He walked slowly into the marina and noticed the boat was empty. He tried the door – it was locked, but he skilfully and without delay picked the lock.

On entry, he went straight to the first port of call – Patrick Sands' organised desk.

He wanted the laptop, but it was nowhere to be seen and this infuriated Zonov. He kicked the chair away from the desk and continued to search the whole of the boat. Eventually, he came across the post-it note Sands had written earlier. He read it and then looked out of the small windows, checking the area was clear.

He quickly placed the note into his jacket pocket and again searched frantically for the laptop, but it was no good. Patrick Sands must have hidden it and the footage.

Zonov left the boat, checked his main phone, then retreated to the Maiden Lane council estate and found a dark alleyway. He sent a text to Anton Loktev to update him on the position.

Hi – completed task – home address searched – no trace – except a note which I will forward shortly by MMS.

Loktev sat and waited at the Russian Embassy as he read the message.

It didn't take long for Zonov to send the photograph of the post-it note. His phone bleeped and he downloaded the MMS, carefully reading the content. He raised his eyebrows. He immediately opened his address book on the phone and scrolled down until he reached 'Z'. He wasted no time in forwarding the photograph with a note attached.

Your thoughts on this please?

Chapter 21

As Patrick Sands slowly regained consciousness, he felt like he had been in the middle of a never-ending nightmare. His vision was blurred, but he could see the image of someone standing over him. The injured journalist tried to focus on the person stood at the foot of his bed as he attempted to turn over, but he couldn't. His left arm was in plaster and his leg in traction. He couldn't remember a thing.

The nurse stood over him and said, 'How are you feeling, Mr Sands?'

He grimaced. 'I'm not feeling well, Nurse, extremely sore.'

She smiled. 'You've had a close run, and you've been heavily sedated.'

Sands was confused. 'What happened?'

'You were run over by a car, and a passing member of the public called an ambulance. At some point, the police will want to speak to you.'

'God, I'm so sore, Nurse. Can I have something?'

'Of course you can', she replied as she pulled the thermometer from her pocket.

Sands cried out, 'My head's sore.'

'Don't worry, it's just concussion. All the tests have

been done and you're okay. The paramedics were initially concerned about your condition at the scene, but the tests are fine.'

Sands was suffering from slight amnesia – not remembering what had happened frustrated him, but he would soon be made aware of the day's events.

'Where am I?' he shouted.

'Guys Hospital. You're in good hands,' she replied.

He was still feeling drained after the attempt on his life, and he started to doze. The rest he needed would be short-lived as a voice interrupted him.

'Mr Sands, hello!'

He saw that it was the doctor.

'How are you?'

'Sore, Doctor, I feel very sore.'

'You will be; you were run over by a car in Covent Garden. If you are well enough, the police are waiting outside with one of your friends – a Mr Beaumont?' He looked at the notes. 'Yes, that's it, a Mr Beaumont.'

Patrick was pleased to hear this news.

'Yes, Doctor, I suppose I should speak to the police.'

The doctor left the room and two plain-clothes officers knocked on the door.

'Come in,' replied Sands.

'Hello, Mr Sands,' they said simultaneously, producing their warrant cards. 'I am Detective Sergeant Wynyard, and this is my colleague, Detective Constable Jones.'

'Pleased to meet you. Forgive me, but I won't shake your hands.'

Wynyard smiled. 'Mr Sands … or can I call you Patrick?'

'Patrick is fine,' he replied as he struggled to make himself comfortable.

'Okay. Do you remember anything about today?'

'No, I don't remember a thing, Officer.'

DC Jones interrupted. 'You're a lucky man. Someone has tried to kill you. There's good news and bad news.'

'Go on.'

DS Wynyard said, 'We have recovered CCTV footage from a nearby shop. It's not great, but we have picked up a registration number, and it's a stolen vehicle. Whoever hit you today didn't want you to be speaking to us. Is there anybody who would want to kill you?'

'No, certainly not, I don't have enemies.'

Wynyard continued. 'We cannot ID anyone from the footage, and the car reversed over you after hitting you the first time. Hopefully it will turn up somewhere, and we may get some forensic evidence. Do you know the driver?'

'No, I do not.'

'I know you're still not feeling well, so I don't intend taking a statement. DC Jones and I are going to make some more enquiries, see if there are any witnesses or more CCTV footage, and then get back to you.'

'Okay.'

As both officers turned, DC Jones said, 'Oh, and Mr Beaumont is outside. Is he a friend?'

'Yes.'

'Close friend or acquaintance friend?'

Sands was becoming impatient and irritated by the attitude of the officers and replied, 'Close friend. Not that I think it has anything to do with the fact someone has tried to kill me, officers!'

Both the officers left and Brian Beaumont entered the room. He looked in a state of total shock.

'How are you, Patrick, are you okay? Where are your belongings?'

Sands replied sarcastically, 'Yes, I'm still alive, Brian!'

It suddenly dawned on Sands that he didn't know where the CD containing the footage was, and he asked Beaumont.

'Leave it to me,' Beaumont replied. 'I'll get the doctor to find out where your clothing is being stored.'

The nurse then entered, and Patrick Sands was desperate.

'Nurse, where will I find all my clothes and other personal items?'

The nurse knelt down and produced a plastic bag. Laughing, she said, 'Don't worry, here they are. What's in them, the crown jewels?'

Beaumont grabbed the bag and clothing and said, 'Where did you put it, Patrick?'

'It's in my jacket pocket.'

Beaumont started fumbling and feeling the pockets. He suddenly sat back and sighed.

'Thank fuck it's still there.'

Sands looked at Beaumont. 'The disc needs to be collected today, and I need you to take it to the boat – get my keys and go, quickly.'

Beaumont collected the bag and said, 'I'll leave straight away and sort it out.'

Sands grabbed his arm.

'Be careful; someone doesn't want us around.'

'Don't worry.'

Beaumont decided to get a cab from the hospital. He was vigilant, constantly checking to see if he was being followed while at the same time wondering what information they should give to the police. As far as he was concerned, the only person that could be involved was Robert Bamford. After all, he was the only man who had made threats against him. But how could he prove it was him? He came to the conclusion during the journey to Sands' boat that they should not mention the footage and keep it quiet.

Things weren't to improve. He eventually arrived at the boat and noticed a light on inside, which was unusual. As he entered the deck area, the door was ajar. There was no visible damage, but the boat had obviously been ransacked. All the drawers had been thoroughly searched, with the contents scattered over the floor.

Beaumont searched furiously for Sands' laptop in every nook and cranny, but to his frustration he couldn't find it. The last thing he needed was the footage to fall into the wrong hands.

He contacted Sands by phone.

'It's Brian. It just gets worse.'

'Why?'

'Your boat's been broken into, and I can't find your laptop.'

'Go to the kitchen table and look under the carpet. There's a trap door in the floor, and it's in a compartment.'

Brian Beaumont rushed to the table, lifted the carpet and opened the trap door. The laptop was intact.

'Thank the Lord,' he squealed.

'I'm relieved it's still there. I don't think we should report this. Can you stay at the boat, clean up and arrange for the collection? Be vigilant, Brian, we're being followed.'

'I'll sort everything. You need to rest.'

Beaumont sat on Sands' bed and looked out of the window towards the office blocks towering above the wharf. He should have been ecstatic, but he wasn't. His only real friend had just escaped an attempt on his life. He reached for his handkerchief and broke down.

He was used to solving problems easily. Even so, this was a different ball game. He was in new territory, and it didn't sit comfortably with him. He slowly pulled himself together and reached up to the shelf, where he found a bottle of Jack Daniels. He poured himself a drink. As he sipped from the glass, he powered up the laptop, eager to get the parcel ready for collection.

Having trawled the computer, he eventually found the inbox and sent an email to Roger Fischer, the FBI agent.

URGENT MESSAGE – FROM BRIAN BEAUMONT – sent on behalf of Patrick Sands.

Dear Roger,

Hi, this is Brian Beaumont. I will be sending the footage today. Patrick is in hospital after an accident, but he will be okay. I will get your number and phone you when it's convenient. Thank you for your assistance in this matter. We will be in contact.

Kind regards, Brian Beaumont.

PS. When you have carried out the clean-up process, can you return the file by email to this address and forward the hard copy back by courier? Sorry, but we are in a race against time.

Chapter 22

Ingrid House Chambers, Mayfair

'Good morning, Mr Rameau.'

Lord Justice Rameau walked into his office and was greeted by his superior, Lord Chief Justice Jackson, who had made himself comfortable behind Rameau's grand oak desk.

The senior judge was keen to keep an eye on the formation of the inquiry team.

Rameau greeted Jackson. 'You gave me a fright. This is a pleasant surprise to see you here at such an early hour, and sat behind my desk. I hope they made you a cup of tea.'

'Your secretary kindly offered, but I'm fine.'

'What can I do for you?'

'Well, I hope your diary's clear of any appointments. Your secretary gave me the go-ahead to see you. I was going to call yesterday, Jacques, but you were out of the office meeting somebody.'

Rameau turned sharply. 'Did anyone tell you who I'd seen?' There was a nervous tone to his voice.

'You sound like a guilty man in the dock awaiting his fate. I hope it wasn't a member of the opposite sex?'

'Not at all, sir. I wish I had the time.'

'I've spoken to the Attorney General this morning and believe they have had several meetings with the government in relation to the inquiry.'

'Well, I guessed the wheels would be well and truly in motion, and I have some ideas about who I need to assist me.'

'Have you spoken to your father about the inquiry? He'll be a proud man.'

Rameau seemed disinterested. 'Not really, sir.'

Lord Chief Justice Jackson lowered his round-rimmed spectacles and said, 'You don't seem to be over-enamoured with heading this inquiry, Jacques. Do I sense something isn't right?'

Rameau snapped back, 'You are right, sir; nerves perhaps, and slight apprehension. This is a great responsibility for me, and people's lives, careers and reputations are at stake.'

'I am coming to the end of my career. Seize this opportunity with two hands and you'll be fine. You're too talented to let this fail. Get a good team and I will be there if you need advice. You are very much the establishment and certainly held in high esteem at No 10. It will not do your career any harm whatsoever.'

Rameau smiled. 'I know, and I will grasp the opportunity, sir.'

Jackson put his arm around him. 'This will be one of the biggest inquiries I have had to oversee and will certainly be subject to close scrutiny by the media. I'm sure the witness running order will be long and exhaustive, and I'll assist you in every way possible.'

'I have no outstanding cases to preside over,' replied Rameau, 'and I presume we could be looking at a time slot well into six months or more for this inquiry.'

'It will be a lengthy hearing.' Lord Chief Jackson paced around the office. 'Do you know the Foreign Secretary, Robert Bamford?'

Rameau snubbed the question and looked at his phone. 'Can I just take this important call, sir?'

'Go ahead, don't let me keep you.'

As he exited the office hastily, Rameau had no intention of entering into any discussion with the Lord Chief Justice about any relationship he may have with the Foreign Secretary.

He entered the sanctity of the washroom and waited in silence – he had not had any incoming call. He waited for several minutes and returned to the office, then immediately changed the subject.

'I don't like this damn vibrate mode on my phone… Anyway, where were we? Yes, I will start my preparations today, and if everything goes to plan, then my team will be in place at the close of play.'

'Thank you, Jacques,' Jackson replied. 'Leave me to liaise with the Attorney General and Charles Chillot.'

Lord Chief Justice Jackson had forgotten once more to raise the subject of Robert Bamford.

'Oh! The Prime Minister has met your father. I just thought I'd let you know.'

Lord Chief Justice Jackson gauged Rameau's reaction and closed the subject. He then opened the door and closed it swiftly behind him, not allowing Rameau any opportunity to answer.

Rameau sighed, sat back in his chair, then leaned forward into the walnut drinks cabinet and turned the gold key. Before reaching inside, he hoisted his hand up towards the window against the light and watched it quiver. He was feeling the pressure.

He reached for his phone and spoke to his assistant, Joan.

'Please switch off all calls and don't disturb me for a couple of hours. I have urgent business to attend to.'

He reached inside the cupboard and surveyed the various bottles neatly stacked. He pulled out a bottle of Chivas Regal Royal Salute, hoping the fifty-year-old whisky would calm his fraying nerves. Released in 2003 to commemorate the 50th anniversary of Queen Elizabeth II's Coronation, it was normally used on special occasions, but in the next few weeks this would be his medicine.

He slowly poured his first glass. The aroma calmed him and he relaxed back in his seat, closed his eyes and took a sip from the crystal glass.

Chapter 23

Downing Street

The Prime Minister hoped it would be business as usual now that the Rameau inquiry had been announced as he mulled over the daily newspapers strewn across his desk. Chomping on his favourite toast and marmalade, he read each paper column by column; the news seemed positive for once. The papers were in a pro Chillot mood and certainly welcomed his decision to call a public inquiry. Even the normally abrasive broadsheets were singing his praises today. For the first time in months he sensed he was perhaps turning a corner as he sipped slowly on his Arabica coffee.

His office door was slightly ajar, and John Smith poked his head through the gap.

'Morning, Prime Minister.'

'Good morning, John. Come in and join me for a coffee.'

Smith entered.

'Prime Minister, there are a few items on the itinerary today, just to keep you up to speed.'

'I've checked the diary. Have you spoken to anybody regarding the inquiry?'

'Yes, sir, I spoke to Lord Chief Justice Jackson and the Attorney General. Everything is in hand, and we must now let the inquiry run its course. Statements will be taken, and I suppose it could be up and running for the New Year. It's in good hands. You may well be called to give evidence.'

'Yes, I am aware of that possibility,' Chillot replied. 'I cannot say a great deal. A futile exercise, but I have no problem.' He continued. 'Any news on Robert Bamford?'

'He's lying low at the moment, and I think he has a few trips abroad coming up. I think the more he is out of the country the better. Oh, and before I forget, you have two conference calls today. The first is with the French President, and the second with some members of the UN. Their names have left me for the moment, but other than that you have quite an easy day.'

Chillot laughed. 'Don't speak too soon and tempt fate.'

Smith laughed.

'By the way,' Chillot continued, 'can you keep the Cabinet up to speed over this inquiry regarding any press approaches? Let's all sing from the same hymn sheet.'

As Smith started to leave the office, the Prime Minister shouted, 'Oh! John, have you seen Bamford socially in the last few weeks?'

Smith turned back and frowned. 'No, Prime Minister, why?'

'Just a thought, that's all. A friend of mine said he thought he saw you in a club. I've forgotten the name…'

Before the Prime Minister could end his sentence, Smith said, 'Not me, he must be mistaken.'

'Oh well, I did tell him you didn't socialise with the man.'

Smith didn't react and kept calm, then left the office. He went immediately to his own office situated at the rear of Downing Street and sat at his computer.

He opened his computer and logged in to his private email account and drafted an email to his brother, Derek Smith, copying in Robert Bamford. It was brief and to the point.

I have just spoken to the PM and he knows about our meeting in the Regal Club – I told him he was mistaken – the meeting was seen by a third party. I am only warning you in case you are approached. JS – DO NOT REPLY.

Without delay, he pressed the send button and then deleted the message from his sent folder. John Smith had his foot in both camps.

Chapter 24

Rameau paced up and down his office, deep within his Chambers. Was the onset of the inquiry starting to worry him? His intake of whisky had dramatically increased over the last few weeks, and those close to him had noticed a change in his personality.

His secretary, Joan, had also noticed a change, and as she entered the office she was careful not to disturb him.

'I've penned a meeting for this week, sir, if that is suitable. I just need a date – regarding the inquiry, that is.'

Miles away, Rameau replied, 'Oh, I'm sorry. Yes, Joan, I'll check my diary.'

She was concerned and said, 'Is everything okay, Lord Justice? You don't seem yourself.'

'I'm fine!' he snapped. 'Leave me alone for a few minutes.'

She shook her head and left the office.

He continued to stroll up and down, rubbing his goatee beard with his fingers. This was the Lord Chief Justice's most important case he would preside over. He reached for his phone and checked it for messages.

Was this the reason for his demeanour? He picked

up a copy of The Times from a large pile of papers prepared each morning and sat down at his desk. He preferred it if his daily newspaper was ironed before he read it – after all, his view was that if they ironed them at his gentleman's club in Soho, then they could do so in his office.

Rameau had already read the circled article referring to Robert Bamford's state of health. He was concerned about Bamford and his ability to give evidence. He would make further enquiries, but reports suggested his state of mind was deteriorating rapidly. He continued to be vigilant in his mission to keep a close watch on developments in the paper and had left a note for his secretary to highlight all articles relating to the Foreign Secretary.

He turned on his computer and waited for it to boot up as he looked through the various articles laid out before him. He waited impatiently as the computer slowly kicked in.

Eventually, the screen appeared and he tapped in the name Robert Bamford – Foreign Secretary. He didn't know where to start as the engine displayed hit after hit – Bamford was indeed a newsworthy character and of interest to the tabloids. Rumours of infidelity and his nocturnal activities far outweighed his political engagements and achievements.

Rameau was fully aware that this inquiry would revolve around the Foreign Secretary, and he wondered how the beleaguered politician would play his cards.

As he continued to surf the Web, bookmarking the articles on Bamford, the door opened unexpectedly.

Annoyed that there was no knock, Rameau shouted, 'Shut the bloody door! I don't want to be disturbed.'

'It's your father,' a soft voice whispered, his French accent unmistakable.

'Sorry, Father, I didn't realise you were dropping by. I had asked not to be disturbed.'

'I can come back later.'

His son didn't reply as he continued to tap the keys on his PC.

Alfred Rameau shuffled into the office and sat down.

'I can come back later, Jacques, but I wanted to congratulate you on the news, and your mother sends her regards. We would like to see you more often, but I suppose you are busy.'

Rameau left his desk and hugged his father. They were very close.

'I'm sorry, it's just been hectic, and I have a few matters to sort out.'

'We are pleased for you – you have come so far – but you look unhappy. I am your father and I know you better than anybody. Surely this should be the happiest time of your life.'

'I'm not happy; in fact, I'm never happy, just content.'

'Have you got a lady friend yet?' his father asked gingerly.

His voice filled with frustration, Rameau replied, 'I have no time, Father. Why do you always ask me this? I have no time.'

There was an uncomfortable silence in the room.

'Is Mother asking you all the time about my personal life? If she is, I wish she would stop it.'

'I think she wants grandchildren.'

'Oh, thinking about herself again. I'll get married

and have children when it suits me. I plan my life now.'

'Don't shoot the messenger; she's just a concerned mother, that's all. She would like to see you settle down.'

'No! She interferes and has her own agenda. Whether I am happy is immaterial!'

Lord Justice Rameau sat opposite his elderly father, frustrated by his comments and eager to get on with his affairs. His life was full, his mind at bursting point as the inquiry grew closer. He didn't like to get into discussions about his life – with anybody. There was always a tension with his pushy mother, who tried to control her son.

The phone rang, and that was Jacques Rameau's chance to get some peace and quiet.

He rudely ushered his father out of the office and said, 'I need to take this – I'll call you later.'

Rameau's father was annoyed by his son's attitude, and as he left he rebuked him in his native tongue. He was normally a laid-back character.

You're a stubborn man, Jacques, and so rude sometimes.

Rameau snapped back at his father, 'Oh whatever.'

As the door closed, Rameau picked up the phone.

He introduced himself, but was met with silence, so he said, 'Who is it?'

The line went dead.

He slammed the phone down. He approached his bookcase, removed a box and placed it in a bag that he kept in a large safe.

As he prepared to leave the office, he said to Joan, 'If anybody calls, I'm not here. Leave my diary free. I'm going for dinner, and I need to see somebody. I won't be back today. Can you tell the other ladies?'

They all looked at each other and shrugged their shoulders. Lord Justice Rameau was acting oddly.

As he walked down the street, Joan looked through the window and shouted, 'Thanks for the apology, you asshole.'

Chapter 25

Once the Norwegian Christmas tree had been erected in Trafalgar Square and the lights were illuminated, there was a definite buzz around the office and Edgerton came into his own. He was quite a party animal for forty something (although he didn't look it). Amongst the various crime squads in London, Christmas was a busy time, but it was also a green light to work and play hard. Edgerton, in particular, loved his annual invite to the Flying Squad Christmas party, and he thought he might invite a few of the Murder Squad boys this year. This was not an evening for the fainthearted. You were guaranteed a bad hangover the next day.

Now divorced, Edgerton still found time to see his two girls during the festive period. He had decided this year he would take them to Regent Street and Oxford Street, and he had a plan. He wanted them to meet Chloe Moran – they would get on well. At every available opportunity he found time to talk to Paula and Natalie on the phone, and neither had failed to notice that their dad liked Chloe. He never stopped talking about her, and they reminded him of the fact. He didn't realise he was doing it – a sure sign, they thought, that he was attracted to the young detective.

As Edgerton entered the office, he flicked the remaining snow from his shoe and said, 'Good morning, ladies and gentlemen, how are we all today?'

Like a finely tuned choir, they all replied simultaneously. Edgerton was in a buoyant mood, ready for a good night out.

'I hope you all have your gear with you, because we'll be leaving straight from work tonight. We'll go straight to Covent Garden and then on to an Indian, then hit the town.'

Edgerton looked at the officers as they hung on his every word.

'On the lash, or whatever you like to call it these days, and I will want a full head count tomorrow. No sickies please. If an old man like me can get in, then all you youngsters can make it.'

Chloe Moran raised her hand. 'But you've had plenty of practice, Guv.'

Edgerton smirked. 'I have, but no excuses please.'

Laughter erupted around the office.

'I might even do a bit of dancing if we end up clubbing it. Show you all some moves. There's still life in the old dinosaur yet.'

DI Palmer banged on the desk. 'Now I would like to see that!'

'On a serious note, you will all shortly be recommended for a Deputy Assistant Commissioner's commendation for your work on the Jenkins case.'

Cheers erupted in the office.

Edgerton continued. 'Shhh... I've just completed the report, and admittedly, I've had to dress it up a little for some of the intellectually challenged ones among us who did fuck all.'

The cheers were replaced with boos from the men.

Edgerton laughed at them. 'No names mentioned, of course. All donations tonight will be gratefully accepted.'

DI Palmer interrupted. 'Can I echo DCI Edgerton's comments? You really are a great team … well, most of you. And remember, tonight Chief Superintendent Watkins will be with us, so I don't want any dirty jokes … well, just a few perhaps. He will join us there. Any of you got any questions?'

Detective Constable Simpson, the new addition to the squad from Bethnal Green, held his hand up.

'Go on then, make it quick, Bob,' Edgerton said, hands firmly on his hips.

'Can I come back after and sleep at the nick?'

'I suppose so, and by the way, if I find out who's been rustling in my office when I'm not in at the weekend, I'll have their guts for garters. And before you apologise, I notice a few red faces sat amongst you all.' Grinning, he added, 'You lot think I was born yesterday. You're lucky I'm a patient soul.'

Edgerton and Palmer retreated to his office leaving a happy team behind. The officers' morale couldn't have been better. Edgerton's motto 'work hard, play hard' was a proven recipe, and it worked. He was a natural-born leader.

As they sat at the desk, they could still hear laughter from the office. DI Palmer closed the door.

Edgerton looked at him.

'Philip, I was checking through the force incident logs and noticed a job near Bow Street. Have you seen it?'

'No, Guv.'

'A car tried to run down a pedestrian. The guy survived. He's a journalist. I think they've recorded it as a GBH. I thought attempted murder would have been a more appropriate classification. The fucking idiot in the car ran him over and then reversed back over him.'

'Who's the OIC?'

Edgerton reached for a pile of papers. He slowly flicked through the logs, licking his index finger at regular intervals. He found the one he wanted.

'Here we are. DS Wynyard and DC Jones.'

'Ah yes, I know Brian Jones, but I've never heard of a Wynyard. I just thought if it was an attempted murder we could have a look while it's quiet.'

'You could call them, Guv, but I think I'd be inclined to let them get on with it. I mean, if it gets messy we could assist, I suppose.'

'I might make a quick call later, or call in. I think they're from Charing Cross nick. We could walk over later before we go out.'

'Yes, Guv, let's make a call. But don't tell Watkins, it'll fuck his night up.'

Palmer left the office as Edgerton reached for the phone. It rang and rang, and he placed it on speaker phone impatiently, muttering under his breath, 'Answer the bloody phone.'

As he spoke, a voice rang out. 'CID office, Charing Cross, can I help?'

'This is Detective Chief Inspector Jack Edgerton. Can I speak to DS Wynyard or DC Jones please?'

The phone was immediately passed over.

'DC Jones, sir, what can I do for you?'

'DC Jones. DCI Edgerton from the Murder Squad. I need to have a chat about the GBH near Bow Street, with the car.'

'Are you from Complaints?'

'No, am I bollocks.'

'I thought we had another complaint, Guv.'

Edgerton laughed. 'So, what can you tell me about the case?'

'Yes, no problem, sir. DS Wynyard is out at the moment, but we're working on it together, and I use the term loosely because we've come up against a brick wall. There are no decent witnesses to work with, no CCTV of any value, and the victim can't remember a bloody thing. There's also no forensic evidence at all. The car was found the next day burnt out – not a trace of any evidence. Of course it was stolen, and the AP never saw the car being taken, so we didn't get anything there.'

'Okay. Who is this journalist?'

'He's a big friend of the Shadow Home Secretary – his name is Patrick Sands.'

'Ah, Mr Beaumont. Have you spoken to him yet?'

'Briefly, sir, but he hasn't given us anything. I have a feeling we're not getting everything. Why? I don't know – perhaps just intuition, but they have something to hide.'

'We could assist you. I think something's going on here. Have you read about the inquiry?'

'I'm glad you mentioned it, and we would be grateful if you assisted. I spoke to DS Wynyard and we both think there's a connection, but our gaffer's shitting it. I'm not having a go at him. It's political, and I would feel the same way. It's a right ball of shit, sir, and the more we dig, I think the bigger it'll get.'

'I'll be speaking with my boss tonight, so just leave it with me. I'm interested in this one. We may let you carry on as OIC, but whatever happens, we'll get it sorted.'

This would be an interesting development.

Chapter 26

Christmas

A London park would be a perfect place to meet and conspire, far away from prying eyes.

The rules were simple in the lead-up to the inquiry – to keep phone conversations to a minimum and avoid identification.

The Russian Ambassador, Andrei Loktev, was placed firmly on the park bench in the obscurity of St James' Park, a safe distance from his residence in Battersea. He was covered by large oak trees, close to the bandstand. His only fear was that the park's police may come across him, but he had a cover story ready.

Looking down at his pay-as-you-go Blackberry, he turned it on before placing it in his pocket and waiting for the start-up tone to sound. This mobile GPS device, if not used properly, could place him in a location too close to home, and the same applied to the others. He unlocked his phone and scrolled through the address book. It contained three simple names. The code names were all part of his elaborate plot to avoid any detection. His instructions were quite clear, and there could be no comeback on the Russian Mafia.

X – Loktev

Y – Zonov

Z – The contact – unknown – his decision was final – the paymaster.

He pressed the highlighted telephone number marked Z and waited for a reply.

The contact immediately recognised Loktev's number.

'Hello, Andrei.'

'Are you well today?' Loktev waited for a reply from the paymaster and the message was brief.

Z was not happy with developments and made it quite clear to the rogue Ambassador.

'I'll keep this message short. The inquiry is about to start. Can you keep me up to date with developments? I need to know what is on that footage. The finance is in place. Please get Y to keep watching every move. We will speak again and arrange a further drop.'

This didn't surprise Loktev. He knew his contact wouldn't be happy. The attempt on Sands' life had been a disaster, but they had to stay with Zonov. He knew too much and came with a good reputation. He immediately contacted him.

'Are you secure?'

'Yes, I am,' Zonov replied.

Loktev's message was also brief and to the point.

'Keep watching both parties closely and the finance will soon be in place. I will keep you up to date with the inquiry and get back to you.'

Loktev terminated the call. He would now make a call to Moscow. They wanted to be informed of every move. The Russian Mafia invested a lot of money in the West End of London.

Chapter 27

The boredom of the last few days was getting on top of Detective Chief Inspector Edgerton as he read through a hotel brochure. He intended to stay in Edinburgh for a weekend and see his girls after the Christmas break. He would break the news when he saw them.

As he flicked through the pages, he noticed DI Palmer walking past his door and he shouted to him.

'Philip. Can you come back into the office, please?'

'Yes, Guv,' came the reply.

'I've just spoken to DC Jones regarding this hit-and-run. Do you fancy a walk to Charing Cross nick, and I'll fill you in on what's happened?'

'I'll just get my jacket.'

Palmer was eager to get his teeth into another case. Like Edgerton, he wasn't at his best during quieter moments. He needed to be stimulated. It was fortunate that it was during the festive period. At least Palmer had quite a few parties to attend.

They made their way out of the building and headed towards Whitehall.

As they walked, Edgerton said, 'This could be an interesting case for us to look at. The victim is a close friend of Brian Beaumont, and with the inquiry coming up I think something's going on. Are you thinking what I'm thinking?'

'I am, but I'm confused. How's Beaumont's friend connected? I suppose all we can do is speak to the lads and get their take on matters.'

'Yes. Let's not tell Watkins until we find out more, though. I might slip it to him tonight when his guard's down and he's relaxed.'

As they walked, it started to snow again. It was already slippery underfoot, and the snow was so dense that Edgerton noticed it starting to settle on the lions as they approached Trafalgar Square.

As they reached Agar Street, the impressive Charing Cross Police Station came into view.

Edgerton remarked, 'I much prefer the old nicks, like Bow Street and West End Central. These new stations are okay, but they have no character. I suppose this is the best of the lot.'

Palmer agreed. 'I know, Guv. I liked the old nicks and the Section houses, but they're on their way out, and that's a load of old bollocks.'

Edgerton, reminiscing, said, 'It's funny you should say that. When we lived in Trenchard House, we could just pop into the market and we were always close to all the nightclubs and bars. Trenchard House is now empty and for sale. I feel rather sad about that. Do you remember when you used to finish work, play squash and have a game of snooker?'

'Oh, the memories,' replied Palmer. 'And the social bar? It was a great place, and all the hustle and bustle of Soho right on your doorstep.'

'I think we've seen the good times in the job. Some of the things we used to get away with when we lived there…'

Palmer laughed. 'When I used to work late, I'd walk home in half blues and didn't get any trouble, unless I walked under the archway next to Raymond Revue Bar.'

'Why?' Edgerton was intrigued.

'The prossies knew I was a cop and they used to offer me a freebie.'

'Did you go for it?' asked Edgerton.

'Give us a break, Guv … no, I didn't.'

Edgerton was in mischievous mode. 'I'm surprised, you tight arse. You could peel an orange in your pocket.'

Palmer hit back. 'Fine coming from you, Guv.'

Both men revelled in the banter.

Edgerton wasn't for ending the conversation.

'Another one… Do you remember when we had those locusts in butter at that Chinese restaurant? I was nearly sick, but you loved them. You used to take birds there if you wanted to get rid of them! You could be cruel.'

Palmer was crying with laughter. 'If I could turn the clock back, rewind… Great times, but we've got a few left, I hope.'

'Just had an idea. Tonight we should start in the Punch and Judy.'

'Nice call. Do you remember we were nearly in tears when Brahms and Liszt closed to make way for the extension to the Opera House?'

'In happier times I took my wife there, downstairs on a Saturday night. Great club for the old jazz, and we got to know the regular doorman. I've forgotten his name, but he was from Brixton.'

'He was the main man, and a great guy.'

Both officers were now at the station entrance. Two large Roman-style columns supported the grandiose entrance and the cream exterior made the vast building a real spectacle.

The front desk was packed with people, and DCI Edgerton and DI Palmer jostled their way to the front of the queue.

Edgerton produced his warrant card and said, 'Can you let me in, please? I need to see two lads in the CID.'

The door opened and they made their way up the stairs to the CID office.

Every desk was taken in the office – all open plan – and Edgerton shouted at the top of his voice, 'DS Wynyard and DC Jones, are you there?'

Immediately both men stood up and beckoned DCI Edgerton and DI Palmer to join them.

Edgerton introduced himself and Palmer.

'Hello, I'm Bill Wynyard and this is Brian Jones. I believe you spoke to Brian earlier?'

'Yes, Bill, pleased to meet you.'

'I'll let you have a look at the file in a short while. Come, both of you take a seat and let's have a chat. Would you like a brew?'

Both men declined.

Bill Wynyard paused, his face a picture of total confusion.

'Detective Chief Inspector Edgerton, I'm totally lost with this one, and I can't see any way forward.'

Edgerton took the lead. 'It's a tough one.'

Before Wynyard could speak, Palmer interrupted. 'Where's Patrick Sands at the moment?'

Jones replied, 'He's still in the hospital. Broken arm

and broken leg, but he should be out soon. To be honest, I don't think he really wants us around. Go and see them, Guv, and you will probably draw the same conclusion.'

Edgerton probed further. 'Does the press know? Have they got wind of this?'

Wynyard replied, 'Not that I'm aware of.'

'Let's keep it that way. We can do some digging, and at some point, when I get clearance, I'll meet with Brian Beaumont.'

As Edgerton spoke, DI Palmer noticed that he was looking around and kept holding his nose. There was a rather musty atmosphere in the office, but Palmer had chosen to ignore it. Edgerton was a different animal and didn't waste any time raising the subject.

'Moving away from the case, chaps, I've got to ask you something. What's that smell? It smells like … well, death.'

Jones casually replied, 'Oh yes, it's the bag next to my tea. It's a ring off a dead man's finger. He'd been dead for about a month when the uniformed lads found him. It must be the remains of rotting flesh left on the ring when the undertaker took it off. The gentleman's next of kin is coming in later to collect it … just a favour for the officer. He's gone home.'

Edgerton's colour drained from his face.

'I think I might be sick,' he said, holding his hand to his mouth.

The officers started to laugh.

Jones said, 'The bog's over there, Guv.'

Edgerton barged through the toilet door.

'He's got a dodgy tummy, boys.' Palmer laughed. 'I can see we're all going to get on!'

In no time Edgerton was back at the desk with his perfume-soaked handkerchief held firmly over his nose and mouth.

In a muffled voice, he said, 'Right, we're fucking off. Next time, you can see us at our place. We have a night out to go to, and I have to eat.'

The laughter had shown no sign of subsiding.

As he left the room, Edgerton turned in the direction of Wynyard and Jones and shouted, 'Animals!'

Chapter 28

After his experience in the CID office at Charing Cross, Edgerton was pleased to get out into the fresh air. He enjoyed an office full of humour and let a lot go by, even if it wasn't always politically correct. Anyone who questioned his methods would be met with his standard reply – *'If it offends, then go and work elsewhere.'*

Detective Inspector Palmer was still beside himself after the incident in the CID office and said, 'Guv, this sets us up for a good night tonight – wait until I tell the chaps. They are going to laugh their bollocks off. I might even get a laugh out of Watkins at your expense.'

'I'm sure you will, Philip. You know, there are two things I dread in the job. Bloody post mortems and the smell of death. It's nauseating!'

'Ditto, Guv,' replied Palmer. 'I was just thinking, I can't wait to see Julian Wallace.'

Edgerton replied sarcastically, 'Dr Julian Wallace, the Home Office Pathologist? Well, he'll have no sympathy – he always has a laugh at my expense when he does the post mortems.'

Palmer looked at his watch. 'It's five thirty already, Guv.'

'That late? We should get back, change and then hit

the town. In fact, I'll phone Watkins now and make sure he's setting off.'

The snow was falling heavier than before as both men headed back to the Ministry of Defence buildings, both seasoned detectives in high spirits.

Their emotions were in stark contrast to those currently being experienced by the Foreign Secretary.

Bamford sat at home in Beak Street off the Regent Street, having spent the last few days mulling over his position. Only he knew the truth about how he'd conducted his private life and for the first time in his life felt helpless. He was still seething with the Prime Minister and former friend, whom he felt had thrown him to the wolves. Tonight, he would hit the town alone. He would find himself a bar and drink himself into oblivion. Only the alcohol and his Prozac could numb the pain and anger he felt deep inside.

His secretary at the Foreign Office was having a torrid time deflecting all the enquiries from the media looking to speak to him about his position. Karen Boyd sat at her desk. She too felt alone. She could see the deterioration in Bamford as each day passed and was increasingly concerned not only about his physical state, but also his mental state.

She called the tipsy Bamford, who was just about to leave his house.

'Robert, it's Karen. We need to talk. This can't go on. I have some emails regarding the inquiry, and we need to get together.' After a pause, she added, 'How are you?'

'I'm fine, Karen, how are you?'

Noticing his speech was slurred, she said, 'You are drunk, Foreign Secretary. What are you doing?'

'I'm just having a drink, that's all. Don't worry, my dear, I'm alright.'

Karen was annoyed. 'I've known you a long time, Robert, and you are not well.'

'I am fine, please just forget it. I need a favour before I leave. Can you give me Brian Beaumont's telephone number from the directory? I need to speak to him.'

Karen Boyd's patience was wearing thin.

'Sir, to phone him at this time is not a good idea. Please do not speak to him with the inquiry about to start.'

In his familiar patronising tone, Bamford said, 'Karen, Karen, Karen,' as he downed another whisky, 'this has nothing to do with the inquiry. It is an unrelated matter, and I need to speak to him.'

His secretary didn't believe a word he was saying. As she reached for the directory, she slammed the phone down on her desk in sheer frustration and for the first time thought of resigning from her post there and then. She was witnessing the slow demise of Robert Bamford, the normally confident and boisterous politician.

She reluctantly gave him the number. She knew he would get it anyway and make the call. She had always had her suspicions about him, but she knew any complaint would fall on deaf ears if she started to pontificate. After all, he was his own man, powerful and many might say arrogant, but definitely ruthless, and nobody got in his way.

She decided to phone her husband, Jonathon, for advice. Karen's instinct told her that Bamford was plotting revenge and she feared for his rival, Brian Beaumont. She was also in fear for her own position if she spoke out. However, she wanted a clear conscience, so she reopened the Commons address book and looked for Brian Beaumont's personal email address, but she couldn't find it.

She sat at his desk and planned her next move. She checked the Web and decided to go to Beaumont's website. She would leave him an anonymous email. She certainly wasn't going to do it on the office computer, though, so she quickly grabbed her laptop and turned it on, frantically searching for an unsecured wireless connection that she could hack into. It was a risky move, but she felt compelled to warn Beaumont. All the networks within the Parliament buildings were secure, so she grabbed her jacket, placed her laptop in its case and made her way out of the building.

Once outside the main entrance, she crossed the road and stood next to the Winston Churchill statue before she left and searched the local streets, looking for the open network she so desperately needed. It didn't take her long before she found one in Whitehall next to an old café. It was close to the Clarence Public House … one of Beaumont's favourite haunts.

She quickly created an anonymous email account using a false name and typed an email.

FAO Brian Beaumont

From a friend – regarding Robert Bamford – watch yourself – I'm sorry, but I must remain anonymous for my sake. Please listen.

She pressed the send button and waited. 'Message sent successfully' appeared on the screen. She turned off the computer and headed back to the House of Commons. Karen Boyd had done her good deed for the day.

Chapter 29

Detective Inspector Palmer was no stranger to inclement weather. Born in Aviemore, Scotland, he was used to the harsh conditions; unlike Edgerton, who preferred a warmer climate. Both were ready for a good night out.

'It's fucking freezing,' Edgerton said. 'I need a hot curry to warm me up.'

Palmer looked at his watch. 'We are off duty, so with all respect, Jacky boy, you are a soft arse – and I say this as a hardened Scotsman.'

Edgerton turned to him. 'C'mon, let's get upstairs. I didn't expect sympathy. And keep your gob shut about the ring in the CID office earlier.'

Palmer giggled like a schoolchild. 'It will go no further, Guv.'

Edgerton was relieved momentarily. 'Good,' he replied.

'No further than Scotland Yard, anyway.'

Edgerton waved at Palmer as a show of defiance.

The two detectives were soon greeted upstairs by the members of the squad, all raring to go, including Chief Superintendent Watkins.

Watkins was upbeat. 'Come on, hurry up, we all want to go. Are you ready?'

He stared at both officers, who looked somewhat dishevelled.

'No, sir, but give us ten minutes.'

Chloe Moran shouted, 'Come on, hurry up.'

'Where have they been?' Watkins whispered to DC Moran.

'Not certain. Charing Cross nick, I think. I'm confident they will tell you.'

'Oh, I'll ask Jack later.'

Edgerton and Palmer didn't take long to get ready.

'Right, we're off and running,' Edgerton yelled. 'We can all get cabs – let me do a quick head count. One, two, three, four, five, six, seven... Three cabs will do.' He took control and led the way.

The office was soon a ghost town as the team headed for the heart of the city. It would be a sluggish journey as they plodded along the snow-covered streets towards Covent Garden.

The Punch and Judy was an old haunt for Edgerton and Palmer and a great starting place for a drink. After that they would follow their noses and perhaps have a nice curry before going to a club. The Murder Squad nights out were always a diplomatic affair – a quick show of hands to decide the next watering hole.

Finally, they were all assembled in the pub and Edgerton found himself at the front of the group.

'I suppose I'll start the rounds then? Are you all shy? This lovely barmaid won't bite.'

One by one the drinks came. Edgerton was in the mood for a short or two, and he ordered his neat Jack Daniels.

Moran stood close and said, 'I'll have the same, Guv.'

He gazed into her eyes. 'Chloe, call me Jack when we're off duty. You know I hate being called Guv.'

She replied sheepishly, 'I know, but…'

He held her hand and said, 'No buts, Chloe, call me Jack … you know I like it that way.'

Her voice crammed with affection, she said, 'I know … hurry then, I'm thirsty.'

Edgerton hadn't been able to stop looking at her since they left the office.

'Take it easy, and while we're alone, you're looking gorgeous tonight … as per usual.'

Moran winked. 'You too, Jack.'

They both raised their glasses and touched them.

The pub was now starting to fill up with other office parties and the atmosphere was building. A good time for the team to relax and de-stress after recent events. They all huddled together in the corner, and as usual Watkins made a beeline for Edgerton. Edgerton didn't bother on nights off about the formality of rank.

'Well, Bob, I'm glad you're out tonight.'

Now in a relaxed mood, Watkins replied, 'Me too, Jack. Thanks for organising it.'

Edgerton, fully aware that Watkins was in a positive mood, made his move. 'I'm having a late one, but now might be the time to ask you something.'

'Run it by me.'

'I've been to Charing Cross with Phil today. Just a follow-up, but there was an incident the other day with a hit-and-run in Covent Garden. Not a normal hit-and-run, but it involved a guy called Patrick Sands.'

'I don't know about this one.'

'Well, he's a close friend of Brian Beaumont.'

'Brian Beaumont? Keep going, you've got my

undivided attention.'

'I think it was an attempted murder, and I think something's going on, so I've spoken to the OIC.'

'Well, why didn't we hear about it?'

'It was recorded as GBH, but I think it's more serious than that. I wouldn't mind having a look at it while things are quiet.'

Edgerton looked closely to gauge Watkins's reaction. He was to be pleasantly surprised.

Watkins gave an immediate decision. 'I trust your instincts, what with this inquiry. Let's have a look and see what we find, but keep me in the loop.'

'I will.'

'Have they got anything to play with?' Watkins asked.

'No, they haven't.'

'Well, work closely with the OIC, and I'll speak to his boss. Now we can let our hair down and have a good night.'

Edgerton was a happy man; Watkins's reaction had been unexpected.

Watkins held his glass up and shouted to all the officers, 'Merry Christmas and a Happy New Year! Here's to a good night.'

Alcohol was flowing freely as the squad sat in the darkened bar, now vibrant and alive. Edgerton's attention was again drawn to his favourite detective, Chloe Moran.

Chloe, still young in service, was stunningly beautiful. Large piercing brown eyes, an hourglass figure and a dark complexion, she had a personality to match. Edgerton had been attracted to her since she joined the Murder Squad, but had never made an advance.

Perhaps she had seen Edgerton's friendliness as just a good working friendship between two professionals. He was flirtatious with all the girls, and she was still impressionable in a job that had many pitfalls, but she was learning quickly under his watchful eye. He guided her, and she had the utmost respect for him. Edgerton's door was always open to all his officers, but one of the team had a hunch based on his many years of working in a close group, and Palmer had hinted several times that he thought they had strong feelings for each other.

'A volcano waiting to explode, Jack,' had been one of his more direct hints when he spoke over a pint and Chloe became the topic of conversation. Edgerton had simply brushed off the comment as office gossip.

Perhaps tonight Edgerton was having second thoughts. Chloe was radiant and sexual, and as the night slowly progressed in a crowded room, their eyes were constantly drawn to each other. Their conversation flowed easily as both felt relaxed in each other's company. This behaviour did not go unnoticed by some of the more nosey members of the team. The night was still in its infancy.

Edgerton sat down with his drink and his phone rang. It was his daughter, Natalie.

'Nat, how are you? I need to come and see you one weekend. How are the studies?'

She was happy. 'They are great, Dad. You must meet my new boyfriend.'

'Has Paula met him? More to the point, has your mum met him?'

'No, not yet, Dad … you can be happy for me, you know.'

Edgerton was a protective father. After all, they were his babies. In his mind, they hadn't grown up, and he had a mistrust of men ... perhaps his job had made him that way.

Paula and Natalie were identical twins, and as they continued their studies at Edinburgh University, he kept a close eye on their progress. It was fortunate that he was amicable with his ex-wife – they had simply grown apart, and Kathryn now lived in Scotland with her boyfriend, Alan.

If Kathryn was happy, then so was Edgerton. She once told Jack, *'You love the job ... and the children and I stand alone.'* The sad thing about the comment was Edgerton knew it was the truth and his marriage was doomed. 'The job' was his life.

Edgerton thought he should meet the boyfriend as soon as possible. He would play the serious father on their first meeting and vet him. He did this all the time, much to the annoyance of Natalie, who was the feistiest of the twins. Paula was much more like her mother and easy going.

Moran looked over at Edgerton as he spoke, and smiled. He returned the compliment.

Watkins looked over and gave Jack a knowing look. He was astute and knew when two people had feelings for each other, but ever the professional, he held court; deep down, he wanted Edgerton to meet another woman. Both he and DI Palmer held the same view on this topic.

Edgerton was starting to see the nice side of Detective Chief Superintendent Watkins and was coming around to working with him, despite having some conflicting views on policing.

In the same city, Robert Bamford continued to drown his sorrows, totally oblivious to the harm he was inflicting on those close to him. He stumbled out of the bar into the cold air and made his way back to his flat. As he reached the doorway, he slipped and fell to the floor in a drunken heap. He had lost control, but he slowly picked himself up and attempted to put the key into the lock.

Eventually opening the door, he banged his feet to shake off the snow and then heard a voice in the distance.

It was Derek Smith, his close friend, shouting, 'Robert.'

Bamford was wasted and his clothing dishevelled.

As Smith approached, Bamford managed to focus and said, 'Hello, Derek.' As he uttered the words, he fell again and Smith picked him up.

'For God's sake, Robert, pull yourself together, man.'

Bamford collapsed again.

Derek Smith was surprised when he turned the lights on in Robert Bamford's house, only to see how untidy it had become. Robert Bamford was normally a tidy man, and everything had its place. Suddenly, he was confronted with this disorder, clear evidence that he was on a course to self-destruction.

He loosened Bamford's clothing and put him to bed.

Smith phoned home, but his wife was unable to speak, so he spoke to Elizabeth, Bamford's eldest daughter.

'Elizabeth, I'm with Robert and he's not well. He's drunk, so I'd better stay the night. Tell your mother he will call you in the morning.'

She wasn't that bothered about the news, which

surprised him.

Smith knew that Bamford had been struggling, but was shocked by the severity of his condition. He looked around the once pristine flat and started to attempt to make it presentable. Bamford's desk was cluttered with newspapers. Nothing unusual there, except that some were highlighted and they were all articles relating to the Shadow Home Secretary, Brian Beaumont. Smith became increasingly concerned.

Smith, now tired, lay on the settee thinking about his own predicament. He needed to talk to Bamford in the morning about the forthcoming inquiry, as he had been called to give evidence. Like Bamford, he was all too aware that he could well be fighting to save his political career.

Before he fell asleep, he sent a text to his brother, John.

John. I'm at Robert Bamford's, and I will be there overnight and will speak tomorrow. He is drunk and not in a particularly good way.

Smith tossed and turned on Bamford's settee, dosing off periodically. The night was still young.

The Murder Squad detectives were now all settled and the drink flowing at a rapid pace as Edgerton shouted up the rounds, one after the other. He wouldn't take long to lead the charge for the Indian restaurant in Pimlico, but the officers were settled in Covent Garden, so he would have to think of an alternative quickly.

Philip Palmer shouted, 'Let's go to the Masala Zone.'

Watkins shouted, 'I've been there a few times and it's a great place. Come on, let's make tracks.'

It was like a procession as the officers left the Punch and Judy and made their way to the restaurant. The heavy intake of alcohol had wetted the officers' appetites, and they were eager to get there quickly. Philip Palmer struggled to hold his footing on the thick frozen snow and fell over. He couldn't stop laughing, and Chief Superintendent Watkins tried to help him, only to suffer the same fate. Edgerton grabbed for his phone and snapped them on his camera. The very sight of Watkins lying on top of Palmer would make a great picture to hang up in the office.

Edgerton came to their rescue and helped both men to their feet as the rest of the officers continued to laugh hysterically. They were so close to the restaurant they could smell the Indian food escaping through an open door as customers left the building.

Palmer said, 'I love this. Nights out like this make my day.'

The door opened and a voice shouted, 'Mr Watkins, how are you?'

Watkins, immediately recognising the man, replied, 'Sabal, how are you? Can you sit us all down?'

'Yes, come on in, you are all welcome.'

All the officers took their place, and Chloe Moran made a point of sitting next to Edgerton.

'Chloe, what are you going to have?' he asked.

'I'm going to have my usual chicken korma.'

Edgerton laughed. 'Not again! You have it all the time. Why don't you try a hot one?'

Chloe hit him playfully on the shoulder and said, 'No way, nothing too hot and spicy for me. I'll leave the hot stuff for later, Jack.'

Chloe was drunk, but she was not alone as they all started where they had left off.

Watkins bawled across the restaurant in the

direction of Sabal, 'Twenty bottles of Kingfisher, when you're ready.'

Palmer looked in the direction of Edgerton and Chloe, and shouted, 'Where are we going later? I want to dance.'

Edgerton replied, 'Let me think … do you all fancy the Los Locos?'

One by one they all ordered their curries and sat reminiscing about old cases as Watkins took control of events in his favourite restaurant.

'And why have you chosen the Los Locos nightclub then, Jack?' Chloe was intrigued.

'Well, it's dark, the music's great and the atmosphere will be awesome, and I almost forgot … you'll be with me.'

Edgerton was aware Chloe was being flirtatious with him, and he enjoyed every moment. She looked into his eyes, not for the first time that night, and he was fascinated. His mind was running away, and he felt the urge to be alone with her.

'Are we going to dance tonight, Jack?'

'In a quiet corner perhaps, if you're lucky.'

Chloe smiled as she continued to toy with him.

She leaned over and breathed slowly, whispering into his ear. 'Are you playing hard to get?'

'Just enjoying the moment – can't wait to get to the club.'

Chloe was fascinated by him. He was much older than her, but seemed so much younger in every way. She couldn't help herself and was under his spell. She, too, wanted to be alone with him and started to fantasise. The presence of her colleagues didn't matter as her inhibitions floated away. She wasn't bothered any more about what people might say and what advice they may give her, as long as she was by his side.

Edgerton had been to Los Locos several times. Its dark caverns deep within the club would give him privacy, and it was a classy venue. One other advantage was that it would certainly be packed, and he could disappear with Chloe without being noticed. Watkins checked the numbers and did a head count.

'Who's coming to the club afterwards?' Watkins was subsequently interrupted by Phil Palmer. 'Oh, by the way, before we leave I must bell Burky. He's on another do, and he will meet us here and then come to the club.'

'Young Steve Burke is probably with a bird, the lying bastard,' Edgerton said.

'Come on, Phil, get him here. We're wasting valuable drinking time,' Watkins replied.

Palmer fumbled with his phone and made the call to the young detective, and said he would soon join them in the restaurant.

Still half sober when he entered, the young man was ravaged by the officers, something he was used to as the resident rookie.

One of them shouted, 'Where've you been, Burky?'

In his high-pitched voice, he replied, 'Soho.'

'With a slapper?' Edgerton said.

Chloe nudged him. 'Behave.'

Burke squeezed up close to DI Palmer, attempting to get out of the verbal firing line.

'Looks like I've got a bit of catching up to do with you boys,' he said.

Palmer handed him a half-empty bottle of lager. 'Get this down your neck.'

He wasted no time. 'Hey, Guv, I've just seen some

blokes near Archer Street. They've been on TV, but I can't remember their names. I'll be wracking my brain tonight thinking who they are.'

Palmer struggled to focus properly as he stared at Burke.

Burke grimaced and declared, 'You're fuckin' leathered, Guv.'

Palmer chuckled. 'Yes, I am. Now come on and get pissed. When I was a sprog I came out early doors with the boys – these new boys … fuck 'em!'

Burke cried laughing. He had never seen Palmer so inebriated.

Chapter 30

As they approached the club, it was packed with partygoers queuing along the front in the freezing cold. The temperature must have dropped to well below freezing, still unusually cold for London.

'I'm not queuing,' Edgerton said. 'I'm showing my Club International card and we'll get in quickly.'

With a quick flash of the warrant card, they were in the confines of the club in no time.

'Extreme circumstances mean extreme measures,' he said, another example of his self-confidence and willingness to break the rules to gain an advantage.

There was a great party atmosphere inside, and everyone was ready for a good time. These were the moments the officers needed to relax and let their hair down. For once they felt like everybody else, and they slowly broke ranks and split into their various groups. The lights flashing and the dry ice dispersing made for a great atmosphere as the Stone Roses started to play. Edgerton grabbed Chloe as the opening verses of 'Made of Stone' rippled along the dance floor. They were both ecstatic as they moved around, singing along with Ian Brown.

The DJ kept the pace going as the dance floor remained crammed with revellers. Edgerton and

Moran needed a rest, and they made their way to the bar where they bumped into Bob Watkins.

'What can I get you, Jack? And you, Chloe?'

Jack shook his head. 'No, I insist, Bob. I will get these. What would you like?'

Watkins had a childish grin on his face. 'Whatever you two lovebirds are having.'

Edgerton shouted up the round. 'Three Bombay Sapphires, please.'

'I'm going to have a bad head tomorrow,' Watkins said.

Chloe looked at Jack and said, 'Let's make this the last one.'

'I'm not going yet, I've only just started.'

Chloe embraced him and said, 'I want to check out your house and everything in it, Jack. After all, you keep promising, so I'm taking the lead.'

Edgerton soon changed his mind. His heart started to race and his urge to be alone with Chloe had not dwindled. Watkins watched on approvingly as the couple entwined in a passionate brace.

Chapter 31

As Edgerton broke away, he grabbed Chloe's hand and, careful not to rouse the attention of the other officers, the couple made their way to a nearby fire exit in the corner of the nightclub. As they exited the club, the arctic wind hit them. Edgerton took his jacket off and wrapped it around Chloe's shoulders. They searched furiously for a cab.

'If I don't find one soon, I'm having my jacket back and you can die of hypothermia,' he joked.

'Well thank you, Jack Edgerton,' she said, and slapped him gently across his frozen cheeks.

Edgerton soon spotted a yellow light shining on top of a cab as it approached through the snow. The warmth inside was welcome, but it would take a while for the couple to thaw.

'Faversham Mews, please, driver – as quick as you can,' said Edgerton.

The driver was puzzled. 'Where is that?'

'Primrose Hill. Does that ring a bell?'

'Ah yes, squire. My knowledge has just kicked in. It shouldn't take long.'

The mixture of drink and fatigue had now started to take its toll on them both as they sat in the back of the dark cab. Chloe showered Edgerton with soft kisses to his cheeks and then moved slowly towards his lips. Her pecks steadily developed into a long passionate kiss as she took control.

She couldn't believe she was alone with him. It had been a long time for Edgerton to be without a girlfriend. He'd had the odd one-night stand: one with a female barrister who demanded sex every day. He had told Palmer about the affair and that he couldn't cope with her unreasonable requests for sex. Palmer had joked at the time, 'Bloody hell, Jack, I'll have her for a week, you ungrateful sod. Do you know how fortunate you are? I'm lucky if I get it once a year these days.'

This situation was different. As the cab pulled up next to his house, Edgerton extracted a twenty-pound note.

Desperate to go inside, he passed the note through the sliding window and shouted to the cabbie, 'Keep the change.'

'Thank you. Merry Christmas!'

As they stumbled into the house, Edgerton fumbled for the light switch and turned it on. Chloe had seen the house several times, but had never been inside. She was only concentrating on one thing...

As he was about to ask her if she wanted a nightcap, Chloe thrust herself towards him with such passion, throwing him against the wall. Edgerton picked her up as she wrapped her legs around his hips, pushing her hands downwards to feel for his midriff. He held her firm buttocks, pushed her upwards and disrobed her in a moment of unbridled lust.

He explored every inch of her slight frame, and as they kissed, she slowly removed his trousers and caressed him until he could wait no longer. His desire to make love to her had reached a point of no return as he tore off her dress and cast it aside, before continuing to explore her silky curves.

Their dreams of being alone now realised and no longer an illusion of the mind allowed Chloe to continue to tease her lover as she caressed every inch of his athletic physique, bringing him to near climax. Edgerton ached and so desperately wanted to be inside her, to feel her warmth. She guided him slowly towards her, anticipating his desire.

Chloe moaned, and as they connected her screams intensified as her lover continued to push her against the wall. She tightened the grip with her long supple legs as the couple moved together, gradually bringing them to new heights of pleasure as they both exploded as one.

Their first encounter had been quick, but better than anything she had experienced before. Chloe enjoyed the moment she had longed for since the very first day she had set eyes on him. Then they both collapsed onto the sheepskin rug close to the fire. They would sleep soundly tonight.

Chapter 32

There was no time to rest as the Murder Squad officers slowly made their way, one by one, into the office after the office party. It would prove to be a sombre occasion as the detectives nursed their hangovers, and it wouldn't be long before Bamford woke up, not remembering the night before. Smith showed his displeasure with him.

'Robert, you made an ass of yourself last night.'

'I'm so sorry. I can't remember a thing, Derek. It all seems strange.'

'I'm going to make some coffee, but we need to talk about this inquiry and get our stories straight.'

Bamford joined him in the kitchen.

'Has my brother been in touch regarding his dealings with the PM?' Smith asked.

'I saw him at the club, but other than that things have been quiet.'

'I noticed you have all the papers with Beaumont's articles highlighted. What are you doing?'

Bamford refused to be drawn on the subject. 'It's nothing to do with you, Derek. It's all in hand.'

Smith, unsure of Bamford's intentions, circled the room. 'This fascination with Beaumont is unhealthy.'

Bamford laughed. 'You must be joking. This is a man who is hell-bent on ruining me and my family, and you expect me to sit back?'

'I understand…'

Bamford interrupted him. 'No, you don't. He's not after you, you're small fish.'

Smith was visibly upset by Bamford's cutting remark. 'That sums you up at the moment, Robert. You're a joke.'

Bamford apologised. 'Just remember, revenge is a dish best served cold – that's all I'm going to say about Beaumont.'

Smith looked at him. 'You're going down a rocky road and it's going to lead to your downfall, and mine. Have you spoken to any of the Russians about this whole mess?'

'I'm trying to sort out matters, but the answer to your question is no. I haven't spoken to them yet.' There was a pause. Then he said, 'I need to speak to Andrei Loktev over some outstanding issues, and he's being awkward and making threats.'

'What threats?'

'Leave it,' Bamford replied in an agitated tone. 'It is nothing that concerns you. It's between me and him. He owes me some money, that's all.'

Smith didn't believe him. He knew him too well. Bamford held up a file and passed it to Smith.

'Have you seen the documents? My solicitor has provided me with these because I need to complete a statement for the inquiry.'

Smith donned his glasses. 'I've not had them, but that's why we need to speak. What are we going to say? That we fraternise with prostitutes at the club?

This is serious.'

Bamford took hold of him by the shoulders. 'You deny everything. The establishment won't allow this to come out – leave the rest to me.'

Smith paced the room and started to tidy the mess. He looked around and surveyed the expensive furniture and paintings that donned the wall. All fine pieces acquired by a man who had wealth and success. He couldn't help but think that all Bamford had worked for was about to be thrown away.

As Bamford watched him, he again mentioned Beaumont, such was his hatred of the man.

'Derek, if there is any dirty work to be done then I will do it. When people fuck about with people's lives there is always a price to pay, whether it is this year or in ten years' time.'

'Can you not let it go?'

'Nothing inspires forgiveness quite like revenge.'

Even though Bamford knew that this could be the end, he still had that inner arrogance, an innermost strength that had got him where he was, and perhaps the visit from his close friend had revitalised the wounded politician.

In the coming weeks, Bamford wanted to know what was happening with the Prime Minister at 10 Downing Street, and he was in the fortunate position of having an ally in John Smith, Derek's younger brother, who had no allegiance to anyone.

Bamford's house was now looking as it should, like that of a serving Foreign Secretary. He thanked Smith as they sat down on the window seat overlooking Beak Street.

'Look, Derek, don't you worry about the inquiry, it

will be all dealt with, and you'll be back in Parliament and I'll be back in the Cabinet.'

Smith reached into his trouser pocket, pulled out a silver pillbox and opened it. He quickly took a tablet and swallowed it as Bamford looked on.

'What's that?'

'My daily dose of Venlafaxine. This whole saga has made me a nervous wreck.'

'It's lucky we know the position at No 10. Chillot isn't aware that I really know John, and I believe he is briefing against me, but I'll sort out that problem at a later date. My first priority is Brian Beaumont. Believe me, he is the greatest threat.'

The phone started to ring and he answered it. It was only a brief call, but he had to leave.

'Going anywhere special?' Smith asked.

'Got to see someone in Soho, then I'll be going to Westminster. How about you, what are you up to today?'

'I'll go to Westminster now. I have to see one of my constituents later. I'll see you there.'

It would be a night to forget.

Chapter 33

Edgerton was first in the office, which was the norm, and he received a call from DC Brian Jones at Charing Cross Police Station. They arranged a meeting that morning. Edgerton was in no fit state to walk to Charing Cross, so it was agreed that both officers would come to the Murder Squad office.

Edgerton sat at his desk with a large Starbucks black coffee and a bottle of Irn-Bru. A strange concoction, but someone had once told him as a probationary constable it was a great remedy for a hangover. It had proven to be a considerable success over the years of attending office parties.

DC Palmer entered the room as Edgerton finished the call.

'How are you, Guv, did you have a good time?'

'Yes, Phil, it was great, but I'm paying the price. How are you?'

'Pretty rough.'

Edgerton looked at him. 'You do look rough, but then again, you always do.'

Palmer laughed. 'Thanks a lot.'

'Before I forget, I've just spoken to DC Jones, and

they're coming up later. The Super has said it's okay to look at things while it's quiet.'

Palmer looked rather surprised. 'That's good news.'

'Watkins was more than happy for us to assist them. He is going to let their boss know. Just good manners, I suppose.'

DI Palmer winked at Edgerton.

'What's up with you, have you developed a twitch?'

Palmer was in an inquisitive mood. 'Well, Guv, you vanished last night.'

Edgerton was guarded with his reply. 'I stayed late.'

'But you back-doored it, Guv, I think, if my memory serves me right, and so did Chloe.'

'Phil, I've known you long enough and you're fishing. Even so, on this occasion, I'm afraid you're barking up the wrong tree, my mate, so let's leave it at that.'

Palmer knew when to stop. After all, Edgerton was his senior officer.

There was a knock on the door and the two Charing Cross detectives were beckoned into the office. Before they even discussed the case, DC Jones handed Edgerton a handwritten report.

'Here, Guv, these are all the details just in case – there's very little to go on. Unless something falls from the sky, it's a no-goer, I'm afraid. I spoke to CPS, and they said there's not enough for an attempted murder. I have my views, but we must go with their decision. I don't think you will get any joy from Sands, and Beaumont knows very little, or it seems that way.'

Edgerton had expected this response.

'So I take it we've drawn a blank on forensics, CCTV and witnesses?'

'Yes, you've hit the nail on the head,' DS Wynyard replied.

Edgerton read the crime report and attached report.

Reference: GBH with Intent C476774 / 2011
Date: 10th December 2011
Location: Convent Garden, London
Time: 11.00
Victim: Mr Patrick Sands
Address: Boat 24, Ice Wharf Marina, King's Cross, London N1
DOB: 10/12/1964
Occupation: Freelance Journalist/Writer/Broadcaster
Description of Suspect: No description
Vehicle Driven by Suspect: Black Audi TT, Registration GIK 4
Recovered Y/N: Yes. Recovered burnt out
Details: C476775 / 2011, refer to Theft of Motor Vehicle. (See separate crime sheet attached)
Circumstances: Motor vehicle left outside takeaway while AP ordering food at the location with engine running and keys in the ignition. The assailant entered the vehicle and left location undetected.
Witnesses: No witnesses traced.
CCTV: Some CCTV footage, but very poor quality. This footage is unsuitable for evidential purposes.
House-to-House Enquiries: All enquiries completed and negative.
Evidence submitted to Forensic Science Laboratory: Nil – Unsuitable for evidential purposes.
Summary: Further enquiries required. Officers now assisted by Central Murder Squad – DCI Edgerton – this crime may require classification. All statements attached.
OIC: DS Wynyard/DC Jones

Edgerton paused and sat back, holding his head in his hands.

'Well, I smell a rat. A journalist gets knocked down and his mate's the Shadow Home Secretary? Do you all agree with where I'm coming from, boys, or is cynical old Jack at it again, coming up with his conspiracy theories? The truth please, chaps.'

All the officers nodded in agreement.

'That's all I wanted. I respect your input.'

Edgerton would soon be in contact with the inseparable friends.

Chapter 34

Edgerton had started to look at the report and dissect the case now that several days had passed since the commission of the crime.

Brian Beaumont needed to visit Patrick Sands. He was waiting to hear news from Roger Fischer, the FBI agent. There had been no reply to the email he had sent to Roger, and he was becoming a little concerned. He had been checking Sands' inbox regularly and he needed good news. Perhaps Fischer was working on the footage and just wanted it finished.

Sands knew Beaumont was becoming a little edgy and said, 'Brian, if we don't hear, perhaps he has been successful in enhancing the footage. Knowing Roger as I do, he's meticulous. He'll do a good job.'

'Yes, I understand,' Beaumont replied. 'Anyway, when can you get out of here?'

Sands was optimistic. 'I'll be out of this godforsaken place in the next few days and could do with a lift back to the boat.'

'Have you had any news from the investigating officers?'

Sands smiled. 'I think they've drawn a blank. An abundance of CCTV, as you would expect in the West

End, but the quality is poor, and as I told them, the windows of the Audi were blacked out.'

'I saw Bamford in the corridor the other day. I suspect he's behind this. It's funny, he couldn't look me in the eye, the devious bastard. If only he knew what was around the corner at the inquiry he might have done a better job.'

Sands' mood changed. 'Brian, get with it. Have you never thought he knows we have something on him? Jesus Christ, that wasn't a little accident the other day. It's not as if they were sending a warning, it was an attempt to shut me up. Whoever knocked me down wanted that footage and then went to the boat. It's lucky you hadn't arrived and they were still there, especially if you had been there with the bag containing the disc, because you would have been next – if you're not already.'

Beaumont's demeanour changed.

'I see where you're coming from. Do you want to come and stay with us when you get out? It may be safer.'

'No, I need my space, but thanks.'

Beaumont whispered, 'Make sure you're protected, Patrick.'

'You don't need to worry on that front.'

Beaumont prepared to leave the hospital armed with Sands' laptop before he made his way to his office in Portcullis House, Westminster.

After saying goodbye, he approached the door, turned and said, 'Well, at least I asked you to stay – it would have put my mind at ease.'

Beaumont waited patiently outside the hospital and waved down a black cab. The cab driver recognised him immediately.

'Hello, Mr Beaumont, it's a pleasure to drive you today, sir. I'm a staunch Tory.'

Beaumont replied politely, 'Thank you for your nice sentiments.'

'And where can I take you?'

'Portcullis House, please.'

En route to the office, Beaumont's phone rang. It was Sands.

'Brian, I just had a call from Roger.'

'Oh great.'

'He sent an email a matter of minutes ago, and he's checking the footage. He should be able to do something with it. If he can't, he has a friend at NASA who might be able to help him. Apparently, they can enhance images.'

Beaumont couldn't have been happier. 'That's great. Look, I'm in a cab, I'll speak later.' Turning to the cab driver, he said, 'Excuse me, young man, could you take me to the Sherlock Holmes?'

The driver, thrilled to be transporting Beaumont, replied. 'No problem, Mr Beaumont.'

The Sherlock Holmes public house was another of his favourite haunts. A traditional English pub, it was an old building filled with nostalgia from the classic detective tales. Situated at the bottom of Northumberland Street close to the Thames Embankment, it was an ideal location and he cherished the atmosphere. It was always packed with locals and tourists who would flock to this mecca. The exterior, kind to the eye, was the embodiment of what a public house should look like, and in all the years Beaumont had frequented the place it had never really changed.

He often joked that one day he might enter and bump into Holmes and Watson. He could sit all day with his pint of Guinness and Ploughman's lunch and stare at the old artefacts, and pictures attached to the walls.

As he sat down with his drink, he opened the laptop and went straight to the inbox. He searched the new messages and noticed Fischer's email. In the subject box, it read:

CCTV FOOTAGE ATTACHED.

He opened it immediately and read the contents.

Good morning, Brian. What is happening with Patrick? Thanks for contacting me. I just need to tell you the package has arrived, and I am reviewing the footage. When I have finished and cleaned it up, I will compress the file and send it back to you by email. You will need to unzip it, and I will then return the package with the original and another cleaned-up version. It looks like some serious **** is about to fly. Listen to my advice as an old soldier. Both of you must watch yourselves, and make plenty of copies. Speak soon. Roger Fischer.

Beaumont shut down the laptop and placed it firmly back in its case. Not being a man to drink alone, he phoned his wife, Isabel.

She answered immediately, a sure sign she wasn't busy.

'Hello, Beaumont Solicitors and Co., Isabel Beaumont speaking.'

'It's Brian, can you speak?'

'Hi, honey. Yes, I'm fine, how are you?'

Beaumont hadn't seen Isabel for more than a few minutes at a time recently.

'I'm in the Sherlock Holmes, alone. I've just come

from the hospital and wondered if you fancy joining me for a drink and some dinner?'

Beaumont sensed her joyous tone as she agreed. 'Yes, I fancy that, it's quiet today. I'll get a cab now. About fifteen minutes.'

His response was equally enthusiastic. 'Great, I shall be near the entrance to the left of the bar.'

He sat alone and waited. To kill the time, he unpacked Patrick's laptop again and browsed the Internet, checking the news.

He felt vindicated; the party faithful were still championing him as their next leader. John Cotterhill, the current leader, approaching his 65th birthday and suffering from prostate cancer, was tired. He'd had enough of being in the middle of this pressure cooker and was aware of Beaumont's potential. Cotterhill knew deep down that he would never be Prime Minister, but he had taken the Conservatives from the doldrums and reinvented them as a leading force in politics. A traditional politician brought up on Thatcherism, he was well aware that the political climate was changing.

'No longer will the Tories be looking up to a Labour government that continues to undermine public confidence and engage in double standards while the country falls to its very knees.'

Cotterhill had delivered the speech to the young Conservatives at a recent conference.

Beaumont was a new breed of a politician. A little more to the left in his views, but nevertheless, he had the utmost respect for John Cotterhill. From similar backgrounds, they worked well together, and Cotterhill had decided to nurture Beaumont by giving him the opportunity to hold a Shadow Cabinet post. Some of the more cynical members were less sympathetic to their ageing leader.

All these thoughts raced through Beaumont's already congested mind as the pub started to fill with customers taking their lunch breaks. Although he was alone in the pub, he received the odd acknowledgment from strangers, but shied away from contact. He didn't need any unwanted attention today.

Isabel finally arrived. As they ordered lunch, she gave him a peck on the cheek.

'We don't see each other much.'

'I know,' replied Beaumont.

'How is Patrick? I tried to phone the hospital earlier, but they were changing his dressings, so I said I would visit him another time.'

'No need, my dear, he'll be out soon. And you're too busy.'

'You seem rather preoccupied, is everything okay?'

Beaumont paused. He didn't want to worry her, and he certainly wasn't going to mention the CCTV footage.

'Everything's fine.'

Isabel could sense his negative tone. 'It can't be. Patrick's in hospital and someone's tried to kill him. I know it's all connected to the inquiry. For God's sake, what's going on? Are we in danger, Brian?'

Beaumont caressed his wife's hand and tried to comfort her. 'Everything is fine, let's just carry on as normal.' He hugged her. 'My love, you've enough on your plate.'

Isabel was inquisitive. 'What have the police done? Have they got any idea?'

'No, I don't think they have a clue.'

'And why have you got Patrick's laptop?'

'It's like the bloody Spanish Inquisition.'

'I hope you're telling the truth.'

'Oh please, Isabel. Relax, and let's have lunch.'

Isabel remained in her seat and chose to change the subject.

Chapter 35

The Strand – Royal Courts of Justice

The pace of the London traffic was almost unbearable for Lord Justice Rameau as his phone rang.

'Good morning, Father.'

'Good morning, Jacques. How are you today?' asked the elderly man.

Rameau felt a little awkward.

'I'm sorry for the outburst, Father.'

'Don't worry; I know you're under pressure. I think I caught you at the wrong moment, and it was rude of me to turn up unannounced.'

His father's voice faded as the connection was lost.

Rameau cursed. He sat in the rear of his chauffeur-driven Mercedes Benz as it continued to plough through the London traffic along the Strand. It would be a route he would become familiar with. This would be an intimidating time for many of the witnesses as they approached the Victorian Gothic building – the work of George Edmund Street, the solicitor turned architect who had created this masterpiece. Rameau had spent many years working on his cases, but he had moved on.

As the car door opened, he stepped out and made his way through the judge's entrance. He looked up at the carved stone cat and dog that watched over the walkway – there to represent the role of the court.

Rameau made his way to the basement, past the robing rooms, to the Old Jury room, almost prepared for the onset of the inquiry. It wasn't far from the delivery entrance, making it easy for the transportation of television equipment, and indeed several witnesses had requested that they arrive this way to avoid the cameras.

The courtroom had now been fully prepared for the hearing and Lord Justice Rameau's office was situated conveniently at the side.

He had spent his whole life giving his all to the legal profession, and this would surely be his finest moment.

He had been inundated with texts and emails from his colleagues, and a handwritten letter from his first tutor at Law School sat on his new desk. It read:

Jacques, cometh the man, cometh the hour – I couldn't think of a better way to describe your new post. Well done. I knew you would get to the top, and I told you so.

James W Killgannon QC

He showed no emotion at such adulation, and those close to him put it down to his steely character.

As he sat at his desk, he ploughed through a mountain of correspondence that had now arrived at his new home. The office was set out perfectly, with no expense spared. He carefully ran his fingers along the packed bookshelf, checking to see if the correct law books were at his fingertips.

As he approached his coffee machine, there was a knock on the door.

Rameau opened it to find his right-hand man, William Bell QC, waiting.

'Good morning, sir. I thought I would come to check out the courtroom before proceedings start. One of the court ushers stated you were in your new office.'

'Thank you, Bill,' Rameau replied. 'Have you checked out your office?'

'I have, sir, and everything seems to be in place. It will make a change not to have to wear my wig. At least there's a whiff of informality about these inquiries.'

'I suppose you have a point. Have you checked the files yet?'

'Yes, I have, sir. All the bundles are together, and of course the witnesses have been sent the files. I think we may possibly have well over three hundred witnesses, and I'm sure the list will grow.'

Lord Justice Rameau remained silent as he opened a small envelope with his letter opener.

As he read the contents, he looked at Bell and said, 'I need a moment alone please, William.'

Rameau sat at his desk and donned his glasses. It was a photocopy, A4 size, and he examined the contents slowly and methodically.

As William Bell QC walked into the courtroom, he heard a noise come from within Rameau's office. It was the sound of banging furniture, and in the background he heard a muffled shriek.

He turned back round and knocked on the door.

'Is everything in order, sir?'

'Yes, sorry, the chair fell over.'

Bell thought nothing more of it and continued to study his new courtroom.

Rameau remained static and continued to stare at

the sheet of paper. There was another knock on the door.

'Yes?' he said, the tone of his voice evidence that he was in a state of shock.

'Sorry, it's me again,' Bell said.

'Come in.'

'I'm ready to go to Gray's Inn for a spot of lunch. Would you join me, sir?'

Rameau, still preoccupied, said, 'I will … just let me collect a few items,' as he opened his wardrobe door.

Bell's attention was drawn to a hooded cloak hanging in the space. He noticed the hood had eyeholes. He was rather surprised as he eyed the purple cloak decorated with unusual patterns and emblems in gold silk weave. The robe had a Ku Klux Klan clan look to it and it made Bell feel a little uneasy. He felt compelled to speak out.

'That's an impressive robe, sir, and very unusual I might add. What is it?'

Rameau closed the wardrobe door quickly.

'Oh, my new robe. I'm a bit of an amateur dramatic in my spare time. I thought I'd told you?'

'No, I don't recall you ever telling me.'

Rameau shrugged his shoulders. 'Well, the robe is for the latest play – a thriller.'

'And the title?'

Rameau calmly replied, 'That's a secret. You must come when rehearsals are over.'

Bell, honoured to receive an invitation, dropped the subject.

Rameau opened the door and looked at him.

'We can go in the car if you get my driver.'

Chapter 36

The day had finally arrived. Brian Beaumont and Patrick Sands had been waiting for this moment for a long time, as it had been difficult to make any progress while Sands was hooked up in a hospital bed.

Beaumont was out of bed bright and early ready to take Sands back home. He organised a wheelchair, as it was a long way to the car park, and he had arranged to keep it for a short while until his friend could walk again. He remained concerned about Sands' personal safety after his previous encounter with the Audi at the hands of Anton Zonov. In fact, he was now looking at his own position, wondering if he too was in grave danger. He had a plan as they eventually arrived at his Jaguar.

'Patrick, please come and stay with us, just for a while.'

'Thanks, but I need to be at home, alone – I need my independence, and I need to write.'

Beaumont laughed. 'Well, that won't be easy in your state.'

Sands paused. 'By the way, have you brought my laptop?

'Yes, it's in the boot, but I haven't checked it for a

few days.'

Sands leaned back and groaned – he was still feeling the pain.

'The least I can do is pull a few strings. Can I try to get the police to keep watch, or at least keep an eye out?'

Sands replied in a firm but polite tone to his best friend, 'Brian, the last thing we need at the moment is unwanted attention. If the press gets wind, they'll start to ask questions, and we don't want anyone to know about the footage, do we?'

'I suppose you're right, but I had to try. As a friend, I couldn't live with myself if anything happened to you.'

'Don't worry.'

Much to Sands' annoyance, Beaumont listened to music all the way to North London. When they eventually arrived close to King's Cross near to Patrick's boat, they both double-checked the area around the barge as they approached, mindful of being followed. After close inspection, Beaumont entered the boat and checked inside while Sands stood in the snow, holding onto his crutches while leaning against the wheelchair, wondering how he would cope. Eventually, Beaumont helped him onto the boat and he was pleasantly surprised.

'Thank you, Brian, the boat is the cleanest I've seen it. You didn't have to do that.'

With a sheepish look on his face, Beaumont replied, 'Isabel did the cleaning. I just did the basics.'

'I should have known!'

It certainly relaxed the pair as they giggled like schoolchildren.

Beaumont threw a newspaper onto the desk. 'I've brought you a paper to read while I go to the office.'

Sands slowly made his way to the table and picked it up, and thanked Brian again for his help. As he tried to turn the pages, he dropped it on the floor. The paper fell open, and as he picked it up he noticed an interesting headline on the second page.

New investigation launched into death of journalist – Egyptian authorities to revisit case

Sands read the article, and the content sent a shiver down his spine.

Chapter 37

A number of days passed, and there had been no word from Agent Fischer. Beaumont stood outside the Mayor of London's office in a pensive mood. He'd just had a brief social meeting with Brian Heath, a fellow Conservative and old university friend. He looked out over the Thames towards the Embankment and ironically towards the MOD building, where Edgerton was planning with colleagues to meet up with Beaumont and Sands.

Stood outside the Mayor's office on the South Bank, Beaumont leaned over the river wall and stared into the murky water. It reminded him of the world of politics, the game in which he had become a lead player – dirty muddied waters, and rather choppy. Mixed emotions came over him as he continued to stare into the abyss, and he said to himself, *Am I happy or miserable? How is this going to turn out?*

As quickly as the negative thoughts entered his head, he shook himself down. He had to have inner strength and be positive – a lesson he had learnt from his father. The confusion caused by the article on Edward Fahy had placed a massive burden on him, and he was unsure what to do.

The next few days would be fast and furious – Anton Zonov, the ever-present hit man, had orders, and he would be watching Sands and Beaumont like a hawk. He had no choice – Zonov was a pawn in a big game controlled by powerful players, who had a lot to lose financially if their operation were exposed. They were running an operation that depended on keeping in with certain members of the establishment.

Ever since Europe became a free zone, the Russians had seized the opportunity to make big money, and London was one of the best cities in which to operate. With a laissez-faire attitude, many of their clandestine operations would go unnoticed.

The next few days would see activity on all fronts – calls from X, Y and Z would become frequent as the inquiry approached and timing became a critical factor, time would be precious, and planning had to be precise on both sides as the Labour government continued to govern. MPs carried out their mundane constituency work and attended their daily House of Commons meetings. Some with small majorities in all parties were unsure if they had a job in the next few months as the general election approached. The usual late-night drinks in the Commons bar and the dinner parties flowed endlessly, and all the time nobody knew what lay ahead.

As he continued to peer across the River Thames, the smoking gun that Brian Beaumont waited for would soon arrive.

His pocket shook as he felt his phone vibrate – it wasn't the normal call from the office, or Isabel asking what he wanted for dinner; it was a text from Sands.

Meet me at the boat. Agent Fischer has sent the footage.

Beaumont felt a shivering sensation down his spine and his stomach started to tighten as the anticipation of what the footage would reveal started to take hold.

In the distance, at the foot of Westminster Bridge, stood a man. Equipped with high-powered binoculars, he focused firmly on Brian Beaumont, watching his every move. Anton Zonov was back on his tail, this time armed with a listening device.

Chapter 38

This was the moment Brian Beaumont had been waiting for, but he was not in a good place. His instincts had now kicked in, and the enormity of this unfolding scandal was taking over his life, but he had to face it head-on.

It would normally be a shortish ride in the black cab as he made his way to see Sands at the boat. His stomach was still churning, and he hastily hailed the cab, clutching his newspaper. At that time of the day, there was no shortage of cabs, and Zonov also hurriedly hailed one and ordered the driver to follow.

'Follow that cab in front and stay close – don't lose it.'

Zonov could be intimidating, and the driver followed his every order.

The cab driver followed Beaumont through the icy roads of the capital as the politician sat reading the daily newspaper. Beaumont, unaware of his surroundings and the unfolding events, read about the inquiry – the biggest one for several years, it was very much on the tip of everybody's tongues, especially the political correspondents who were networking 24/7 to get an edge on their competitors. All had strong ties in the world of politics. He was aware that they would be watching his every move, and he could ill afford anyone finding out about the footage.

His progress through the London traffic was typically slow, and Sands' patience had reached its limit. He was unwilling to wait any longer as he sat at his desk, overlooking the wharf. He placed his fingers on the keyboard, hands shaking, and his fingers slipped on the keys – the nervous tension was overwhelming. He turned on his revolving chair, searching for his whisky bottle, and after locating it he poured a large neat double. It was unusual for him to drink in the morning, but this was a special occasion.

He had to open the email, and there was a simple message from Fischer.

The footage is now ready and good quality (unzip the file, it's large) – don't reply to this email – for your sake, any further contact regarding this by payphone.

The file started to download as Sands sat drumming his fingers on the desk, watching the download bar move slowly across the screen. There was a tap on the door as Beaumont arrived and Sands laboured over to open it.

'Come in and sit down. Get a drink, quickly,' he ordered.

As Beaumont's hackney carriage left Ice Wharf, Zonov's cab waited at the corner of the approach to the wharf with the Russian sat in the back seat. He left the cab quickly and made his way to the boat.

Zonov stopped and quickly made his way to the stern, placed the wall microphone contacts onto the cabin where Sands and Beaumont were sitting, and then crawled away. It was an incredibly risky operation, especially in daylight hours, but the stakes were so high that risks had to be taken. The hooded hit man made his way to the sanctity of an alleyway and placed the earphone into his ear. He would listen and make notes as both men began to talk.

The file was immense and still downloading. Both men were poised, waiting for the file to be ready.

'I think the clean-up operation was successful, Brian.'

'I hope so.'

The footage was finally downloaded. One click of the mouse by Sands, and it started. It was now crystal clear as the film started to roll. It was no different than last time. Bamford stood out quite clearly in the footage, but as the camera moved and the other parties came into shot, both men stared at each other.

Beaumont didn't know whether to rejoice or cry. Edward Fahy still in his mind, he closed his eyes.

Sands nervously croaked, 'It's Lord Justice Rameau with one of the girls … what the…'

Beaumont was astounded and seemed somewhat disappointed, or was he hiding his feelings of sheer disbelief and the thought of what action he should now take? The fact that Bamford was in the footage was always going to have catastrophic consequences, but now Rameau was also involved it would become a national scandal. It would shake the establishment to its very knees.

Both men knew each other very well. They could judge each other's reactions, and that didn't help matters. A feeling of deep paranoia overwhelmed them as they remained glued to the screen.

'Is this why they tried to silence me?'

Beaumont was confused. 'I don't know – let me think. It's all fuzzy – do they know what we know? They must do.'

Sands remained silent, still dazed. He stopped the footage and both men contemplated.

'I've watched both men,' Beaumont said, 'and Rameau continues to lead the inquiry regardless of the fact that he's in the club with Robert Bamford.'

'Do you think they are in it together?'

Beaumont snapped. 'They might be. Look at them both in a brothel with girls. This fucker continues to lead the inquiry knowing that he's involved.'

'Do they have an association? Listen carefully, I know that both men know they are involved, but Bamford is arrogant. Does he really know about the footage? If he doesn't, he'll think he's bombproof and that he can control the inquiry. The same applies to the Lord Justice, and if you watch the footage, you cannot prove an association between Rameau and Bamford.'

Sands pressed the play button as Beaumont spoke.

'You have a point. They are in the same room but at opposite ends, but look at you, you're hardly the picture of health – someone has tried to kill you, and perhaps I'm next.'

Sands sat with his head in his hands. 'We must call the police and reveal all.'

Zonov listened as silence took over the boat. He smiled and continued to make notes on a small pad. He would soon report back to Loktev. As the footage continued to roll, he continued to eavesdrop on their conversation. He showed no emotion and remained detached.

As the camera scanned the room, Sands stopped the

217

footage again. Slowly moving the mouse along the mat, he rewound the footage and stopped it.

'What do you see?' Beaumont looked closely at the screen.

'Hang on, I can see a window. It rings a bell … and I think I know where this place is – Soho. Do you fancy a trip?'

Beaumont stood up and made a dash for his coat.

'I'll have to take you in the wheelchair, Patrick.'

'I'll use my crutches and struggle. It's only a quick trip, I'll manage.'

Zonov, still listening in the alleyway, panicked for a moment. Should he get the device now and risk exposing himself, or leave it in place until they left? He decided on the latter, but he had been forced into a corner and had to make a call quickly. As he didn't have time to make it from the secure phone, he would have to break protocol.

Chapter 39

Zonov reached inside his jacket pocket and took out his Blackberry. Mindful of alerting any of Sands' neighbours, he quickly dialled Loktev's number, which soon connected.

'Andrei Loktev.' His tone was abrupt, as he didn't recognise the number displayed on his phone.

'Hello, Andrei, it's Anton.'

'Why are you phoning me on this number? You have put me in a bad position – you know the rules.'

'I had to. I'm at the boat, and they have found the location – they are coming to Soho. Make the necessary calls – I had to call you on this line.'

There was no response from Loktev, and the call ended. He was furious with Zonov.

Loktev would have to make calls and close the Soho location, or warn the Russians.

Zonov's work for the day was finished, but he decided to make his way to Soho. His precise location would be Archer Street, and he would wait to see if there was any unusual activity. He hoped Sands and Beaumont would struggle to find the club.

The backstreets of Soho were narrow and perfect

hideaways. With the mangled old fire escapes hanging from these alleyways people rarely ventured into them – perfect for the Russian Mafia to set up their brothel, and perfect for the likes of Bamford and Rameau to frequent without any real chance of being detected.

Before leaving Ice Wharf, Zonov deliberately came out of his hiding place and pulled his hood firmly over his head. He looked around to ensure the jetty was clear and boarded the barge, still scouring the area before removing the listening device. Careful not to leave any prints, he pulled on his gloves again to make sure they were firmly on his hands. It was very quiet, with most of the residents at work – perfect conditions for Zonov to leave the scene undetected.

He left the wharf on foot and walked in the direction of King's Cross Station.

Zonov wanted a newspaper, so he quickly entered the newspaper booth located next to the station and bought The Times.

Eventually, he found a cab and jumped in, shouting to the driver in his deep Russian tone, 'Trocadero Centre.'

Unravelling the newspaper, he saw the headlines were still dominated by the Rameau inquiry and the current state of the European Union countries. However, there was an article on Brian Beaumont which caught his attention. He may have been following Beaumont and attempted to kill Patrick Sands, but he had a respect for Beaumont – it was a perverse respect that would shock any normal-minded person.

Although Zonov regarded himself as a professional hit man, in reality he was a psychopath – the self-styled hit man had created this persona to give him the feeling of well-being. He was drawn to power whether it was legitimate or not, and he took the view that honest people were fools. This was an ideal that had caused friction between himself and his parents, who had worked tirelessly for very little in the old Russia. Zonov vowed never to make that mistake.

The article in The Times was clear and to the point.

Brian Beaumont – A man for all seasons

There was no doubt Beaumont was the man of the moment, but in the next few days and in the light of recent developments, his resolve would be tested.

Zonov had many attributes, but a conscience was not one of them.

The article covered Beaumont's career, which had been fast-tracked, and the papers were aware of his desire to push for the inquiry, with the popular media backing the Conservatives. The media had run out of patience with Charles Chillot, and his former champions were now deserting him. The Bamford affair was another knife in the scabbard waiting to be drawn. The inquiry was also prominent in the papers, and Lord Justice Rameau had currently completed his team of Queen's Counsel to assist him.

Chapter 40

A place in the city where a red light shines

Zonov had every right to be concerned as he approached Archer Street in Soho. Beaumont and Sands were already there, so he decided to stand and watch from the corner.

'Patrick, how do you know we are in the right place?'

'Trust me. I take photographs, and I know Soho like the back of my hand.'

A typical backstreet right in the heart of the city, no one would venture into this part of town, or if they did, it would be by pure chance.

Sands eventually found the location right in a small corner of the alleyway. It looked like an old warehouse with a double black door. Almost derelict, with a big window above the door, the premises were secured with a padlock and chain and three locks. Graffiti covered the surrounding walls and there was a stench of rotten litter.

'This place is a dump,' Beaumont said. 'It can't be here.'

As he reached for his phone, Sands confirmed this

was the place as he pointed to a small CCTV camera located at the top of the door and an old buzzer.

Zonov moved into the bottom of Archer Street, his vision made difficult as steam billowed out of the drains.

Beaumont was becoming increasingly uncomfortable in these surroundings. It was worlds apart from those he was used to, but Sands was enjoying the experience. He looked ready to investigate, and the fact that he may have a story wasn't far from his mind.

As the duo continued to explore, they were being watched from the window above the door by one of the Russian doormen. As Sands started to take photographs with his mobile phone, the man at the window returned the compliment. The one-way glass was perfect for him to watch all the activity outside. The doorman stood and watched. They had been informed of an impending visit by the Russian Ambassador, Andrei Loktev.

The inside of the brothel had been renovated to the highest standards and was run with military precision, only being open to a select few. The outside of the club was intended to look derelict to avoid unwanted attention.

Beaumont wanted to leave.

'We must leave, and leave now. We can't be seen here, and I have a meeting at the House of Commons later this afternoon.'

Progress was slow as the duo left the street, and negotiated refuse sacks and the abandoned rubbish skips left at the side of the road.

Sands, now tired and hobbling on the crutches, was

happy to leave, and as they emerged slowly from the mist, Zonov retreated. The time had come for him to return to his home in Hampstead and make contact now that the stakes had once again been raised. A decision had to be made.

Zonov was confused as to why Beaumont hadn't told the police immediately, or at least informed somebody of his findings. The question had to be asked. However, he was certain about the fate of both men, no matter what course of action they were about to take.

Chapter 41

A cab took Sands back alone, but Beaumont was still concerned about his friend's safety. Sands, however, had no intention of being mollycoddled, and as the pressure increased, he was becoming more entrenched in current events.

When he arrived, he struggled to get on the boat. When he finally entered, he carried out a thorough check. He then looked at his phone and found several voicemails. The most important was a message from Roger Fischer.

Hi, buddy. Hope you are well. By the time you get this you'll be back in good working order. Ring me immediately, and don't worry about the time difference.

Sands picked up the phone. It rang for a while before Roger Fischer answered.

'Hi Roger, it's Patrick speaking.'

'Hi there, buddy. Hope you are well. Have they caught the bastard?'

'No, I just called to thank you for the footage, it's worked out well. Needless to say it reveals a lot, but I don't want to say too much in light of what's happened.'

Fischer was a seasoned FBI agent and knew the

score. 'Not a problem. All I can say is, be careful, and keep a spare disc well hidden – you never know.'

'I must say we were surprised how quickly you cleaned it up.'

'Well, to be honest I didn't go to the FBI – I thought about it, man, but hey, it was too risky. In the end, I went to an old FBI buddy who worked in the Forensic Audio Video and Image Analysis Unit – FAVIAU, to be precise.'

'I appreciate it, I really do.'

'Yeah, an old friend, Billy Davies, who used to work out of Quantico did it. Going through the FBI could have been messy, and he works for himself so that was the safer bet for us all. All he did was maximise the clarity of the original video signal, it was a simple as that.'

Sands was becoming tired and said, 'I need to sleep, Roger, but thanks again.'

'You go get some sleep, and don't forget to put a spare disc somewhere.'

Sands laughed. 'Okay, I will. For your information, if they are successful next time I'll hide it in Brian Beaumont's safe.'

'Okay, I'll remember that. Bye, buddy.'

Beaumont's taxi slowed down as they entered the Houses of Parliament entrance close to where MP Airey Neave was murdered, and they were beckoned by the armed officers to show their identification.

He had an hour to play with before a pre-arranged meeting with the party leader, John Cotterhill. Armed with his newspaper, he headed to the central lobby to his favourite seat at the entrance to St Stephens's Hall. There he could watch the clock and would see

Cotterhill arrive from a distance. The history of the building filled him with warmth and a feeling of contentment. He would meet other MPs as they passed, and he could sit and look at the statues in the lobby as they watched over him.

As he sat down and started to read, he heard the unmistakable sound of footsteps, louder than anyone else's in the house. Footsteps as loud as his deep voice came closer as Arthur Betram, speaker and close friend of Beaumont, approached from the east corridor.

'Good morning, Brian.'

'Your shoes are loud and you have a voice to match, Arthur, and that is why you are the speaker.'

'Fancy seeing you here – I think you should set up an office nearby.'

Beaumont laughed, and Betram pointed to the large marble statue of William Ewart Gladstone.

'You spend more time in here than him, dear fellow.' His voice echoed around the grandiose hallway.

Betram sat down by the side of Beaumont and, in his usual friendly manner, placed his arm around his shoulders.

'How are things? We must catch up and have lunch.'

'Things are manageable, and the inquiry is starting soon; hopefully everything should work out fine. We will have lunch; I'll hold you to it.'

Bertram sighed. 'Brian, you have done well, and the press speculation is very much on our side. The party's flying and we must keep the pressure on until the election. You are the future leader, and I think, deep down, Cotterhill is happy that you're the man. He has more pressing things on his mind, and he's been a good leader, but you have the energy to take us forward.'

Beaumont wiped a tear from his eye. He valued the speaker's opinion. 'Very kind words, Arthur, and I appreciate your support.'

'How is Isabel?'

'She's fine, but a little concerned that we don't have much time together, and with the inquiry and the other things going on she thinks I'm a little preoccupied. Patrick's accident hasn't helped.'

'Send her my love, and spend a little time with her or take her to dinner one night – I have a friend in Kensington who has a nice restaurant, and he'll look after you.'

'Thanks, I will. I have a meeting with John Cotterhill on the hour just to bring him up to speed with things, and then I must see Patrick.'

'Send him my regards, and if you need anything, you know where I am.'

Beaumont was eager to have the meeting and leave as Betram left the lobby. He looked into the eyes of Gladstone's most elegant statue. It fascinated him that the former Prime Minister had long gone, but still commanded a presence in the lobby as if he were alive – He knew that all the great leaders had to endure periods of pain and sorrow before achieving their goals, and it spurred him on. He now felt an inner strength and believed he should be the leader of the party. It was his time, and he would grasp it with both hands. He knew he had to decide quickly what to do with the footage – if he held onto it for too long, he knew he could be the one under fire, and the finger would be pointed at him.

But who could he really confide in, apart from Patrick Sands? He couldn't tell Cotterhill yet, but the thought of throwing Bamford to the wolves didn't concern him. He was concerned with Lord Justice Rameau and the power the man might hold. After the visit to Archer Street, he was also well aware that there was a murky world out there, and he wanted to find out more. He decided he would return to Soho alone, under the cover of darkness.

These moments of silence were precious to Beaumont as he browsed through the newspaper. He sat back and waited for the arrival of his leader. It was unusually quiet in the lobby, the silence only interrupted by the muffled sound of the Westminster traffic and the occasional voice from distant chambers, but it was a soothing atmosphere in these great halls.

Beaumont heard the sound of footsteps. They were instantly recognisable.

John Cotterhill shuffled towards him, stopping every few yards to catch his breath. Age catching up with him and with his deteriorating state, Beaumont knew that his days as a leader were numbered. He had been kind to Beaumont and pushed him forward into his new role as Shadow Home Secretary.

As Cotterhill appeared at the entrance to the lobby, Beaumont quickly left his seat and approached him, offering him his arm.

In a laboured voice, Cotterhill said, 'I'm not in the knacker's yard yet – I can manage. But thank you even so.'

They both took to the bench and sat beside each other. Cotterhill, wearing a neat black pinstripe suit, reached for his pocket and pulled out a beautiful polished gold pocket watch, and checked the time.

Beaumont was always impressed by Cotterhill's

dress. Even in bad health, he was immaculately turned out. Ever the statesman and so professional in his image, he was always in awe of the man.

'Things are moving quickly with the inquiry. How are you standing up, Brian? A bit of an inane question since we are in the driving seat, but nevertheless, I thought I would see how things are.'

'Fine, but more importantly, how are you, John?'

'Oh, the dreaded cancer,' Cotterhill replied. 'The prognosis isn't great. I feel fine at the moment, but there will come a time when I won't be able to carry on.'

Beaumont was knocked for six. He thought Cotterhill was meeting him for a casual update.

'Yes, but…'

'Brian, this is a topic that must be discussed. That time will come; sad, but a simple fact of life, and it needs to be addressed, which is why I wish to spend more time with you leading up to this inquiry.'

Beaumont was stunned, but at the same time honoured that Cotterhill was discussing this matter with him.

Cotterhill continued, holding Beaumont's arm. 'You are a gifted politician, and I've got to a point where I've taken the party to where I wanted it to be. I had a remit and think I've achieved everything – if not more – than the party asked of me, and I am proud. I wanted to be Prime Minister, but I know that it's not going to happen, and I need to take a back seat and spend time with my family. Brian, you remind me of myself in younger days, and if I am to leave then it must be you who takes my place, and I'll do everything to make that happen.' He paused. 'Yes, you must take the reins.'

Beaumont sat quietly, tears welling up in his eyes.

'I'm so grateful for your belief in me.'

Cotterhill smiled and placed his arm around Beaumont.

'When the time comes, I cannot see anyone standing up against you in any leadership campaign. Everyone in the party backs you, and it would be a foolish man who stood up against you … and we must remember that any candidate who thought about doing so would surely be thinking about his future if he lost and his prospects of sitting on a Cabinet under your leadership. So in short, the path is laid, and I tell you now, seize this with both hands … I know you will.'

Cotterhill pulled out his handkerchief and wiped Beaumont's eyes. It was a display of the man's caring side that people rarely experienced.

Beaumont was now on the path to reaching his goal. To be the next Conservative Prime Minister he needed to take stock and plan carefully before making his ensuing move.

The two experienced politicians sat in the peaceful central lobby, surveying their surroundings, both content with their positions. Finally, Cotterhill made his exit.

As he was leaving, he turned to Beaumont and said, 'A weight has been lifted off my shoulders, and I am a happy man.'

As he hobbled out of the lobby, Beaumont experienced mixed emotions of elation and sadness. He put his head in his hands and waited for silence, and then started to weep uncontrollably. He wept until his tears dried and he wiped his face. It was time to be strong. He had no time to waste.

He ambled back to Portcullis House before returning

home. Beaumont always tried to visit his office just in case there were any messages, but when he arrived it was quiet. The girls had gone home. There was a message left on a post-it note on his desk.

Brian, please contact DCI Jack Edgerton at the Murder Squad on the following number. Jane x

Edgerton, a man of his word, had wasted no time in contacting Beaumont, so he decided to phone him back straight away. Beaumont was very careful – he had to be – but he had been waiting for the call.

'Detective Chief Inspector Edgerton. I just received your message. It's Brian Beaumont. I presume you need to talk to me. What's it about?'

'Hello, Mr Beaumont,' Edgerton replied with an element of surprise in his voice. 'Thank you for returning my call. I need to speak with you and Patrick Sands regarding the incident in Covent Garden. I can come to see you, or you can come here, whichever is most convenient.'

If Edgerton had been surprised by the call, then Beaumont was even more so by the latest development.

'Oh, Detective, you surprise me. I thought DS Wynyard and DC Jones were the investigating officers?'

'They are still investigating the matter, and it is highly likely that DC Jones will be with me. I need to keep you in the loop so to speak, tell you what stage we are at, and I need to clear a few things up, that's all. It's nothing to worry about, Mr Beaumont, just following force procedure.'

'No problem, Detective. Did you want me to contact Patrick and meet you? Would tomorrow be okay at my office at Portcullis House?'

'That is perfect. Just around the corner. I look

forward to meeting you.'

After hanging up, Beaumont circled the office and decided he must ring Sands immediately. After getting no reply, he decided to get a cab and make his way to see him at Ice Wharf.

En route, Sands made contact with him.

'Hi, Brian, I've got a missed call.'

'I'm on my way to see you. The police want to speak to us both. Are you at the boat yet?'

'Two minutes away.'

'I'll see you there.'

On his arrival, Sands had already prepared a Guinness for Edgerton as he entered the boat. He was keen to find out what had happened.

'We have to see a DCI Edgerton tomorrow morning, 10 a.m., Portcullis House.'

'He's not dealing with the case,' Sands replied.

'You took the words out of my mouth. Those were my initial thoughts. Don't forget, we must make sure we get our story straight when we see him.'

Sands looked panic-stricken. 'Jesus Christ, what about the CCTV?'

Beaumont remained calm. 'We don't need to mention the footage from the brothel. Not yet anyway.'

'Okay.'

'It's very simple. Let Detective Chief Inspector Edgerton investigate and just play dumb. We're doing nothing wrong.'

Patrick replied with some trepidation, 'I'm happy with that.'

Both men sat late into the night drinking and preparing themselves for the meeting.

Tonight Isabel would sleep alone in Camden Town

as Beaumont set up camp at Sands' boat for what would be a heavy session.

Chapter 42

Portcullis House

Edgerton was ready for his meeting. Dressed in his black suit, he had decided to wear his favourite Boss shirt and silk tie that Chloe had bought him for his 49th birthday. She had impeccable taste; it was his favourite tie.

The office phone rang and Chloe answered it. She then passed it to him and said, 'Brian Beaumont, Guv,' and smiled.

'Good morning, Mr Beaumont. I'm just about to set off and we will be with you at 10 a.m. prompt.'

'Good morning, Detective. I will be with Patrick in a meeting room we have set aside close to my office, but I'll meet you at the Despatch Box.'

Edgerton was puzzled and looked at DC Jones. He mimed, 'Is he taking the fucking piss?'

The detectives were just as puzzled.

'Sorry, you've lost me.'

'It's the café in Portcullis House as you enter. Don't get it mixed up with The Adjournment, which is a restaurant, or the informal café known as The Debate.'

'I won't, Mr Beaumont. See you soon.'

Edgerton put the phone down. He looked at the detectives now gathered in the room. He couldn't hide his feelings.

'He must be having a laugh. I'm going to the office where they house the MPs, and they have a restaurant and God knows what else. What a fucking joke! Look at me in this shithole, and they talk about taxpayers' money. It's one rule for one and one for the other.'

'You have a nice office, Guv,' DI Palmer said.

'Now I know your 'avin a laugh. DC Jones, let's go and mingle with the bigwigs.'

He was greeted with roars of laughter.

It was a brisk walk to Portcullis House, but today they were hampered by the thick snow on the ground, made even more treacherous by the freezing conditions overnight.

As they passed through security, they entered the main atrium. It was an impressive sight.

The security guard greeted DCI Edgerton as he showed his warrant card.

'Can you tell me where the Despatch Box is, please?'

'Just over there,' came the reply.

Edgerton, accompanied by Jones, entered the coffee shop and immediately recognised Brian Beaumont. He had seen him in the newspapers and on the television many times since their last few meetings at the charity functions. Jones recognised Patrick Sands. Both men were dressed in suits; it was clearly going to be a formal meeting.

As everyone shook hands, Beaumont said, 'Can I get you all a drink? Tea or coffee, which do you prefer?'

Edgerton and Jones gratefully accepted a pot of tea. They eventually found themselves in a meeting room close to Beaumont's office.

Edgerton opened his file. 'Thanks for today, gentlemen. Patrick, are you happy that Mr Beaumont is present with you, and for me to go through all the information?'

Sands smiled. 'No problem, Detective.'

Edgerton wasn't intimidated by the fact that he was sitting in the same room as a Shadow Home Secretary, or that he was an ex-lawyer. He wanted to solve a crime and had tunnel vision. If he had any fears, they would be short-lived. Beaumont played the game; he was courteous to Edgerton and showed him the utmost respect.

'Well, Patrick, I'm going to be honest and ask you a simple question.'

'Fire away.'

'Do you have any enemies?'

Sands fired back quickly, 'No.'

'Right then. We found the car and it was burnt out. No forensics and no witnesses.'

'Do you know of anyone who might want to hurt Patrick, Mr Beaumont?'

'No, sir, I don't.'

'To be quite honest, whoever tried to run you over, Mr Sands, didn't mean to injure you. I think it was an attempted murder, period.'

Sands agreed and Beaumont nodded.

'There are no witnesses, and am I right in saying that you didn't see the driver?'

'No, Detective, I didn't. It happened so quickly.'

'Right, that's all I wanted to know.'

DC Jones looked at DCI Edgerton in anticipation of his next question. He had researched the detective after his first visit to Charing Cross and was now fully aware of his pedigree.

'Mr Sands, you are a freelance journalist, aren't you?'

'Yes, I am.'

'Well surely you have a few enemies then, don't you?'

'I've upset a few people over the years, and they probably deserved it, but not to the extent that anyone would want me dead.'

'Okay. Can I you give you a scenario then? Assuming you are both close friends, and please don't take it the wrong way.'

Beaumont and Sands looked at each other but made no reply.

'I read the papers, Mr Beaumont, and the inquiry into Robert Bamford is imminent. It's no secret that the knives are out, and people may have a lot to lose. And let's be honest, you are very close friends, aren't you?'

'Yes, we are, Detective. Please carry on, although I'm not sure where you are going.'

Edgerton continued. 'My theory is that the attempted murder on your friend may serve as a warning to you in this matter. I'm sorry to be blunt, but I can't think of any other way of putting it.'

Sands interrupted. 'You think Robert Bamford is involved, Detective?'

DC Jones jumped in. 'Well, he has a lot to lose.'

'Mr Beaumont,' Edgerton said, 'has Robert Bamford threatened you?'

There was a long silence. Edgerton detected that both men were hesitant. He knew he wasn't far from getting something out of them.

Sands couldn't help but speak out. 'Brian, please tell him.'

Beaumont sighed. 'Look, Bamford is not happy with me and he's made a veiled threat. I just think he said it in the heat of the moment when the Prime Minister announced the inquiry. Come on, surely you don't think he would do something like that.'

Edgerton smiled. 'I'm not saying anything, I'm simply investigating. Like a debate, I'm throwing in some possibilities to see if they take us anywhere.'

Beaumont was impatient. 'Yes, I understand, but it's politics. These things happen every day, and things are said. God knows, if I treated every threat as an attempt on my life, then I'd become paranoid.'

DC Jones was now enthralled by the toing and froing and wanted a piece of the action.

'Mr Beaumont, I think this matter is quite serious. It's in the papers every day. If you backed down or vanished, then Bamford could well be in the clear. I think that gives him a motive – and he's threatened you?'

Beaumont looked shocked. 'I don't know what to think. I know Bamford's a few things, but I've never marked him as a cold-blooded killer. It's absurd, Detective.'

'Well it's a line I will look at, and I need you both to cooperate fully with me.'

'We will,' both men replied.

'Mr Beaumont, I'm concerned enough to ask if you both require protection – again, I must recommend you consider it while this is ongoing.'

Beaumont and Sands had discussed the matter previously and their minds were made up. There would be no protection.

Edgerton closed the meeting.

'Thank you for your help,' he said, and handed both Beaumont and Sands his business card.

'Here's my mobile. Don't hesitate to call me if you hear anything, and watch yourselves. If there are further developments, I will contact you.'

Beaumont reached inside his jacket pocket and pulled out a business card followed by his fountain pen. He leaned over the desk and wrote on the card, and then handed it to Edgerton.

'This is my card, and I've written Patrick's mobile number on it for you.'

Edgerton took it and shook his hand.

'I must say, that is an exquisite pen you have there. It's a beauty. Better than mine, I think.'

'Thank you, Detective, it was a present from my wife – a Monte Blanc.'

Edgerton was impressed. As Sands and Beaumont left the room, he hit the two friends with a low baller.

'Just a quickie, chaps. Did either of you know Edward Fahy?'

Both men remained silent. Edgerton smiled. He then proceeded to end the meeting on his terms.

'A strange death, I think, and I believe he was keeping close tabs on Bamford. It's a funny world, Mr Beaumont. If you have second thoughts about protection, then give me a bell.'

Edgerton left with Jones, while both Sands and Beaumont went his office after their chat with the detective.

'Thank the Lord that's out of the way,' Sands said, relieved.

Beaumont was a little more cautious. 'Edgerton's no fool. He's suspicious, and I don't think he will let go. I do admire his tenacity, though. And he mentioned Fahy.'

Sands agreed. 'I think we should go away and be vigilant. Do you think Bamford is involved?'

'Well, I didn't want to say he would do something like that to the DCI. The last thing I need is Edgerton crawling all over the Houses of Parliament and interviewing Bamford. There's enough scandal as it is. Do I agree with Edgerton?' Beaumont paused. 'Yes, I do. I think Bamford's lost the plot, and I'm at a loss. The inquiry will finish him off, don't worry. I just hope he doesn't know about the CCTV footage.'

'He can't do, unless we have been followed or bugged.'

Beaumont laughed. 'Bloody hell, no way have we been bugged; we're not in the Soviet Union!'

Patrick didn't respond. After a lull, he said, 'I will ask you one question. Why did someone try to kill me? There is something going on whether you like it or not.'

Beaumont needed to get back to the office.

'Let me sleep on it,' he said.

Beaumont left the room and entered his office. His secretary, Jane, was sitting stony-faced at her desk.

'Good morning, Jane.'

'Good morning, Brian. You need to look at this.'

She handed him a piece of paper.

'This was sent through to your website address. I was going through your emails…'

Beaumont noticed that the sender's email address read freindanon@...

FAO Brian Beaumont

From a friend – regarding Robert Bamford – watch yourself – I'm sorry, but I must remain anonymous for my sake. Please listen.

Beaumont felt a knot in his stomach as he read through the email. Edgerton was right. He thanked Jane and sat on his desk with the paper copy. He opened his wallet and pulled out the business card DCI Edgerton had handed to him. He thought about the consequences of his actions if he did phone the detective, and he decided he must speak to Isabel first. The matter had reached a critical point. He forwarded the email to his wife and rang the office.

'Are you taking me to dinner, Brian?'

Brian was in no mood for small talk. 'Isabel, read your emails. I've just sent you one, tell me what you think.'

Beaumont sat impatiently, hearing her tapping away at the keyboard.

'I've got it, just let me read it.'

Isabel remained calm and was quite matter of fact about the anonymous email.

'It's very simple. You must contact the police straight away and let them deal with the matter.'

Beaumont agreed. 'I have DCI Edgerton's card with me. I spoke to him this morning, as you know, and it's purely coincidence when I see this email has come through.'

'Brian, just phone Edgerton. The person who sent it has remained anonymous, so they must know what Bamford is capable of.'

'Unless someone else wants to cause trouble and is stirring things.'

Isabel lost her temper. 'Let the police decide and get

on with your daily business. I must go, I have a client waiting.'

Chapter 43

Although the office within the MOD building was a temporary measure, no expense had been spared when it came to the main operations room. However, it was still a far cry from the eloquence of Portcullis House.

DI Palmer was busy getting the Perspex boards ready. He was sure it wouldn't be long before the next murder fell their way. Edgerton was convinced Palmer had a disorder when it came to tidiness around the office. Everything had to be in order. Every file, every paperclip and every statement had its place. Edgerton had his own filing system. He believed that if it was behind a cupboard door, it was tidy, much to the frustration of Palmer, and sometimes Chloe Moran, who wasn't far behind Palmer when it came to an orderly office.

Chloe couldn't abide a grimy PC. She scoured the office with her duster and screen wipes, looking for any officer with a filthy screen. Edgerton was a mischievous character and regularly wiped the screens with his fingers, finding the effect was better when he'd just eaten his favourite bacon sandwich.

Edgerton had now arrived back after his meeting with Beaumont and Sands, and Palmer was eager to check on his progress.

'How did it go, Guv?'

'Okay, but there's nothing come to light. I think Robert Bamford is involved.'

'Don't tell Watkins,' Palmer said with a wide smile. 'He'll shit himself. He'll think it will fuck his promotion up.'

'Well, I'd rather be friendly with Beaumont. After all, he is the Shadow Home Secretary, and the way things are going, he'll be the Commissioner's boss after the next election. That's if he's not in No 10 by then.'

'Good point, Guv'.

Edgerton felt his phone vibrate. He looked at the screen, which displayed *number unknown*. He didn't like withheld or unknown numbers, but he answered it anyway. It was Brian Beaumont.

'Hello, Mr Beaumont.'

'Hello, Detective. I'll come straight to the point. I've had an email which I must show you.'

'Can you read it out to me?'

Beaumont proceeded to do so, and waited for Edgerton's response.

'Who sent it?'

'It's anonymous.'

'My email address is on my card. Send it to me and I will have a look. It doesn't surprise me the sender wishes to remain anonymous.'

'No problem, Detective, I'll send it straight away.'

Edgerton sat at his desk and beckoned Palmer over to sit next to him, pulling a chair from across the room.

'Philip, have a look at this.'

It didn't take long for the email to come through to Edgerton's inbox. Palmer waited as it flashed before his eyes.

'Well, what are your thoughts?'

'Interesting,' Palmer replied. 'Could be a hoax – then again, it could be real. I suspect the latter to be the case. I read an article the other day in one of the tabloids. I use the term loosely because I suppose it was more of a titillating story, with pictures of Bamford, mocking his downfall and his current state of mind. Let's speak to Watkins, and perhaps it might be a good time to see Bamford.'

Palmer left the office and closed the door. Almost immediately there was a knock on the door.

'Come in.'

As the door opened, Edgerton was pleasantly surprised to see Chloe enter. She turned and shut the door, then approached slowly and leant over the desk.

She whispered in his ear, 'I have a surprise, Jack.'

Edgerton whispered back, 'And what might that be?'

'I'm going to book a table at Quo Vadis for me and my favourite detective.'

Edgerton mischievously replied, 'Why, have you met someone?'

She poked him. Chloe must have heard him talk about the restaurant; it was in his top ten. He didn't waste any time in taking her up on her offer. In fact, he couldn't hide his pleasure as he embraced her and gave her a peck on the lips. It was surely a sign that the two detectives had a lot in common. Any misconceptions that it had been a one-night stand soon evaporated as she left his office.

Edgerton had reservations about contacting Chief Superintendent Watkins, afraid what his reaction might be when he briefed him on the email sent to Brian

Beaumont. Would the matter be a political hot potato for him? He took the bull by the horns and made the call.

'Jack, just the man. I was just about to call you – you've saved me a job.'

'What is it?'

'I just wanted an update on things. I know it's quiet.'

Edgerton took his chance. 'Guv, there has been a slight development in the case of Patrick Sands. I have a hunch that the Foreign Secretary might be involved. Brian Beaumont has had an anonymous email warning him about Bamford, and I still think they are hiding something. Both have declined any sort of protection.'

Watkins' reaction again shocked Edgerton. 'That's great. Keep digging, and if you come up with anything more concrete later, speak to Bamford. If there's enough, then nick him. And another thing Jack, if you get the chance come and see me later at the Yard.'

This style was right in line with Edgerton's way of thinking. He ended the call in a happy mood. His boss was backing him, and he had a date with Chloe to look forward to. The thought of a nice quiet romantic meal in a great eating house and then another night alone together was just what the doctor ordered.

He placed the phone back on the receiver and loosened his tie. His mind was firmly fixed on his date with Chloe. He checked his mobile and there was one simple message from DC Moran – *Speak to me later, and we'll arrange a time. Chloe x.*

Chapter 44

Palmer, not a man to waste time, made his first call to Patrick Sands. He couldn't get a reply, so he broke protocol and phoned Beaumont.

'Sorry to bother you. It's Detective Inspector Palmer speaking.'

'Detective Palmer. Are there any further developments?'

'We'll be making some further enquiries, and at some point be speaking to Robert Bamford.'

Beaumont was uncomfortable.

'It will be a chat – very informal, just to get his side of the story, and if he's involved, it may stop any further threats.'

'Have you spoken to Patrick, Detective?'

'No, I couldn't get him.'

Beaumont held court and didn't voice his opinion on this latest development. Palmer sensed his disapproval of the news.

'If that is the case, I will contact him myself, if that's okay?'

'Thanks. I will report back to DCI Edgerton, because he will be dealing with matters.'

The call ended. He immediately called Sands and

again, but there was still no reply. He left a brief message.

Detective Inspector Palmer then called Edgerton, but it just rang out.

Edgerton had gone shopping. As he strolled through the bustling crowds of shoppers in Oxford Street, he couldn't hear a thing. The repeated echoes of police sirens bouncing off the skyscrapers and the London traffic made it difficult to even concentrate. He was in 'switched off' mode, and nothing was going to interfere with his plans as he continued to browse through the shops looking for a suitable outfit to impress Chloe when they met for their next date.

Palmer was sitting at Edgerton's desk, waiting for a reply when Chloe Moran walked into the office.

'Where's the Guvnor?'

'I'm here!' replied Palmer.

Chloe let out a girlish laugh. 'No! I don't mean you. DCI Edgerton.'

'You tell me, Chloe. He's out participating in some retail therapy. He must be going somewhere. Do you know where?'

She couldn't hide her embarrassment and blushed.

'No comment – if I did know, I wouldn't tell you.'

Palmer wasn't the jealous type. He knew that they were out together. He was pleased for his friend; he wanted to see Edgerton happy. He had been without a lady in his life for too long.

It was a good time to for Palmer to catch up on some correspondence and he looked at a large pile of internal delivery envelopes. Nestled deep within another pile of papers was a printed sheet of paper. It had been taken from the Internet. He read the article with interest.

Rameau inquiry will uncover what is wrong with modern politics

As the inquiry led by Lord Chief Justice Rameau is about to start, there is no shortage of opinions on what is wrong with modern politics in the United Kingdom.

Some high-flyers must be cowering as they prepare to give evidence in a case led by one of the country's leading judges, renowned for his independence and impartiality.

Few in the establishment are against this inquiry. Lord Gilbert recently said on a BBC programme, 'The voting public is growing tired with politics, living their lives in a difficult economic climate and possibly being more accountable than they have ever been. They expect people in public office to live to the same rules, which many aspire to. However, recently, certain Members of Parliament have acted inappropriately, and I believe well below the standards set by Parliament. Coupled with the current economic climate, it is up to us to clean up our act and do it quickly. I really hope this inquiry is the start of this process.'

The list of witnesses will be endless: the Prime Minister, the Foreign Secretary, Robert Beaumont, the Home Secretary and leaders from the foreign embassies. The list goes on and on, and the cost to the taxpayer will run into millions of pounds.

Palmer continued to read, but he was most interested in the final paragraph.

Many speculate about the outcome, but don't be surprised if certain members of the government end up facing criminal charges.

He sighed. 'What the fuck is going on?'

Chapter 45

Andrei Loktev was in a pensive mood, and still annoyed that Zonov had contacted him on his personal phone. He had a lot to lose in his role as Russian Ambassador, and he needed to meet his contact quickly to get a decision. Zonov was a trusted ally, and he was the man to carry out and complete the operation. Beaumont and Sands had now become a thorn in their sides.

The main man at the Archer Street brothel was Stepan Oborin, thanks to his close friend Anton Zonov. He controlled the brothels.

Loktev's days as a Russian Civil Servant were now long gone. He was in too deep, allowing himself to fall into a world of criminality for personal gain. His salary was attractive, but he struggled to maintain his lavish lifestyle without help from the Russian Mafia. It was a two-way deal, and he was paid handsomely.

Before the meeting with his contact, Loktev was certain of one thing – a plan had to be devised to get rid of Sands and Beaumont quickly, without any mistakes. The matter had dragged on for too long.

Leaving the Embassy, he made his way to a quiet area with his secure phone, where he made contact with

Z. He sat on a park bench close to Kensington Palace as he made the call – the reply was brief.

'No contact to be made. A parcel will be placed in the Embassy first thing tomorrow morning and will be sealed for your attention. Open it, then pass on to Y who must carry out the instructions as soon as possible.'

'But…' He was immediately interrupted.

'Listen carefully. Payment instructions are in the package, and if this is acceptable, then further contact will be made to arrange two payments.'

The line went dead. Loktev immediately made contact with Zonov by text.

Make contact immediately.

Zonov, now back in Hampstead, scampered around to find his phone and picked up the text. Hampstead Heath would be the nearest place, and he grabbed his leather coat and made a quick exit. As he walked towards the Heath, the wind cut through him like a knife. It was almost as cold as the Siberian winds he had encountered in previous trips to this wilderness in his Russian homeland. It was so cold that he took shelter behind a tree and held his jacket tightly closed at the neckline. He opened the phone to contact Loktev and waited for a response.

Loktev answered.

'What do you have for me?'

'Tomorrow afternoon at 1400 hours I will make contact to arrange a meeting – repeat, 1400 hours.'

'Okay,' Zonov replied, and terminated the call.

Tonight Loktev would not return home, but would go back to the Russian Embassy and sleep in the office. He wanted to be waiting for the parcel first thing in the morning. He couldn't risk some mischievous night porter opening the package. He knew the Embassy would close at around 11 p.m., so he would make his way there around midnight.

From the privacy of Kensington Park, he made his next move and phoned his driver to arrange collection, asking him to meet him on Kensington High Street.

'Take me close to Soho – St Giles High Street, outside the Intrepid Fox will do; I have an urgent meeting. Then pick me up in one hour after the drop-off at the same place.'

The driver, smartly dressed in his chauffeur's outfit, tipped his cap, mindful not to say too much. The elegant black Mercedes rolled through the streets of London towards Soho as the Ambassador made a call to the club in Archer Street.

The Intrepid Fox was now in full swing. From its beginnings in the heart of Soho in the 1960s, the pub had gained legendary status. Frequented and idolised by the Sex Pistols, everybody knew of its existence. Although the Russian political climate had changed radically, Loktev was fascinated by the free-and-easy attitude of people who frequented this great watering hole. Their dyed hair, in a vast array of different colours, and eccentric dress code were at odds with his values as a Russian citizen, but he liked this culture. It was a breath of fresh air. No restrictions and no boundaries – total freedom to express yourself.

Loktev looked somewhat out of place in his attire as he drank his pint of lager, but he didn't care. He contacted Stepan Oborin on his phone and made his way to the brothel around the corner. Always careful to conceal his identity, he placed a scarf around his face and pulled his flat cap down firmly to obscure his eyes.

On his arrival at the brothel, the door opened slowly. It was a strange environment. A walk up the staircase revealed a club that was majestic and tastefully designed. It oozed class and opulence, which masked the seedy activity taking place. The stunning hostesses looked as though they had just fallen from the catwalk as they plied the elite with bottles of Cristal champagne. The booths, filled with lap dancers all dressed in uniform, were in narrow corridors adorned with mirrors, which led to the suites where the prostitutes worked, right in the very heart of the building. A red light shone down the hallways, where the girls would lead their clients for nights of pleasure.

The monies would be paid in cash discreetly into the hands of Oborin, where it would then be laundered in the usual clinical fashion. The main corridors were protected by a thick steel door, to be closed in the event of a raid – it was a place where the clients could seek refuge. A smack on the wrist for licensing breaches and other misdemeanours would be a small price to pay to cover up the true inner workings of the club.

Oborin greeted Loktev with his customary tight hug and led him into the small office, but not before offering him the services of one of the working girls. Loktev politely declined.

Oborin passed him his mobile phone, which contained several pictures taken earlier that day. The images of Beaumont and Sands didn't surprise Loktev, but concerned him. All it proved was that action had to be taken swiftly and efficiently.

Loktev transferred the pictures to his mobile phone and said very little, but the words he did utter were straight to the point.

'Watch the security and keep it tight. If they visit again, just leave them outside, and any calls from the authorities, close up. If you need more men so be it, but keep me informed. This is important.'

Oborin took in every word and nodded.

Loktev headed for the bar area and sat down, studying the photographs carefully again while he ordered another beer. He sipped his bottle of Grolsch as he mulled over the content.

Chapter 46

A large bubble-wrapped envelope was thrust into the hands of the porter. Before he could even check the name, Loktev snatched it from his grasp and ran to his office, eager to check the contents.

For the attention of Andrei Loktev – Russian Ambassador – Private and Confidential

Loktev leaned over the desk, reached for his paper knife and cut through the taped envelope. He took a deep breath. When he finally managed to open it, he exposed an old newspaper clipping from the Evening Standard, with a circle around the headline on the front page.

Friday 29th August 2008
Serial killer on the loose – Police link murders in Mayfair and Camberwell

The article had a typed message attached.

Read the article and research – use your imagination and eliminate two further couples not connected to Beaumont and Sands. They must reside in affluent areas of London. The serial killer has re-emerged. Then eliminate Beaumont and his wife Isabel, and finally Sands. These must be carried out quickly and efficiently before the inquiry starts.

A separate piece of paper was also attached with the payment details.

Payment for services will be completed by wire – £250,000 before and £250,000 after completion. The monies are deposited in offshore accounts – forward your secure account details urgently as arranged previously.

The final line read:

I will be in contact.

Loktev had expected the outcome, but was rather surprised by the method. There was now going to be a series of murders – innocent people targeted for no reason apart from the fact that they fitted the victim profile of the previous murders in Camberwell and Mayfair. He doubted whether £500,000 was enough for the two of them or for such an elaborate plan, and he would have to meet Zonov in person.

The enormity of their task kicked in as he slowly slumped in his settee at the side of his desk. He donned his headphones and leisurely increased the volume as the tones of Wagner rang in his ears. This was a scarce moment alone and a time to reflect.

If he were caught, his reputation would be in tatters. Surprisingly, cracks were starting to form as he slowly developed an aching conscience. He rested his tired eyes, rubbed his temples and tried to think of an escape route if things went horribly wrong. He was well and truly in the grip of the Russian Mafia. He was on their payroll, and any hint that he was about to sing to the authorities or any sense that he was becoming weak, Loktev's life on this earth would be cut short. The thought made him feel physically sick. He had to fend for himself, but he also had a responsibility to his wife and two young girls. He feared for their safety. He must soldier on and display the inner strength that had helped him climb up through the diplomatic ranks.

He also had other problems to deal with. Loktev had been invited to view CCTV footage in the club; Oborin had become infuriated with Bamford's conduct after several complaints from the girls. The Foreign Secretary was increasingly demanding free sessions and pushing his political weight, making threats to Oborin. He was becoming a thorn in their side and demanding money to keep the operation running smoothly. He had now been on the Mafia payroll for quite some time, and Loktev's patience had run out a long time ago. He hoped this would be a problem that would sort itself out.

As he sat in his seat, he slowly dozed and fell into a deep sleep. It would be a frenetic few days for him as the plan was unlatched.

Chapter 47

Zonov waited for a response from Loktev and prepared for the inevitable. He looked up at the painting on the wall – Moscow snowfall – and moved it to one side, exposing a wall safe.

With several turns of the dial, the safe opened, revealing cash and a small stash of uncontaminated white snow on a mirror in a bag – pure cocaine.

He needed a lift, and cocaine was the drug of his choice. He placed it on the table and meticulously divided it into four equal lines before rolling a ten-pound note and inhaling line after line. A quick intake of breath and he was alive – he felt invincible, and over the next few days his intake of the stimulant would increase to dangerous levels.

It wouldn't take long for him to receive the call. It would be a grave mistake to call from home.

'Meet me now at Hyde Park. Speakers' Corner.'

Zonov's mind was racing and he was already planning ahead. On a high, the drug enhanced his murderous tendencies, giving him the confidence to carry out his assignment, but he was unaware of the task that lay ahead as both men made their way to Hyde Park on this early winter's evening.

The scene was set. As the wind died and the temperature rose in the heart of the city, a fog descended over the park, the Speakers' Corner sign now barely visible as Loktev arrived. Zonov still making his way, Loktev paced the grounds, careful not to attract attention as he held his overcoat tightly shut, the contents of the envelope safely inside his pocket. Disturbed by the odd bird circling for scraps and dog walkers oblivious to what was happening, it was a perfect setting for their meeting. He had his script firmly implanted in his mind, and already had a feeling of how things must go forward, but he had to place his trust in Zonov.

Then there was the issue of the money. Loktev may not be contracted to kill, but he needed something to fall back on, and £250,000 would be the sum he required; the other half would go to Zonov.

He soon spotted another figure emerging through the mist, and he approached. It was Zonov, and the men greeted each other and started to walk the perimeter of the park. The night was now closing in as they discussed the plan.

'Anton, this is quite uncomplicated. Study the newspaper and carry out the request. It is easy. The money will be split fifty–fifty – the full amount being half a million. One hundred grand will be paid immediately, and the final instalment of one hundred and fifty grand will be paid when the job is complete. We will get two hundred and fifty thousand each. Are you satisfied?'

Zonov was filled with anger.

'No, Andrei, that is not sufficient for my part. You are just the middleman. I want a total of three hundred and fifty thousand, one hundred and twenty-five thousand now and then the balance after completion. Tell the contact no more and no less. It is simple or I stop, and he must accept the consequences.'

Loktev had expected the response, but if an agreement were to be reached, he would have to return to the contact. For his part, he would do very little for such a big reward.

He stayed in Hyde Park, eager to contact Z. This was a cunning plan being masterminded by a person who held a grudge against Beaumont, a person whose career was in danger of meltdown and who had reached the end of a road, with no place to go, no place to hide, and the only way forward being a last act of desperation to save himself from a national scandal exposed by the inquiry.

Loktev knew that this was the only way out, but it didn't stop him having his doubts about the plan. He was corrupt and dishonest in every sense of the words, but he was not a cold-blooded killer. He sat and waited long enough to allow Zonov to leave, and then made the call to Z.

'Can we speak?'

The reply was immediate. 'Yes, we can.'

'It's regarding the funds. We need to meet, now.'

'If I have to – location please?'

'Hyde Park, Speakers' Corner. What's your ETA?'

'Fifteen minutes. And cover up – you will not see my face. Stand at the sign and I will pass and speak. I will say clearly, "Cold day, sir," and you must reply, "Colder than Moscow, dear fellow." We will then make contact.'

'Fifteen minutes.'

Loktev awaited the arrival of Z, also known as the

'customer'. He made his way to the entrance to Hyde Park and crossed the road, entering a nearby café. He was so cold, and with fifteen minutes to spare, he needed warmth and a cup of tea before he went back into the park.

Checking out every customer in the café was easy since it was quiet. Only three workmen, but he was still on his guard as he drank his tea. It wasn't long before he had finished and headed back to the park. As he entered Speakers' Corner, he noticed movement in a small wooded area and nervously entered the bushes, flicking the snow which coated the branches. He wondered who might be lurking within. He couldn't take any chances. As he progressed quietly into the middle of the wooded area, the noises were getting louder and he was ready to pounce. Suddenly, from nowhere, the trees started to shake and a large flock of pigeons flew into the open, terrifying him and covering him with snow.

He shouted in his native Russian tongue. He brushed himself down and waited. There was total silence and he sighed with relief – a false alert, or so he thought.

Deep in the woods, Zonov watched Loktev's every move. He knew that in his killing games no one could be trusted, and he was eager to see whom Loktev was meeting. He lay in wait.

His heart still pounding, Loktev now stood at the Speakers' Corner sign awaiting the arrival of Z, knowing it wouldn't be long.

Zonov was now perfectly poised deep in the undergrowth, where he had the perfect vantage point.

Chapter 48

As the temperature continued to plummet, Loktev became impatient as a ten-minute wait turned into twenty five minutes. He fumbled in his pocket and checked his mobile phone; there was still no sign of his client. He made another call and there was no response, but he persevered. He couldn't let the meeting slip by.

Then he heard a voice in the distance.

'Cold day, sir.'

Loktev instinctively replied, 'Colder than Moscow, dear fellow.'

The men shook hands, both with their scarves covering their faces. Loktev knew his client, but they couldn't be seen here.

Zonov watched as the men spoke. He was frustrated. The dialogue between them was uttered in nothing more than a whisper. He looked at the man closely. Neatly dressed and wearing a black scarf around his face.

'My man wants more money – the job is off if you don't pay him!'

Loktev looked at his client and made no reply. Both men hesitated.

'How much does he want?'

'An extra one hundred and fifty thousand for his

part, or the job is off – there is no leeway.'

Z was resigned to the fact that he was in a corner and had to pay. 'I will pay the money later – the job is still on. Just remember, no tricks. If the job is not completed, there will be consequences for both you and your friend.'

Loktev agreed. To reiterate his position, Z spoke again.

'Do you hear me loud and clear? The job must be completed before this inquiry starts. No mistakes, no fuck-ups – do you understand the plan?'

'Yes,' Loktev replied.

'We will speak again.'

There were no handshakes during this meeting. Loktev was quite clear in his mind of the position he was in, and he was keen to speak to Zonov again. He had to think of himself.

The client made his way through the park, while Loktev went in the opposite direction.

Zonov waited for the right moment to come out from the woodland to follow, but it wouldn't be easy. He had to pick up his pace to catch up and watch his every move. Darkness was now closing in, which made his task even more treacherous as he struggled to find his footing on the frozen ground. It was like an ice rink as he tried to run to make up ground. Almost out of breath, he finally caught up, only to be left standing alone as his target got into the back of a black Mercedes.

He tried to catch up with the car on foot to get the registration number, but it had gone.

Zonov was still at a loss as to who the man was behind the scarf.

Chapter 49

December 2011
Holland Park, London

Considering it was late December, this day was like no other. The trees in Holland Park were now stripped bare, all the fallen leaves floating in the bitter wind. The snow started to fall, and a blizzard developed as the snowflakes chased across the gardens like a fast-approaching wave. The sky was a dark grey as the temperature continued to drop.

Through the thick snow falling from the sky a female jogger appeared, wearing skin-tight jogging pants and a yellow fluorescent running top.

Rebecca Labelle loved the park and was just coming to the end of her long run. It was her only source of relaxation after a long day in her interior design shop on Kensington High Street. As she approached the monument not far from the entrance to the High Street, she noticed a figure near a tree. She wouldn't normally watch for people and wasn't the slightest bit suspicious, but this was different. This person was out of place, hiding in the shadow of the trees next to the Lord Holland Statue, and she felt violated. She could feel the eyes of this figure staring right through her, so she accelerated quickly and kept turning around to check.

The person had vanished, and she whispered to herself, 'Rebecca, stop being paranoid.'

Zonov waited – the elaborate plan was now playing out.

Rebecca decided to pass the shop en route home and check in with her sister, Pippa, who had decided to work late. They were partners and had run the business for a couple of years. It was a successful company which had flourished in this affluent neighbourhood.

When she arrived at the shop, she popped her head through the window and said, 'Can't stop – is everything okay? I'll see you tomorrow about 7.30.'

'Okay, see you tomorrow,' her sister replied.

Rebecca wasn't far from her house so she slowed down to a brisk walk – it wouldn't be long before she arrived at her fashionable regency-style terraced home on Royal Crescent.

It was going to be a relaxing night tonight with her husband Jeremy, a freelance journalist, so she decided to pick up a bottle of wine from the local off-licence.

The long run had exhausted her and she was hungry, so it was time to spoil herself and buy some chocolate from the newsagents near to the Crescent. As she entered the shop, she noticed the papers and thought she would have a sneak preview.

Ali, the shopkeeper, shouted, 'Becky, are you going to buy it?'

Realising she had no money, she said, 'You won't believe this, but I have no money; I've been out for a run.'

Laughing at her, he said, 'Don't worry, drop it in tomorrow.'

She grabbed a Mars Bar and The Times, and left the

shop, shouting back, 'Thanks, Ali, you're a star.'

Having a quick glance at the front page, she saw a picture of Brian Beaumont MP and the headline:

Beaumont on course to root out corrupt officials

She was just as inquisitive as the next person, and it stopped her in her tracks as she read...

After recently resigning from his position on the House of Commons Select Committee, Brian Beaumont Labour MP, the Shadow Home Secretary, called for a wider, more detailed public inquiry into government corruption, and now that it has been announced, he welcomes the inquiry to be conducted by Lord Justice Rameau. Beaumont, in a press release, has stated that this is the only way to gather evidence into allegations of corruption. He also added that he would fully cooperate with the inquiry and help to uncover the truth...

When she arrived at the entrance to Royal Crescent, she saw Jeremy's BMW sports car parked outside their house, and as she walked up the steps, she noticed mud smeared everywhere and the door slightly ajar. Rebecca didn't think it strange – perhaps he had taken the dog for a walk. But she was surprised that Bobby, their pet Dalmatian, was not barking.

As she opened the door, she shouted, 'Jeremy, I'm home.'

There was no response.

'Bobby, Mummy is home,'

Still no response.

She thought Jeremy might be in the back washing the dog, so she continued to creep forward through the hallway. She shouted again, but there was no answer and she started to become more anxious with each step. Her anxiety would soon be overtaken by a feeling of complete horror.

As she entered the kitchen, there had been an obvious struggle and drops of blood were on the floor at the side of the sink. There was a silence that sent a chill through her body. Rebecca suddenly heard a panting sound, and as she stooped down towards the floor to pick up a broken plate, she saw Bobby lying there panting, his eyes open, struggling to find his next breath. There was a large wound to his neck, and she grabbed a tea towel to stem the blood flow.

She started to sob as her dog lay there, wheezing and choking. It was the most gruesome sight for the young lady, and her mind was a daze. She couldn't begin to fathom what had happened – it was a living nightmare.

She screamed repeatedly, 'Jeremy, where are you?'

There was a deathly silence.

Her dog went quiet and Rebecca knew there was nothing more she could do. Covered in blood, she crawled across the kitchen floor. The reality of the situation had now hit her, and she reached up and took a stainless steel knife which lay on the chopping board next to the kitchen sink. The white floor tiles were covered with bloody drag marks as she pulled herself towards the entrance to Jeremy's office.

Rebecca's home had become the scene of a most evil act. She was in a terrified state of mind, thoughts racing through her head. In a matter of hours her whole life had changed, and she sobbed uncontrollably, shouting, 'Jeremy, please answer. Where are you?'

Rebecca was now at the entrance to Jeremy's office and she noticed the door was closed, so she reached up and turned the handle slowly. The silence was interrupted by the squeaking hinges, and as the door opened she saw Jeremy lying on his desk, with a deep laceration to his throat and a stab wound to his chest. His lifeless body just lay there. No movement. No breath. All life sucked from his body.

Rebecca screamed, the whole series of events causing her to be sick, her stomach twisted with fear and pain. She stood up and ran over to him, hugging him as she wept. She knew he was dead. A sudden feeling of anger came over her. Who had carried out this act? Thoughts of what might have happened were now racing through her mind. It was time to call the police, so she nervously picked up the phone from Jeremy's desk and started to dial 999. The line was dead. She stopped and tried to think. All she could hear was the continuous dead tone coming from the speaker.

Confusion had now taken over as she began to search the rooms downstairs to find her mobile phone. She paused and tried to gather her thoughts, and then screamed out, 'Where the fuck is my phone?' It suddenly came to her that she had left it in the bedroom before going for a jog. Still breathing heavily and shaking, she ran upstairs, leaving bloody footprints behind her.

She opened the bedroom door and saw her Blackberry on the bedside cabinet. Grabbing it, she turned around and felt a draft as a heavy blow descended upon her. It came from nowhere. Rebecca was now in a state of semi-consciousness, everything blurred. The knife she had in her grasp fell to the floor. She tried to move, but couldn't. It was as if everything was in slow motion. Then she felt a strong grip around her throat and could hear heavy breathing. Confused and frightened, she tried to struggle, but she was overcome by the sheer strength of her assailant. She tried to turn to see her attacker, but it was impossible as she was lifted off the ground and thrown from side to side.

The grip around her loosened unexpectedly, and as she opened her eyes she saw a bright glint flash rapidly in front of her eyes. It was a large knife. Rebecca Labelle was now fighting for her life. Grabbing the knife with her hand was impossible, but she tried desperately to save herself. The blade slid, cutting her hand. She felt helpless. Then came a punch to the chest that was delivered with such ferocity that it knocked her to the ground. As she turned to look up, another blow descended on the top of her head and everything went black.

Park Terrace was now shrouded in a blanket of silence. A home in one of the most affluent areas of London had become a murder scene. Two lives erased in the blink of an eye. It was a bloody mess.

Chapter 50

New Scotland Yard

Eventually, Edgerton was called up to see Chief Superintendent Watkins, and he decided to take the lift. As the door opened, he was greeted by an old colleague.

'Hi, Jack, you're back – nice to see you.'

'Oh yes, you come down, and I go up. You're looking good.'

The lift eventually arrived, and as the doors opened Edgerton's phone bleeped. It was a text message from Philip Palmer, the office manager at Homicide and Serious Crime Command.

Please phone as a matter of urgency.

The phone bleeped again and there was a message from Chloe.

Just arrived at the Yard checking some exhibits

'Bollocks,' he said under his breath, not realising there was a female behind him. 'Oh sorry, my dear, I hope you didn't hear that.'

He replied to the text.

I'm here will speak soon. There's been an incident.

He made a quick entry into the reception where he

waited to see Bob Watkins. Edgerton couldn't decide whether to phone Palmer back straight away, but he was a laid-back type of character, and when he used the word urgent it probably meant urgent, so he phoned him immediately.

Eventually, Palmer answered the phone.

'There's been an incident in Royal Crescent near to Holland Park,' he said. 'I need to speak to you about it. The lads are at the scene liaising with the Fire Brigade because there's been a fire at the house, and I'm not sure about the state of the scene and what's happening.'

'Right, find out ASAP what happened, and once the blaze is sorted, get the scene taped. I don't want every man and his dog trampling all over it. And then bell me back. Is there anybody in the house at the moment?'

'It's still a bit sketchy, Guv. I'll get straight back.'

'Please do, Phil, and I'll get to the scene and see you there.'

Edgerton was happy with the call, as it meant he could make his excuses and leave the meeting.

Watkins appeared from nowhere.

'Hi, Jack, please come in.'

Taking off his coat, Edgerton replied, 'Hello, Guv. I'll be right with you.'

After exchanging the usual pleasantries, Watkins said, 'How are things? Is there anything to report?'

'Nothing really, it's been quiet. Chloe's just sorting out some exhibits on the Jenkins case while we're here, but no, not really. How long is it until we have to move back to the Yard?'

'Six to twelve months,' Watkins replied as he stood at his pristine desk.

He was a small man and spoke with a slight lisp.

Dressed in his pinstripe suit, he was immaculate, and Edgerton often wondered how many suits he had. He looked more like a barrister than a senior police officer.

'You look a bit edgy, is everything okay?'

'I could do with getting off. I've just had a call from Phil Palmer; there's been an incident in Kensington which I need to go to.'

'What is it?'

'It's a possible crime scene. Phil's there at the moment, but I really need to get there ASAP. Can I phone you en route, Guv, and give you a SIT report when I get there?'

Watkins ushered Edgerton out of the door. 'I'll leave you to it, Jack. I might give Phil a bell myself. If you need me, I will come, but I'm supposed to do a bit of shopping with my wife tonight. I'm under orders.'

Gathering his coat, Edgerton said, 'See you later.'

As he entered the lift, he phoned Chloe Moran and told her he had just had a call from Phil Palmer.

'We need to get there ASAP. Royal Crescent – if you don't know where it is, tap it into the satnav and I'll see you in the office.'

'I told you it wouldn't be quiet for long, Guv; you tempted fate.'

'I know, you're right.'

As he hung up, his phone rang – it was Philip Palmer again.

'Hi, Guv. I can tell you a little more now. It's looking like a double murder here. I'm liaising with the chief fire officer at the moment, and the house is pretty safe. Luckily the fire started at the rear, and they were alerted quickly so the scene looks like it's intact, but it looks like an abattoir. The shithouse has butchered the dog as well, Guv.'

Edgerton sighed. 'What do you think, Phil, a burglary gone wrong?'

'Not sure, hard to tell. It doesn't look as though anything's been stolen.'

'Is there anything else to report?'

'No, not at the moment. The ERU are here and are just getting their suits on, and the area's all taped off. I've taped off the alley at the rear as well, and got the uniform lads to cover the scene with the logbooks. The Fire Brigade's sending their lads up to liaise with the ERU.'

Edgerton's mind was now working overtime. 'Phil, make sure you get the TSG lads down. I want a full search of the area, and if the press are sniffing, forward them on to me and I'll liaise with the local Borough Commander and the Guv.'

'Ok, Guv.'

'And we need to contact the relatives when we can, and please get the Home Office Pathologist out and check the status with the ERU – sounds like we've got a messy scene here.'

'Okay,' Palmer replied. 'Anything else, Guv?'

'A brew would be nice when I get there, if there are any witnesses with a kettle?'

'No problem, see you later. I've got some of the lads checking with witnesses, and I'm sure they'll locate a brew stop.'

'Bye, Phil, see you in about half an hour. I trained you well,' he quipped.

Chloe arrived at the office. Edgerton sighed, looked at Chloe and smiled. 'It's going to be a late one. I promise we'll get together one day.'

'I know,' she said, and smiled.

Both detectives started to make their way to the scene.

Edgerton looked at the Sat Nav.

'Chloe you've typed in Camden by mistake.'

'Oh sorry I went there the other day. A slip of the finger.'

'It's been a long time since I've been to Camden,' Edgerton said. 'I keep meaning to go back now that the Roundhouse has been renovated.'

'I've been there a few times, and I've seen Paul McCartney there.'

'Is it nice then?'

'Oh yes, it's fantastic, but not being a grey dinosaur I wouldn't remember the old venue, would I?' she replied with a broad grin on her face.

Edgerton frowned. 'I went to see The Stranglers and Patti Smith in 1977 at the Roundhouse, and I intend on seeing them again when they return – what a band.'

'I like them as well … I might come with you.'

Edgerton was surprised. 'You never told me!'

'Well perhaps we can go together? I have a few of their albums … love 'em!'

'Which ones?'

'No More Heroes, Rattus, Greatest Hits and Suite 16.'

Edgerton let out a scream. 'Amazing! I'm shocked. You kept that quiet. We shall watch them together.'

They soon arrived at the entrance to Royal Crescent and were greeted by a uniformed officer standing next to the crime scene tape. It was dark, but the sky was lit by the portable floodlights aimed at the house. There was still steam rising from the address and it was enveloped in a thick fog. The whole scene was eerie.

'Look at these houses!' Edgerton said.

They were beautiful, immaculate and almost identical. All terraced and white fronted, they were decorated with an array of different plants in boxes under the windows. All the front doors were black and shiny, and as Edgerton approached he could see his reflection clearly. All the brass fittings shone brightly, and everything looked so clean.

This only added to his repulsion at what he anticipated was around the corner... How could this happen in such a neighbourhood?

Chapter 51

Murder Scene

As Edgerton approached the door at Park Terrace, Royal Crescent, he heard a shout from behind and realised it was DI Palmer.

'Hi there. Have you had a look inside yet, Guv?' he asked.

'No, I'm just going in. By the way, have you found any witnesses?'

'Not a thing, Guv. No one has seen anything, but I'm going to check if any of these houses have CCTV – there's got to be something!'

'With all this wealth, there's got to be CCTV,' Edgerton agreed. 'I bet these places are getting screwed all the time.'

He felt a tap on his shoulder, and as he turned he was greeted by Dr Julian Wallace.

'Hello, Detective Chief Inspector Edgerton, how the devil are you?'

'I'm fine, and glad to see you, Julian. You should get a desk in the office, it would make life easier.'

'Couldn't agree more.'

'I've not been inside yet, but I've been briefed by DI

Palmer. Are you aware of the circumstances?'

'I've been briefed by the Evidence Recovery Unit and I'm sure you have some ideas about how you want the scene managed, but I want to see inside and take it from there.'

'Well let's get in,' replied Edgerton.

'We also need to liaise with the FIU guys, bearing in mind we've had a fire here. I'd like to hear their thoughts.'

'I agree.'

All the men donned their J-suits.

'I hate these things, they make me sweat like a pig,' Edgerton said.

Edgerton reached for his Chanel-soaked handkerchief and held it to his nose as he entered. Once inside, the detective was surprised to see no real fire damage in the hallway, although he could smell the strong stench of damp smoke. There was also the unmistakable smell of death...

Palmer closed in on him and stopped everyone in their tracks.

'Sorry, Guv, can I have a word?' Edgerton leaned over and DI Palmer whispered in his ear, 'Just a thought, and I don't want to pre-empt any thought you may have, but I'm mindful of the murders in Camberwell Grove a few years ago. I know the method is slightly different, but I just hope 'the Barber' hasn't made a comeback.'

'Yeah, the thought had crossed my mind. I'll have a look at this line of enquiry. Dr Wallace was involved with the cases, so we'll get his input.'

As they walked into the scene, Edgerton turned around and said to Palmer and Dr Wallace, 'No taking the piss.' He then raised his handkerchief to his nose again.

Dr Wallace laughed. 'I see you haven't changed, Jack.'

DI Palmer laughed as Edgerton replied with a muffled grunt from behind his perfumed handkerchief.

In the kitchen, the forensic teams were working with the Fire Brigade.

As he entered, Edgerton removed his handkerchief and shouted, 'Hello, guys, how are you? I'll speak to you later, I'm just checking the scene.'

As he looked down at the kitchen floor, he noticed the dead dog and looked at Palmer.

'What the fuck is this, Phil?'

The Dalmatian lay in a pool of blood, its face distorted.

'Whoever's done this is a psychopath, Guv; that's why I mentioned the other murders.'

Edgerton remained silent, slowly surveying the scene, looking up, then down.

He turned to Dr Wallace. 'What do you think?'

'Well, it's different, isn't it? I'm wondering whether the dog attacked the offender when they entered.' He looked at the dog more closely and could only find one deep laceration.

Edgerton turned to DI Palmer. 'Phil, what are the names of the victims?'

'Jeffrey and Rebecca Labelle.'

'They're obviously very wealthy. Is there any sign of a break-in?'

'I don't think there is, Guv. It looks like Mr Labelle was murdered initially and then the offender waited upstairs in the bedroom and attacked her when she checked the rooms. Both victims have suffered horrendous stab wounds. We'll come across Mr Labelle soon, Guv.'

Edgerton shone his torch on the bloodstained floor next to the dead Dalmatian.

'I can see the odd footprint. Some belong to the girl, but the others must belong to the offender. I'd say it's quite a big man, looking at the shoe size.'

Palmer agreed. 'Yes, I think so. Jeffrey Labelle is through here, chaps,' he said as he pointed towards the office. 'There's been quite a struggle – he has several defence wounds to both hands. I don't think we should actually go in the office until the forensic boys have finished.'

Edgerton peered through the door and looked at the victim lying on his desk face upwards, with a deep cut to the throat, his arms flayed and legs crossed. He looked at his chest and noticed a stab wound where his shirt had been torn. He had suffered massive blood loss. Edgerton saw there was also slight smoke damage as he ran his finger along the wall.

'Why's the fire not taken hold? Have you spoken to the Fire Brigade?'

'There's mainly smoke damage, Guv,' Palmer replied. 'He tried to torch the place; they've found accelerant by the door.'

'It stinks of petrol. Has anything been stolen from the property or ransacked?'

'Not sure, really. I can speak to the other boys later, but I've not had time to do a thorough check.'

Dr Wallace jumped quickly into the conversation. 'It's going to be a while before the bodies are released for post mortem. Jack, are you coming to the post mortems?'

'I suppose I'll have to, Doctor.'

Palmer laughed.

'Good day, Guv, how are you?'

Edgerton turned round and saw that it was Fred Constance, Head of the Evidence Recovery Unit.

'Have you found anything, Fred?'

'Nothing at all. There are quite a few footprints, but gloves have been used in the commission of this. The offender is a male and quite powerful by the looks of things.'

'I couldn't agree more, Fred,' Dr Wallace said.

'So you're the SIO?' Constance asked.

'I am,' Edgerton replied.

Constance beamed. He was a happy man. 'Well, Guv, it looks like a premeditated murder. It's not a burglary gone wrong.'

'Well, chaps, we've got a right mess here. Let's have a run-through of the scene as best we can, and then get back to the office and re-evaluate things.'

He was in a place where he felt comfortable; he currently had a double murder on his hands. It wasn't long before his phone started to ring. He checked the display and saw that it was DS Wynyard from Charing Cross Police Station.

'Hi, Guv, see you've got your hands full. I've just seen the log.'

'Yes, it's a double murder. I'll see you about the Sands case, but carry on as normal. It doesn't change anything, and I'll still be able to oversee things.'

'Have you got much?'

'The forensic boys are at the scene, and we're having a scrum-down back at the office. I'm with the Home Office Pathologist at the moment, so I'll keep an open mind.'

'Okay, Guv, I'll let you get on and get back to you later.'

As quickly as the phone went dead, it rang again. It was Chief Superintendent Watkins.

'Hello, Guv.'

'Go on, what's the score?' Watkins asked.

'Well, Guv, not a lot at the moment.'

'You don't think there's…'

Edgerton interrupted. 'I know what you're going to say. Is there a connection with the Camberwell Grove murders?'

'How did you know?'

'DI Palmer asked the same question. I'm not sure, unless he's changed his MO. No hair has been removed from the victims, but the ferocity of the attacks bears the same hallmark, and there appears to be no motive.'

'We can go back to the office and meet, can't we?' 'If you don't want to attend the scene, we can see you later.'

'I must go, and then I'll meet you back at your office. Looks like it may be a late one.'

Edgerton laughed. 'Just when we thought it was going to be a quiet Christmas.'

Watkins laughed. 'It's always that way, Jack.'

Edgerton continued to examine the house carefully, and as he looked through the elegant rooms, he noticed a picture on one of the walls. He beckoned over DI Palmer and pointed to it.

'Look at this photograph. Mr and Mrs Labelle are in the foreground with the Foreign Secretary, Robert Bamford. Not sure about the other couple. He gets around Bamford, doesn't he?'

'We've now dealt with a couple of incidents, and his

name keeps cropping up,' Palmer replied. 'Looks like we may have to pay him a visit.'

Edgerton took the picture from the wall and looked at the back. There was a sticker that read: The Photograph Agency.

'It looks like some charity ball, doesn't it?' Palmer said.

Edgerton agreed.

Palmer wanted to head back to the office. 'Are you ready?'

As he approached Fred Constance, Edgerton replied, 'I'm coming now, Fred! Have you anything to report?'

'No, not really. We have some good footprints in blood and we're in the process of photographing them, but this guy is forensically aware. I think we'll draw a blank on fingerprints, and the weapon hasn't been found. Not yet anyway.'

'Okay.'

'Oh, there are a few other things. I spoke to the boys from the Fire Investigation Unit, and they've found the source of the fire quite easily. Luckily, it didn't take hold. Look, Jack, I know Phil's had a word with you about a link with the previous murders, but I wouldn't count it out. I know no hair has been taken, but the ferocity of the knife attacks ... well, they are similar, and then there's the motive element. Perhaps 'the Barber' has changed his method, although I don't know why he should have been away for so long.'

Edgerton remained silent.

'What do think?' Constance said.

'I'm going back soon, but keep me informed and tell me when the bodies are released.

You know, Fred, I'm not sure about any connection. It's been too long, but I hear what you say.'

His phone started to ring. It was an unknown number; *probably the press*, he thought. He decided he would leave that role to Mr Watkins. He was certain they would be looking for a slant on this story, and he was confident they would want to link the murders.

His final call was the bedroom, and he took his time climbing the stairs, looking for any clues. As he entered, he saw Mrs Labelle.

'What a fucking scumbag!' He was angry.

He looked at Rebecca lying there, covered from head to toe in blood, again with severe injuries to her chest. The white carpet and whitewashed walls made the scene look so much worse. There were blood splatters on the ceiling and all the walls, and he could smell perfume on the victim.

Edgerton soldiered on…

Chapter 52

As Edgerton sat alongside, he looked at the officers gathered ready for the briefing. He began to fumble with his hands as he spoke to DI Palmer.

'These bloody laser pointers, Phil. Turn it on for me, will you?'

The seasoned detectives filling the room started to laugh.

'Right, chaps, we've got a killer on the loose,' he said, and pointed to the board.

There were two photographs taken from the house of the victims, a poignant reminder of how life could be taken so quickly and viciously.

'Both professional people and both brutally murdered, without any motive. You will find a pack which has been prepared for you, so read carefully. The couple were both stabbed repeatedly, and the dog was also killed, or butchered might be a more appropriate term. As you can see, we have very little evidence at the moment, but the killer was male, and we shall have to determine whether he worked alone. Dr Wallace will be carrying out the PM tomorrow, which I shall attend, and if you look at the boards you can see the crime scene photographs, carefully prepared by the Crime Scene guys under the supervision of Fred Constance, so please acquaint yourselves with him if you have never met.'

As the officers scoured the room, they were surrounded by photographs that exhibited the horrendous scene at Holland Park. Even the most experienced murder detectives were surprised by the ferociousness of the attacks.

As Edgerton sat and prepared to make another statement, one of the officers said, 'Can I make an observation about 'the Barber' murders?'

Edgerton replied, 'I was just going to raise this subject, and at this moment in time let's keep an open mind. I have my reservations about this theory, but let's do the basics. I want house-to-house enquiries carried out, and any CCTV examined. Just good old basic police work, and keep your ears to the ground. We have no murder weapon, but we can surmise that it was possibly a large kitchen knife. The search at the scene by the Territorial Support Group has yielded nothing.'

It would be a long day as the Murder Squad started to prepare the investigation. Not much to work on, Edgerton waited for the arrival of Chief Superintendent Robert Watkins.

He was passed a note, and after reading it said, 'Dr Wallace, sorry to bother you. The bodies are ready for release, so can you get back over there and make sure you supervise the removal? I don't want any problems. I'm going to speak to the relatives and get the Labelles identified. Can you keep me informed, and I was wondering if we could get started tonight on the PM?'

Dr Wallace was amused. He was used to Edgerton's work ethic.

'Yes, Jack. Would you like anything else while I'm doing that?'

Edgerton chuckled and immediately fired back. 'Sarcasm is the lowest form of wit, Doctor.'

'It is, but afterwards, you can buy me a bloody pint if the pubs are still open.'

DI Palmer interrupted the conversation. 'Jack, we've got a Pippa Hawksworth in the waiting room with Rebecca's mother and Jeremy's father. They are obviously distraught. The Family Liaison Officer's with them. They picked them up earlier. They know the news.'

Edgerton remained silent. It was the worst side of police work, and meeting the relatives never got any easier. He opened a file, double-checking all the details, and then looked at Palmer.

'Phil, I am right. Rebecca's father died, and Jeremy's mother also. None of these deaths are recent, are they?'

'No, Guv, all their parents were retired, and Pippa runs a business with her sister and saw her just before she went home.'

Edgerton lost his cool momentarily. 'When I get this animal, I'll fuck him up.'

He purposely made his way to the waiting room and was immediately greeted with a hug from Pippa. She wept at the loss of her sister as the detective continued to hold her tightly.

Rebecca's mother, Angela, said, 'Chief Inspector, please catch the person who killed my daughter.'

Sometimes, there was a procedure to follow and Edgerton was warned by some never to over-commit when dealing with victims. He ignored the rule.

'Mrs Hawksworth, Mr Labelle, I can assure you I will use every resource at my disposal to catch this person.'

Edgerton had now reached a point where the family would have to identify the body at the mortuary, and it was not an event he relished. It wouldn't be far to travel, but he needed to move on with the case, and it would be a quick process. He always liked to get the identification over with, and then he would witness the post mortem. This whole ghastly process was for him a necessary evil.

He hated the clinical smell in all the mortuaries and the overwhelming feeling that fell upon him when he was surrounded by the deceased. It didn't matter that they were all tucked up safely in their separate compartments. The strong smell of stainless steel added to the unwelcome atmosphere, not to mention the surgical tools that were all laid out ready to be used on the next body. Some officers liked post mortems, but Edgerton could never understand why.

If Dr Wallace thought there might be a chance of getting a pint with him after such a grisly procedure, then he would be sadly disappointed.

It was a slow drive through the streets of London to Kensington Mortuary, passing the shops' glowing Christmas lights, and Edgerton couldn't help but think how the grieving families in the back of their cars would be denied many Christmases and celebrations in future years. Like all the cases he dealt with, the victims' lives changed forever and things never got easier. He often spoke to Detective Inspector Palmer about this subject, and how he found it so difficult to come to terms with.

As they arrived at the mortuary and Edgerton sat the family in the peace and tranquillity of the chapel, Dr Wallace prepared the victims for identification.

Edgerton entered the mortuary and approached the two bodies, both covered in white blankets. The Home Office Pathologist slowly pulled back the covers so that both faces were visible.

Edgerton looked closely at the corpses. Rebecca Labelle looked like an angel. There were no visible injuries to her face, and he was thankful as he touched it gently and made a sign of the cross. He was not religious, but felt compelled to show the utmost respect.

He then turned to Jeremy Labelle, who had a horrendous facial wound on the right side, possibly caused when he defended himself against the attacker. Dr Wallace carefully moved his head to the injured side, covering the wound. Edgerton smiled at him, knowing he was equally sensitive in these situations.

Edgerton approached the families while they prayed in the chapel, and the identification of both victims was a quick but painfully emotional affair. It brought him close to tears. He was now more determined than ever to catch this killer. As he stood with Dr Wallace, there was a knock on the door and Chief Superintendent Watkins entered. He was very matter of fact in these situations and showed no emotion. He agreed to take the families back where they would spend the night with a Family Liaison Officer close at hand.

This was the moment Edgerton dreaded as Dr Wallace prepared for the detailed post mortem of the victims. He stood with his handkerchief at the ready.

Chapter 53

It had been a long night for the Detective Chief Inspector as he sat with his feet up on the desk, and it was only 6 a.m. He read through the files relating to 'the Barber' murders, examining every detailed report and crime scene photograph.

He had never noticed that death in all the cases was almost instant after one lethal stab wound had been inflicted. Whether they had suffered before that fatal blow was not for debate, as all the victims had serious defence wounds.

As he checked all the reports, the cause of death was by bleeding as a result of a single stab to the heart, which had severed the aorta. This wasn't a coincidence, and such detail had never been released to the general public as a matter of strategic planning carried by the original Senior Investigating Officer. Edgerton continued to keep an open mind as he put the papers down and drank his strong black coffee. This would keep him going over the next few weeks.

He expected the officers in at about 7 a.m., but he would soon be joined by Chloe, who always came in early. Since their night out, their time together had been scarce, but at least they were in work together so they had time to talk about the case.

There was a knock on his door, and his face lit up when he saw that it was Chloe.

'Hi there. You only needed to be in at 7 a.m.'

'Don't overdo it, Jack … oops sorry, Guv.'

Edgerton laughed, as no one else was in the office. He grabbed her and kissed her on the cheek.

'Would you like a coffee?'

'That would be great I just need to get some papers from the main office,' she replied.

There was another knock on his door after Chloe left the room. It was Dr Julian Wallace.

'Good morning, Jack, how are you today?'

'Tired. So, are you happy with the cause of death for both?'

'Well, I've checked and checked again, and they both died due to the aorta being severed.'

Edgerton passed the files to the Home Office Pathologist who started to read as he turned on the kettle.

After examining the medical evidence, Wallace looked at him and said, 'Six deaths, all with an identical cause of death. Either pure coincidence or a well-rehearsed method of killing.'

'I don't believe in coincidence, Doctor, I think this killer might be back – slightly different method, but nevertheless, back with vengeance.'

'DI Palmer was right then.'

Edgerton shouted out to Chloe, 'Come here.'

She entered immediately, 'What can I do?'

Edgerton tapped on his computer and said, 'Do you know PC Smithers? He used to be at Carter Street.'

'I think you have spoken about him.'

Edgerton printed the officer's duties off the

computer and handed them to her.

'Can you get him to come and see me now? He's on early turn.'

Chloe left the office.

Dr Wallace said, 'The name does sound familiar.'

'He worked on the murders in Camberwell and was very friendly with the profiler on the case. Let's speak to him.'

Dr Wallace looked out of Edgerton's window. As he noticed the snow-covered statues, he said, 'Bloody hell, Jack, you have a great view here. If I were you, I wouldn't want to go back to the Yard.'

The phone rang, and Edgerton answered immediately.

'Hello, Guv, it's Fred Constance.'

'Just the man,' Edgerton replied. After a few moments, he said, 'I'll speak to the lads at the Fire Investigation Unit. Before I forget, did you work on 'the Barber' case?'

'No, Guv, I didn't, but I have read about it a little. There are similarities, but no hair cut off, so it's a difficult one. I wouldn't like to make a call one way or the other.'

Edgerton looked at his grey notebook with an old coffee stain and scribbled down in big capital letters the word 'LINK'. As he placed the note over his keyboard, Chloe entered the office and said, 'PC Smithers can't get to see you, but he will be in touch, Guv.'

'He's a busy bastard,' Edgerton replied.

Chapter 54

Knightsbridge

'Christmas is too expensive,' two shoppers were muttering to each other outside Harrods as David and Lizzy walked arm in arm, catching up on some timely Christmas shopping.

Knightsbridge, London was a wonderful spectacle as a white blanket of snow covered the capital after a week of heavy snowfall. The trees were coated in frosty snow and the smell of roasted nuts and mulled wine from the stalls added to the seasonal atmosphere. The speedy pace of London was slowly coming to a standstill as cars struggled to navigate the snow-covered roads and pedestrians were forced to walk at a snail's pace.

The country was in a recession, but there was no visible sign of it in this part of London. Knightsbridge was packed with shoppers, prepared to part with their well-earned readies. A procession of extravagant cars lined Brompton Road – Bentleys, Rolls-Royces and an Aston Martins, to name but a few.

Last year, the Christmas shopping was left to the eleventh hour, but Lizzy and Dave had made a conscious effort this time to be organised. After all, it was going to be a hectic year for them both.

'I wonder what your mother would like this Christmas?' David said.

'I'm not sure,' Lizzy replied. 'She seems to have everything.'

'I've been thinking for a while we should go to Harrods and buy her some perfume.'

'She'd like that, and a nice piece of jewellery?'

'Perhaps some Chanel No 5. She would adore it, especially when she goes away.'

'I'm so jealous, filled with envy,' said Lizzy, giggling. 'I've never been on the Orient Express.'

David had lost his parents at a young age, and Lizzy's mum and dad were his adopted parents. He adored them, but had an especially great fondness for Lizzy's mother, Adrienne, the wife of John Kinlan a, self-made multi-millionaire. John had made his money in shipping and now lived in the stockbroker belt of London, Virginia Water on the Wentworth Estate, home to some of the wealthiest people in the city. He often played golf with him on the West Course at Wentworth and Sunningdale, John's main club.

'Well, Lizzy, if you are so desperate to go on the train, then perhaps that is how we should spend our honeymoon.'

'David! I want sun and lots of it.'

David looked at her and they embraced – they were a happy couple, both working in London as successful stockbrokers. Lizzy had recently been promoted within her company, and the couple's lives were hectic as they prepared for a move to New York, which was part of the deal – one she could not refuse. David had applied for another job with a rival bank, and it was going to be exciting times – brand new life, new city, fresh adventures.

However, David was going to miss their three-bedroom flat in the fashionable part of Notting Hill. He had fallen in love with this part of London after watching the film so simply named after this little gem in the borough of Kensington and Chelsea.

Lizzy, with her flaming red hair, eccentric dress sense and little round glasses felt at home there. She often browsed through the second-hand bookshops and loved the vibrant social life associated with the place. Mixing in the cafés with writers, playwrights and the odd rock star complemented her lifestyle.

She still had an ambition to open a gallery to show her artwork, which had been given good reviews from local galleries. While David played golf, she would walk for hours and visit the London art galleries, lapping up the atmosphere of these temples of genius, her favourite being the National Art Gallery, where she would sit for hours staring contently at Van Gogh's Sunflowers. The naivety of his style fascinated her, and it fitted in with her idea of how art should exhibit an exposition of bright colours that leapt out at you. This was therefore the decorative theme that ran through the home they both shared. It was a 24/7 life for David Lowsley and Lizzy Kinlan in Notting Hill, and the heart of Westbourne Grove in the Hill Villas was a dwelling any person would aspire to live in.

Before they made their short trip home, they entered the perfumery at Harrods arm in arm, where they were hit by the warmth and accompanying odour of all the different perfumes combined together to add to the feeling of opulence within this great hall.

As they dodged the salesgirls, they made their way to the counter and started to test the vast array of perfumes, eventually deciding on Chanel No 5 for her mother. Lizzy then indulged herself with a free manicure while David wandered off to the sports department. He refused to be dragged into having a manicure with her and had no intention of hanging around. Looking at the golf clothing and golf clubs was his idea of a good day's shopping. Perhaps he might find a present for Lizzy's father. He was in his element while testing new clubs in the golf net, and was so entrenched in his thoughts that he missed several calls from Lizzy, who had now finished.

Eventually, he answered his phone, and Lizzy said, 'What are you doing?'

'I'm in the golf net, my dear.'

'Okay, I'll see you up there. Then we must go home.'

Lizzy appeared and watched David at the golf net still hitting golf balls to his heart's content. She waited impatiently and then insisted they make their way to get a black cab to Notting Hill.

'Come on, I find this hitting a ball into a net thing a pointless exercise. You can't even see where the ball is going.'

Muttering under his breath, David said, 'Much better than having your nails filed!'

Lizzy turned and gave him a frosty look.

As they walked through the automatic revolving doors, they felt the bitter cold air hit them as the chilly wind continued to blow, picking up the snow in its wake.

David hailed a cab and they both jumped inside

hurriedly. The warmth of the radiator was so refreshing. It was time to get home, relax and have their evening meal. Relaxing in the cab, they huddled together – it would be a short trip, or so they thought. The traffic was still slow.

David said to the cabby, 'Can you turn up the radio please? Give us something to listen to while we're stuck here.'

'No problem. Is 5 Live okay? It's my favourite.'

David smiled. 'We have the same taste,' he said as he listened intently. 'Lizzy, it's Brian Beaumont. Do you remember we met him at the charity function at The Savoy?'

'Oh yes. What's he talking about?'

Beaumont was being interviewed about the ongoing public inquiry into allegations of corruption within the Labour government. He was being grilled, but stood his ground with the presenter.

'Look, this is not about one-upmanship. There's a clear line, good and bad, and the public has a right to know. I have been a tireless campaigner for this inquiry since resigning from my post as Chairman of the Select Committee.'

The presenter said, 'But with respect, Mr Beaumont, your Select Committee didn't prove a great deal. Will the public inquiry make any more progress?'

'It's been a while since that Committee finished and published its findings,' he snapped. 'A public inquiry has more scope, and there is new evidence which will be made available that wasn't there at the time, and it must be investigated. I still believe our hands were tied.'

'Mr Beaumont, will you be giving evidence?'

'Of course I will. I have told the Prime Minister I will. I have been accused in certain quarters, including the media, of playing party politics, but again, I must reiterate my stance. If MPs are indulging in corrupt activity from any party, and let me repeat any party, then they must be dealt with accordingly.'

'Did you always think there would be an inquiry?'

'Of course I did. The pressure from the public and the press was mounting – it was always a case of when, not if.'

The presenter continued. 'If you get an outcome, of course, your party will bear the fruit, won't they, Mr Beaumont, and possibly you as well? After all, there are rumours you have aspirations to be a future leader of the Tory party, if not a future prime minister. Am I barking up the right tree, Mr Beaumont?'

'Look! What happens will happen. First things first, let us get this inquiry completed and restore some trust – that is my main goal.'

'Thanks for your time, Mr Beaumont.'

And the interview ended.

David looked at Lizzy. 'I like Beaumont; he's like a dog with a bone. He'd get my vote if he was the leader.' Lizzy wasn't into politics – she didn't even vote. David was met with a wall of silence.

At around 7 p.m. the cab arrived at Westbourne Grove, the snow still falling heavily.

Hill Villas was an old building from the Edwardian period that had recently been converted into luxury apartments. David and Lizzy had bought the penthouse flat with a spectacular roof garden, which had a panoramic view of London. They had never experienced a London summer in their new flat, but might just get one chance before they left for New York; they longed for those hot summer nights on the rooftop. Lizzy already had ideas for themed parties, barbeques and perhaps some lingerie parties with her female friends. She was a social animal – unlike David, who was an introvert.

Around 10.30 p.m., after a light spaghetti bolognese, the couple relaxed on the settee and watched a nice film – Return of the Pink Panther. The day's shopping had taken its toll and they were ready for an early night.

David went upstairs to get ready for bed, and Lizzy turned the lights off. While completing her usual ritual of turning on the dishwasher and shutting the blinds, she heard a noise outside that stopped her in her tracks. She shouted up to David.

'David, can you hear a noise outside?'

'Hang on,' he replied.

Checking the front bedroom window, he then shouted down to Lizzy.

'It's the car alarm. Can you turn it off please? I'm in my boxer shorts.'

David ran to the top of the stairs and threw the keys to Lizzy as she slipped on her overcoat and slippers.

After leaving the apartment she couldn't be bothered waiting for the lift, so she walked down the three flights of stairs to the main entrance onto Westbourne Grove where their White Range Rover Sport was parked in the street. As she opened the front door, the arctic wind cut right through her. As she approached the car, indicator lights flashing through the falling snow, she tried to speed up, but to no avail since it was so icy. With cold hands, she fumbled with the remote control, and after several attempts to push the buttons, the alarm turned off. After pressing the remote button once again to reset the alarm, the car lights flashed and alerted her to a moving shadow in the background. As she turned around she saw a dark figure hiding in the forecourt of a basement flat next to the Villas.

All she could see was an outline, but as she got closer she saw that the figure was dressed in black with a hoody. Her suspicions were aroused immediately.

'What the hell are you doing there?' she asked.

There was no response, but the figure moved away from the basement steps and slowly approached her.

Lizzy said again in a more desperate tone, 'What are you doing?'

There was a stony silence. Anton Zonov continued towards her, his face hidden by the darkness of the night and the fog caused by his heavy breathing in the cold air.

Without warning, Lizzy was set upon with such speed that she didn't even have time to shout. She felt a punch to the back of her head, which knocked her down, throwing the keys from her hand to the floor as she let out an ear-piercing scream. Another blow was delivered to her stomach, which winded her, rendering her helpless. As she doubled up, she felt another blow, which landed heavily on her back – a powerful punching sensation, followed by excruciating pain, sent Lizzy into a state of utter panic. She felt a deep burning sensation in her midriff followed by a feeling of fear.

This unprovoked attack was quick, ferocious and delivered so quickly and skilfully that she never had a chance. Then a lull. The attack had ceased, or so she thought.

Still in a semi-conscious state, she heard the car

alarm bleep and was then thrown into the rear of the Range Rover by her assailant. Her eyes stinging, she tried to wipe them with her bloody hands. She now lay on her back, motionless, breathless and in a state of confusion, and thought only of escape.

The interior light inside the car was shining as she struggled to catch every breath. Now fully aware of her precarious situation, Lizzy thought of David and let out a screech. The car door suddenly slammed shut and she felt her attacker straddled over her. With heavy breathing and sweat droplets hitting her face, a sudden feeling of hysteria came over her as she tried to struggle free. In this time of need David was so far away. The situation she found herself in was hopeless. She was overcome by this person's strength and in one sudden movement, she felt another deep punch to her chest and then a wrenching feeling from within. Still struggling to breathe, her life was fading rapidly as the assault continued.

No words, no threats, no insults were uttered by this hooded monster. Anton Zonov was in full swing, and not for the first time.

Lizzy Kinlan lay still, covered in blood, eyes wide open … lifeless.

David was still upstairs, oblivious to what had taken place, and shouted down to Lizzy.

'Lizzy, are you done?'

He was greeted with a stony silence, but thought nothing of it. He prepared to shave and turned on the radio – his favourite, Classic FM.

The only visible signs of any crime were the blood splatters on the snow, which slowly faded as the flakes started to fall. The huge figure of Zonov again appeared from hiding, having waited in the dark shadows. No one was in the vicinity, and it was quiet. It was time to check the car and retrieve a can of petrol he had noticed earlier in the rear seat. Clicking the remote, the car was now secure.

From nowhere an elderly lady came into view, walking her poodle towards the hooded figure next to the Range Rover holding a set of keys, and as she approached, Zonov paused.

'Hello, how are you? It's a cold night, isn't it?'

A muffled reply came from under the hood. 'It is, have a good night.'

The woman continued to walk her dog.

Now free to make his next move, Zonov approached the entrance to Hill Villas and crept up the stairs to avert attention, eventually arriving at David and Lizzy's apartment.

The house key on the fob was inserted deliberately and methodically into the lock and turned until the lock clicked. Zonov then pushed open the door with his gloved hands and placed the petrol can on the floor.

Now that he was in the flat, he could see that there was a hall light illuminated, which he quickly extinguished. In the darkness, there was a hint of light from upstairs and the sound of running water, and the classic Elgar coming from the radio in the bathroom.

The radio then went quiet and the running water ceased.

David finished shaving and rinsed his face. He heard the creaking footsteps and assumed it was Lizzy back in the house.

'Thanks for that,' he shouted, still wiping his face. 'Finished in the bathroom now, my dear.'

Placing the towel over the bath, he opened the door and was confronted by the killer holding a knife. David lunged at Zonov, and a violent struggled ensued. David was a golfer and a talented sportsman. Six foot and of athletic build, he would be a match for anyone and to overcome him would be difficult.

In the struggle, the knife fell to the floor and they both wrestled, knocking over ornaments on a set of drawers with their flaying legs. The hood came away, and the violent struggle continued, with punches being exchanged. David grabbed an ornament and managed to hit the intruder in the face. Blood appeared on the carpet – the blow had wounded his attacker. The brawl continued as both men tried to reach for the knife that lay on the floor.

The wound angered Zonov, and he managed momentarily to get the better of David and get him in a neck hold. David struggled to breathe as the crushing sensation on his windpipe became stronger and stronger. His eyes bulging, he was losing the battle for life. As he continued to fight for every breath, the knife was now in the hands of this cold-blooded killer.

In a matter of seconds, the bladed weapon rained down on his head and neck. One, two, one, two, one, two… Now that David was in no position to fight back, Zonov withdrew the shiny blade and diverted his attention to the chest area, where he delivered one final stab wound with a twist, which penetrated deep into his victim's heart at such speed that David's death was instantaneous.

It was time to clean the scene – no trace could be left. With four murders in the space of a few days, the police wouldn't be far behind. Zonov ran to get the petrol can and soak the scene. He did this in a clinical fashion.

With the door ajar, he threw a flaming rag inside and then the door was swiftly closed. The flat was quickly engulfed in flames. This time the fire took hold quickly and the area was soon cloaked with flames.

After exiting the flat and still panting, Zonov approached the car and unlocked it. Lizzy's dead body lay in the back like a mannequin. The keys were thrown inside, and the contents of the petrol can emptied onto the seats. He then threw the empty petrol can inside, followed by an ignited match, and the car was ablaze. The suspect fled from Hill Villas along Westbourne Grove and then turned back. The darkness of the night was illuminated by a red flame burning, and the noise of house alarms was deafening.

Mission accomplished – no remorse, no going back.

Chapter 55

Soho

Robert Bamford stood on the street corner – a dark place in the heart of Soho – with his large hat placed firmly over his head. He slowly pulled a cigarette from his pocket and waited. Eventually, he heard the familiar sound of stilettos on the concrete pavement approaching. The working girl, wearing a long overcoat, stopped.

'You want business at your place tonight?'

Bamford replied, 'No, I want it here. I want it now.' He opened his wallet, full to the brim with clean crisp fifty-pound notes.

He disappeared into the dark alley with the girl, careful to keep his anonymity. After his brief liaison – a habit that had now taken over the politician's life – he would again return to Beak Street and drink heavily. The whisky would numb the pain he felt, and the night would be long...

When he woke, still fully clothed, the phone rang.

Still half-asleep, Bamford said, 'Hello, who is it?'

'Good evening, Foreign Secretary, this is Detective Chief Inspector Jack Edgerton from the Murder Squad.'

Bamford sounded surprised. 'What can I do for you, Chief Inspector?'

'Can I speak to you about an ongoing investigation into the attempted murder of Patrick Sands?'

Bamford's mood changed dramatically. 'What the hell are you talking about?'

Edgerton had dealt with high-profile suspects before and wouldn't be deterred.

He hit back. 'I need to speak with you, that's all.'

'Are you arresting me, Chief Inspector?'

'No. But if you force my hand, I will.'

'I will bring a solicitor. Where can I see you?'

'Tomorrow, about 11 a.m. at Charing Cross Police Station, if that's convenient?'

Bamford replied with a hint of sarcasm in his tone, 'I'll see you there.'

Edgerton was shattered and needed an early night. It would be a busy day as he continued to look at the evidence gathered from the Kensington murder scene. Still at work at such a late hour, he decided to sleep over at the station. He couldn't face the trip to Primrose Hill and all the messing around. It was fortunate that he regularly kept spare clothes at the station along with a camp bed for such occasions. He could invariably watch TV before he slept and prepare himself for the next day. As he settled down, he lay still and listened to the sirens blaring away in the background and vehicles passing beneath his office window. It didn't stop him dosing off into a deep sleep with the TV still on.

When Edgerton woke, he felt rather refreshed. Known not be the greatest sleeper, he often boasted that he needed less sleep than the Right Honourable

Margaret Thatcher. He made a grab for his phone, still on charge, and as he turned it on he was surprised to see no messages or missed calls. It was a relief, as he had a busy day ahead. Before he even had chance to dress properly he heard shuffling from the incident room, and he opened the door.

Chief Superintendent Watkins entered.

'Morning, Guv,' Edgerton quipped, rubbing his eyes.

'Have you slept here?'

'Yes,' he replied, and as he looked at his desk to arrange the files, the fax machine bleeped. It was the report completed by Dr Julian Wallace.

'Like a brew, Jack?'

'Yes, please,' he said as he waited patiently for the fax to feed out the full report.

Edgerton handed him the report and the files from 'the Barber' murders.

'What are these?'

'The medical reports on the Labelle murder and 'the Barber' murders. I'm getting ready, Guv. Have a close look, in particular at the causes of death, and tell me what you think when I get back.'

Watkins' interest was suddenly aroused as he sat at Jack's desk with the thick crumpled files.

Edgerton returned while Watkins continued to read and looked through the daily log on his computer.

'Is there anything interesting on the log?'

Edgerton paused. 'No, it's been relatively quiet. Just a serious fire in Notting Hill. The Fire Brigade are still fighting it. I'll keep an eye on that one.'

Watkins didn't reply as he continued to read the files. Edgerton noticed that his attention was drawn to the autopsy reports. He was intrigued.

'Well, what do you think, Guv?'

'There's a connection. The causes of death are all the same. I'm concerned that the method has changed in that no hair was taken in Kensington, but with the time gap, perhaps the lunatic now has another fetish. Am I right in thinking that no DNA has ever been recovered?'

'No, nothing at any of the scenes. Perhaps he's just been released from prison and started up again. If that is the case, and he slips up, we'll get him. You know who might be a good man to get on-board?'

'Go on, run it by me.'

Edgerton knew there was a history of some sort between the two men, but went for it anyway.

'PC Smithers from Carter Street Police Station. He was on the Camberwell Grove murder and knows the case.'

Watkins looked at Edgerton and frowned. 'I can't stand that man, Jack, and he's trouble.'

Edgerton defended Smithers. 'I know, but I don't think you treated him well. He's a good cop, and I know you can't deny that.'

Watkins must have been in a good mood. 'I'll leave it with you, but warn him not to fuck about with me again, or he'll be out on his arse.'

Edgerton entered the incident room where all the officers were working on their particular tasks. The phone rang in the main office and Chloe Moran answered it. Edgerton could tell by her reaction that something was wrong.

When she placed the phone down, he said, 'Go on, give me the news.'

'That was the control room at Notting Hill.'

The penny dropped. Edgerton knew what she was about to say.

Chloe gave him the news. 'The Fire Brigade has only just made the house safe in Notting Hill and entered with the local cops. It was a bad fire, and they've found two bodies. One in a car parked outside and one inside the house. That's all they have at the moment.'

Edgerton said, 'Right, guys, keep me up to speed. I'll see Watkins. I think our friend's at it again.' He paused. 'How come they didn't spot the body in the car straight away?'

'It sounds like the place is gutted,' Chloe replied.

Edgerton approached Watkins, and just as he prepared to tell him the news, Watkins interrupted.

'Yes, Jack, I just had a call on my mobile and I heard you in the office. We need to be kept fully informed, and when we get any further information, we can go to the scene.'

'Can you hold the fort?' Edgerton asked him. 'I have to see the Foreign Secretary at 11 a.m.'

Watkins grinned. 'That should be interesting. I'll look forward to hearing his response.'

'I'll go to Charing Cross nick and see the boys, and can you keep me posted? I can always check the log while I'm there.'

Watkins pointed to the door and replied, 'Go, Jack, everything will be fine.'

As Edgerton's back was turned, Watkins gave a smile of appreciation in his direction. He really valued his presence; he could not have had a better detective on his payroll.

Chapter 56

Edgerton started the walk alone to Charing Cross Police Station, knowing he would get there well before his 11 a.m. meeting with the Foreign Secretary. It would give him time to mull over the last few days and consider what lay ahead. He couldn't help but think that the Notting Hill fire would link up, and he was now faced with a challenge.

He decided to phone ahead and speak to DS Bill Wynyard at the station.

'Hi, Bill, it's Jack Edgerton. I'm on my way to see Bamford at 11 a.m.'

'Is it okay if I sit in?' DS Wynyard asked.

Edgerton was obliging and replied, 'Of course, but I have to see him at eleven. Its hectic here and there's been another incident in Notting Hill this morning.'

'Oh yes, I heard about that.'

It was only 9 a.m., so Edgerton thought he would relax in the National Art Gallery in Trafalgar Square. He decided he would sit on the bench and face John Constable's 'The Hay Wain' and make notes before he interviewed Robert Bamford. He couldn't think of a quieter spot at that time in the morning. It wasn't the first time he had visited the gallery, and it wouldn't be the last.

He had seen the painting before, and as he sat down opposite, the sheer size of it astonished him, the detail almost photographic in its finish. He longed to touch it and check out its smooth brushstrokes.

The security guard at the gallery, a retired police officer, recognised Edgerton as he scribbled on his pad.

'Good morning, Jack. Preparing for another case?'

Edgerton greeted him as if he did not know him, and the guard, a little confused, said, 'You don't recognise me?'

Edgerton apologised. 'I'm sorry, it must be old age.'

'Jack Croft, ex-Flying Squad.'

'Bloody hell, you old bastard, you look different in a uniform! I've never seen you look so neat and tidy.'

'See you've kept your humour. It's great to see you again.'

Both men shook hands vigorously.

Croft knew as an ex-police officer that Jack must have a lot on his plate.

Robert Bamford had decided not to bother with a solicitor and walked the short distance from his home in Beak Street to Charing Cross Police Station. Again, he would wear his hat to avoid being recognised by the public. Just like his enemy, Brian Beaumont, he had now become a well-known name for all the wrong reasons, but unlike Beaumont, who generally received adulation from the public, Bamford had become public enemy number one, and with the latest developments, it didn't look as though things were going to get any easier.

Edgerton waited for the Foreign Secretary and soon introduced himself to the politician.

'Pleased to meet you, Mr Bamford.'

'Good morning, Chief Inspector.'

Edgerton's manner was formal as he escorted Bamford through to an interview room and waited for DS Wynyard to join him.

Bamford was on the defensive immediately.

'Detective Chief Inspector, I haven't got a clue what this is all about, I really don't.'

Edgerton watched Bamford's body language closely and noticed he was sweating profusely.

As Detective Sergeant Wynyard entered the room, Edgerton began to question Bamford.

'Foreign Secretary, I'm investigating the attempted murder of Patrick Sands in London on 10th December 2011. Do you know anything?'

'I don't. Who is Patrick Sands?'

'He is a good friend of the Shadow Home Secretary.'

'Of course, I know Brian Beaumont, but I've never heard of a Patrick Sands.'

'Do you have an alibi for the date in question?'

'I'm sure I have. I'll get my secretary to check the diary and provide you with all the details.'

Edgerton read the papers and looked at the anonymous email sent, but decided not to disclose the information until a later date.

Bamford looked at Edgerton and said, 'Where is this leading, Officer?'

'On the day the public inquiry was announced did you threaten Mr Beaumont in the toilets?'

'I deny this. Brian Beaumont is attempting to ruin me. I may have had words, but have never threatened the man.'

'You do have a lot to lose, with the inquiry looming.'

Bamford was in a defiant mood. 'Mr Edgerton, sorry,

Chief Inspector, do you think I would try to kill a politician's friend to get back at him? This is preposterous.'

'Mr Sands is a well-known investigative journalist, and you have not heard of him?'

Bamford was becoming increasingly irritated with Edgerton's line of questioning.

'If you have any evidence, and I doubt you have, I ask you to arrest me now.'

Edgerton remained calm. 'I have no intention of arresting you. I am simply investigating a serious matter and need to speak to witnesses. If you wish to leave, then you may do so. I merely seek your cooperation on the matter, that's all.'

There was a pause, and DS Wynyard was clearly becoming increasingly uncomfortable sitting in front of the Foreign Secretary.

'Look here,' Bamford said, 'I will provide you with my alibi, and it's sound. What do I think of Brian Beaumont? I hate the bastard more than anyone, but that does not make me a killer, and I hope you're not looking at me because of the press speculation about my private life. There are a lot of rumours out there, and mistruths. Now, if you have finished, Detective, I'm a busy man and need to get back to Westminster, unless you have any other silly questions.'

Edgerton stared into Robert Bamford's eyes. 'Thank you for your time. If you can provide me with your alibi that would be great, and if I need to speak to you again I will contact you.'

He went to shake his hand, but Bamford refused and started to leave the room.

'One last thing, Mr Bamford, I have a picture to

show you.'

Edgerton showed him the picture he had taken at the murder scene in Kensington.

'That is you, Mr Bamford, at some sort of function with a couple. See them?'

He pointed to the Labelles.

'I go to many charity functions and have photographs taken with people, Detective.'

Edgerton smiled. 'But they don't all end up in a casket six feet under after being murdered, do they, Mr Bamford?'

'The next time we speak, I will have a solicitor present.'

The officers looked at each other.

'Strange man. We may have to revisit him another time,' Wynyard said.

Chapter 57

Beaumont checked his phone, and saw that it was inundated with messages.

There had been developments in Notting Hill, so Edgerton went straight up to the CID office to check the log. His fears were confirmed as he slowly read through it. It was one of the longest he had seen, and he scrolled and scrolled until he arrived at the last page.

Detective Chief Superintendent Watkins arrived at scene and liaised with FIU. Two bodies are still in situ at the scene of fire. One in a burnt-out Range Rover and one in the house.

Coroner informed. ERU is on the scene liaising with SIO and DI Palmer. Fire at this moment in time extinguished and scene is safe. Extensive damage to the interior of building and, after inspection, the Fire Brigade has confirmed it is now safe to search.

Detective Inspector Palmer at the scene.

DC Moran at the scene.

Home Office Pathologist Dr Julian Wallace has arrived and is liaising with SIO Ch. Supt. Watkins.

TSG are now at the scene. They will carry out a detailed search of the garden and the surrounding area.

CID officers are conducting preliminary house-to-house enquiries.

CCTV footage seized – poor quality. In custody of DC Moran.

Short message from Chief Superintendent Watkins (SIO). The deaths are being treated as suspicious.

Press Office aware and have liaised with SIO.

Witness – Annette Barker just contacted the police by phone. She heard screaming coming from the scene before the blaze started while she was walking her dog. Details passed to DC Moran at the scene...

As he turned around, DC Jones was standing over his shoulder.

'Looks like this killer is on a roll.'

Edgerton looked drained. He had to return to the office.

As he started to stroll, he attempted to text his old colleague PC Smithers since he hadn't heard a thing, but it was way too cold. The snow continued to fall and blow horizontally right into his face. It felt like he was being peppered by pellets, such was the force of the wind. It was an opportune time to take shelter, so he entered the little café at the side of St Martin-in-the-Fields Church, which overlooked Trafalgar Square. The feeling of the warm air on his icy face was indeed refreshing for the detective. His hands now warm, he sent a text and contacted Patrick Sands to update him.

Sands answered the phone.

'It's Jack Edgerton, Patrick. I've just interviewed Robert Bamford.'

'Oh! And what did he say?'

'He denied any involvement and denied threats ever being made. I'm just keeping you up to speed.'

Sands appeared almost disinterested in the update.

'We are still looking at it, but there isn't a lot to go on at the moment.' Edgerton sensed Sands' disinterest. 'If you hear anything, please contact me, and the same with Mr Beaumont. I presume you will inform him of our conversation?'

'Of course I will.'

The phone line disconnected.

Edgerton knew he was being hoodwinked by Sands. He started to get a feeling... It would come every now and again, and would eventually lead to a development. It made him uneasy; something wasn't right.

He once told Chloe Moran, 'These feelings come every blue moon. Why? No one will ever know. I think some detectives are born with a sixth sense, and when it happens, you must embrace that feeling and follow your instincts. The rest will follow...'

Edgerton would only ever share such a profound statement with those he considered close. Great detectives were few and far between, and his ambition was to create an elite squad.

The phone rang; it was Watkins. The picture that appeared on his display had now been changed to that of Watkins himself, which was evidence that over the last few weeks Edgerton was mellowing and indeed starting to admire his superior.

'Good morning, sir.'

'Hi, Jack. How did you go on with Robert Bamford?'

'I drew a blank.'

'That doesn't surprise me. If you are coming back now we're going to have a meeting about the Notting Hill job, just to bring you up to speed. I know you'd normally like to visit the scene, but it's a state and all the groundwork's been completed. The photographs are all up and ready.'

Edgerton agreed. 'I can give this scene a miss, I think. I appreciate the help, Guv. I'll be fifteen minutes. When is the PM?'

'The bodies are still in situ, because of the state after the fire. I've liaised with Dr Wallace, and he'll be at the scene and supervise the recovery of the bodies. The PM might be tomorrow. Are you up for that?'

Edgerton laughed nervously. 'Oh yes, I love 'em, Guv. See you later.'

He sat and finished his piping-hot tomato soup. He wasn't relishing the thought of walking through the cold air, but he braced himself.

Chapter 58

Murder Incident Room

The officers prepared for the arrival of Detective Chief Inspector Edgerton. Chief Superintendent Watkins scoured the main office, checking that the HOLMES computers were all up to date and the office was tidy. He too was meticulous, and today they had a special visitor. The case was being closely followed by the press and speculation was rife. Managing the press wasn't easy at the best of times, but the responsibility had been passed to Deputy Commissioner Roger Evans, who needed to speak to the officers.

Watkins checked the Perspex boards all meticulously prepared with more crime scene photographs and those of the victims, their personal details written neatly in capital letters. The photographs were a necessity, but now depicted two hideous murder scenes.

The officers took their place and waited for Chief Superintendent Watkins, DCI Edgerton and the Deputy Commissioner.

Dr Julian Wallace was used to these meetings and sat beside Chloe Moran, who was somewhat nervous.

Fred Constance sat back as though he didn't have a care in the world as he twiddled his handlebar moustache, but he was an excellent investigator and one of the best in the business when it came to combing a crime scene. The senior officer heading the Fire Investigation Unit sat alone in the corner. It would be his first meeting with the Murder Squad officers, and Jonathon Bellsden was relishing the challenge that lay ahead. After all, he had shot up through the ranks since joining the service in the early 1980s.

Chloe Moran looked through her file and checked all the reports. She wanted to be prepared for any questions.

She then looked over to the office manager, DI Palmer, and said, 'Are we ready to set up the conference call with Joanne Wineford from the Metropolitan Police Forensic Science Laboratory?'

DI Palmer laughed. 'Yes, I think I've got the hang of it!'

There was suddenly a knock on the door and the entire office stood to attention. The trio finally entered the room, and all the officers sat down.

Roger Evans headed proceedings. 'Good morning, ladies and gents, I think you know me. We'll keep this informal and recap on what's happening and what we are getting in at the moment. I'll leave most of the talking to Jack and Robert, but I'll be dealing with the press. I will be doing a press conference later on, and as you are probably aware, most of the crime correspondents have made a link, just as some of us have. I'm not confirming a link as yet until we are certain, and I know Jack has his reservations. I suspect they've all been working overtime with their various sources, but we must treat their views as mere speculation. We run the show here. Okay, Jack, away you go.'

Edgerton stood up and started to stroll around the room.

'Firstly, I can tell you with both these murders we have very little at this time. I will attend the post mortem tomorrow in relation to the murder of David Lowsley and Lizzy Kinlan.' He pointed to the board. 'We have two murders in affluent areas with no apparent motive, and as it stands, no fingerprints, no CCTV and no witnesses. All the victims have been stabbed, and the cause of death is indeed identical to 'the Barber' murders, and a pattern has been established. The fact that the aorta was severed in every case concerns me, but it doesn't prove a definite link with the previous murders in Mayfair and Camberwell Grove. We may have a copycat killer putting us on the wrong track and playing games.'

Watkins nodded. 'I agree, this is a complex one. Of course, we will have to wait for the result of the PM on David and Lizzy.'

Dr Wallace looked closely at his reports. 'If I may?'

'Go for it,' Edgerton said.

'I think it unusual that the aorta was severed on every occasion. It's not something I have come across before, and if there is a copycat killer, how would they know about the other murders? These details were never leaked to the public, unless a police officer or someone who had access to the information is involved in some way.'

Detective Inspector Palmer said, 'I think this is where we are at the moment, until we get further information.'

All the participants agreed.

Detective Chief Inspector Edgerton looked over at Chloe Moran and smiled.

'Chloe, can you update us?'

Chloe took a deep breath. 'None of the searches at the scene have yielded any new information, and the squad is still engaged in house-to-house enquiries and statement taking. None of the victims appeared to have any enemies, and this is where it becomes a little cloudy.' She paused. 'There are no signs of a break-in and the attacks have been carried out by a male of large build. The wounds on the victims at the Kensington scene are extensive, and the murder weapon is a sizeable knife; we think a large kitchen knife. I'm sorry I cannot give you any more at the moment.'

Robert Watkins shouted, 'Thanks, Chloe,' and looked at the phone.

'Hello, Joanne, can you hear me?'

Joanne Wineford replied, 'Yes, hello to you all. Go ahead.'

'Have you any news on the forensic side?' Watkins asked.

'We have no real news. The fingerprints are negative, and the blood at the scene matches the victims, so we must wait for the second scene. However, I understand the evidence has been destroyed by a fire in Notting Hill. We have found some fibres at the first scene and we're still working on that side of things. I must warn you that the scene at Notting Hill will yield very little due to the fire damage.'

Fred Constance said, 'I echo your thoughts.'

Jack Edgerton had now loosened his tie and was chomping on a custard cream. He held up the picture and showed it around the office.

'See this?'

Everybody looked puzzled.

'I found this at the Kensington scene. Of the Labelles and Robert Bamford at a function; you might think so what? I have a hunch about Bamford, as I'm dealing with another matter involving a Patrick Sands who was nearly killed the other week in Covent Garden by a stolen car, and he is a close friend of Brian Beaumont. Note there is an inquiry coming up, and they are enemies. It's just a hunch, that's all.'

The Deputy Commissioner said, 'I agree. We must look at all angles.'

Jonathon Bellsden held his hand up.

'As you know, the culprit tried to torch both scenes and was successful on the last murder in Notting Hill. Petrol was used on both occasions, but we have no container. We of course will work with you if there are any further developments. It's not always easy to torch a place, and I am optimistic he will make a mistake. Keep patient.'

'Thanks for the input,' Edgerton said, 'and thank you, Deputy Commissioner. Let's keep interviewing any witnesses and pray he doesn't strike again.'

He stood at the window as the meeting came to an end, hoping for a break in the case. As he pondered, Zonov was sitting at his desk reading the newspaper's headlines.

Serial killer strikes for second time in Notting Hill

Zonov laughed and said to himself, 'Take the bait.'

Chapter 59

'As I stand here outside the Royal Courts of Justice, I can sense an atmosphere of anticipation. If you look around as the camera turns, this inquiry has captured the imagination of many. That's why we see the scaffold being erected for the various news channels from around the globe that will be following this event.

Lord Justice Rameau will head the inquiry, and it is a politically sensitive area for the governments that, one might say, are in the middle of a crisis. At some point, Brian Beaumont will give evidence, and that will no doubt be one of the highlights. After all, the Shadow Home Secretary has been instrumental in the setting up of this inquiry. His evidence will be absorbing, and there is speculation that he may produce a smoking gun. This would be catastrophic for the government, so it will certainly be an entertaining and pivotal moment in politics.'

Andrei Loktev watched the evening news with interest as he donned his coat. The first part of the plan had gone well, and he needed to speak to Zonov and the contact. As the inquiry approached, tensions were high. They could not allow it to take place, and no mistakes would be tolerated by the Russians. Loktev, however, was still concerned about Robert Bamford, who had proved to be a thorn in their side. Loktev had a plan he would share with none of his colluders.

Loktev left the Embassy and drove to Shepherds Bush, where he would make a call from within the sanctity of Shepherds Bush Green to the contacts. His first task was to leave a message via text for Anton Zonov.

Go to a safe place and call X.

As soon as Zonov received the text, he made his way to Hampstead Heath and called Loktev. His first priority was the money; it always was. After all, he was a paid assassin, and it was his livelihood.

'Is the money in place?'

Loktev replied, 'It is all okay, don't worry. I have read the news, although it's a little short on detail. I see that you saw my man on the inside. They seem to think the murders are connected after all.'

'Yes, that's a plus, but on the negative side, the fire didn't take hold in Kensington.'

'I have spoken to him since your conversation and he told me they don't have a great deal of evidence, so there isn't a problem. You mustn't fuck up again, Anton.'

Zonov was relieved. Loktev then gave the final order.

'The inquiry is imminent. Get rid of Beaumont and his wife quickly, and then Patrick Sands. If there is anything else that gets in the way, clean up. We can't have any trails. Check your account tonight. An instalment is on its way. I'm meeting the contact at Shepherds Bush Green very soon regarding the concluding stage. That will be our last meeting.'

Loktev had grown to mistrust Zonov and the feeling

was entirely mutual. Once Zonov returned to his flat, he would make his way to Shepherds Bush and join Loktev.

He left his flat immediately, opened his lockup and prepared his Suzuki Hayabusa motorbike. He had to get to the meeting place quickly and watch Loktev. He wanted a hold over the contact, and he needed to see them meet at Shepherds Bush Green. He could then follow.

He left Hampstead Heath and negotiated the roads with such difficulty that he turned around and abandoned the bike close to his flat. It would be easier to get a cab.

He phoned Loktev again and asked him if he had met the contact. He was still waiting at the Green, so Zonov made his way there, asking to be dropped off at Shepherds Bush Empire. He could then scour the vicinity with his binoculars. He saw Loktev waiting patiently on a park bench and noticed a black Mercedes pull up, but it was obscured by a large oak tree covered in snow.

Zonov, usually the cold-blooded killer, became nervous. This would probably be his last chance to find out who was organising these elaborate hits. The person must have been so desperate. He manoeuvred his way around the trees and tried to get the vehicle registration, but visibility was poor. He noticed that it was chauffeur driven and then suddenly, he saw the figure approach. He needed to follow the man back, but as he zoomed in with his binoculars, he got a good look at the man's face, which had previously been uncovered. Wearing a hat was insufficient disguise on this occasion.

Zonov's job was almost complete. He could relax now

because he recognised the man who was meeting Loktev and locating him would be uncomplicated. Loktev had to leave quickly to prepare for his final assignment.

Chapter 60

Beaumont Solicitors and Co.,
Regent Street, London

As the afternoon closed in, Isabel Beaumont sat at her desk contemplating life. She was concerned about her husband Brian, and Sands after the events that had taken place.

She placed her head in her hands and muttered, 'How am I going to get away on time?' The desk was piled high with outstanding legal cases for review, and she needed to get home quickly tonight. After all, she had a dinner party to prepare, and she couldn't be late. She looked up and snarled at her assistant, Anne.

'Can these cases wait, or are they urgent? I really need to get away tonight.'

'Please don't worry, they can wait until later in the week. There are a couple of case files which need tidying up, that's all.'

'Sorry for being so curt, I just feel rushed.'

Anne Franklin, stunningly beautiful and in her late thirties, was a bit of an entrepreneur and ran a cleaning business as well as working for Isabel. They were close, and she worried about Isabel taking on too much work.

'Chill out,' she said.

'I keep telling my husband if we're having dinner parties then to make it a weekend, not on a Monday night – it's sod's law that it will all go wrong if it's in the week. But as usual, he never listens, he just goes on and does his own thing; he's a stubborn old thing.'

Anne said in a sympathetic tone, 'I understand, but you know what men can be like.' She paused. 'I've not seen or spoken to Brian for a few weeks, is he well? The only time I see him now is on the television.'

'He is a typical MP, and now the cameras are in the house. They can't stay away.'

They both laughed loudly.

'To be honest, I'm a little worried about him – he's obsessed with the Rameau inquiry, and as it has progressed, he seems to have something on his mind all the time. It's so frustrating, and I want to help him.'

'He's not the worrying type, at least that is how he comes across to me.'

'I agree, but that's my concern,' replied Isabel.

'Don't worry, it will all be fine.'

'Yes, but he doesn't normally hide his feelings. Something's not right, and his friend was nearly killed by a car recently and I think it is all connected with this damned inquiry.'

'I'm a dummy when it comes to politics. He should see the police.'

'It's in hand. Anyway, stop me from being a misery and change the subject! Regarding the job here, I need to speak to you about doing more hours, if you still want them?'

'I'd rather not at the moment, with the cleaning business. It's so busy.'

Isabel was happy for Anne. 'It's not a problem,' she said, 'I was just wondering from your point of view, but I'm glad the cleaning has taken off as well. If it changes, and you do want more work, give me a shout.'

'Who's going to be at the party tonight?'

'I don't think you'd know anybody.'

Anne became increasingly excitable. 'I bet it'll be full of important people – what I would give to be a fly on the wall!'

'It will be a bore, the usual rhetoric, and I'll be in the kitchen cooking,' Isabel replied.

'But all parties take place in the kitchen; it's the place to be.'

'Not if I have my way,' Isabel replied, smiling.

'Is it couples, singles? A mixture? Maybe if I were to go, I could meet the man of my dreams – a sugar daddy perhaps!'

Isabel smiled as her inquisitive nature took hold.

'Are you available again?'

'Since the divorce I can't settle. I still have feelings for Jim, but I must move on.'

'Come to the party, I insist, and help me in the kitchen. After all, I am a novice when it comes to cooking.'

Sounding rather sad, Anne said, 'So you don't want me there for my scintillating company and banter?'

'Of course I do, stop feeling sorry for yourself. 'Isabel looked pensive. 'Let me think now, who's going tonight? Well, there are quite a few couples, and the odd bachelor – Paolo De Francesco.'

'Is he nice? It's a classy name.'

'He is, and he's an artist. Everybody says he looks like George Clooney.'

'Does he?'

'Yes, he does. He's very handsome.'

'Anyway you know what it's like, all the men ignore me to get to you, all of them falling at your feet.'

'Anne, stop exaggerating. I'm sure you're attractive to all men – you really feel sorry for yourself today, don't you?'

As she sat in the chair, she spun around and picked up a piece of blank paper. She looked hard at the embossed letterhead. It read: *Beaumont Solicitors and Co. Senior partner, Mrs Isabel Beaumont.* She sighed with a feeling of self-gratification. She was thinking it only seemed like yesterday that she had been living in a student flat in Moss Side before completing her law degree at Manchester University, and now she was running her own law firm. Her dream to be self-employed had turned into a reality. Her life had changed so quickly, and she was now in the fast lane.

As a young student she had had aspirations to go and work as an advisor to Amnesty International, but her life had taken a completely different path to the one she had mapped out for herself. Perhaps it was just fate, she thought.

She gazed at the old grandfather clock mounted high on the office wall. It was now 4.30 p.m. and was starting to go dusk. Isabel stood up and walked over to the window in her dimly lit office and looked out onto Regent Street towards Piccadilly. The traffic was moving slowly through the snow now that rush hour had arrived, and she could see the flashing multi-coloured advertising in the distant Piccadilly Circus casting their lights upon the busy street. It was a scene reminiscent of the old postcards she would send to her mum and dad when she visited London for weekends away while living in Manchester.

The sight of the bustling Regent Street made her feel anxious again; if she were to get home in Camden Town on time, then she would have to get to Piccadilly Underground quickly.

In a rushed tone, she said to Anne, 'Can you phone Brian for me on his mobile and just tell him I'm on my way home?'

'I will if I can get hold of him, he is the Scarlet Pimpernel.'

'Has everyone left now?'

'Yes.'

'I'm really going to have to shoot off now, so I would be grateful if you could lock up the office.'

'No problem; and I'll see you at the party.'

Isabel grabbed her bag from the desk and rushed towards the coat stand in the corner of the office. It was a cold night, so she quickly grabbed her knee-length overcoat and noticed a black woollen hat and matching cashmere scarf hanging up. She didn't recognise them, but it was so cold she thought they might come in handy.

As she walked out she showed the hat and scarf to Anne and said, 'Are these yours?'

'No; they probably belong to one of the girls in the office. Sometimes the cleaners put them there if they've been left behind.'

'Well, I'm borrowing them. I'll see you later.'

She wasted no time as she left the main reception and entered the communal hall leading out onto Regent Street, and immediately she could feel the chilly air rush into her throat as she took a deep breath. It was so cold she quickly donned the hat and scarf. As she walked into Regent Street, her phone rang. She looked at the display and saw it was the office number. It must be Anne phoning about Brian.

'Hi, did you get Brian?'

'Yes,' Anne said. 'He'll meet you at home later. He said he won't be far behind you.'

'Oh thanks, Anne, you're a star. What would I do without you?' Isabel smiled. 'I rather like this hat and scarf. I will have to find out where the owner bought them and will pay a visit to the shop. See you later.'

She ran her fingers over the thick black woollen scarf; it was just what she needed on this cold night.

Regent Road was packed with Christmas shoppers and there was a real atmosphere as Isabel walked towards Piccadilly Circus, the Christmas lights twinkling in the night sky. She looked up at them and smiled. She decided tonight she would catch the tube to Euston and then jump on the Northern Line to her destination, Camden Town. It was a short walk home, just under a mile from the station at Camden High Street. Isabel was relieved. The temperature had now dropped well below freezing, and as she approached Piccadilly Circus, she noticed the Statue of Eros had frozen. She thought how nice it looked against the backdrop of Piccadilly Circus; a real Christmas scene.

The tube would be busy tonight, and as she went down the escalator deep into the Underground, she gazed at the billboards as she passed them, one by one, thinking she might watch 'Chicago' at the theatre with Brian next week. They loved the theatre, but had never seen the production, and every time she passed the billboard advertising the show it niggled at her that they still hadn't seen it. Little did she know her husband had been on the lookout as well.

Eventually, she caught the tube and settled on the Northern Line, where she read her new book, 'North and South', but by the time she had read a few pages she was nearly at the station. The train was typically busy, as most of the passengers getting off at Camden would be checking out the late-night Christmas market or browsing through the many trendy clothing stores in the area.

It was a pleasant walk, which she enjoyed, especially in the snow. Eventually, she reached her house in Camden Square, an early Victorian stucco-fronted villa with a beautiful front garden, which she had tended every weekend until the snow arrived.

As she entered the house, it was quiet. She checked her phone to find a text from Brian:

Get the food started, darling, won't be long now xx.

Chapter 61

Camden Town

Isabel's mood soon changed – perhaps she was now ready to have friends round. The walk along the snow-covered streets of Camden and the bustling atmosphere revitalised her. Christmas was here, and she was glad to be seeing Brian again – in the last month, time together had been scarce, and she missed him dearly.

Her feelings were in stark contrast to those of Robert Bamford.

In the last few weeks the speculation had now taken its toll – dependent on anti-depressants, his whole demeanour had changed. Drinking heavily and suffering from bouts of paranoia, he had become isolated. His marriage was gradually breaking down, and he was becoming obsessed with the inquiry – his past was finally catching up with him, but there was no repentance as he continued to take money from the Archer Street brothel to inflate his already vast income. Bamford lived a life which required huge sums of money and it was filtering through his fingers as quickly as water from a tap. Notes strewn across his desk with childlike scrawls on them, the once proud man was living in near isolation – all his appetite for life had deserted him, and it was doubtful whether he would remain in his position as Foreign Secretary for much longer.

His once close allies had deserted him, and he was left in the wilderness. His parents had passed away and there was no longer a shoulder to cry on. As a young man he had had a close bond with his mother, and he could no longer go for walks with her alone as he did in his thirties, to ask for advice. This man had become a social pariah.

A simple press statement released by Charles Chillot's office read:

Robert Bamford is currently recuperating after a short illness and will soon be returning to his duties within the Foreign Office. While he is absent, the role of Foreign Minister will be carried out by his Junior Minister.

A copy of the statement lay on Bamford's desk, stained with tobacco and a whisky glass mark. It had been screwed up in a fit of anger, and he was struggling to cope with his inner feelings. A man who had everything continued to free fall and he was slowly losing his self-dignity, oblivious to the consequences of his actions. He laid the blame on others and was becoming increasingly aggressive towards those who sought to help him.

Chillot now regarded him as a lost cause – a liability even – and a danger to the future of the Labour party. His advisor continued to play off both sides against each other as he misunderstood where his loyalties lay. Only time would tell as to how Bamford tried to redeem himself. He had risen from the ashes on previous occasions.

A quote from a political commentator in previous years commented on him as a future leader and aspiring government figure.

A wounded Robert Bamford is a dangerous animal.

Only time would tell if the commentator had got it right.

As he sat in silence, slumped in his chair, the opposite was true for the Beaumont household as all the guests, now full of Christmas cheer, started to arrive. Isabel had no time to spare to prepare for them. It was an inconvenience, but it didn't matter. It was time to change, and she threw her coat, together with the borrowed hat and scarf, onto the coat stand at the entrance to their home in the huge Victorian hallway. Looking at her pristine Rolex Oyster, she realised she didn't have a great deal of time and again shook her head in disbelief at the thought of Brian organising a dinner party at a most inconvenient time.

Finally settled in the kitchen, she heard the door open and saw Brian arriving with a crate of wine.

'Hello, how are you coping?' Brian asked.

'Thanks to you I'm struggling, so I suggest you get changed and roll up your sleeves.'

Brian left the kitchen and whispered under his breath, 'Nice to see you, Brian.'

Isabel would cook a simple meal for her guests; after all, they were regular visitors. Perhaps they might end the night playing their favourite game, Jenga.

The smell of her stir fry sizzling in the huge wok slowly started to spread around the house, and it wasn't long before Brian came downstairs looking eloquent with his cravat tucked underneath his shirt.

'Mmmm, let me try it, test your cuisine.'

As he leaned over with his fork, Isabel prodded him and shouted, 'Out, now!'

'Have you had a bad day, my dear?'

'Not at all. Let me do the cooking, and you see to the guests and lay the table. They'll be arriving soon, and knowing Patrick, he'll be the first to get here. You'll start talking, and I'll end up doing everything. When Anne arrives, send her in. She agreed to help me.'

Brian scurried to the dining room and started to set the table. It would be a welcome break for him, his mind still occupied with the latest events and his recent announcement that he would soon be giving evidence to the public inquiry.

Isabel shouted to him to return to the kitchen and said, 'Open the window, it's like a sauna in here. At this rate I'll to have to change again.'

'Okay, my dear, anything else you would like me to do? After all, I am at your beck and call tonight.'

'Just make yourself useful. After all, this entire evening is your idea.'

'Where's the broom?' he muttered. 'I'll stick it up my arse and do some cleaning.'

He was sensible enough to speak such words at a safe distance. As he left the kitchen, he noticed the yellow post-it note with the list of guests. The heading read: BRIAN'S PARTY!!!

He laughed to himself. Was Isabel being sarcastic? He browsed the contents.

Patrick Sands
Tom and Gaynor Worthington
Ian and Victoria Pearce
Anne

Ian and Michelle Pascal
Paolo de Francesco
Tony Smythe-Higgins

All the names were written in Isabel's elegant handwriting.

As Isabel had predicted, Patrick Sands was the first to arrive. Brian answered the door.

'Hello, Brian. I'm looking forward to a stiff drink tonight.'

'I bet you are. How are you feeling now?'

'I'm a little sore, not sure about the crutches though.'

'Have you had any more contact with the police?'

'No, not really. What's going on with these murders? Bloody hell, there's nearly one a week now.'

'I know. Edgerton's investigating the two murders in Kensington and Notting Hill.'

Sands reached into his pocket. 'I've been thinking about things, and I have spoken to Roger Fischer about the security of this footage.'

He took a spare USB stick and his laptop out of his shoulder bag. 'Let me just copy the CCTV for you, and please keep it in your safe. To be honest, that's why I've brought the laptop tonight. After the break-in I daren't leave anything on-board. I'm sure someone is hanging around the boat. If the party finishes late I might stay over, if that's okay? I can do without battling through the snow in my condition.'

Beaumont took the USB stick, and when he returned to the room said, 'Anyway, what were we talking about? Yes, that's it. I've read about the two murders, and it's funny, I was asked by a reporter about this the other day. I get the usual questions about London and crime being out of control. They're all panicking that these murders are linked with the ones a few years ago.'

'The Barber' murders, very interesting indeed.'

'Have the police offered you protection?'

'Yes, they have. I refused.'

'I wonder if it's because I know you.'

Their conversation ended abruptly as Tom and his wife Gaynor entered.

'Hello, everybody,' Tom shouted.

It wasn't long before all the guests arrived and the dinner party started. As they all sat together in the room, Brian Beaumont introduced everyone. It would soon be time to relax as Isabel came in and took over proceedings, while Beaumont opened his favourite wine. Isabel carefully organised all the guests around the large dining table.

Patrick Sands sat close to the door, a sure sign that the bachelor would be called on at any time to go into the kitchen and collect any missed utensils. He sat next to Brian and Isabel whilst Tom and Gaynor Worthington sat on the other side. The friendly neighbours were always joking, and Tom, the charismatic architect, invariably liked to indulge others with his love of old buildings, especially Sands.

Ian and Victoria Pearce were both mathematics teachers and rather more serious characters, so Brian thought it appropriate to sit them next to Ian and Michelle Pascal. They were both QCs and had always got on with the Pearce family. Beaumont regularly commented that opposites attract.

Isabel was true to her word after her earlier conversation with secretary and friend Anne. She would be flanked by the other single men – Paolo De

Francesco, the good-looking artist, and the author, Tony Smythe-Higgins, who was recently widowed.

Anne seemed attracted to Paolo as soon as she set eyes on him – Isabel had warned her, perhaps a little perturbed by their age difference.

As the meal started, Anne was intrigued and asked Pascal, 'Ian, do you know Lord Justice Rameau?'

Michelle Pascal interrupted immediately. 'He has met him, but I know him well, although only as a young barrister. Why?'

'I was just wondering, that's all. I have a cleaning company and we clean his residence in Islington. I've only met him on the one occasion.'

'Rather you than me,' Michelle replied, and laughed.

'Oh dear, why?'

'I'll be diplomatic with my reply, as I've not seen him for years and our paths haven't crossed since his meteoric rise. I always found him strange, that's all. Just a woman thing; call it intuition.'

Anne shrugged her shoulders. 'Oh well.' She thought perhaps there was a touch of professional jealousy and tried to close the subject.

'But he is a first-class judge and has a good reputation,' Ian said.

Tom Worthington was now starting to enjoy the flowing wine and he looked at Patrick Sands. They had met on several occasions before.

'How are you, Patrick,' he asked, 'apart from your little brush with the car?'

Worthington had a dark sense of humour and Patrick appreciated him making light of the incident. He laughed and Beaumont joined in.

Isabel said, 'You cruel devil, Tom.'

341

'I'm fine,' Patrick replied. 'Are you still president of the Wagner Society?'

'I am,' Tom said. 'You must come to one of the meetings. You'd love it, and bring Brian along.'

'I will, don't worry.'

Patrick sat back, drinking his Sauvignon Blanc; he was getting quite tipsy.

Isabel jumped in. 'In your condition you can stay; I'm not letting you go home like that, especially with your injuries.'

'I surrender, I surrender.'

Beaumont lifted a Christmas cracker and said, 'Come on, let's pull the crackers, and Paulo, no cheating.'

De Francesco was enjoying the company. Anne couldn't keep her eyes off him. Everything Isabel had said was true; in fact, she thought he was better looking than George Clooney. She melted every time she looked at him.

The doorbell suddenly rang.

'Have we got a gatecrasher?' Beaumont said.

He looked through the peephole in the door and noticed a group of small boys and girls with two adults all dressed up in beautiful festive clothing.

He opened the door. 'What can I do for you then?'

A little angelic voice said, 'Can we carol sing, sir?'

Beaumont knelt down. 'Yes, my dear. Can you sing my favourite carol?'

'And what's that?'

'Silent Night, young lady.'

'Oh yes,' she replied.

'Good. I will leave the door open and my friends will all listen.' Beaumont ran back into the room and said, 'Quiet, listen!'

The young children started, their voices so beautiful as they sang.

'Silent night, holy night,
All is calm, all is bright…'

All the members of the party joined in with the festive spirit. This was surely going to be a Christmas to remember.

As the children finished, Isabel said, 'C'mon, get your money out,' and passed around the empty bread basket.

They partied until late into the night, and after a long game of Jenga, which Sands had to watch and referee to avoid an argument, the guests left one by one until the final trio were left exhausted and ready for bed – Brian, Isabel, and Patrick Sands.

Chapter 62

The Beaumont residence – Camden Town

They weren't to know that in the dark of the night Zonov waited patiently outside their house, lurking in the trees, for his moment... Dressed in black, with his hood covering his face, he was inconspicuous. The only sign of his presence in the vicinity was his warm breath billowing into the cold air. It would be a challenge for him to enter this house, as it was well secured, but he would stalk every corner, every crevice, to find a weakness.

This kill would be the most important, and he knew he would only get one chance.

Zonov knelt down and weighed up his options. Then he noticed the kitchen window ajar. This would be his opportunity. He listened and waited for total silence.

Beaumont and his wife were now comfortably in bed reading as Zonov climbed through the open kitchen window, making every effort not to make a sound. Before he climbed onto the kitchen sink he again paused and listened in the pitch-black. The last thing he wanted was a confrontation with two people – that would be a disaster. Sat motionless, he continued to listen. He had learnt over the years that his ears were his best weapon in the darkness of night. Pausing, he adjusted his latex gloves and then pulled a small torch from his pocket attached to a cord. It was a precious gift, given to him by his late grandfather.

Like a cat hunting its prey, he climbed from the kitchen worktop onto the floor and wiped away any footprints before shining the torch around the darkened room. He couldn't hear anything as his breathing became faster and heavier. Adrenaline was now pumping through his body.

He felt his pocket – his knife was in place, again his weapon of choice. He only had a short time in which to plan his attack on the Beaumonts, so he moved into the hallway and waited at the bottom of the stairs upon hearing faint voices coming from upstairs. An air of progressive panic came over Zonov as he prepared for his ultimate move. He wanted the Beaumonts alone so he could pick them off one by one, but he would need lady luck on his side tonight to make the kill quickly.

He knew that patience was a virtue, and if he had to wait for hours then that is what he would do. He heard a noise from the bedroom. Suddenly, the voices became louder and clearer as the bedroom door opened, and Zonov retreated to the kitchen and waited. He heard Brian Beaumont talking and then footsteps on the stairs. Beaumont was getting closer, and Zonov, like a lion, crouched low in his den as he waited for his victim. Securing his hood, he prepared his lock knife and hid at the side of a large freezer close to the entrance to the kitchen.

Beaumont entered the room, and as he opened the

fridge, the light from within lit the kitchen. With speed and accuracy, Zonov raised the knife and stabbed Beaumont in the neck and chest, turning the knife with such precision. Beaumont was stunned. No time to shout, no time to scream, no time to plead. It was another clinical attack as Zonov wrapped his arm around Beaumont's face with ease. The kill had been simple and much easier to execute than Zonov anticipated, and he maintained his death grip on Beaumont until there was no more movement. He slowly lowered Beaumont's lifeless body to the floor and attempted to remove the knife, but the blade had snapped. Zonov would have to leave the blade embedded in his victim.

Zonov shone his torch and found a set of kitchen knives in a block on the kitchen worktop, and took one quickly. He extinguished his torch and approached the kitchen entrance, waiting patiently for a minute. There was calm. Calm before the next storm.

He had a very short space of time to ponder his last kill while he stalked Isabel, still in the bedroom oblivious to the fact that her husband had just been brutally murdered. He was satisfied with his work thus far. It was business as usual for Zonov – he treated it as a natural occurrence done in a professional manner for the sake of his client. He didn't differentiate between his actions and those of a stockbroker who had a good day in the city.

He was an intellectual psychopath with no conscience.

Zonov could relax now. Time was on his side. He believed he had rid himself of his main threat, so he took a deep breath and prepared to complete his assignment. As he crept up the stairs, Isabel was alerted by a creak in the old staircase and felt uneasy. She hid in a dark shadow and waited, hoping it would be Brian.

Zonov appeared and Isabel made the first move, striking him with an old antique shillelagh. She had intended to strike him on the head, but she made a fatal error by hitting his shoulder instead, sending him into a rage as he came face-to-face with his prey. She tried to strike again, and knocked the small torch from his grasp. He grappled with her and with ease disarmed her. She was petite and no match for this monster.

Her dressing gown had now unravelled. She tried to punch Zonov, but he threw her to the floor like a rag doll. As he looked for his torch, Isabel managed to get herself up and run into the bathroom, where she sought refuge by locking the door and leaning against it.

It would only be a matter of seconds before Zonov broke it down.

Patrick Sands, who had been fast asleep in the spare room, was woken by the disturbance. He slowly moved from his bed, still incapacitated. He could hear the screaming, but felt helpless as he opened the door slightly. He couldn't see Isabel and fumbled around in the dark, looking for a weapon. He wondered if the intruder knew he was at the address.

The struggle between Zonov and Isabel continued. Now armed with a small pair of scissors – no match for the large kitchen knife in the hands of her assailant – Isabel held them up as Zonov started to kick at the door. She knew it would soon give as his foot penetrated the flimsy door panel.

She seized her chance and, with the scissors in her clenched fist, repeatedly stabbed his right leg. Zonov screamed as the sharp scissors struck his shinbone. Bleeding profusely, her attacker was now in a psychotic rage, and as he entered the bathroom his clinical approach to previous murders disappeared as he pulled his leg away and smashed the whole door down, knocking Isabel to the black and white tiled floor.

His knife now on the floor, Zonov punched Isabel as he shouted abuse in his native Russian tongue. Bloodied and battered, they fought, but Isabel refused to give up her battle for life. She kicked and screamed as Zonov showered her with a flurry of heavy punches as Sands tried to leave his room.

Zonov then picked Isabel up from the floor and forced her head into the bathroom sink and against the taps, rendering her unconscious. So powerful was the manoeuvre that it smashed the sink, and water started to spray all over the bathroom from the exposed pipes. He then picked up the knife and cut Isabel's throat, before driving it into her chest and turning the knife slowly. Blood gushed from the wound and covered him. This had been a fight he had not anticipated as he sat in a bloodied state.

Zonov stumbled down the stairs and checked the front door. In a state of panic, he cleaned himself quickly, using anything he could get his hands on. He found an old towel and a black scarf hanging on the coat stand next to the front door and then returned upstairs. As the bathroom continued to flood, covering the floor in a bloody mess, he gave up – it was an impossible task. The carnage he had left behind was so bad he couldn't clean up the scene, as the water was now cascading down the stairs from the damaged sink. He again ran down the staircase to the porch, where he had previously left a can of petrol, and methodically showered every room.

Zonov continued to pour the petrol, oblivious to the fact that Sands was also at the address. Suddenly, he heard a noise from upstairs and froze. As he listened carefully, he could hear noises as Sands dragged himself from the small bedroom onto the landing. Sands could hear Zonov so he retreated back into the bedroom and sat in the room.

Zonov charged up the stairs, picking up the discarded shillelagh, and ran into the dark bedroom where he saw Sands cowering in the corner. Zonov didn't have time to plan this attack. Caught unawares, he showered Sands with blows until the room went silent. He had surely killed the journalist at his second attempt.

Sands lay on the floor and held his breath – it was the only way he could survive.

Zonov paused and threw the weapon to the floor. Sands' deception had been successful.

He then made his way down the stairs and ignited the curtains in the living room with a lighter before making his exit. Zonov was annoyed – the murder had been quick but disorganised and his leg was badly injured. As he left the house, the red flames burned. He quickly threw the towel and the scarf into a bag and left the scene as neighbours started to come out.

He would have to leave Camden rapidly. Zonov hastily ran down the street, got into his jeep and drove back to Hampstead Heath. He needed to clean himself.

Sands waited for Zonov to exit, and then managed to stagger out of the house and fell into the arms of a female neighbour. The night sky lit up with the red flames and the cold air momentarily faded as the intense heat penetrated the atmosphere. Sands lay in the woman's arms and looked up into the sky. He started to drift away as he heard the distant sound of sirens.

On his return to the flat, Zonov ran a bath. He noticed he had cuts to his arm and leg and one above his left eye. While the bath filled up he showered and then put all his clothes into the bath. As they soaked, the water gradually turned a bloody red.

He emptied and cleaned the bath with bleach and placed the clothes in the washing machine. A nearby bucket filled with bleached water was already prepared into which he threw his boots.

As he dried himself down, he looked in the mirror and took a deep breath. He had lost his cool and needed to gather his thoughts quickly.

He shouted loudly in his native Russian tongue, 'Fuck, fuck, Anton, what have you done?'

Chapter 63

Jack Edgerton was still up watching a film when his phone rang. It was a withheld number, a sure sign something was wrong.

After introducing himself, the dulcet tones of a male said, 'Hello, Detective Chief Inspector Edgerton, we have one for you at Camden Town.'

Edgerton stood upright and rubbed his eyes. 'Okay, I'll be there. Can I have the address, please?'

The officer replied, 'Camden Square, Guv. You'll know the address because it's on fire. The Fire Brigade's there now.'

Edgerton dashed out of the door, got into his car and left for the scene.

Meanwhile, Zonov left his flat to find a twenty-four-hour shop to purchase more cleaning fluids. As he left Hampstead Heath, he travelled along Rosslyn Hill towards Belsize Park Tube Station and noticed blue flashing lights and a police roadblock ahead. It was too late to turn round; he would have to bluff his way through.

As Zonov approached, he opened his window and was greeted by a traffic officer with a slashed peak. He reminded Zonov of a Russian officer and he uttered,

'Tosser,' under his breath. The officer greeted the Russian.

'Hello, sir. This is a routine roadblock, so if you could just pull over?'

Zonov wasn't really that concerned.

As he pulled over, another officer approached him and said, 'We are carrying out a road check. Can I have your name?'

'Anton Zonov. I have my documents here.'

'Thank you.'

The officer inspected them closely. Then he went to check the tax disc and looked into the vehicle, shining his torch. He waved to another officer and then approached Zonov.

'Thanks for the documents, Mr Zonov; they appear to be in order. Have you had an accident? I can see you have a cut.'

'I just do a little boxing, sir.'

The officer smiled. 'Can you step out of the car?'

Zonov remained cool. As he stepped out of the jeep, the officer leaned over to the passenger seat and produced a small wrap.

The officer showed it to Zonov and said, 'This yours?'

'Yes.'

'What's in it?'

Zonov was almost relieved. He thought the officer had wanted to speak to him about the murder; a minor drug violation didn't concern him.

'It's a little coke, Officer, for my personal use.'

The officer looked at his colleague and said, 'Get the van.'

Before Zonov could speak, the officer said, 'You're

under arrest for possession of a Class A drug, Mr Zonov. You don't have to say anything, but it may harm your defence...'

Before Zonov knew what was happening, he was in the back of the police van being searched.

Growing increasingly concerned with his plight, he said, 'What about my jeep, Officer?'

'We'll take it to the nick.'

As they drove back to the police station, Zonov remained calm, but he knew he needed to get away quickly. He'd already decided he must use his phone and call Loktev. As far as he was concerned, this murder had proved to be the most difficult, but he was happy in the sense that he had managed to kill the Beaumonts and Patrick Sands at the same time.

He must get this charge out of the way; after all, it was only possession of a small quantity and he just wanted to be on his way. Time was precious.

Zonov had again attempted to torch the house, but this time the Fire Brigade had been quick on the scene. As Edgerton arrived at the scene, he could see some flames and smoke rising as he passed under the yellow and black crime scene tape. He stood and watched, taking in the enormity of the situation before approaching the lead fireman.

'Detective Chief Inspector Edgerton. What's the score?'

The fireman smiled. 'We'll be done soon, Officer, then we can do a search and I'll report back to you.'

'Anyone inside do you know?'

'Yes, there is, but one got out. He's going to the Burns Unit at Chelsea and Westminster.'

'Any name?'

The fireman shouted orders to his men and then said, 'No name. He was rushed off by the ambulance straight away.'

Edgerton paused and then approached the uniformed inspector at the scene.

'DCI Edgerton, Murder Squad. Get on the radio and ask the control room to get all my available men to the scene.'

The inspector wasted no time in carrying out the order.

The scene in Camden Square was frenetic, with officers shouting as the firemen worked tirelessly to control the fire. The Metropolitan Police were inundated with calls, and

stretched with a serious incident near Belsize Park, which had resulted in Zonov's incarceration at the roadblock.

As the desk sergeant looked at Zonov, he said, 'Do you want to make a call?'

Zonov was desperate and took the chance. When the phone was handed to him, he dialled Loktev's number.

'Where the fuck are you?' Loktev shouted.

'I've been arrested for possession of cocaine, but I'll be out soon. I cannot say too much. All the parties are now asleep.'

Loktev now wide awake and paced his room, wondering what had happened. However, he got the gist of the message. Zonov had to leave…

Chapter 64

St John's Wood Police Station

Zonov lay in his cell on the uncomfortable blue plastic mattress. There was a strong smell of urine, and he could hear shouting from the other prisoners. He wasn't perturbed by the conditions; he had been arrested in Russia on many occasions, where conditions in the jails were much more brutal.

When he eventually started to doze, he was awoken by the sound of voices and the clink of keys. As the door opened, he jumped up from the mattress and was escorted to the fingerprint room, where he had his DNA taken. He found this process rather humiliating and became increasingly annoyed. He looked menacingly at the officer as he completed the procedure.

For no reason he pulled away and said, 'You do that to me where I come from, and I kill you.'

The officer laughed and ignored him. It wouldn't be long before the hefty Russian was back in play. Charged and bailed to appear at court.

The news channels were slowly closing in now that the fire raging in Camden Square was firmly under control. The newsrooms were inundated with calls from the public and close sources were working overtime to provide information. The country was being informed via all the channels that there had been a serious fire at the home of the Shadow Home Secretary, Brian Beaumont. The reporters at the scene were scrambling for information as they stood behind police lines.

John Cotterhill, the Conservative leader, was woken by the news and watched with horror. He tried to call Beaumont, but it went straight to voicemail.

Foreign Secretary Robert Bamford lay fast asleep in his Beak Street residence as Prime Minister Charles Chillot was monitoring the incident from No 10.

Chillot phoned John Smith, his advisor, in a state of panic and asked him to attend Downing Street immediately.

One by one, the Murder Squad officers arrived at the scene as Edgerton monitored the address. Edgerton was no fool, and he knew that this was now unfolding into a national scandal. He wracked his brain as to who might be behind these callous murders. He was in no mood to be played for a fool.

Chief Superintendent Watkins soon turned up looking exhausted and said to Edgerton, 'I've heard the news. Are they still in there?'

'I don't know yet. We can go in when it's safe. Expect the worse, Guv.'

Watkins looked at the emergency vehicles all lined up in the square, lights still flashing.

'I've got all units on standby. I need someone to go to the hospital. We have one casualty there at the moment in the Burns Unit.'

Chloe Moran turned up and surveyed the carnage.

Visibly shocked, she said, 'What can I do?'

'Thanks, Chloe,' Edgerton replied. 'Can you get to Chelsea and Westminster Burns Unit? We have a casualty there, and give me an update when you arrive. Take your time.'

Edgerton was then approached by two paramedics, who whispered in his ear.

He turned to Watkins and said, 'As I expected. There are two bodies. We have another murder on our hands.'

He was approached by DI Palmer and was relieved as all the trusted members of the squad appeared one by one. By now, he had almost expected the inevitable.

The lead fireman approached and said, 'Are you ready, boys?'

Edgerton opened the boot of his car and took out his major incident box, throwing the J-suits to his colleagues as they prepared to enter Beaumont's residence.

As the fire faded, the cold night air returned to the scene and the snow started to fall once more.

Loktev was content. He thought the last piece in the jigsaw had now been put in place, and he waited to make contact to arrange closing payment. He wanted the matter finished.

Edgerton prepared himself, again with his perfume-soaked handkerchief at the ready as they approached the front door. As he surveyed the hallway, he was surprised that the fire damage was only restricted to certain rooms. He turned and thanked the lead fireman who accompanied them for their efforts. The heat within the house was almost unbearable, with steam still rising from the floor. Edgerton approached the kitchen and could see the body on the kitchen floor covered in blood.

He was the first to enter and saw that it was Brian Beaumont. He stepped back and hyperventilated, shocked to see the body of a man he had only spoken to days ago. He knelt down and looked at Beaumont's distorted features. His face painted a picture of utter fear. It was obvious by his wounds that he had suffered a violent end to such a promising life.

Edgerton said, 'We now know these murders are all connected to this inquiry.'

Chief Superintendent Watkins also knelt and put his head in his hands.

'Oh my God,' he whispered, strong words from the shocked Chief Superintendent.

DI Palmer was indifferent as he examined the body. Still fully clothed, it was a grotesque sight as he visually examined the chest wound and severe defence wounds to Beaumont's hands. All the officers were alerted when a loud bang came from behind as Dr Julian Wallace entered the room.

'Hello, gentlemen, I see I've caught you just at the right time.'

Edgerton pointed towards the body. He produced a large pair of tweezers from his Crime Scene suit and lifted the torn clothing from around the chest area.

He looked up at the officers. 'Very interesting. Look here, these are very similar injuries to those inflicted on the other victims. As you can see, there is some blood loss, but not as much as I would expect.'

Wallace probed and said, 'Ah, as I expected. The blade is still embedded in the victim. That says a lot about how the attack was carried out.' He turned to

Edgerton. 'What are the odds on the other victim having similar wounds, I wonder?'

Both Watkins and Edgerton said, 'Pretty good,' as Wallace continued the detailed examination.

'Am I right in believing there is another person who survived?' Wallace asked.

'Yes, Doctor,' Edgerton replied. 'He's in the hospital; Chloe Moran is taking care of him.'

After a short pause, he rubbed his head and said quietly to himself, 'And I have a good idea who it is.'

Wallace smiled. 'Ha! He's made his first blunder then, hasn't he?'

As the Evidence Recovery Unit started to arrive en masse, the officers were joined by Fred Constance.

Edgerton shook his hand. 'Bloody hell, Fred, you look wide awake. Do you ever sleep?'

As soon as they got upstairs, they were faced with bloodied water all over the floor. Edgerton entered the bedroom where Sands had been sleeping. He then turned his attention to the bathroom, were Isabel lay dead on the floor. He closely examined the bathroom door, which had been damaged, and as he looked down he saw a small torch still shining. Careful not to contaminate the evidence, he shouted to Fred Constance.

'Fred, there's a torch in here. I don't think you can miss it, just bear it in mind.'

Edgerton looked at the torch again and noticed a small inscription on the bottom. It was difficult to read, so he shouted, 'Magnifying glass, please?'

'I always come equipped,' Dr Wallace said. 'There you go.'

Edgerton looked closely at the torch and said, 'It's

gobbledygook to me. Any ideas, chaps?'

Wallace looked at the engraving: AZ. 'It's just some initials, I think.'

Edgerton took a picture with his phone. He felt this was his first real break.

Palmer said, 'Well, Guv, at least we've had some luck this time, unless it belongs to the victim, which I very much doubt.'

Edgerton looked closely at lsabel and noticed that the method of attack was indeed related. Acute blood loss around the chest area, which indicated similar injuries to those suffered by Beaumont.

'What do think, Jack?' Watkins asked. 'Surely there must be a connection?'

'I need to think about this.'

As Edgerton knelt beside the body, he knew the inquiry was the driving force behind these crimes. He was sure they were not connected to the previous murders, even though the method was again strikingly similar.

The blood covering Isabel had now congealed, and Edgerton knew the lady had been involved in a monumental struggle with her attacker. He looked up at the other officers and sighed.

'This girl fought to the death. What a shame; a young life just finished for no reason.'

He could not hide his sadness. Her clothes shredded, she lay like a mannequin, her body covered in lacerations and deep scratches. He examined her bloodied fingernails, a sure sign that at some point she had scratched her attacker.

Edgerton's phone bleeped and he saw that he had a text from DC Moran.

At the hospital. Victim Patrick Sands. Speak later.

He thought the other officers were making a judgment too soon about any connection with 'the Barber' murders, and now that a high-profile politician had been slain and a second attempt on Patrick's life had been made, there was something much deeper going on. His thoughts turned to Robert Bamford. As the case was gathering momentum, Edgerton believed he had a motive. The inquiry was imminent and Beaumont was his arch-enemy. He decided he needed to revisit Robert Bamford, but he would wait. He had a gut feeling that he would not share with anyone.

Edgerton decided to walk round the scene slowly, and as he entered the living room, he noticed this area had been particularly damaged by the fire. One of the Evidence Recovery teams was placing items into evidence bags.

He asked, 'What's that?'

From behind the mask, the voice answered, 'Think it's the hard drive from a laptop. I presume the shell melted in the heat, but I'll send this to the lab to see if they can recover any data.'

He needed to phone Chloe Moran. He was keen to speak to Patrick Sands and was growing increasingly concerned about his safety.

He shouted over to Chief Superintendent Watkins, 'Guv, I need an armed guard at the hospital for Patrick Sands.'

'Why, has something happened?'

'No, Sands is the victim. I'm just worried something might happen.'

'Okay, Jack,' Watkins replied, realising the gravity of the situation. 'I'll get onto SCO19 and arrange an armed guard. Please tell Chloe so she's expecting them.'

Chloe didn't have a chance to speak to Patrick Sands as the hospital staff tended to his injuries. He had again defied death, suffering first-degree burns and head injuries, but the mental scars would be much deeper as he started to come to terms with the death of Brian and Isabel Beaumont.

Chloe waited outside his room and soon received a telephone call from Edgerton. She was pleased to hear his voice and wanted to be with him after their previous encounter at his house.

'Hi, Guv.'

'How is Patrick faring up?'

'He'll survive. I've not spoken to him yet.'

'Well, I'm happy about that. Just to let you know, SCO19 are on their way to keep guard, so when they arrive, you can get back to the office. It'll be nice to see you.'

'Yes, you too. I enjoyed the other night by the way.'

Edgerton replied in a soft voice and a different tone than he would normally adopt, 'Me too. We need to get together again soon.'

Chloe was happy to hear his response. She was so engrossed she had forgotten all the formalities of rank.

As they spoke, Sands lay in his bed contemplating what had happened. He was no different to Jack Edgerton, and his thoughts were very much focused on Robert Bamford. He would have to tell Edgerton everything about the CCTV footage. He then thought about the laptop he had left at Brian's house and panicked. He hoped Brian had placed the USB drive in the safe.

He shouted to Chloe Moran. 'Detective, Detective,

please come in, now!'

Chloe entered the room immediately and was confronted by a hysterical Patrick Sands.

'Where's the laptop, DC Moran?'

'What laptop?'

Sands lost his temper and shouted so loudly that he grimaced with pain.

'The fucking laptop I left at the house. Where is it?!'

Moran held his hand and consoled him. 'Patrick, I'm sorry, I've not been to the address, but I'll find out.'

Sands was clearly distressed. 'Miss Moran,' he shouted, 'give Detective Chief inspector Edgerton the following message. Tell him my laptop should be in the main living room. I handed a USB stick to Brian, which he should have put in his safe. I don't know where it is, but he needs to find it and my laptop. It has CCTV footage on it. When he finds it, I need to speak to him.'

Patrick Sands was becoming increasingly agitated and the doctor soon intervened.

'Mr Sands, you need rest.'

Moran said, 'I'll speak to my boss, but please rest, and we'll interview you when you're ready.'

She waited for the armed guard to arrive after the medical staff decided to sedate him.

Chapter 65

The newspapers and twenty-four-hour news channels were in full flow as the news about the death of Brian Beaumont was now out in the open. In the coming days there would be much speculation about how he died and why he was the victim of a serial killer. The press had already made their minds up.

As Edgerton studied the evidence, he received a call from his friend Joe Smithers. He was happy to hear the dulcet tones from his old friend.

'Well, Jack, looks like you've got your hands full at the moment.'

'Yes. Will you come and join us?'

'Of course I will. I understand they're trying to make a connection with 'the Barber' case?'

'Yes, they are, but I'm one of the sceptics.'

'Me too. I don't think it's the same guy.'

Edgerton took his chance. 'That is why I need you. You can at least help us while we deal with this case. Anyway, I've okayed it with your governor, and there will be plenty of overtime.'

Smithers agreed. 'Is Watkins alright about it? I didn't think he'd want me on-board.'

'You've made my day, and don't worry, the

Guvnor's fine.'

Edgerton was back to the drawing board as he went through all the evidence. All the victims had stab wounds to the aorta. This was the same method used by 'the Barber', but he was at a loss as to why the killer would reinvent himself. He was only too aware that the chances of the same method being replicated were almost impossible, especially in this case. He thought there must be another reason, and he had to base it around the death of Beaumont and the attempted murder of Patrick Sands. Edgerton had always realised that the face of policing had changed, and he could no longer rely on the word of an informant or an admission. He knew that he had to break the case with solid evidence that placed the murderer at the scene.

He wasn't going to waste any time with this case, and he phoned Detective Chief Superintendent Watkins.

'Hello, Guv. I have a plan. I think I have enough to move on with this case.'

Watkins was intrigued.

'We have very little evidence at the moment, but I believe Robert Bamford is one of my only leads. I want to arrest him on suspicion of murder and interview him. If he's clear, then so be it, but I can't afford to lose evidence if it's him.'

There was a pause. Then Watkins said, 'Jesus, Brian, the shit will fly if you arrest the Foreign Secretary, but we must go with it.'

'Look, Guv, threats have been made, and I have an email saying so. I have the grounds, and if I didn't at least bring him in, then we would be neglecting to carry out our duties. He's threatened Beaumont and that's enough.'

Watkins thought about it while Edgerton continued to argue his case.

'Look, we can nick him, quick interview and search his address, then 47(3) bail him to come back in a month. Let him out to play and see what he brings us.'

Watkins let out a nervous laugh. 'Well, there go my chances of promotion to Commander. Bring him in, Jack.'

'I know I'm right on this one.'

Watkins sighed. 'Try to keep it low-key for once.'

'I'll go with Phil Palmer, Guv. And by the way, Joe Smithers is joining us!'

Watkins' day was complete. 'I've got three of you to contend with now. Just a warning, Jack. I agree that Robert Bamford has a motive for the Beaumonts' murder, but I don't honestly know where the other two murders fit in.'

Edgerton simply brushed the comment aside and replied, 'Well, we'll find out.'

He already had a plan in mind to arrest Robert Bamford. He contacted his adversary Fred Constance and briefed him on his plans. There was no doubt that upon his arrest the backlash would be immense and although the Prime Minister had almost abandoned his Foreign Secretary, it wasn't the sort of publicity the government sought.

As Sands remained in his hospital bed heavily sedated, now surrounded by an armed presence, Chloe Moran returned to the Murder Squad office and met up with DI Palmer and Detective Chief Inspector Edgerton, who continued to plan the arrest of the Foreign Secretary.

Edgerton had now made a conscious effort not to

read the newspapers or watch the news. He didn't want any distraction that would take him off course. Various commentators were now hitting the airwaves, each having a different slant or theory on what had happened. He was well aware that their views were all politically motivated.

The detective contacted DS Wynyard and made provisions for the custody office at Charing Cross Police Station to be ready for the Foreign Secretary's arrival. After all, it was only around the corner from the Foreign Office in King Charles Street just off Whitehall.

Edgerton decided Chloe should go with Fred Constance and search the address of Robert Bamford while they carried out the arrest discreetly at his office. He certainly didn't want to alert Bamford, so he made a call to Bamford's secretary and asked to speak to him regarding another matter.

She informed Edgerton he would be back to carry out some constituency work later. This was an ideal time for the detective to strike.

As he sat in the office with the door ajar, he shouted, 'Any news on the PMs, chaps?'

He heard a shout return from the office.

'Dr Wallace is supervising the removal of the Beaumonts, and he will contact you when they're in place. I'll sort out the identification, Guv.'

'Master Parrington, you are learning quickly. By the way, do you fancy the PM as well? After all, I'm busy. I'll get someone to go with you.'

Eager to please his boss, the graduate entry detective sergeant replied, 'Yes, leave it to me, Guv, all in hand.'

The atmosphere was now frantic as the detectives worked tirelessly to gather the incoming information.

The information boards were crammed, and the HOLMES computer operators typed at a frenetic pace to enter new information as it was continually fed into the office.

Edgerton shouted to the officers, 'Keep it up, and keep me posted. Any positive leads, I want to be informed. If I don't reply, text me or whatever, just please keep me in the loop. If you get any press enquiries, then refer them to the Press Office at the Yard.'

His voice, drowned out by the banging of keypads, was greeted with the usual positive response that the lead detective demanded.

DI Palmer shouted to Edgerton, 'The car's ready, let's go.'

Edgerton was biting at the bit as he scurried to get his coat.

He looked at Chloe and said, 'I'll keep in touch. You meet up near to Beak Street and be ready for the search. Fred Constance will follow you there.'

As the officers made their way to Westminster, Robert Bamford entered the office in a somewhat upbeat mood, much to the disappointment of his secretary. She felt increasingly uncomfortable in her boss's presence and was even more concerned about his demeanour. Since the death of his rival, he had shown no emotion. He almost seemed to revel in the fact that Beaumont, his nemesis, had gone. Karen Boyd now accepted that her days working for this man were numbered.

As Chloe Moran approached Beak Street, she had time alone to wait for Fred Constance and his team from the Evidence Recovery Unit, so she phoned DCI

Edgerton.

'Guv, I told you earlier about the USB stick at the Camden address. I'm not saying you forgot, but I know you have a lot on your plate.'

'No, Chloe, thanks for your concern. Fred's left a member of his team at the scene and he's having trouble locating the safe, but I'm sure he will find it. As for the laptop, we must wait and see. It looked in a poor state when I saw it, but I must confess I am a bit of a thicko when it comes to computers.'

Edgerton was met with laughter. Chloe was relieved that he hadn't forgotten.

As the duo approached the Foreign Office, Palmer said, 'You know, Guv, I have butterflies in my stomach.'

'Me too, Phil, but we'll get through it.'

The Foreign Office building was similar to those that surrounded it. It was a grand, imposing structure representative of other government buildings, with a presence that oozed power and authority. This didn't make their task any easier.

As they swiftly breezed through security, they were soon eye-to-eye with the Foreign Secretary in his office. Edgerton wasted no time.

'Mr Bamford, I am arresting you on suspicion of the murder of Brian and Isabel Beaumont. You do not have to say anything…'

The Foreign Secretary remained surprisingly calm and held out both his hands.

In a mild voice, he said, 'Would you like to handcuff me?'

Edgerton was surprised by the beleaguered politician's reaction and replied, 'No, I trust you will stay with me and my colleague.'

Bamford remained tight-lipped as Edgerton phoned Fred Constance to instruct the teams to start their search.

After DI Palmer requested the Foreign Secretary to take a seat, both men commenced a detailed search of the suspect's office. It was an impressive room, but surprisingly sparse and very tidy.

Palmer whispered to Edgerton, 'Wish they were all as easy as this. Not like the usual shitholes we have to search.'

Palmer was immediately drawn to the computer at Bamford's desk, and he opened up the homepage. He opened the settings and pressed the search for recent websites visited.

Both address searches revealed very little evidence for the detectives. He was rather disappointed as he relayed the news to his superior. Watkins remained surprisingly calm. Unless he got a full confession from Bamford, it was highly likely that the Foreign Secretary would be released without charge. Bamford remained tight-lipped, refusing to answer questions after his arrest.

As they left the office to make their way to Charing Cross Police Station, Karen Boyd handed Edgerton a note. It read:

Please contact me in the office. We need to speak.

Edgerton sat next to Robert Bamford in the CID car as they made their way to the station and looked at him scrutinising his every move. He eyed him up and down, but the politician gave nothing away. He resembled a blank canvas – nothing there that might give the detective an edge as they approached Charing Cross.

As the police station gates opened, Edgerton turned

to the Foreign Secretary. 'Is there anything you'd like to say, Mr Bamford?'

Bamford smiled. He remained silent, refusing to answer any questions which might implicate him in the murder of Brian Beaumont. It made Edgerton feel uneasy. Time was now running out for the detective, and as soon as he was booked into the custody suite the clock started to count down. The Police and Criminal Evidence Act was a thorn in his side.

As he stood in the charge office, he felt his phone vibrate and grabbed it quickly. The custody sergeant continued to book Bamford into custody.

'Sorry, Sergeant, must take this,' Edgerton said as he scurried out of the custody office into the nearby fingerprint room.

It was Fred Constance from the ERU.

'Hi, Fred, what have you got?'

Constance sounded disappointed, and Edgerton's heart sank.

'We've had little joy at Beak Street, Guv. The house is clean, and he has no computer at the house, which I find rather surprising.'

'He's saying fuck all.'

'Okay then, do you want the good news next?'

'C'mon, I've no time to fuck about,' Edgerton replied impatiently.

'Okay, the laptop hasn't been examined, but Gerry has located the USB stick in the safe at Brian Beaumont's house. Whatever is on that stick is of utmost importance. They're nearly finished with the blood samples, and the swabs taken upstairs in Camden are from a third party. There was lots of it, so they should have a DNA profile ready soon.'

Edgerton sat down and breathed deeply as he took in the news.

'Great. Please pass on my thanks to Gerry. It must have been like looking for a needle in a haystack.'

'It was, but luckily the safe had been shut but not locked. It was in the kitchen in one of the cupboards behind the cereals.'

Edgerton had to act fast.

'Fred, can you get that stick to me quickly? And if you can make some copies I'd appreciate it. Patrick Sands is still heavily sedated, so he's out of the game. I need to check this myself.'

'No problem, sir, consider it done. And while I'm en route, I'll chase up this DNA.'

Edgerton thanked Fred as he prepared to contact Bamford's secretary.

Detective Inspector Palmer entered the room.

'What's the score on the doors, Guv?'

'I'll tell you in a minute, Phil.'

Edgerton dialled the number to the Foreign Secretary's office, and Karen Boyd rather hesitantly answered the phone. The Detective could detect that she was upset. She burst into tears, and he tried to console her.

As she gathered her thoughts, she found inner strength and said, 'I'm glad it's all out, Detective. I feel partly responsible for Brian's death. I did try to warn him with an anonymous email.'

Edgerton was sympathetic. 'There's nothing you could have done, my dear. I did find out about the email, but what can you tell me, what do you know?'

'Ah, to hell with it, my career is over, but I cannot say if he was involved in the death of Brian. After the initial Committee report, Robert was fine, but when Brian pushed for the full public inquiry he just changed. He became fixated with him, and I told him so. But I was powerless.'

Edgerton tried again to calm the politician's secretary.

'Anything you can give me will help, even if it's a hunch,' he pleaded. 'Do you think there was any truth in the allegations levelled at Robert by the Select Committee?'

'Of course, Detective. I never saw Robert with these women, but I'd take calls sometimes and I knew his private life was a mess. He mixed with the Russians and became friendly with the Russian Ambassador, Andrei Loktev. I warned him several times, but he dismissed it. On one occasion, such was his arrogance that he told me to remember my place. He was ruthless.'

'Who were the women?'

Karen became even more distressed. 'They weren't normal women. He would ask me to draw large amounts of cash, and I knew what it was for. They went to a brothel and fraternised with high-class girls, and I saw him one night in Soho. He wasn't the type of man you could approach.'

Edgerton kept his thoughts to himself as she continued. This would have certainly given the politician motive to kill Beaumont, since there was no doubt Beaumont had been on a mission to finish his career.

'Karen, do you think he killed Brian?' Edgerton asked confidently.

'No, no, Detective, he couldn't have done it himself. He wouldn't have done it himself. He would have had someone else do his dirty work. Anyway, he was with his constituents on the night of the murder, and then he had dinner with his friend John Smith at a gentlemen's club in Soho. They used to meet regularly.'

'Who is John Smith?'

'The brother of Derek Smith MP. He's the Prime Minister's advisor and has his feet in both camps. He's a two-faced bastard.'

'Yes, I read there was a lot of friction between Chillot and Bamford after the inquiry. So why should Smith be so friendly with Robert?'

'Oh c'mon, Detective, wake up and smell the coffee. It's the game of politics. Smith has a good number with the PM and didn't want to lose his friendship with Robert. He just played dumb when it came to their dealings with Robert over this whole mess, but I suspect he thought it might blow over. I'm surprised Robert didn't dump John when the inquiry was announced. After all, he is the PM's advisor.'

'Is there anything else you can tell me?'

'Nothing at all, but if I hear any more I will tell you. I would predict in the next few days they will be announcing Robert's resignation. Good luck with your investigation, and tread carefully.'

As the conversation ended, Edgerton heard sounds from the office next to the fingerprint room. As he entered, he saw DI Palmer and Fred Constance sitting in front of a laptop. They inserted the USB stick and the footage started. All the detectives watched closely, their eyes cemented to the screen.

'The quality is good,' commented Edgerton as he continued to observe.

'Don't know this knocking shop, Guv, and I've seen a few in my time,' Palmer replied.

Constance, twirling his moustache, broke the ice. 'The birds are nice, boys. Not the normal slappers you see in King's Cross.' He pressed the pause button. 'Oh look, there's Derek Smith MP. He's in for the bullet.'

Palmer sarcastically sang, 'Another one bites the dust,' as the footage continued.

Edgerton watched the whole footage and then returned to the custody area to brief the sergeant, who stood tall at the desk. Edgerton was a content man. He knew Bamford was against a wall, with all barrels pointing at him.

'He's waiting for his brief, Guv, and then you can interview. He's coming from Kensington, so it shouldn't be long.'

'Can you do me a favour and phone my Guvnor to brief him at the office? I was waiting for DNA, but it doesn't really matter because he has an alibi. I think he's involved in some way. This could be a bail to return to at a later date, Sarge.'

The custody sergeant playfully saluted Edgerton and beamed.

Chapter 66

Charing Cross Police Station

Detective Inspector Palmer prepared the interview room as Edgerton sat down and made notes. Palmer was meticulous as he lay down the tapes and seals in order and prepared the laptop. Both detectives were fully prepared for a negative interview from Robert Bamford. He had refused to speak to the officers, but Edgerton was confused. This was his toughest case.

As he sat writing, he looked up at Palmer as he dimmed the lights and moved the chairs.

'Phil, I'm thinking about this. Do you think Bamford is involved in the murder?'

Palmer was forthright with his boss. 'So far, on what we have, he may be involved, so we must investigate. Based on the CCTV he is involved in illegal activity, and it happens that the CCTV was in the hands of Patrick Sands and Brian Beaumont. The rest is history.'

'Good analogy.'

'But he obviously didn't actually kill Beaumont did he, as he has a solid alibi?'

'And…?'

Palmer continued with his theory. 'So now we have

to look at the other murders. Why would Bamford kill the Labelles and Lizzy Kinlan and her boyfriend? It doesn't add up, although he was in a picture at the house. I am confused about this aspect, Guv. Perhaps they all had some dirt on the bastard. And then of course we have the outstanding DNA, and the initials on the torch left at the Camden town address. Who is AZ?'

Edgerton rubbed his head. 'Let me think.' He tapped his fingers on the desk. 'Of course that's if AZ are initials, and we're not certain. We need Bamford to talk. We need to know who the other people are in the footage, and I'm sure that will lead us to the killer. He must be confident, because his chauffeur-driven Mercedes is waiting outside so he must be expecting to go home.' He scribbled on his pad. 'What about the link with 'the Barber' case? I have a hunch, but I need your view.'

Palmer sat down. 'Look, it's just a hunch, but I think the other murders are a smokescreen to take us off track. How they knew how to replicate the MO confuses me, and why samples of hair were never taken from the victims remains a mystery, but I no longer believe they are connected. And by the way, I don't give a fuck what the press thinks.'

Edgerton nodded. 'I agree. I'm glad I'm not alone.'

'I did fall for it at first, but with time I've moved away from that theory.'

Edgerton laughed. 'Well, I've always had my reservations.'

There was as sudden knock on the door. It was the custody sergeant.

'Hi, guys. Mr Bamford has had his consultation, and

he's ready if you are?'

'Bring him in; let's get started,' Edgerton said.

As Bamford entered, he sat down next to his brief while Edgerton placed the tapes in the tape recorder and waited for the bleep. The interview commenced, and he went through the usual formalities. Bamford looked confident.

Edgerton looked at the suspect and said, 'You know we have CCTV footage. Have you anything to say, Mr Bamford?'

Bamford remained steadfast and folded his arms.

'No comment,' he replied in the sternest of tones.

Edgerton turned the laptop and started the footage.

Bamford watched the film begin, and Edgerton noticed his expression change. His whole life was disintegrating in front of his very eyes.

Edgerton pressed the pause button.

'C'mon, Mr Bamford, you must have something to say?'

As before, he replied, 'No comment.'

The solicitor interrupted the interview. 'Detective, I need a break to consult with my client for a few minutes.'

Edgerton replied assertively, 'Be my guest, take as long as you need. The footage will still be here when you return.' He turned off the tapes.

Edgerton felt nothing but contempt for the politician.

He looked at Palmer and said, 'The man is still full of his own self-importance. I'll throw the bastard to the dogs.'

As quickly as their brief chat ended, the duo returned to the interview room and Bamford sat down.

Edgerton restarted the tapes and the solicitor said, 'My client will not be answering any more questions, Officer.'

'Fine by me, but I will run through them anyway.'

Edgerton then paused, and with a tone that oozed sheer aggression, he moved his chair closer to Bamford, just inside the politician's comfort zone.

'Mr Bamford, I will repeat the caution and remember it. You do not have to say anything, but it may harm your defence if you fail to mention, when questioned, something which you may later rely on in court. Anything you do say may be given in evidence. Do you understand?'

Bamford laughed and then remained silent. He was in a defiant mood.

Edgerton continued to show the CCTV footage while Bamford stared at the wall. For the next few hours Edgerton and Palmer fired questions at Bamford and got nothing in return. It was a frustrating time for them.

Before the interview finished, Edgerton put one final question to the Foreign Secretary.

'Mr Bamford, why are you taking money from this man stood at the bar?'

Bamford turned his head away and Edgerton noted a change in his expression.

He replied loudly, 'No comment.'

The interview ended.

Edgerton walked into the custody office a frustrated man, but he always knew Bamford would not make life easy for him. He read out the facts.

The custody sergeant smiled and said, 'I suggest when he's bailed he leaves in the back of a van. Hope you have a contingency plan, Jack. You'd better tell him to cancel his chauffeur.'

Edgerton peered out of the window onto Agar Street, now packed with press waiting for an update.

Palmer laughed. 'I think you need to get onto Bob Watkins. They do all that shit at Bramshill.'

Edgerton wasn't interested in dealing with the press, he had a job to do. He wanted to look at the footage again and identify the other people. He hoped for another break, and he waited patiently for the DNA evidence to be processed at the Forensic Science Laboratory.

He decided to phone Chloe. She was evidently pleased to hear from him.

'How did the interview go?' she enquired.

'Not great. He refused to speak, but the CCTV is interesting. We all need to have a scrum down at the office and review this tape. I'm sure we'll have a DNA result in the next few days.'

'I'm watching the news, Guv; they're waiting for him outside the nick.'

Edgerton laughed. 'They are wasting their time. He'll soon be safely tucked in back at Beak Street, courtesy of a section van. He's an arrogant man. He deserves what he gets.'

'By the way, Joe Smithers has settled in. He's taken up two desks, Guv. I take it it's a permanent move?'

'Old Billy two desks.'

'What?!'

'He's not changed. He likes his space, but he's a good tec.'

'We'll have to have a drink when we have some time.'

'We will have one in the next few days. It would be nice to box this off first.'

Edgerton said his goodbyes and made his way back to the MOD building with DI Palmer, whilst Robert Bamford was under siege at his home in Beak Street.

Aylsa Mews, Beak Street, London

The phone rang constantly, as did the doorbell.

Bamford shut himself in his dark room, away from distractions. His life now ruined on both a political and personal level, he opened the whisky bottle and reached for the medicine cupboard. He wasn't going to suffer the indignity of explaining his actions to his Prime Minister or his family, who had almost disowned him.

John Smith frantically tried to contact his friend while advising the Prime Minister. The Labour party was in a bad place.

Robert Bamford arrested in murder probe

Brian Beaumont murder – police deny link with 'the Barber'

Death of a rising star

Crunch time for the Labour government

Just some of the headlines that were splashed on the front covers as Andrei Loktev watched proceedings. The fact that Patrick Sands had survived at Zonov's hands in Camden Town had serious ramifications. They were now in a place that they never expected to be and the only way out would be to eliminate Sands before he spoke to the police. Loktev arranged another meeting with Zonov, this time in person at the Russian Embassy. Loktev was furious, as was the contact.

As Zonov made his way across London, Robert Bamford considered his limited options as he continued to lay siege in his London residence.

The Russian Embassy

Zonov finally arrived and received a frosty reception from the Ambassador.

'The contact is refusing to pay the final amount now that Sands is still alive. He is in a vulnerable position.'

Zonov was incandescent with rage. 'We can still eliminate Sands, Andrei.'

All protocol stopped. Meetings in the Embassy and unsecured telephone calls were taking place as the conspiracy started to slowly collapse.

Loktev said, 'No, this is impossible. My contact at the Yard has told me Patrick Sands is under armed guard. It is impossible to get close to him. He holds all the information.'

Zonov showed his displeasure but remained silent. Loktev sat turning in his revolving chair, pondering.

'Anton, I will have to devise a plan. We must do something before it's too late.'

Zonov didn't trust Loktev and he certainly didn't trust the contact, but at least he now knew his identity. He had a plan, and England was not a safe place for Zonov to be. He would prepare for his exit, but he wanted payment first. He played his hand.

'Andrei, please tell me who the contact is?'

Loktev laughed and replied, 'You will never know who it is. Do you think I am stupid?'

Zonov also laughed. 'You are a bigger fool than I thought.' He stood up. 'Make sure he pays the money, for your sake.'

'You're bluffing.'

Zonov slammed the door as he left. As Loktev sat down, the door opened and Zonov returned.

In one final attempt to get the matter back on track, he said to Loktev, 'I will think about this. There is a solution, but you must contact him and tell him that payment must be made. If not, then he will face the consequences. Let me also remind you that I know who he is and where he lives.'

Loktev was shocked. 'You cannot know him.'

'The Mercedes, the chauffeur-driven car… Do think I'm stupid? Do you think I ever trusted you and your contact? This is business, my friend. I have done a job, and I want the money.'

'Remember your vulnerability,' Loktev threatened. 'Detective Chief Inspector Edgerton is closing in. I have contacts, and you're in the same place as me.'

Loktev was not wrong as the murder inquiry gathered pace.

Chapter 67

Murder Squad Incident Room

As all the officers gathered, Edgerton received a call from Joanne Wineford at the Forensic Science Laboratory.

'Hi, Guv. We're working quickly on the blood sample and should have a profile very soon.'

'Can you rush it through, Joanne?'

'Roughly speaking, once the Lab has received a biological sample, there are five steps that we need to perform to generate the DNA profile: screening and sampling of the sample, extraction of the DNA, DNA quantitation, PCR amplification and electrophoresis. Each of these processes can take anywhere from a few hours to a few days. We're trying, and I will get it to you soonest.'

Edgerton was impatient, but understood her predicament. He couldn't hide his disappointment as he replied, 'Thanks, Jo, keep me posted. I'm desperate for something.'

As Watkins entered the room, he said, 'How are you, Guv?'

'Okay really since having my ear chewed off by the

Commissioner and the press.'

'Oh, why?'

Watkins laughed nervously. 'Well, their arses are going regarding Bamford. It's the usual political bullshit. I'm getting rather tired of it all. Do they not see we have a murder to investigate?'

'Well, Guv, I'm on your side. You're coming round to my way of thinking. All they're bothered about are their own careers.'

'Thanks, Jack. If it were a normal case, no one would blink an eye. I know what's the right thing to do and that's to get the man responsible for these atrocities locked up.'

Edgerton sat down and opened the laptop. 'Come on, get everyone in while I link this thing to the big screen. We have a show to watch.'

Soon the incident room was packed with all the officers as the CCTV footage started. As the girls appeared on the screen, Edgerton pointed out the suspects.

'Right, chaps, there is Bamford, and you can see Derek Smith MP in the picture. As the camera pans around you can see some other faces. The footage is quite good, but I don't know the other characters, and I don't know where the club is. We still can't speak to Patrick Sands, and that's a bummer.'

Chloe Moran interrupted. 'I think it's an Eastern European operation, Guv, by the looks of the characters.'

Watkins agreed.

One of the officers looked closely and said, 'That face looks familiar, and so does the other, but I can't think who it is. It's a little grainy, isn't it?'

'Well, I suppose we will have to sit tight on the case at the moment,' Edgerton said.

Chief Superintendent Watkins looked at the group of officers gathered and said, 'Well done, chaps, you're working hard. By the way, what's happening with Bamford?'

Edgerton replied, 'He's section 47(3) police bail to appear at Charing Cross in a couple of weeks, Guv.'

'How about sticking a tail on him?'

Edgerton smiled. 'I like it, Guv. I'll get on to Surveillance and have him followed. You never know where he might lead us.'

Edgerton was desperate to speak to Patrick Sands, who still lay in his hospital bed.

'Sorry, Chloe, you've drawn the short straw. Can you see Patrick at the hospital and if possible get something out of him?'

'No problem,' she replied.

As they left the office, Jack turned to her. 'If it's all quiet, we can have a bite to eat if you fancy it? There's not a lot we can do tonight.'

Chief Superintendent Watkins chirped up, 'I'm leaving now. I'm going to have an early one. Remember, it's a long day tomorrow. And can someone chase up the pathologist? I think he does the post mortems on the Beaumonts in the morning.'

Edgerton replied, 'It's in hand.'

As the office slowly cleared, the detective needed a little time alone. DI Palmer said his goodbyes, and Edgerton loosened his tie, leant back and closed his eyes. He was exhausted, so he dimmed the lights and took his small bottle of whisky out of the drawer.

Whenever he was asked why he had it, the officers

always got the same reply: 'It's purely for medicinal purposes, chaps. We all have times of need.'

As the lights were low and he sat in the peace and tranquillity, he looked outside his window towards the London Eye. The snow was falling again. He had never seen weather like it before in the capital. He was a master of the power nap as he checked his watch. He didn't have time tonight, but the view was just the tonic. The snow so heavy it had settled on the dolphin lamps lining The Thames embankment. Edgerton was mesmerised by the beauty of the lamps which had lined the river since the late 1800s. As far as he was concerned, they were just as iconic symbols of the city as its more high-profile monuments such as Big Ben, St Paul's Cathedral or Westminster Abbey.

As he looked down out of his window, he saw a tramp shuffling through the snow. No footsteps, just two lines left behind.

Edgerton opened the window and shouted, 'Oi, come here.'

The tramp continued, oblivious to the detective's presence, and he shouted again. This time he caught his attention, and he waved the whisky bottle. The tramp came closer as Edgerton threw the bottle into the gardens outside the MOD building. The tramp looked up with his long, wispy matted beard and waved.

Edgerton had made his day. He sat back in his chair and continued to take in the view.

He turned on the news and watched briefly. He'd had a belly full all day as he pressed the red button to turn it off.

As he looked at Big Ben, he saw that the time was approaching 8 o'clock, and he sent a text to Chloe.

Everything okay at the hospital?

Chloe returned the text immediately.

Patrick Sands is still sedated and all is secure at the hospital. On my way back, Guv.

He couldn't wait for her return. He fancied a nice quiet drink with his colleague and his new lover. Edgerton had always enjoyed his work, but now it was a sheer joy.

The peace and serenity he experienced as he awaited her arrival was a far cry from the turmoil Robert Bamford was experiencing. The recent months had taken their toll on him, and as he sat on the edge of his bed, he whimpered as he scrawled on a piece of House of Commons letterhead paper. The words were filled with misery and regret from a man who had everything. It was brief and to the point as he slowly swallowed the concoction of tablets helped down by the whisky he held in his quivering hand.

The flashlights from the cameras occasionally flashed through the curtains as Bamford lay on his bed and closed his eyes. As he lost consciousness, the bottle slipped from his grasp, coming to rest on his suicide note. The ink ran slowly.

To all my family and friends who may read this note,

I'm not a murderer, but I have lived another life and for that I am deeply sorry. I can no longer stand the pain that burns deep within me, and I think the world is a better place now that I am gone. I'm sorry things couldn't have worked out better.

Please forgive me, and remember, deep down I loved you all. Robert.

The press continued to wait outside as the scandal took another dark turn.

Chapter 68

As Edgerton woke in his Primrose Hill residence with Chloe by his side, he gathered his thoughts. It was early, but his mind was alert. He crept from his bed, leaving a note on the side. They had spent another good night together.

Edgerton made his way to Camden Town tube station to get to work. He hoped he would receive the news about the DNA from the Forensic Science Laboratory. He would be on Joanne Wineford's case all day if he had to. He was still nervous as he checked his phone. The last thing he needed was another murder to contend with, but it had been a quiet night. He wanted to go in alone and review the case to see if he had missed anything. He was meticulous.

As he sat at his desk, wading through the papers for 'the Barber' case, the phone rang, and he answered it immediately.

Much to his surprise, it was Joanne Wineford's assistant, Becky Jenkinson.

'Good morning, Becky. Why are you in so early?'

'I'm working on the samples with Joanne from the Beaumont murder scene, and I have some good news.'

Edgerton was eager to hear her findings.

'Go on then, let me have it.'

'Okay, sir. I created the DNA profile and ran it through the system, and it came back 'no match', which is not unusual.'

Edgerton groaned with disappointment.

'Hear me out,' replied Becky. 'After that I left it for two hours, then ran it through again, and I now have a match. He was only arrested the other night in Hampstead for possession of a Class A drug by a PC Alex Scrafe.'

'And his name?'

She replied slowly and with conviction, 'Anton Zonov is the name, sir. He is a Russian national.'

Edgerton laughed. 'AZ.'

Becky was pleased with Edgerton's reaction. 'I will email all his details to you now. I suppose you will be paying him a visit? He only has one address, in Hampstead Heath.'

Edgerton wasted no time in contacting the control room.

'Please get all the chaps in as a matter of urgency and I'll wait for them. I also want TSG and the ERU.'

He decided to phone Bob Watkins himself, and was elated when he answered, still half asleep.

'Guv, we've had a breakthrough. Get to the office as soon as you can.'

'Why, what's happened?'

Edgerton had no time to waste as he replied, 'Just get here. We have our man.'

This was the break he had been waiting for, and no sooner had he put the phone down than the email from Becky Jenkinson came through.

He shouted out at the top of his voice, 'PC Alex Scrafe, you are a beauty!'

He prepared for the arrival of the officers as he read the email from the Lab closely. Zonov certainly fitted the bill.

Name: Anton Zonov
ID: White European
Date of birth: 21/01/61
Place of birth: Khrushchev, Moscow, USSR
Occupation: Unemployed (not verified)
Height: 6'4"
Build: Muscular
Eyes: Hazel
Address: Aitcheson House, Flat Two,
Hampstead Heath, London
No marks or tattoos
Arresting Officer: PC Alex Scrafe
Offence: Possession of Class A Drug (Cocaine)
(See picture attached)

Like a finely tuned army, all the officers arrived ready for their briefing. Edgerton didn't want to waste time on this arrest, so he handed the email to all the personnel and briefed them. All the officers knew their roles, and it wouldn't be long before Detective Chief Inspector Edgerton, DI Palmer and Detective Chief Superintendent Watkins were knocking on the door at Flat Two, Aitcheson House.

The TSG officers all waited at the rear of the premises dressed in their body armour, and an armed patrol from the Diplomatic Protection Group was on standby at the foot of the stairwell. Watkins and Edgerton were not prepared to take any chances.

At 0645 hours, Edgerton knocked on the door. There was no reply.

Watkins said, 'Go on, Jack, belt the fucking door. Wake the bastard.'

Edgerton duly obliged and the door opened. He noticed a suitcase at the entrance.

'Going somewhere?' he asked.

The officers were surprised by Zonov's calm reaction. 'I've been expecting you.'

Edgerton was still on guard. He'd always been warned to be cautious when dealing with prisoners who showed no emotion. Zonov displayed an inner confidence as they entered the flat, and DI Palmer wasted no time in handcuffing the suspect.

The detective showed Zonov his warrant card and said, 'You're under arrest on suspicion of murder.' The caution was delivered in the usual quick and efficient manner.

Zonov smiled at Edgerton and said in his soft Russian tone, 'Well, I finally come face-to-face with the infamous Jack Edgerton.'

Edgerton smirked. 'I will take that as a compliment, Mr Zonov.'

Another knock on the door came and the rest of the team arrived. Edgerton decided to stay for the search with Zonov.

He said to the Russian, 'We're going to search the flat inside and out, so tell me if there is anything I need to look at.'

Zonov replied, 'I will let you decide, Mr Edgerton.'

As the ERU combed the flat, it wasn't long before Fred Constance's colleague, Kevin Parr, produced a black bin liner.

Edgerton said, 'Anything in that?'

Parr was a veteran detective in the ERU. He winked.

'Possibly clothes, Guv, and they're all sealed now. There's a strong smell of bleach. It's always a good sign! When we leave, the forensic boys will do the house thoroughly.'

Edgerton decided to leave with Zonov, and as Watkins left with him he said to Fred Constance, 'Anything you think is of value, please bag and seize it, and I want any computers.'

Edgerton turned to the handcuffed Zonov. 'Do you have a lockup, Mr Zonov?'

'Yes, the number is on the key attached to the main fob.'

Edgerton examined the keys and threw them to Constance. 'Fred, I'll leave this is in your capable hands. By the way, we're going to Paddington Green nick.'

Edgerton felt quite confident he could close the case as he left for Paddington Green with Watkins. He found that cases were just like life. You get your bad breaks, but when the good ones came along they tended to flood in as all the pieces slotted together.

En route, he received an important call from Westminster Hospital. It was the news he'd been waiting for. Patrick Sands was ready to talk to the officers. He immediately called Chloe Moran and asked her to see Sands, as she was particularly good at interviewing witnesses.

Edgerton continued on his way to the station, and Watkins decided to go into the interview with him. In the last few weeks Edgerton's respect for his senior officer had reached new heights.

As they drove through the early morning traffic,

Anton Zonov looked at Edgerton and said, 'Mr Edgerton, I want you to be honest with me, and what you say will determine whether I cooperate with your investigation.'

Edgerton was sceptical. He didn't want to show his hand.

'In simple terms, what evidence have you got against me?'

Edgerton looked at Watkins and received a nod.

'DNA, and it puts you at the scene. No outer on this one, my friend.'

'Thank you, Detective, you will receive my full cooperation.'

Both the detectives were taken aback by the suspect's willingness to help them. He seemed quite relaxed for a man who was in such a perilous position. Edgerton thought perhaps the Russian felt he was in corner and there was no place to go. The police would not be allowed any deals with this case.

Westminster Hospital

Patrick Sands' situation was woeful as he came to terms with the loss of his friends. He was a broken man.

When Chloe entered, he was pleased to see the female detective. She had a calming manner, and her striking looks made him feel at ease. She offered her heartfelt condolences and held his hand. It was a nice touch in such difficult circumstances. She was, as Bob Watkins described her, a natural. She explained to Sands that a man had been arrested. For the first time in days the injured man received some good news. It was a line he could cling to as he started to tell Chloe the tale. It wasn't going to be as complex as she thought.

She said, 'Go on, Patrick, take it from the top.'

Sands took a sip of water from beside his bed and began.

'Well, it wasn't long ago that Brian finished the Select Committee, and I spoke to him about the report. Everyone knew that he wasn't happy with the findings, and he knew Bamford was corrupt. Brian was a good friend – like a brother – but he was a politician and an ambitious one at that. He saw political capital in the setting up of an inquiry and outing Bamford. This would surely bring the government down, and as the push gained momentum, Brian was sent the CCTV footage, which I presume you found, Detective?'

'We did.'

Sands continued. 'So we looked at the footage, and although it was poor, we were flabbergasted by what we saw.'

As Sands spoke, Chloe took notes in shorthand.

'Perhaps we were guilty of not telling the authorities straight away and that will live with me forever, but I am a journalist and could break the story.'

After a pause while he wiped the tears from his eyes, Sands continued.

'And after that we spoke about the footage in St James' Park, I think we must have been followed. Then things got progressively worse. My houseboat was broken into and subsequently there was an attempt on my life. Someone must have known about the CCTV. We thought it was Bamford, but how could you prove this?'

In an encouraging tone, Chloe said, 'That's great. Then what?'

'I sent the footage to a friend in the USA. Roger

Fischer works for the FBI, and he sent the footage to NASA. When it came back we couldn't believe who was on the tape. Obviously we saw Robert Bamford and Derek Smith, but when we looked closely, in the background we could see Lord Justice Rameau with a working girl.'

Chloe Moran stopped. 'What did you say?'

'Yes! I said Lord Justice Rameau, the very man heading the inquiry into Bamford, and other corrupt government officials. Was it coincidence or did they know each other? Perhaps we panicked and decided at some point Brian would let the truth out into the public domain, but he never had the chance. Rameau complicated matters. Whoever killed Brian never wanted the CCTV footage to be released to that inquiry. There were too many people who had a lot to lose.'

'What about the other murders?'

Sands shrugged his shoulders. 'That is a mystery, Ms Moran.'

'Who do you think made an attempt on your life?'

'I do not know, but when we saw the CCTV footage, I recognised the club and its location and I went with Brian to have a look.'

'How did you find it?'

'I take photographs in London and recognised the street through a window in the footage. It was in Archer Street, Soho.'

Sands reached for his phone and opened his album.

'Look, I took some pictures.'

'Can you send them to me by Bluetooth? I will certainly need those.'

Chloe Moran was still in a state of shock. She needed to contact Jack before he interviewed Zonov.

Chapter 69

Edgerton was preparing for the interview with Zonov when he received a call from Chloe Moran.

'Hi, Chloe, how are you?'

Chloe tried to remain calm. 'Are you with anyone, Guv?'

'Yes, I'm with the Chief Super.'

'I have something to relay, so I suggest you go to speaker phone.'

As he turned the phone to speaker, she read the full statement she had just taken from Sands. In all the years the detectives had worked they had become hardened, but nothing could have prepared them for this. Edgerton went into combative mode.

'Let me think. I need you to liaise with DI Palmer. We can't leave here. Check this brothel in Soho, and if it's kosher, draw up a request for a warrant and get to the Magistrates Court with Phil. Are you with me?'

'Yes, Guv,' she replied.

'Get the ticket, then go mob handed and raid the fucking place. Leave no stone unturned and retrieve any evidence from the shithole, and if anyone gives you shit then they can come in on suspicion of murder. It'll be a while before we can get it sorted this end.'

Edgerton took a breath. 'Under no circumstances mention the Lord Chief Justice, whatever you do. When we get any more information, then we can act.'

Chloe was on a mission. She didn't even reply as she left the hospital to see Palmer.

As the ERU finished the house search, Fred Constance sat down and sighed. Kevin Parr joined him and patted him on the back.

'Are you okay?' he said.

'This has been the busiest few days in my whole career, Kevin.'

As they unzipped their suits, Fred said, 'C'mon then, give me a list of items found at the address for Edgerton. He's about to interview Zonov.'

Parr started to read the exhibits list. 'One laptop, with the engraving E. Fahy on the base at the side of battery. One bin liner containing boots, black trousers, black hooded sweatshirt and gloves, all soaked in bleach. One post-it note containing notes. Envelope containing photographs of Brian Beaumont and Patrick Sands, and finally, one hat (clean) and scarf soaked in blood in a separate bag. Various correspondence including plane tickets and an envelope containing information on 'the Barber' murders. Two mobile telephones. One laptop, the property of Anton Zonov, and two wraps containing a white substance.'

Constance looked over the sheet and wasted no time faxing it to Paddington Green Custody Office, where Edgerton waited sipping his coffee.

There was a tap on his shoulder and the jailor said, 'Guv, the prisoner Anton Zonov would like to see you in his cell.'

'Come with me, Officer, we'll see him now.'

As they walked down the cell corridor, Edgerton could hear other prisoners shouting. As the cell door opened, he saw Zonov sitting on his blue mattress in the sparse detention room.

'Mr Edgerton, I have been thinking. You will receive my full cooperation, but I need to know if you can help me.'

Edgerton knelt down. 'There is very little I can do. The system doesn't work that way, but you will help yourself if you tell the truth. I can then tell the presiding judge that you fully cooperated.' He turned to the police officer. 'Get me a pencil and paper, and bring it here.' He turned back to Zonov. 'You can tell me everything when I do the taped interview, but I'm certain you haven't acted alone. As we speak the brothel is being raided, and I need to know who your co-conspirators are. Please write them down.'

Detective Chief Inspector Edgerton handed Zonov the paper and pencil. It didn't take him long to write down the names. Edgerton looked at the paper.

Andrei Loktev – the Russian Ambassador – my contact

Lord Justice Rameau – I never met him, but he is at the centre of the conspiracy.

The notes came as no surprise to the detective. He needed to contact Palmer and get the two men in for questioning. The net was slowly but surely closing in.

Edgerton walked down to the custody office and passed on the information to Chief Superintendent Watkins. Watkins remained composed, which impressed Edgerton. Other men would have cracked under the pressure.

'Right, Jack, I need to contact the Press Office and the Commander now. The Commissioner will have to deal with this.'

'I understand.'

Watkins shook his head. 'You know, the fallout will be huge. What the fuck is going on with these people?'

Edgerton was sympathetic. 'All we can do is investigate matters. I don't regard these people differently to anybody else. It's plain and simple, I swore an allegiance to the Queen when I joined the job, and if it upsets certain quarters, then tough shit.'

'You have a simple philosophy, and I admire you.'

Before Edgerton could interview, he needed to secure the arrests of Lord Justice Rameau and Andrei Loktev; the two missing pieces.

Edgerton returned to the cell and opened the hatch. Zonov looked up.

'Why the link with the other murders?'

'It was a smokescreen, and we had information on the original murders. I changed it slightly to make the investigation process more difficult.'

'Some of the information came from within. The method used by 'the Barber' was never in the public domain.'

'Then you have a leak. You will have to ask Andrei.'

Edgerton left the cell block and made contact with Palmer, who was sitting in the incident room with Chloe when the phone rang. He checked the display.

'Hello, Guv, how's things at Paddington?'

'Phil, I need you to make at least one arrest, possibly two. You'll need two teams, and the searches at their addresses will have to be done simultaneously. One of the suspects will have diplomatic privilege, so we're going to have to do some checks. Keep it on hold until I get back to you.'

'That's a fucking joke, Guv.'

'Touché,' he replied, and put down the telephone.

Edgerton approached Watkins. 'What are we going to do about Loktev?'

'I've been thinking. It's a serious offence, so we're going to have to get his immunity waived through the Foreign and Commonwealth Office, and I'm going to have to contact the Diplomatic Protection Group. We can't just go in and lock him up on Embassy premises.'

Edgerton was frustrated. 'What! We can't touch him?'

'It's up to the Foreign and Commonwealth Office and the Chief Crown Prosecutor, Jack. It's a serious case. Then they go to the head state. If they refuse to waive his immunity, we're fucked. The best scenario is that he's asked to leave the country. Not to mention I'll be writing for England.'

Edgerton was angry. 'Can we not lock him up?'

Watkins pulled rank and said, 'Jack, listen carefully. Loktev can be detained if he is a danger to himself or the public, but I'm not making that call. Neither are you.'

Edgerton paced the room and kicked one of the chairs.

'Look, I'm as frustrated as you are. Rameau can be arrested and then I'll roll on with Loktev.'

'I'll speak to Phil. Even so, Loktev will know everything once Rameau is arrested.'

Watkins sympathised. 'You know better than anybody, justice and fairness don't go hand in hand.'

Edgerton took a deep breath and held his hands behind his head.

'Get me a coffee, Guv, and I'll speak to Philip Palmer.

Hopefully, by the time we are finished Rameau will be here.'

As he sat at his desk waiting, he looked through the files. He was now resigned to the fact that 'the Barber' may be on the loose, unless he'd died. He was still interested in the case as he flicked through the papers. As he closed the file, he saw a signature at the foot of a post mortem report. It read DC Brian Martin. A thought crossed his mind and he contacted Chloe.

Chloe thought he was checking her progress with the arrest of Rameau and was slightly defensive.

'Hi, Chloe,' he said. 'We now know a little bit about DS Martin, don't we?'

'Yes, the exhibits man.'

'Go on then, go through his career.'

'He was a DC, then went to the Diplomatic Protection Group. I can't tell you anything else other than that he was promoted.'

Edgerton thanked her and put the phone down. Chloe was confused by the call. He then phoned the personnel department at the Yard and had his file pulled.

As he spoke to the personnel officer, he had a text from Fred Constance asking that he contact him.

Edgerton said to the helpful lady, 'Can you tell me DS Martin's duties when he was on DPG?'

'That's easy. He was on the bikes initially, then he was posted to the Russian Embassy in Kensington. He left when he was promoted.'

Edgerton had a hunch and made a discreet call to the Embassy. It was a risky call to make, but he went ahead with it. Eventually, the call was answered.

'Hello, it's DS Brian Martin,' Edgerton said. 'Can I

speak to the Ambassador if he's there?'

Edgerton was immediately connected to his office, and a lady answered.

'Hello, Brian. How are you?'

'Fine.'

'Andrei has been trying to get hold of you. He'll be glad you called.'

He was then connected to Loktev, who took control of the conversation and fell right into Edgerton's trap.

'Hello, Brian. We need to talk about these murders. You know that Anton's under arrest … no one knows you gave me any information so you must keep quiet. I have diplomatic privilege and shall remain silent. You need to do the same. You will be paid when everything dies down.'

'Andrei, I must go,' he said, and put the phone down.

That was enough for DC Edgerton. He didn't hesitate in contacting Martin's senior officer at the Yard. He would deal with him when he returned from the interview with Zonov. The fact that Edgerton had come up against a brick wall with Loktev left a bitter taste in the detective's mouth.

Chapter 70

'Well, Jack, we have two interviews left, then we might have cracked it,' Watkins said.

'Not quite. We have another visitor en route, but I'll tell you after the interview. It'll become evident as we progress.'

Edgerton remembered that Fred Constance from the ERU had left him a message, so he called him back.

'Jack, did you receive the exhibits list from Zonov's flat?'

'Yes, I did. Just about to read it before we go into the interview. There have been a few developments, not all to my liking.'

Constance sounded upbeat. 'Well, you will like this. We've had a look at the laptop with the name Edward Fahy etched on the base, and it's full of incriminating information on the lot of them.'

Edgerton reflected for a moment. 'Go on…'

'Fahy was an investigative journalist.'

'We'll have to speak to him then.'

'That's impossible, he's dead. Fahy died in a diving accident off the west coast of the Sinai Peninsula, and

Zonov was in the area at the time of his death.'

'I take it you are looking at some airline tickets?'

'Yes, return tickets, Guv. Sharm el Sheikh International Airport – Heathrow International Airport at the time he drowned.'

'It's coming back now. I think it was in the papers, or somebody told me. Fred, you're a good man, and shave that tash off.'

Constance laughed. 'Well, we're on our way to see the judge, and by the way, Dr Wallace did the post mortems and the MOs were the same again. I'd love to know how Zonov did it.'

'He's a professional killer.'

Zonov's life was over. He was facing life in a Category A prison for his crimes, and he remained cold, showing no remorse. He didn't intend to make it difficult for the officers as he handed them a prepared statement before the interview commenced. There was nothing in it that would enlighten the detectives.

Edgerton was prepared for a long interview as he took his jacket off and prepared in the usual meticulous fashion. After the usual formalities, the questions flowed from the detective's mouth effortlessly.

'Please lead me through the events in your own words.'

'Mr Edgerton, I will do my best. I have known Andrei Loktev for years, and I would consider myself a mercenary. Most would call me a contract killer, and I worked with Andrei, who had strong connections with the Russian Mafia. I do not wish to talk about their activities, as I do not wish to put my family's life in danger. There were several people who had a great deal to hide, and my initial contract was to follow Edward

Fahy, who was about to break a story involving the brothel in Soho. There was a lot to lose and my instructions were to neutralise him and then get any information he had. I followed him in London and ascertained he only had information on his laptop.'

'How did you know this?'

'I entered his house, just as I did with Patrick Sands, but there was nothing there. I placed a listening device in his flat.'

'And you killed him?'

'Yes. I made it look like a diving accident near the HMS Thistlegorm wreck.'

'Was Jacques Rameau behind this murder?'

'I could not say, sir. At this time I took instructions from Loktev, but I presume it must have been Rameau. He was going to be named in the story.'

Watkins said, 'Go on...'

'It was a successful hit and things went quiet, then Brian Beaumont started pushing for the inquiry. The Select Committee was never going to expose anything, but Andrei asked me to tail Beaumont and his friend Sands to see if I could dig anything up. It was I think a precautionary measure on behalf of the Russians.'

'Do you know the Foreign Secretary, Robert Bamford?' Edgerton asked.

'Not personally. But he used the brothel, and he'd been taking money from us on a regular basis. Loktev was fed up with his behaviour.'

'Go on...'

'After following them, it became evident they had the CCTV footage, and at some point it was going to come out. I never knew who the contact was, as I worked through Andrei. You can check my phone. We used code names. Andrei was careful to protect his identity, which didn't surprise me.'

Watkins asked, 'Why?'

'That's just the way we carry out business, Mr Watkins,' Zonov replied with a smile. 'Then it was decided that Sands had to go, but the first attempt failed in Covent Garden, and then we tried unsuccessfully to retrieve the footage from the boat.'

'Did you steal the post-it notes from the houseboat?' Edgerton produced the yellow note written by Patrick Sands.

Zonov examined the writing, paused to take a drink and looked around the room.

'Then, Mr Edgerton, we found out that the CCTV was so damning that Loktev gave me instructions to kill Sands and the Beaumonts. They knew too much.'

Edgerton flicked through his files. 'And the other murders, what about them?'

Zonov smirked. 'This was an elaborate plan to make the murders look like the previous ones in Mayfair and Camberwell Grove.'

Edgerton held up the newspaper cuttings found at Zonov's flat.

As Zonov looked at them, he said, 'Yes, and of course I knew the MO. It was passed to us by a police officer, a friend of Andrei, and the rest was simple. The first two murders were purely random to act as a smokescreen.'

Edgerton became annoyed. 'Why did you kill innocent people?'

Zonov showed no emotion as he answered, 'We had to make it look as though the serial killer had re-emerged, reinvented himself. That is why no hair was taken from the victims.'

Watkins said, 'How did you find out about the judge?'

'I had tried to find out in the past and failed. Then, when Andrei met him in Shepherds Bush I saw him and recognised him from the newspapers.'

'And then what?' Edgerton asked.

'Nothing. I needed leverage, just in case. I didn't really trust Andrei towards the end. The bottom line is that the inquiry was about to start, and the judge must have had it all planned. He was using the girls in Archer Street, and he was finished. There were a lot of people using the club. I never knew how the CCTV footage came into the hands of Brian Beaumont, but I always presumed someone from the club must have sent it anonymously.'

Edgerton produced the small torch and showed it to Zonov. 'Can you explain this?'

'I left it at the Beaumonts' house. It didn't go as planned, and his wife put up a fight. That's when I cut my leg, and then I confronted Patrick Sands. That was not intentional, as I didn't know he was staying at the house. The torch was a present from my native Russia, Mr Edgerton.'

As Edgerton continued to interview Zonov, Watkins had to leave. The Russian Ambassador was sitting pretty in the sanctity of the Russian Embassy as a free man. Watkins didn't hold much hope when it came to the fate of Andrei Loktev. It would become a diplomatic row if the wrong decision were made. He had visions of him being told to pack his bags and return to a hero's welcome.

As he entered the custody office, he immediately

recognised Lord Justice Rameau talking to the custody sergeant at the desk. It wouldn't be long before the whole pack was rounded up. Derek Smith MP would be the last to be arrested as the net closed in.

The Murder Squad was at full stretch.

Zonov continued to cooperate with Edgerton well into the afternoon as Lord Justice Rameau languished in his cell, a far cry from the elegant chambers he usually frequented.

As Watkins prepared to leave, he looked around the custody office. It had been taken over by his squad as they rushed around the various rooms. He looked at the custody officer.

'It reminds me of the New Year sales!'

The custody sergeant said, 'I was hoping for a quiet day's work so I could get an early dart, and you lot have fucked me again.'

Both the officers laughed. Watkins knew he had a battle on his hands with Loktev, but he would give it a good run. He owed it to his officers.

Edgerton soon left the charge office, keen to speak to Rameau. The officers had changed their plan and searched his residence in Islington and his Chambers. Edgerton had also instructed his officers to search his office deep within the Royal Courts of Justice. He thought it might be a sensible move.

If the period before the full scandal broke out was a prosperous time for the press, then the present was even better as the uncut affair gained momentum with the arrest of Rameau and Bamford. On the instructions of the Commissioner, the Metropolitan Police were giving very little to the press.

As the press and paparazzi camped in Beak Street,

Karen Boyd contacted Jack Edgerton with her concerns. She had not seen or heard from the Foreign Secretary since he returned home. This was unusual, and she was becoming increasingly concerned. It appeared that his family had given up on him.

Edgerton arranged for a local patrol to attend his residence, and they would meet Karen Boyd there. It was the least he could do for Bamford's assistant.

The Prime Minister and the leader of the opposition, John Cotterhill, continued their tributes to Brian Beaumont and his contribution towards politics. The Prime Minister tried to keep the statements brief while the investigation gained momentum.

Edgerton sat in the office with Palmer as they looked through the statements and evidence. He liked to keep up to date with every aspect of the investigation as he ploughed through the physical and documentary evidence.

Palmer said, 'I take it you didn't go to Edinburgh to see your daughters?'

'I haven't got around to it with all this. I'll be in bad books again.'

'Me too. I wouldn't recognise my missus.'

'It's a difficult job, isn't it? Long hours, grief, little reward and dealing with the worst society has to offer. But you know something, Phil?'

'I know what you're going to say.'

'I love it, but I must be mad.'

'We're all mad, Guv. Anyway, back to business. What about Derek Smith?'

'Make some checks at Portcullis House and we can pay him a visit. I'd like to leave Rameau until the end.'

'What's happening with Loktev?'

Edgerton laughed. 'It is very complex. The Guvnor is dealing with it, but it's a travesty. As Ambassador he has full diplomatic privilege; what a fucking joke. We may be able to make a move, but we need clearance, so don't hold your breath. I never thought anything would happen to him. The Russians are hardly going to cooperate with us.' Edgerton was ready to feel another collar. 'C'mon, Phil, do those checks, then get on the snow chains. We might need them.'

Palmer looked out as the snow continued to fall.

'I love a white Christmas.'

Beak Street junction with Carnaby Street, London W1

Karen Boyd stood under the archway at the entrance to the famous street, anxiously waiting for a marked police car to meet her. The activity outside Bamford's address had not subsided, even though the snow continued to fall. Suddenly, she felt a tap on her back. It was DS Wynyard.

'Hello, I presume you are Karen Boyd.'

She was surprised.

As he pulled out his warrant card, he said, 'DCI Edgerton asked me to meet you.'

'No, you just shocked me. I was waiting for a police car and a uniformed officer.'

DS Wynyard comforted her. 'Jack thought it might be prudent to go to the rear in plain clothes. We need to avoid the press if we can.'

As the pair started to trudge through the dense snow that lay on the ground, Karen said, 'There's an alley that leads to the back. No one will know this route, so we should be fine.'

Wynyard held his collar together with both hands to avoid the snow falling down his back.

As they approached the rear door, he wiped the snow from the French doors, but couldn't see anything. He tried to tap on the door, careful not to attract attention from the reporters at the front of the house.

'When was the last time you tried to call him?' he asked.

'I've tried his mobile and home number every half hour, but I can't get him. His family hasn't seen him, not that they care any more.'

Wynyard paced the back garden. 'Let's take the bull by the horns.'

He slowly pulled out his asp and flicked it open. He approached the French window and smashed the glass, then leaned inside to unlock it so they could enter. The house was in darkness as they approached the front of the house. He could see the odd camera flash through the closed curtains as he approached the bedroom. He could smell whisky as he entered the bedroom, only to be confronted by the sight of Robert Bamford lying on the bed. Bamford was deathly white and lay motionless, with the whisky bottle still in his hand. Pills were strewn across the dressing table, and a note lay beside him. Wynyard read it.

'Where are you, Officer?' Karen shouted.

'Stay there, Karen. Don't come in.'

Wynyard examined Bamford's face with a torch. His lips were blue, and he had been in the job long enough to know when a dead man lay before him.

Wynyard read the note again and couldn't help feeling sad. He left the room, approached Karen and put his arm around her.

'Let's go downstairs. I don't want you in there.'

She could sense bad news was about to be delivered by the detective and braced herself.

'Robert's dead. He's killed himself.'

Karen broke down and cried. 'He was full of pain, but why kill himself?'

'I don't know; perhaps we'll never know.'

Wynyard contacted Edgerton. It wouldn't be long before the news broke.

Chapter 71

Main atrium – Portcullis House

As Edgerton rummaged through his tray at the X-ray machine, he laughed as Palmer struggled to put on his belt.

'Bloody hell, Phil, you need to get back in the gym.'

'With respect, Guv, piss off.'

Edgerton looked ahead. 'I hope it's our last visit here. It feels like my second home.'

His phone rang and everybody turned round, giving him a disapproving look. Edgerton stopped the call. It was DS Wynyard.

'There's a surprise,' Palmer said. 'Another noisy ringtone, Guv.'

'It's a classic actually. Hanging Around; you must have heard of it.'

'The Stranglers, Guv; I've heard it many times. Great tune.'

'You never cease to amaze me, Mr Palmer.' Edgerton moved to a quiet corner within the main atrium and called the Detective Sergeant back; he had a crisis on his hands in Beak Street.

Edgerton was upbeat. 'Everything okay, Brian?'

'Guv, I'm with Karen Boyd. The wheels have well and truly come off.'

Edgerton paused. 'Why?'

'Well, I'm at the house. I have the press at the front waiting for a story and a dead Foreign Secretary upstairs. Other than that, things are fine.'

As Palmer looked on, Edgerton became ashen-faced as he digested the news.

'Don't worry, Guv, he's not been murdered. He's taken his own life, but he's left a note.'

'I suppose he denies any involvement in the murders?'

Wynyard read the note as Edgerton listened intently.

'Right, I'll contact Watkins and he'll liaise with you. Obviously the shit will fly again. It's never-ending, but that's not my concern. I'll speak later, Brian, and keep your head up.'

Edgerton and Palmer made their way upstairs to the office of Derek Smith and awaited his arrival. He must have been expecting a visit from the officers as they sat outside, since it wasn't long before he arrived. He was immediately greeted with the flash of Edgerton's warrant card.

Derek Smith, invited them into his office and offered them a drink. Edgerton was shocked by his reaction.

'What can I do for you, chaps? It's not about my speeding ticket is it? Sorry, just having a joke. I was expecting you.'

'Mr Smith, you are close friends with Robert Bamford, are you not?'

'I am.'

'You must have read the news, sir. We are investigating several murders, in particular the death of Brian Beaumont.'

'He was a promising politician, Detective, even though we were on opposing sides.'

'Can you tell me when you last entered the brothel in Soho, Mr Smith?'

Smith's expression changed. 'This is preposterous, Mr Edgerton. You firstly accuse Mr Bamford of murder, then you dare to come here and accuse me of going to brothels.'

Edgerton reached for his jacket and pulled out an envelope.

As he showed Smith a CCTV still, he said, 'That is you, isn't it?'

'I didn't know it was a brothel.'

Edgerton's patience with the MP was slowly running out.

'The picture is a still taken from substantial footage of you in the brothel. I don't need to spell it out, do I?'

Smith laughed sarcastically. 'I'll speak to Robert Bamford. This is a conspiracy to get rid of us.'

'You won't. Your friend has killed himself, so I suggest you stop fucking me about and answer my questions honestly.'

Smith staggered as his legs buckled.

Edgerton looked at him. 'I know you had nothing to do with the murder of Brian Beaumont, but you certainly know about the club. You will of course have to do the proper thing and resign, but I suggest you help me first. I'm sure you know a few things. The choice is entirely yours.'

Smith said impatiently, 'Okay, I will cooperate with you.'

'Did you know Lord Justice Rameau?'

Smith sighed. 'Not really. I saw him a few times at the club. Robert didn't know him, and I only knew his face.'

'Loktev – Andrei Loktev. Did you know him?'

'Yes, Detective, I knew him very well, as did many other people who frequented the club.'

Edgerton walked around the office and then looked at Smith.

'I just want to make a simple observation. I look around and all I see are people who evidently have everything and then squander it all.'

'Have you ever strayed, Detective, or done something that isn't in the police handbook?'

Edgerton smirked. 'I'm no angel, but I don't beat on and tell people daily how they should live. That's why I'm not a politician.'

Smith sat at his desk as the reality of his situation dawned on him. His marriage and his career would soon come to an end.

He collected some papers and said, 'Am I under arrest, Detective Chief Inspector?'

'No, but I would like you to assist me at the office. I need all the information you have. I'm sure you will have to face some sort of internal investigation. I think that's enough?'

Smith nodded. 'I suppose I'd better prepare some sort of statement. If you could wait, it will be very brief.'

Edgerton took a chair and sat beside Detective Chief Inspector Palmer.

As Smith prepared his laptop, Palmer whispered to Edgerton, 'Why are we not arresting him?'

'I think enough lives have been wrecked for one day. Arresting him is a futile exercise. He'll cooperate, and

I'm sure I have my man.'

'Do you think Bamford and Smith were just caught up in the middle of this conspiracy?'

'Yes. It looks like Bamford was always involved, and the evidence points that way. They were in the wrong place at the wrong time, but they knew the risks.'

Smith said, 'C'mon, let's get the show on the road, and then I'll send the draft to the PM. Do you like it, Officer?'

Edgerton read the email draft.

Dear Prime Minister,

In light of recent events, I am tendering my resignation as a member of the Labour party. I therefore do not intend to stand for parliament at the forthcoming general election.

May I also take this opportunity to thank my constituents and colleagues for their support and generosity during my career as a Member of the House.

It has been a great privilege to serve as a Member of Parliament.

Yours sincerely,

Derek Smith MP

'It's short and sweet, Mr Smith, but probably the best course of action.'

Edgerton was keen to shut the case. He knew he had his killer, but his sights were set firmly on Lord Justice Rameau.

Chapter 72

A complex but detailed Anacapa chart awaited
Edgerton on his return to the office, carefully prepared
by Chloe Moran, linking the telephone calls of all the
suspects. As he mulled over the contents, he shouted
Chloe into the office to thank her. He also wanted to
check the footage on the late Edward Fahy's laptop.

'I doubt whether it will be possible to interview
Rameau tonight, so we must go out for a drink.'

Chloe was thrilled. The detective was exhausted and
needed a break; he made one final request.

'I need a simple request from the mobile providers
as soon as we can. Locations are required for the calls,
and that should pinpoint them all. It will take a while,
but we can keep Rameau while we make enquiries and
then get a further extension if need be.'

'Yes, leave it with me. Where are we going, Guv?'

'We can go to the Steakhouse in Leicester Square, if
you fancy it?'

'Sounds good.'

Edgerton continued to dissect all the statements and
noticed that a copy of the yellow post-it note had been
found in Lord Justice Rameau's office in the Royal
Courts of Justice.

This was incriminating. He again browsed the

contents. He couldn't help thinking what if things had been different. If the CCTV footage hadn't been sent and Patrick hadn't made the note, then Beaumont might still be here. Edgerton's thoughts turned to the CCTV footage and who might have sent it. As he looked at the envelope, he noticed it had been posted in the borough of Westminster, but no fingerprints were found on the package.

Palmer entered the room as Edgerton continued to inspect the envelope.

'Philip, who do think sent the package to Beaumont?'

'I don't think we will ever know, Guv. Did they do it as a favour or did they set Beaumont up?'

'Or was someone after Bamford or Rameau? Perhaps the person who sent the package was closer to the action than we imagined. Somebody who would never face prosecution... Just a thought, Philip my friend...'

'Yes. Obviously the person had access to the CCTV and was in a position to send it. They must have used the club or been a member of staff. Could Smith have sent it? Loktev? Was Bamford taking money from the Russians and they wanted him finished? I don't think the Russians would have wanted to compromise their operation, Guv. Whoever sent it wanted the brothel closed and to bring down Bamford.'

'We will have this conversation again in a few months and there will be no winners. We haven't heard the last of Loktev. Have we looked at all the other footage in Soho?'

'After the arrest of Zonov, the footage was destroyed along with any other evidence at the club.'

'That's why we needed Loktev; he always held the ace, didn't he? They knew the club was going to be raided, but that was not the main focus of our attention.'

'Yes.'

'He'll be on a plane with his family very soon, I've no doubt.'

'It's a tragedy, Guv, but we just need to put together the final pieces and move on.'

'Perhaps we could revisit 'the Barber' murders?'

'That could be fun,' replied Palmer.

'It could be, I don't know. I thought I'd seen it all. I wouldn't have thought a little seedy club in the heart of Soho where a red light shines could be at the centre of a national scandal.'

'Well, Victor Hugo made a quote which sums it all up for me.'

'Why, what did he say?' enquired Edgerton.

'We say that slavery has vanished from European civilisation, but this is not true. Slavery still exists, but now it applies only to women, and its name is prostitution.'

'It's a poignant quote, and I like it. Where do you get them? You were thick as pig shit when we trained at Hendon.'

Palmer shrugged his shoulders.

Edgerton stood up and went into the murder room.

'Come on, everybody, do what you have to do and get home. Let's recharge our batteries and get ready for an early start tomorrow. I want you all in at 0600 hours, and we'll start building a solid case against Rameau.'

Palmer said, 'I'll stay a little longer, Guv, and deal with Derek Smith, then lock up.'

Edgerton patted him on the back as he left. Palmer stood and looked out of the window.

As darkness fell over London, he watched Edgerton and Chloe leave together. He was happy that his boss had found companionship. A broad grin appeared on his face as he closed the blinds.

At last, Jack and Chloe could spend a little time together, but the job would be the topic of conversation for most of the night. It would be difficult to switch off. A constant flow of calls came in from Chief Superintendent Watkins regarding the case as he battled to persuade the authorities to allow an investigation into Loktev. Now that Watkins had described his mission to bring Loktev to justice as easy as 'pissing in the wind', Edgerton resigned himself to the fact they would never get their man. Watkins still continued to impress Edgerton as he fought off the press as speculation increased over the scandal, which was now snowballing.

The sudden death of Robert Bamford hadn't helped Watkins in his quest to prosecute Loktev, and Chillot had now intervened. He had gone on the national news that night to make a public statement. Cotterhill, furious over the loss of his Shadow Home Secretary, was moving in for the kill. He demanded the Prime Minister's resignation, citing his inability to manage his Cabinet. Public opinion was on his side. The Lord Chief Justice remained silent while Rameau was incarcerated. John Smith would have some difficult questions to answer in future months. Downing Street was not the best place to be.

This was the least of Edgerton's problems as he made himself comfortable with Chloe. He knew the

Steakhouse well. It was one of his favourite restaurants, and he'd visited it many times on Squad functions. It was the first time they'd had a chance to talk after Chloe had spent the night at his, but the conversation was very much on the case.

Zonov had now been charged with all the murders, and the evidence against him was compelling. He would surely enter a guilty plea.

As they devoured their fillet steaks, Edgerton said, 'What happened with the bleached clothes?'

'Well, he'd destroyed the DNA with the bleach, but they have a technique called LCV which can trace blood that's invisible to the naked eye, and the clothes were full of it.'

'Ah, so we have the other DNA and a full confession, not to mention his torch.'

'We also have records of large amounts of money being wired to accounts. One account has been traced back to Rameau following seizure of his laptop.'

'And the telephone calls made from the Zonov's mobile and Rameau's phone. It didn't matter that we never had Loktev's phone because the number was in fact registered in his name.'

'I hope the providers can give us the information soon in relation to where the calls were made from. The warrant we obtained should speed up the process. Oh and, Guv, I had a call from Roger Fischer from the FBI.'

'Oh the CCTV guy Roger Fischer?'

'Yes. He's coming to the funeral. He'd like to meet up with Patrick and yourself. He's devastated.'

'I look forward to meeting him. And how's Patrick?'

'He's getting better by the day. He has a Family Liaison Officer who's assisting him. It's going to be a hard road ahead for him. They were like brothers.'

Edgerton held her hand and said, 'And how are you?'

'I thought you'd never ask.'

'Of course, I know it's been a hard few weeks, but at least it's nearly over.'

'What do you think will happen?'

'Ah well, Smith will retire with a nice pension, and Loktev will go back to Russia while Rameau and Zonov rot in prison. As for the rest, well, they'll have to pick up the pieces.'

Chloe was surprised. 'You sound very matter of fact.'

Edgerton was candid. 'Of course it's sad, but it's real life. I have no sympathy for Bamford. He knew the game, and he was a hypocrite. I feel sorry for his family and then of course our friendly Detective Sergeant Brian Martin, who was feeding information to Loktev.'

'And what will become of him?'

'He's under the jurisdiction of Internal Affairs, so I suspect he'll be thrown in jail if he's convicted, as an example to us all.'

'Not a place I'd like to be as a cop.'

Edgerton laughed. 'The thought of having crushed light bulb in my mash every day and watching my back in the shower doesn't appeal to me either.'

Chloe laughed.

'Why are you laughing?'

'I'm sure you'd make a good lover to some jailbird.'

'Bloody hell! Let's change the subject.'

They both sat at the window overlooking Leicester Square, watching the Christmas shoppers and partygoers pass by. Edgerton scrutinised their faces as the occasional one looked in at them. They were all happy as they went about their day-to-day lives. London always carried on despite playing host to a political scandal that no voter would ever experience again in a lifetime.

Meanwhile, Jacques Rameau's fall from grace was starting to dawn on him as he sat in his cell. He counted the cracks in the tiled wall – it reminded him of a toilet. He grasped his head in both hands, pulling on his locks as he started to break. There was no light, no view from this enclosed cell as he battled to make himself comfortable on the hardened mattress. The faint cries of other detainees rang in his ears, making it impossible to sleep as he tried to construct a plausible defence before being allowed to see a solicitor. His mind was crammed with thoughts. His career was over, and he would surely be disowned by his strict parents and cut from any inheritance. Law was his life, and he would now face the biggest battle of his life as he prepared to pit his wits against the celebrated Detective Chief Inspector Edgerton.

He pressed his button and waited for the police officer to approach his cell. When the officer arrived, he demanded his right to have a pencil and a paper and his codes of practice. He would not be giving up his life for anybody.

Edgerton, oblivious to Rameau's inner battles as he continued to feast, took another call from Watkins, who was back at his office at the Yard working into the night.

He was furious, and Edgerton listened patiently as his Chief Superintendent ranted.

'I'm up to here with all this. They're dragging their feet over Loktev. No one will decide.   It's the typical hot potato being lobbed around. As for Bamford, everyone seems to be shitting themselves about the fallout after his suicide. I did remind them that it's not our fault, and he shouldn't have been shagging around.'

Edgerton tried to calm him down. 'Guv, it's happened now, there's nothing we can do. We must concentrate our efforts on building our case against Lord Justice Rameau.'

'Who do you want to conduct the interview with tomorrow, it's your choice?'

As Chloe listened to the conversation, Edgerton said, 'Chloe is ready to do this one with me.'

Watkins was agreeable.

Edgerton ended the call and looked at her. 'I was going to ask you sometime…'

'Spend the night at mine?'

Chapter 73

Blackheath, South London

As dawn broke, the skies cleared and the stars slowly faded, followed by a sharp drop in temperature.

The police courier parked his van outside the Ministry of Defence and made his way up to the Murder Squad mailroom with a large crate full of letters and various parcels. He entered the room and started to separate the internal and external mail, deliberately placing them in different pigeonholes.

There was only one letter for Detective Chief Inspector Edgerton marked for his urgent attention, posted in Heathrow the previous night. It was tucked neatly into his pigeonhole for collection that morning.

As Edgerton woke, it was peculiar to be in a strange bed, especially one that came out of the wall. It was 6 a.m. He turned and surveyed Chloe as she lay naked, entwined in the bed sheets in her small but elegant studio apartment. He was in a happy place as he looked at the mass expanse of snow that lay over the heathland. He hoped this would be his last day of interviews and hoped for some time off with Chloe over the Christmas period; and he still yearned to see his daughters. They were currently home for Christmas now that university had finished for the holidays, and they were staying at their mother's in Golders Green.

Edgerton phoned for a taxi and woke Chloe. He whispered his goodbyes in her ear, followed by a kiss, and prepared to leave for the office.

The rest of the squad would be preparing for work as he entered the MOD building. He completed his usual ritual and entered the mailroom, taking the single letter from his pigeonhole. As he glanced at the writing, it looked so familiar that it caught his attention, so he immediately sat down and pulled out the envelope that was originally sent to Brian Beaumont containing the note and CCTV footage. The writing was identical, so he donned a pair of latex gloves and patiently opened the letter. It contained a CD, and this time the note attached was small.

The final nail in the coffin, Mr Edgerton. Have a good day.

Edgerton turned on his computer and opened the two documents contained in the folder. The first piece of footage was clear and showed Rameau meeting Loktev in a park. Edgerton was bewildered by its significance, although it did prove the connection as he moved on to the next file. It was a sound recording of Lord Justice Rameau on the telephone. He listened to the slightly distorted footage.

'Yes, that is correct. The inquiry will be starting in the New Year, so the operation must be finalised before Christmas at the latest. That will allow for things to settle. Beaumont and Sands have to go to sleep. The footage and all traces or copies should be returned to me if possible. If the footage can't be found, then you know what to do. Keep me informed.'

The line then went dead.

The note that had been sent did indeed place Rameau in a difficult position, but frustratingly Edgerton was no closer to finding out who had sent the recording. This was going to be one of his most complex cases yet. He had been involved in many over the years, but he had the satisfaction of knowing that it was on the verge of being detected, although he remained disenchanted with the politics that surrounded Andrei Loktev's position.

His deep sense of injustice would reach a new low as he took a further call from Chief Superintendent Watkins. He knew straight away that something was wrong; he could sense it in Watkins' tone.

'Hi, Jack, it's Bob here. I'm going to cut to the chase. Andrei Loktev left the Embassy, then collected his family and left the country. He took a late flight the other night on a one-way ticket to Moscow, which pretty much tells us what his intention is.'

'It doesn't surprise me, Guv. He'll never come back.'

'I agree. I think we should just soldier on.'

'It would have been nice, but we have most of the main suspects.'

'I'm sure there will be speculation about Loktev and cries for him to return to the UK and face trial at some time in the future, but that's out of our hands.'

'Did he leave a note or anything?'

'Not a thing. He just left,' replied Watkins.

Edgerton was unruffled, which surprised Watkins. He knew that his lead detective would want all the suspects rounded up. Perhaps he was starting to mellow, he thought.

'Well, Guv, I know where I am. I'm going to get on

with Rameau and then after the interview we should all meet and talk about the case. I've no doubt the CPS will want a case conference on this pretty soon.'

'Good luck, Jack. I'm sure you'll crack it.'

Edgerton thanked his supervisor and headed towards the murder incident room. He beckoned Chloe to come into his office.

'Are you ready?' he asked.

'As ready as I'll ever be,' replied the young detective.

She felt nervous but confident. Since joining the Murder Squad after a short spell in the CID at West End Central, she had grasped the role of a murder squad detective quickly. This would be her finest hour.

'I'll take the lead, but by all means jump in or make notes. DI Palmer will be monitoring the interview on video and relaying information if we miss anything.'

Chloe smiled. She appreciated his support. 'Can you hold my hand?'

'Later perhaps, my dear.'

She looked at him as he prepared the papers.

'I know about Loktev. I'm so sorry.'

'Don't worry, we'll soldier on.'

'I just know how much you wanted him to face justice, that's all.'

'I know, and I appreciate your concern. Loktev will always be looking over his shoulder, and one day his crimes will come back to haunt him.'

'I can't see much of a future for the man in his homeland.'

Murder investigations had become routine for Edgerton and interviewing suspects second nature, but interviewing Lord Justice Rameau would present a totally different challenge for the detective. As the judge consulted his solicitor at Charing Cross Police Station, Chloe and Jack entered the underground car park at the MOD and loaded the pool car with case files and exhibits. Edgerton paid close attention to Edward Fahy's computer files loaded on a disk and went through the list as Chloe placed each one in the boot. He could prove that calls were made to Loktev, and the recording of the telephone call would be damning, but getting Rameau to admit to the full conspiracy might prove difficult.

Detective Inspector Palmer had now secured the trust of Anton Zonov, who had been remanded to Belmarsh High-Security Prison, and his willingness to turn Queen's evidence would prove vital to the prosecution case.

Chapter 74

Edgerton prepared to open the laptop that belonged to the late Edward Fahy and was astonished by the content. Now that Anton Zonov had admitted to the crimes, including the murder of Fahy, the Egyptian authorities were reopening the case. Whether he would have to stand trial was another matter, but Edgerton would give his family all the help they needed; they wanted closure and had always suspected foul play. He was rather surprised to find that Fahy had uncovered such widespread corruption going back several years and managed to sit on it.

As he went through the files one by one with Chloe Moran, he was surprised to find how deeply Bamford had been involved in the whole racket. There were hundreds of images of Rameau entering the brothel and without doubt the CCTV that had been sent to Brian Beaumont was much less incriminating than the footage Fahy had been sitting on.

Edgerton turned to Chloe and said, 'How do you feel about today?'

'I'm fine. This footage helps the case, and I think we have Rameau tied down to the payments and the calls made from the phones we have found.'

'I know Zonov is a murderer, but it's surprising how genuine his evidence will be. He has nothing to hide, and it's clear as day that the whole thing was a conspiracy.'

With a sad expression on her face, Chloe said, 'I don't know, Jack. All this carnage to protect someone's career and reputation? I must be on another planet.'

Edgerton sighed. 'You're right. You're learning quickly. There's nowt funnier than people. You think that when you get into higher positions the fall from grace can be that much higher, but it's ironic that these people set the rules which we are supposed to adhere to. Hardly the greatest of role models for young kids.'

'Yes, but there are a lot of hard-working, honest people. These are just rotten apples, Guv. They'll turn around for help and no one will be there, I suppose.'

Edgerton agreed. 'That's the name of the game. Greed and power is the order of the day.'

He continued to trawl the evidence found on Fahy's laptop as they prepared for their date with Rameau.

'How do you think Rameau will conduct himself?' Chloe asked.

'Who knows?' he replied matter-of-factly. 'These people are unpredictable, but he's on the back foot.'

Just as Edgerton was making his move, Rameau made his way to the cell to speak to his solicitor, Walter Perkins. He had known him for years, but he would be straight to the point with him over this whole matter.

Rameau seemed more concerned with his parents' state of mind and asked Perkins, 'How are my mother and father, Walter?'

'They are devastated, Jacques. The press is hounding them. What did you expect?'

Rameau was resigned to the fact they probably

didn't want contact with him, but he thought he might broach the subject.

'Will they come to visit me?'

Perkins was forthright with his old friend. 'Now is not the time to talk about these things. The wounds are still raw. There's lot of evidence against you. I really don't know what to say about the case. Phone calls, money transfers and now they have the footage taken from Edward Fahy's computer.'

Rameau was defiant. 'Does that make me a murderer?'

'No, but that is not the point. As you know, you are going to be found guilty of conspiracy and I don't need to tell you that is just as bad. God, Jacques, get in the real world.'

'I'm not admitting my involvement. I have too much to lose.'

'Then we must make a defence. It's a long shot, but I can't see you getting the result you seem to long for.'

There was a pause as Perkins drank his coffee. He could no longer hide his frustration with his friend and client.

'What were you thinking? How did you think you could pull this off? You had everything that anyone could want and you've thrown it all away. Why? Why? Why? Let me try to make some sense of this whole sordid affair.'

Rameau remained seated. He showed no sign of emotion in response to Perkins' outburst.

'Jacques, what has become of you? You are different from the man I used to know and love.'

Rameau bowed his head. 'I know. Words can't change anything. I'm in this predicament and I must face the consequences.'

Perkins circled the consultation room and ran his fingers through his hair, a sure sign of his frustration.

'Look I'll try my hardest, but you will have to help me on this one.'

The room was silent.

Then Rameau asked, 'Who will be conducting the interview?'

'Detective Chief Inspector Jack Edgerton from the elite Murder Squad.'

'I've heard the name. They've picked their best, haven't they?'

'You could say that. He's ex-Flying Squad and a tough detective. He's been around the block and won't be intimidated.'

In another room in another part of the station, Edgerton would not have known how the disgraced judge was reacting to his incarceration and consultation with the renowned solicitor, Mr Perkins. He had found this whole process draining, mainly because it was put under the microscope by the press.

The Conservative leader was still demanding the resignation of the Prime Minster, but Chillot was refusing to be drawn into such an argument. However, the papers had run a headline that showed some concession on the part of the PM and spelt the end for Lord Justice Rameau.

Prime Minister appoints new judge and new inquiry into government corruption

Whether this headline would appease the British public was another matter; they would make their decision at the forthcoming election. Such was the interest in Lord Justice Rameau that the world's press had again descended on the capital. Everybody loved scandal and there was no shortage of it in Westminster at the present time. Edgerton tried to carry on as if it was a normal case, but he had now become public property and was not overly comfortable in this new role.

Before he left for the custody office to book into the interview room, he went to turn off his phone and saw that there was one final message from Detective Chief Superintendent Watkins.

I'm on the other end of the phone if you need me. Good luck, and we'll have a drink later and discuss the whole case over a few drinks. Bob.

Edgerton thought it was a nice touch and thanked him via text. He was happy with the whole team. They could do some damage in years to come.

He wasn't nervous, but a little apprehensive about his meeting with Rameau. He had made a point of not introducing himself to the judge. He had left the junior officers to deal with his requests while in custody. He entered the interview room with Chloe and phoned the custody sergeant.

'I'm ready for Jacques Rameau, if you can bring him in.'

'He's finished his consultation and he'll be on his way,' the officer replied.

As Chloe prepared the tapes, Edgerton phoned DI Palmer.

'You ready? Are the cameras working, Phil?'

Palmer replied, 'Yes, put your earphones in and we are ready to go, Guv.'

'Great.'

Palmer jumped in before hanging up the phone. 'I know it will work out. I'll keep my fingers crossed.'

Edgerton made himself comfortable as he sat next to Chloe. There was a knock on the door.

'Come in,' he said.

Rameau entered with his solicitor. Edgerton remained seated and sat on his hands. He had no intention of shaking hands with Rameau.

Perkins looked at Edgerton and said in a formal tone, 'Good morning, Detective. I'm Walter Perkins QC and this is my client, Jacques Rameau.'

'Hello, this is Chloe Moran who will be conducting the interview with me today. I'll go through procedure, then we can get started.'

Edgerton looked at Chloe and said, 'Ready?'

The tapes started to bleep. Edgerton smiled at her and shook his head. He had always commented that the noise that came out of the tape machine before it kicked in sounded like a scalded cat. The interview commenced.

Edgerton was straight to the point.

'What car do you use, Mr Rameau?'

'I have a Bentley, Mr Edgerton.'

'No, in your capacity as Lord Justice?'

'Oh sorry, I use a Black Mercedes.'

'Is it chauffeur driven?'

Rameau look puzzled. 'Well, yes, it is.'

Edgerton produced some CCTV stills taken on various dates and laid them on the desk in front of Rameau.

'Is this the car?' he asked.

Rameau replied, 'No it is not.'

'Think again, Mr Rameau. This one here was taken

at Shepherds Bush. We have verified that with your driver and taken a statement.'

Rameau was non-committal. 'Well, if he says it is, then I suppose I must have been there.'

Edgerton carefully reached into an envelope and took the photographs out, and placed them all on the table face down. Rameau looked at his solicitor as Edgerton turned each photograph over one by one. They had all been taken at the murder scenes, and depicted horrendous injuries.

The colour drained from Jacques Rameau's face and he was visibly knocked for six. Edgerton also included a picture of Rebecca Labelle's dead Dalmatian. There was a long silence.

Rameau covered his face with his hands and then rolled up the sleeves on his J-suit.

'Well then, have you anything to say?' Edgerton asked.

Rameau remained silent.

Edgerton continued to probe into Rameau's past and took directions from DI Palmer through his earphone.

Chloe watched on and then took the Anacapa chart from her folder.

'Mr Rameau, we have confiscated a phone which I will show you.'

Rameau examined the phone and, without invitation, replied, 'Yes, that is my phone.'

'When you open the address book there is only one number, and this is marked 'X'. This belongs to Andrei Loktev, the former Russian Ambassador.'

'Okay.'

'There have been at least thirty calls made to him,

and my chart shows that calls have also been made between all three people over the period when the murders took place, and they have all been pinpointed to particular areas. The other two people being Andrei Loktev and of course Anton Zonov, who is currently awaiting trial.'

Rameau was resilient. 'I can't explain myself, Ms Moran.'

Chloe then produced detailed financial records showing payments made to Loktev, and again, Rameau pleaded ignorance.

As she grew frustrated, Edgerton stepped in.

'Have you ever spoken to Andrei Loktev?'

'I may have done.'

Edgerton produced the laptop and played the footage that had been sent to Brian Beaumont prior to the politician's murder. He watched Rameau and noticed his demeanour change. He sensed that he could soon break him into submission.

'Mr Rameau, have you ever spoken to anyone about the murders or discussed planning them on the telephone? Before you answer, I suggest you think very carefully.'

'I have never murdered anyone, Detective.'

'I've never suggested you personally murdered anybody.'

Rameau looked hard at Edgerton. He felt the Detective may be calling his bluff. It was like a game of poker, toing and froing as the men tried to read each other's minds.

Rameau took the bait. 'I've never spoken to anyone about any murders.'

Edgerton smiled as Perkins looked on. He slowly

opened the laptop and a file.

'Please listen to this clip.'

After the tape recording came to an end, Chloe interrupted.

'Would like us to play it again, Mr Rameau?'

For a man used to summing things up in complex trials and making judgments, the judge for once, was lost for words.

Edgerton moved on to the footage collected by Edward Fahy and went through every file. Rameau had made a catastrophic error in answering easy questions and remaining silent for any difficult ones put to him. As Edgerton produced the statement under caution made by Anton Loktev, the wind was taken from Rameau's sails. The evidence was compelling and the CPS had no hesitation in charging the disgraced judge.

Edgerton wanted to see the case through to its natural conclusion and accompanied Rameau to the photograph and fingerprint room where the admin was completed. After suffering the final indignity of having his DNA taken, Rameau looked at Edgerton.

'Would you have done the same, Mr Edgerton, if you had been in my position?'

Jack smiled. 'No, I wouldn't, but you were free falling from a great height.'

Rameau laughed hysterically. Edgerton looked at him as his laugh slowly died into an uncontrollable sob. As far as the detective was concerned, these were the cries of a man full of self-pity and no remorse. It was time to go home.

This Christmas Eve had been one to remember. It was time to celebrate.

Chapter 75

Lord Justice Rameau charged with conspiracy to commit murder

Jack Edgerton sat at home, content having read the daily paper. He was ready for some time to himself after a busy Christmas. At least he had spent some more valuable time with Chloe and been able to see his daughters. He had one final meeting regarding Operation Steadfast, the name given to the inquiry by Chief Superintendent Watkins. It would be informal and Edgerton could go through the case. There had been a few developments since Rameau was remanded to Wandsworth Prison. He had kept them close to his chest and there would be no better place than to return to the Sherlock Holmes. It was ironic that the pub had been one of Beaumont's favourite haunts.

As he gathered his belongings he remembered to pick up a copy of the Moscow Times, which had mysteriously found its way onto his desk via the internal mail. The headline was short and sweet.

Former Ambassador found dead in Moscow flat
Andrei Loktev, the Former Russian Ambassador based in

London, was found dead in a run-down flat on the outskirts of the capital. The police are treating his death as suspicious…

He had arranged to hook up with Chloe after the meeting, but he wanted to see his boss and his trusted ally Detective Inspector Palmer to have a good debrief without the formality he had encountered at previous meetings held at the Yard. He also wanted to leave early and get to the pub to have his lunch alone. Patrick Sands had sent Edgerton and his team a letter of sincere thanks after his ordeal, a great gesture from a man who had lost his closest friends in the most horrendous circumstances and yet had shown incredible strength. Edgerton had not totally lost his faith in the human race.

London still had the feeling of Christmas as the snow refused to thaw. As he trampled through the snow on the Embankment he came to the bridge and saw a familiar figure sitting at the corner with an old supermarket trolley and what appeared to be a mountain of cardboard boxes. The rugged face looked up.

'How are you?' Edgerton asked.

The detective was surprised when the man in his early eighties replied, 'I never forget a friendly face, sir. Thank you for the drink that night.' The man was well spoken.

Edgerton sat beside him.

'I know your name, Mr Edgerton. You are the detective in the newspapers.'

Edgerton laughed and smiled affectionately at the tramp. 'You have a good memory for a face.'

'Your daily paper is my saviour, my bed sheets every night, and I get to see every headline.'

Edgerton reached for his pocket and pulled out two twenty-pound notes. He handed them to the man and said, 'Take care. What is your name?'

'Thank you so much. My name is Edward, or Teddy to my old soldier pals who I served with, sir.'

Edgerton stood up and waved goodbye. Then he turned back to Teddy.

'You know where I am. See you soon, old soldier.' He saluted the man.

Edgerton had mixed feelings as he continued towards his destination, but he was sure they might meet again.

As he entered the Sherlock Holmes he was surprised to see Philip Palmer and Bob Watkins already seated at a table.

As he sat down, he shook his colleagues' hands and said, 'Hope you had a good Christmas, chaps, and I see you've bought me a nice pint of lager.' Edgerton raised his glass. 'Here's to a great Christmas, and I hope you all have a Happy New Year.'

'Are we eating now or later?' Watkins asked.

Palmer interrupted. 'Let's get this over with and then we can relax.'

All the officers agreed and Edgerton started his summary. He had his own thoughts, but he would cover every aspect of the case.

Before he started, he said, 'I have a confession, and it might make your day.'

The officers looked at him nervously. He reached inside his jacket pocket and threw the Moscow Times on the table.

'There you go. What did I tell you, Philip?'

Watkins snatched the paper and read it out aloud.

'Well come on then, what have you got to say?' Edgerton said.

Palmer said, 'At least justice has been done to some extent.'

Watkins was elated. 'Go on then, let's go through everything, and give us your thoughts.'

Edgerton took a huge gulp of lager and proceeded to summarise the case.

'The whole case started in Soho as far as I'm concerned. The operation was run by the Russian Mafia and many of the girls worked between both the clubs in London and the Algarve. It turned out that Bamford and Smith made many trips over there. They certainly had a taste for brothels and the high life. This had been going on for a few years and when we found out, Edward Fahy had been onto them for a while and word got out. This is where it gets a little hazy for me. Did Rameau order the death of Fahy? The answer is yes. Fahy was his only threat at the time and the only known person to have any ammunition on the whole outfit, and although he didn't know many people in the Mafia, he had strong connections within the club in Soho. The Select Committee was a non-event in the great scheme of things. In fact, I'd say it was a joke, and the Russians knew it and so did Rameau, but if Fahy's scoop had been published, then the whole pack of cards would have come falling down. So when the Committee finished I think they were surprised when Beaumont kept pushing and pushing. Initially, Zonov was employed to tail the politician just to see what he was up to. They were satisfied with the clinical way he had disposed of Fahy and he was thought to be a safe pair of hands. Out of all of them Zonov was the most dangerous in terms of killing, an absolute fucking lunatic, but he was intelligent as well. That made him worse than other murderers I have dealt with.'

'Who sent the footage then?' Watkins asked.

'I'm nearly there. Bamford had nothing to do with this whole conspiracy, but got dragged into it through his own greed. The only man who managed to stay on the fringe of things was Derek Smith. It was a total coincidence that Rameau was going to head the public inquiry. He would still have had to silence Sands and Beaumont when it became evident they had the footage, so he went for it. It was an elaborate plan and it fooled us all for a while, thanks to a bent copper.'

'He's up for trial soon,' Watkins added.

Edgerton continued. 'At the same time, Robert Bamford was taking money from the Russians in return for a promise of keeping the authorities away from the place, and the Russians fell for it. Well, they did until he kept raising the stakes and asking for more. Loktev was becoming increasingly pissed off with Bamford and it was him who sent the footage. He wanted him out of the equation, and when he checked those excerpts, the quality was so bad it only showed Bamford and that was enough.'

Palmer said, 'That makes sense.'

'Think about it, boys,' Edgerton said, 'Loktev didn't know Sands would get a friend to clean up the footage to such an extent that every other person came into view. It was a disastrous move on his part, and as it turned out a deadly mistake by Brian Beaumont and his close friend, Patrick Sands. Remember, Loktev knew he had a get out of jail card if the shit flew, and as it turned out he left with the money, or most of it, when he returned. But I believe the Mafia got rid. You don't fuck about with those boys, as history will tell you.'

Edgerton was in full flow. 'Once the footage was out they had no choice but to eliminate Beaumont and Sands, and I think it was Rameau's idea to create this elaborate series of murders to look like 'the Barber' had returned. Inside information on the cause of death came from DS Martin, who had worked on the case and befriended Loktev when he worked for the DPG at the Russian Embassy. The plan that Zonov put in place was a good one, but it was always fraught with danger. Murderers will always make mistakes, but when they commit multiple murders then their chances of being detected increase, and poor old Zonov made several mistakes.'

'I don't think he could ever have got away with it,' Watkins said.

'If he had torched all three addresses properly he would have destroyed all the evidence, and I believe we would still be here scratching our heads, lumbered with a load of purely circumstantial evidence. But he did fuck up and the forensic evidence nailed him. Also, they were sloppy when it came to the use of mobile phones, and how Rameau believed he could offload large amounts of money to pay for the hits is beyond me. Although they had been close, Zonov was losing patience with Loktev and, rightly so, he did not trust the man. That is when he tried to find out the identity of the main conspirator, Jacques Rameau, which he did, and Zonov's evidence will prove invaluable when Rameau goes to the Old Bailey. I suspect he will eventually enter a guilty plea.'

Chief Superintendent Watkins agreed.

'As for the officer who nicked Zonov, if he were here now I'd kiss him. If it weren't for his gold old-fashioned bit of policing we would never have got a DNA match. The main players were sloppy with their willingness to leave evidence lying around, but we still had to crack the case and prove it beyond all reasonable doubt. There will always be criticism, Guv, over the death of Robert Bamford. We have been vilified in certain quarters over this, but only by a small minority of his supporters who I would imagine were not there during his darkest days. I can deal with all that and after all, he decided to take his own life. It was his decision.'

Palmer looked at Edgerton. 'He made his bed.'

'It is a man's own mind, not his enemy or foe, that lures him to evil ways, Phil.'

Watkins was happy with the outcome.

Edgerton turned to him and said, 'Well, you're in the know. What will happen to the world of politics?'

'Not a lot will change, as you know. The country's had scandals before. I think there will be a new government and the leaders will step down. I think the judiciary may look at things and then the rest will be left for the new public inquiry. That will take two years, and by then the dust will have settled.'

Edgerton's phone rang and he excused himself to take the call.

When he returned, he said, 'Come on, let's have a few beers, then I must go.'

Both the detectives smiled at him.

Palmer said, 'Who's the girl, Jack?'

Edgerton laughed. 'You both know her well. Come on, boys, let's let our hair down while it's quiet.'

The End

davidwilsonauthor.com

Follow david wilson on twitter @DaveDmc111
and on Facebook
www.facebook.com/whenaredlightshines

Coming soon...

**Part II of the Detective Chief Inspector
Jack Edgerton series**

Lightning Source UK Ltd.
Milton Keynes UK
UKHW010637160920
370007UK00001B/233